Dilmunia

Rasool Darweesh

Translated by Dr Mohammed A. Alkhozai

Dilmunia

Olympia Publishers
London

www.olympiapublishers.com
OLYMPIA PAPERBACK EDITION

A CIP catalogue record for this title is
available from the British Library.

ISBN: 978-1-80074-242-0

This is a work of fiction.
Names, characters, places and incidents originate from the writer's
imagination. Any resemblance to actual persons, living or dead, is
purely coincidental.

First Published in 2022

Olympia Publishers
Tallis House
2 Tallis Street
London
EC4Y 0AB

Printed in Great Britain

Dedication

Unsuccessful writers are those
who fish over the water.
No one is worthy of presenting this novel,
To none but you,
Khowla.

"Quite often, publishers tend to snatch the manuscript from my hand as I reread it, I made more amendments. I still believe that any text is incomplete and that the writer does not finish his novel but discards it."

Marquees

INTRODUCTION

Modern life, with its cement edifices and wide avenues, has mutilated one of the largest prehistoric necropolises known as Dilmun Burial Mounds. As I was one of the dwellers of the areas surrounding these tumuli, I discovered a spoken relationship between the living and the dead. The problem with the living denizens is that they do not appreciate and respect the privacy of their ancestors, to the point that they have intruded on their resting places as an outcome of modern civilisation. I had to walk between these graves and apologise to their inhabitants. During this strolling, I found myself unintentionally collecting my breath and relaxing at only one specific tumulus lying on the west end of this huge cemetery.

As silence fell on the place, I found myself listening to that stillness. I discovered that silence does not breathe and throb except when all the five senses cease functioning together. There, I learnt a new language, and a quite unusual conversation developed there, urging me to dig and remove the sand and stones, and delve into that tumulus in a desperate attempt to reach the source of the new dialogue and unique language.

I received an invitation from the dwellers of the graves to visit them at a suitable time; I unhesitatingly accepted it. However, when I returned to my own people and their present life, this dialogue dissipated and another haughty dialogue conducts more of a barbaric mob called erroneously "modern" or "scientific". For all this, I was asked by those interested in the subject to research the truth about these burials and their impact on the people of Dilmunia and its successively changing names.

I did not know where to start from and make my first step as there was nobody, whether human or non-human, to usher me to the path to tread. I made several visits to the site and waited for the silence to arrive. It was not long, as if it were waiting for my return. It said that I was the first man from the West called Adam to distinguish between the stone and the mud and was inspired by the spirit of the burial place and loved as a man.

All this led me to do some research on European travellers to the Middle East, particularly those who invaded the Arabian Gulf and deciphered its mysteries in Dilmunia. I found the traveller, or rather, he found me. I followed him, trying to verify stops in his life since his town of birth and then moving to another town in middle of the eighteenth century, ending his tough trip to the Middle East with its stops, ups and downs and events.

Away from these events and before going deep into them, I cannot but express my profound gratitude to the Ministry of Culture in Copenhagen, Ministry of Culture and Tourism in Istanbul and The Bahrain Authority for Culture and Antiquities in Manama for supporting this work and aiding the resolution all the difficulties I encountered. I also extend my appreciation to all museums and public libraries for their cooperation and patience. Furthermore, I should not forget to mention the efforts made by the translators and proofreaders and their invaluable assistance.

Finally, this work took me more than two years to

accomplish, compiling and translating old documents, some of which were in very bad condition. I would beg the gracefulness of the reader for his understanding and acceptance of this work of fiction called Dilmunia.

The Interpreter
19/9/2014

Part 1

(1) The Interpreter
February 1760

The Merchant stood in front of three of the country's dignitaries placed by the current social norm as rulers and judges. He stood as a wounded lion smashed in his pride versus an old retired diver. That made him more dignified and respectful in his society.

At the time, the Chief Justice Shaikh Albalbul said:

"The honourable businessman standing in front of you, the doyen of the Al Jubur family, is representing the defendant accused of killing your son at sea. He is also representing all the sailors on board that dhow when the incident took place where your young son fell victim. My dear sir, the voyage set out two months ago during the summer season. Your son, aged eighteen, wished to accompany the trip as he was keen to know all about pearl fishing in order to prepare himself for the future. It was the inevitable fate and the wish of God that your son met his destiny. Honourable Sir, let us hear what the witnesses have to say in order to reach a verdict that satisfies all parties according to the rules of the Sharia."

The judge beckoned in the accustomed manner with his left hand to the audience, at the white stone courthouse, to come forward to give their testaments on the incident. The puller volunteered first to give his testament and narrate the incident. He was a young man, mid-thirties in age. The sun tanned him, and the salinity of the sea polished him all over.

His face was of the same colour as his body which was smooth, nearly hairless, except with a few spots of hair spread here and there like seasonal turf.

The judge told him to stand up and repeat the swear after him, "Puller, Yousif, put your hand on the Holy Quran and say, 'By God I swear to tell the truth and nothing but the truth.' Tell us then what happened on board the dhow."

"I am Puller, Yousif; I was responsible for Diver Abu Rashed who was diligent and hardworking. He used to dive ten times every morning. As Nasser was an impetuous young man who wanted to learn everything, he asked repeatedly to dive to fish for oysters after his second attempt. As he saw the oysters brought aboard the dhow, he became more eager to dive. The diver would dip into the sea, tied to a robe that he would shake, signalling to the puller to pull him up. As he was at the bottom of the sea, I kept an eye on the rope to shake so I could pull him to the deck of the boat. I was concerned when this did not happen and found that the rope was light and loose. I cried dreadfully and the divers went down looking for him. After a while, we found him floating at the stern, lifelessly. That was an act of fate. God bless his youthful soul."

The puller was in tears looking at the diver Abu Rashed and then at the judge and the Merchant. The judge asked the diver to testify. He endorsed what the puller said, not deviating from the truth.

Meanwhile, the Merchant was absent-minded and stunned. He was gazing at the ceiling as if counting the wooden logs. His eyes moved downwards to the alcoves in the courthouse and the closed windows and faces in the audience. When his eyes met those of the judge, the latter waved his right hand to wake him from his slumber.

The judge turned to the skipper, or the "Nokhuda", who was sitting on his left near the Merchant. He repeated the same avowal statement. He told him to tell details of the incident of the death involving the young Nasser, son of the Merchant. He recalled, "Gentlemen, the deceased was my companion throughout the voyage, as it was agreed with his father before we set sail. Before noon, he went and sat next to Yousif. I could not hear what they were saying. It seemed they agreed on something. Then he moved astern of the boat and disappeared from our sight. When we missed him, we looked all over the boat and only found him one hour later, floating. I have my doubts that Yousif had planned something for him."

Then, the judge addressed those present. "Doubt is not conclusive proof for a judicial verdict that abides by the law of God and the tradition of His Prophet. The Ruler shall not ratify a verdict based on doubt."

Then he turned to the doyen and the Merchant, perhaps to agree with him on this case and to find a way out for this judicial issue. He implicitly gave way to them to express their views. The Al Jubur doyen was the first to speak. "In my capacity as representative of the divers and their families, and as the situation has been proven that it was deliberate murder or not. As risk is an outcome of adventure, and to avoid strife and its unpleasant results, I would like to propose one of three solutions. The first of these is a pardon, as it is the magnanimity of humans as explicitly advocated by the Holy Quran. Or that the Merchant demand blood money. Or the third solution, which is abhorrent to all of us, is retribution if the crime is proven."

The Merchant shook with anger and stood red in the face, moving his head kerchief which surrounded his white gear around his neck falling on his velvet, he said in a sharp voice, "As for me, let me tell you one of three things, no more."

They all rose to their feet, awestruck. The Merchant repeated his demand deliberately. "I would give you the choice of putting the moon in my right hand or secondly, bringing back my son alive."

Then he was silent and looked them in the face, pointing to the doyen, saying, "Thirdly, I cut the throats of all your family."

The appointed court dispersed; all its members anticipated appalling concern. Problems reveal the metal of humankind. Adversaries fear the sudden onslaught of their opponents. When man is ill, tranquillity dies. After all this, the judge tried to heal the wounds and reach the land of safety.

(2) Adam
March 1760

The phenomenon of migrating from the countryside to urban areas, later known as the great escape, became widespread. Thus, we decided to do the same and join the others. Behaviour of the herd protects us from committing errors. We stayed behind due to the illness of my father and the wolves waiting to jump over his properties and heritage. We were hoping to move from the country and hide in the uproar of the town. Then my mother recalled our history, engraved in her entity, with some awe. She spoke in detail of her concern about our known future:

"My son, once upon a time there was a king called Alfred, who ruled over the empire of Great Britain in the ninth century of Our Lord. With his intuition and wisdom, he claimed that God created the universe in the shape of a triangle of equal laterals. One lateral to be ruled in the name of princes; another lateral in the name of the Church; the third side that is horizontal represents the peasants who serve the other two other sides of the triangle. The king, with all his power and might, stood at the top of the triangle. He bestowed many church lands to many princes, and archbishops became exorbitantly wealthy, becoming princes in their own right and discarding their habits, turned into princes, ruling the land as ungodly secular feudal lords. They issued indulgence certificates for those who paid or donated land. It was obvious they used religion for their own advantage and allowed prohibitions such as marriage of bishops. Peasants lost their freedom involuntarily and owned nothing but their own lives. When they sold land, everything on it was consequently sold."

What I know now is that we were living in a modest house, but others saw it as an aristocratic rich house. People know things by their contraries. The house was in the middle of a large orchard with water flowing unrestricted. Cherry trees lined up tightly against each other, with flowers of all kinds growing. On its lawn, the cattle grazed. A short wooden hedge surrounded the orchard where some jasmine shrubs climbed. Everyone envied us this blessing. At the time, my crippled father was in a struggle with illness and resisting death with obstinate willpower. One day, accepting the invitation, the Angel of Death came and took his soul. That was an expected matter. What is expected comes without any surprise.

When the old man passed away, competing feudal lords vied over the vast cultivated land that was appropriated by legal law and hand lying law. My parent inherited it from his father. He and my mother worked hard for a long time and when it bore fruit, he employed some peasants while he became the landowner.

My mother had no intention of confronting the mogul feudal lords who combined against us. She was aware that those who fear evils are entrapped in them. At the time, the concept of feudalism had developed into an echelon of upper landowners who gradually became stronger, making peasants work and live on the land. This ended in slavery when the peasants became part of the private property, or a mere thing. Eventually they became taxpayers on all that they owned over the whole year.

The Church sent us one of its aides. This emissary was short on speech but very rich in attire. I did not like him at all. There is a thin line between dawn and night, between truth and falsehood; if you can get rid of the church aides, you shall be able to see. You shall be in a position to discover your interlocutor quite easily. "My honourable lady, there is a giant scheme that can preserve your present and your hereafter. A project that consecrates the meaning of service to humankind on land and in the sky and maintains their rights in this and a later world," said the emissary.

"How? Isn't the church a place of worship? A place of holding Christian rituals? Does it prohibit meddling with houses of worship in all faiths and outlaws demolishing them? Is it going to be turned into a commercial centre or a ban?"

"Religious trade is more profitable and luckier, my Lady. It is an everlasting trade with God. Ascribing properties to the Church is an act of endowment, where acts of charity do not stop but are duplicated by the passage of time and revolution of the wheel continues for years."

His logic excited me; it is the principle of religion trafficking. One may deal with humans — he may be right or wrong — but dealing with God is a kind of coercion where man has no choice but to obey if he wants to be saved. Oh, my God! What is this man talking about? Has revelation been sent again, and Christ is resurrected? We continued our conversation with him in fun.

"I do not understand! On the other hand, perhaps I do not want to understand. Stupidity is a blessing bigger than understanding in many instances."

"The Church shall grant you an instrument of indulgence that forgives all your sins. You shall be reborn on the Day of

Judgement, on the same day you were born on earth. You and your son shall be granted a pardon that will warrant happiness in this world and the heavens as well."

"If we do not pay, shall we be punished? Will misfortune inflict us before death or after?"

"All I know, my Lady, is that the church shall excommunicate you; the will of God is implemented through us in this world, and He shall ordain and enforce punishment in the hereafter."

The war of wills is more forceful than the war of nerves. Fear began to overcome my mother. I do not think it was a weakness of faith but rather caution of an outcome. To meet their objectives would be to give up reason and fortunes, and in confrontation, there are unthinkable results. We all understood each other and the emissary was aware of our inner thoughts. The word has an extraneous and intrinsic meaning.

The Church did not stop at that as it forged an alliance with the feudal lords gaining, more gold out of it. It terrorised the people and enticed them at the same time. If the feudal lord and the slave paid one tenth of their property, they were entitled to receive an instrument of indulgence. He who refuses shall be excommunicated and shall receive a document written on papyrus leaf. It shall not grow old or be extinguished. In addition, the recipient has the right to take it with him to his grave.

We all felt the diminishing numbers of farmers. This was an unplanned decrease. It was impossible for some of them to pay this tenth. Many of them found a way out by moving to urban centres, as this was the lifebelt. They thought mirage was a light of hope. We followed them as we could not resist those powerful property owners. We found ourselves in an undeclared truce. In the towns, the sun of freedom rises. We know about scientists, thinkers and philosophers. Life in towns is worth pursuing. This became apparent as some thinkers and philosophers preached the motto of "Render to Caesar the things that are Caesar's and to God the things that are God's". The educated pioneers bore the responsibility of fighting the Triangle of Terror, ushering the way to the age of reason. All components of society, men and women, had the right to education, and society entered a new era of reformation; the advancement of human society based on the right of sharing goodness and equality.

(3) The Interpreter
Mid-March 1760

The children invade the sandy courtyard of the house with their comfortable noise and naughty behaviour. They bring life to that mud house and to the fatigued body of the doyen of the Al Jubur family, who is thrilled and moved to life with their homecoming to the family house, the Big House, as they call it. They push the main door, and its squeak is heard all over the house, declaring the beginning of a beautiful chaos. They run barefoot on the white sand with joy filling their hearts. There, on the far southern end, stands a huge tree, proudly embracing the sky.

On the left a two-storey, old house stands with a main entrance and a staircase with its eight uneven steps which take you to the roof with its double-wall parapet built of stone and sea stones. The outer wall is shorter, serving as protection against rainwater, while the other one serves as protection against the wind, channelling the air inside the house as a natural air conditioner. On the ground floor no one can intrude, except by raising and pushing one of the shutters, as if to ask permission from the building, not its occupants. The sandy veranda is in the middle of four adjacent rooms, as if keeping an eye on them. On the farthest left, the Doyen, Al'ameed, is laying on a cotton bed placed on a bedstead made of palm tree branches. Here, the nonagenarian grandfather meets his grandchildren, who surround him and exhale some of their souls to invigorate him. It seems that souls have a language without letters; something that we cannot grasp.

The four children try to make their grandfather sit against the wall before their father arrives. Three of them are doing good while Rashed is gazing at a two-metre distance, moving his sight from his grandfather's face and the place where his leg is amputated above the right knee. The old man deduces bewildered signs from Rashed and repeatedly says, "This is the tax of life, my son."

"What tax and what life, grandfather? Some of our parts die so that we can live with an incomplete whole!"

"What a child you are, always uttering these words. I hope the future is yours, rising with your strength."

Moments pass like previous ones and unanswered questions remain in the heart of the youngster before his mind. What a life is this that a man loses parts of his body to remain alive, sacrificing what is materialistic to rectify what is spiritual. The life that lives on us is warning of a greater danger. The Al Jubur doyen deducts these problematic questions by his cleverness and experience fn the mind of the young man, Rashed. The extreme rhetoric is to answer without a question being asked, "Freedom and dignity, my son."

"Sacrifice is dignity! Shortcoming is perfection… These are part of your glossary that I cannot understand."

"Later, you shall understand that life pushes us to pay a ransom for a crime we did not commit, as a good offering."

The doyen smiled when he recalled the heresies of the Merchant and the sycophancy of the Nakhuda. However, the sane is he who keeps a distance between him and the disputant. Just like that mock trial; the powerful do not abide by its rulings and the weak succumb to its consequences.

The children interrupted that vague conversation, and with their innocence, the youngest of them climbed over his grandfather's shoulders, aiming for the head, that shining dome not without some stains. While Khowla, who was approaching twenty and starting to reach mental maturity, sat next to her grandfather. The middle child embraced his grandfather's lean chest. During that family scene, Rashed stood as a witness, documenting warm familial situations. The question of "who stole the grandfather's leg" still needs an answer.

Khowla tries with her innate nature to attain knowledge from her grandfather's long experience. She is about to find answers to all her questions and inquiries. She can find these in religion and society, and the answer comes. Time becomes so precious sitting next to her grandfather and father.

The curtain fell down on the usual scene with the roaring voice of the father of Rashed, Abu Rashed. The man, in his forties, entered solemnly, and all the throats dried up and all breath was lulled in fear. He was a man with narrow shoulders and an obtruding chest and a strong, lean, soft hand. Anyone shaking hands with him feels its cruelty and then feels safe afterwards. The sun with its heat and the sea with its salinity have changed his complexion, turning it into a dark skin. The climate had an impact on his soft scalp. He had big lustrous eyes, but his nose was like that of an eagle in its sharpness. He had a hairless chin, with the remains of a few hairs, reminiscent of a once-upon-a-time beard.

Abu Rashed entered, bowing down and kissed his father's head, as if smelling it to inspire wisdom and patience. The doyen smiled, inviting his son to sit next to his amputated leg. Khowla came to her father, who stood in esteem for her. She imprinted a kiss on his head and he reciprocated by kissing her between the eyes. He asked her to sit next to him. Then the man glimpsed the grandchildren and its meaning was received. The eye could sometimes be more perceptive than the tongue. The message was delivered faster than lightning. They all left the veranda in full joy, while Rashed stood by the door, awaiting the outcome of the meeting with his father in the presence of his sister, Khowla, hoping to know the secret of the amputated leg.

The doyen invited his family to have dates and coffee. Khowla hurried out, bringing what he asked for. She had intuition and good common sense, so she prepared everything before her father's arrival. The young lady brought what he had asked for. Before the doyen started posing questions, Abu Rashed began drawing plans for his daughter, Khowla. As if I see you made responsible for our faults, as if I see your future different from that of your comrade. I did not find anybody worthy of you in the eyes of anybody in our village, or neighbouring villages. Man's eye is his address; I have never met anyone worthy of you. A father looks into the eyes of young men for his goal and wishes well. The doyen interrupted the string of thoughts of his son and started asking questions, "When will the next diving season start, Abu Rashed?"

"After the next Friday prayers."

"What about our debts?"

"They are and we too are at the mercy of God."

"What did you do with the *Nukhatha*? Will you amputate his hand before he amputates your leg?"

"Perhaps he can cut off my leg, and after that ill-omened trial, the *Nukhatha* shall try to satisfy the Merchant, and then the whole matter will be referred to the Ruler himself."

"How was the impact on the commons? God forgive the

Merchant and protect the *Nukhatha*."

"How do you wish them well after all that they did?"

"Please know, my son, that the adamant in faith is soft in heart."

Rashed picked up this part of the dialogue, guessing that his grandfather's leg met its doom either before or after one of the diving jaunts. That was his first impression, and he had to discover the secret. He was always hopeful and was optimistic when he realised that he had held one end of the string.

Here, the tone of the voices of Abu Rashed and his father went down as their hearts were troubled. The man briefed his father about the consequences of the trial and hoped that God's hand would come to their rescue or may represent it. "Father, at times of distress, and in order to face injustice, one even desires the aide of the devil."

Here the doyen interrupted him. "Do not you ever give up the mercy of God."

The relationship connecting Abu Rashed with his father, representing a tie between a man and his parent, could never be severed. It was a sacred bond between two generations. It was more of a friendship tie of high value.

The quick encounter soon ended. The doyen called his grandson, Rashed, to do his homework in the presence of Khowla. He was in a position to transfer to the child all the knowledge he possessed, in addition to gained experiences. He was preparing him to be a better person. He became lettered and able to decipher the heaped-up manuscripts in the family house. The grandfather was building hopes on his grandchild. At the same time, Khowla was in a race to understand life with its sweetness and bitterness.

(4) Jackson
April 1760

I held her hand in mine, shaking, and offered my sympathies on the demise of her husband. She pulled her hand away disapprovingly and the black gloves remained in my fingers. Part of her black dress revealed her body, exposing rosy whiteness. She did not bother about the glove, but the incomplete beauty moved me. However, the widow looked down upon me, and I took the lead. "I am Jackson, a realtor, a friend of the deceased."

"It seems you are a friend of my late husband at a distance. He never mentioned you to me. I have never met you."

"It seems that worldly matters create intimacy and cut its connecting line. Despite our friendship, your late husband and I rarely met."

"We shall see if that is true."

The Mass was about to start; the coffin was still at the altar where all worshippers were in black, giving the place a sombre serenity. I took a seat in the first row on the right hand of the woman and her son on the left. I thought his name was Adam. The service began in the usual manner, with church organ music followed by hymns and prayers, when silence fell on all. The mourners flocked in a line, casting their final looks at the deceased and offering their sympathies to his family. It was important for me to stand next to them. I thought that would comfort them and make them feel peaceful and would remove the idea from their minds about social climbers and those controlling the estate of her husband. After the funeral, I went with them to the house of the deceased. The woman was trying to show neutral sentiments and be an iron lady in front of strangers, especially those vying for his estate. She wiped all signs of sadness from her face, except that her face refused to hide it. Rattling in her voice was apparent. I preferred to keep quiet, except rarely when I had to be open to her. "Madame, this is life with people coming and departing; but please remember that your husband's estate has become a target for vying noblemen and the clergy. You should be cautious. I find it more useful to sell the property of the deceased instead of facing all those parties."

"You are talking about three issues: the first is to face the avidity of the Church; secondly, that I stand against the nobles; thirdly, that I sell our property at a price you decide; is that not so?"

Her comment did not come as a surprise to me as it was expected. I made it clear to her that some professions do not suit the feminine nature of women, as it is very difficult for women to take that as a career. Given the fact that her son was still immature, it would not be that easy for this widow to manage her property by herself. How would she follow up operations of farming and harvesting and then marketing with all its intricacies, not knowing anything about farming and trading?

Two days later, the woman invited us to lunch at her place. I was the first to arrive, expecting something to happen. Around the big table sat a number of guests. On the woman's right sat her son Adam and next to him, a young woman called Carina and her father. Then the chief farmer and next to him one of the very well-known brokers and then two priests. After dinner, I was expecting the woman to reveal her objectives and future plans regarding her property. However, she said, "Gentlemen, I would like to extend my sincere gratitude to all of you for expressing your sentiments towards the deceased and his family. I know that sorrows bring loved ones together. On this occasion, I shall talk to all of you, despite my knowledge of the consequences of doing so. I shall talk to the priests as clergy, to the brokers as businessmen, to the neighbours as individuals with whom we share love and esteem. Then, we shall decide what we shall do with the inheritance. If the Church has a share, the priests shall have that; if the brokers have a share, they shall have theirs. We must bear in mind that the Church believes it has the right to obtain funds in order to issue indulgence for man to take with him on the Day of Judgement. As this is an ecclesiastical claim, there are people who believe that this is not one of the rights of the Church. There are some who believe that they believe in the Creator and the good deeds are what man is to be compensated for on the Day of Judgement. Many people uphold and believe in this precept."

One of the priests, moved by what he heard, got inflamed and wanted to retaliate. "My dear lady, never ever would the Church corrupt itself. Monies paid to the Church are for man's own benefit in his life and death. I can find that the good lady is about to reiterate the same strayed Lutheran doctrines that we adamantly object to and that according to the law, it is illegal and punishable by law[1]."

---

[1] The German monk Martin Luther King (1483 – 1546) was the first to stand up to the Church's indulgences.

The woman asked the priest to allow her continue speaking and not to be interrupted. "If you want to build me a house in heavens, please build me a house in the hearts of all human beings. Let the people have the choice and freedom of worship. Had it not been for bread, man would never worship God. You have been feeding the people with empty words instead of educating them and enticing them to go to church through your conduct, not by your lip service. Not all Christians carry the church in their hearts. You claim to have divine forgiveness for humans; tell me, please, about your deeds in the service of humankind?"

The priest was full of rage and stood fuming threateningly. He then left with his colleague. That was one hurdle removed from my path to reach the property of the woman. Her son and the workers were the only ones left on her side. My colleague wanted to seize the opportunity and proceeded to address her. I prompted him as to what to say. He was a professional liar. He knew that when a knight is smiling at a time of misery, his smile is immortalised in the memory of the woman. He insolently insisted on telling lies, believing that women have the rare ability of trusting him; the more he tells lies, the more they believe him and their hearts are enlivened. "My dear lady, we would like to manage your business and stand with you against all hungry wolves with their eyes on your legacy. There are matters of farming and business that you cannot face alone."

The woman paid no attention to his false speech, turning to address her guests. "Honourable guests, my son Adam wants to pursue his education in town, while I want to return to my big family that I miss a lot. Accordingly, after prolonged consultations, I have decided to leave the farmlands in the capable hands of our neighbour, the father of Carina, until our return from town. He has full knowledge of the secrets of the land and I have no doubt that he shall maintain our interests. Very shortly, we shall announce the engagement of Carina to Adam. Their marriage ceremony will be held after the end of the mourning rituals when we return from town."

(5) Abu Rashed Al Jubur
May 1760

I hurried between meandering lanes, ending up at the eastern quarter, then walked northward to the house of the *Nukhatha*, whose boundary wall, unlike the rest of the houses, had no adjacent neighbour. This may have been due to fear and suspicion. What I know is that people live next to each other just like birds of the same feather flock together. I knocked on the door made of heavy *nabq* wood, with nobody answering. I repeated knocking three times and was certain that those within could hear the knocking. I drew back two steps, thinking of my father's amputated leg and the incident of Nasser's death and its impact on the history of Dilmunia. I realised what I was undergoing and bit my lower lip, trying to gain more serenity and hoping for a quick recovery.

The door was opened ajar, slowly without squeaking. The Servant protruded his head and part of his neck.

"Who is there?"

"Abu Rashed."

"What do you want, Abu Rashed?"

Silly questions are normally raised to test the patience of the responder and to tease him. I am not one of those easily aroused and usually control myself. I prefer to talk cautiously.

"I came to see the *Nukhatha*."

"His name is *Mr Nukhatha*."

"Yes, I would like to meet Mr *Nukhatha*."

"What are you talking about? He is in a long meeting with the Merchant. He may end soon or later, after few hours. I will tell him them wait until I get back."

I chose the shade to sit in and leaned against the wall. I wondered about the way of life on this meek island, divine in its creation and satanic in its human aspect. Who had enacted this law of the jungle? Who controls us on our land; why all this injustice? I was torn by these woes. Pearl fishing has endless woes.

It is difficult for me to doubt or accuse the Puller, Yusif, of murdering Nasser. It is a framed lie. Out of this incident, the *Nukhatha* wanted to increase his wealth and enhance his power, although he is still under the authority of the Ruler and the Merchant. He must be planning; it must be a long-term dreaming. But he who looks between his steps shall be shocked by life. The Merchant is the one who manages the affairs of the island, and the Ruler remains the scarecrow against the wind.

I was taken by surprise with my eyes closed, when the Servant tapped on my right shoulder and nodded to me four times, asking me to enter to meet the *Nukhatha*.

"The Boss is waiting for you. Please follow me."

"All right."

The Servant moved, and I followed him as if going to my doom. He was wearing a short shirt, a *thawb*, off-white in colour. He was bare headed with thick, fuzzy hair. I glanced at the wide gap between his hair and shoulders, indicating that he was concealing meanness and docility reflecting in return the vanity of his master. The Servant opened the door of the reception hall and I stood by the door. The *Nukhatha* was sitting in the centre with a large red cushion that he used as his desk, with lots of ledgers. The *Nukhatha* was immersed as usual in his books, revising loans and debts. He was dressed in a snow-white *thawb* and a head-kerchief adorned with gold thread. I was not deceived by his cleanliness; man's filth is inside him. He frowned, red-eyed and feigning anger in order to strike awe his interlocutor. I began, "Peace be upon you."

He raised a frowning face with deep lines on his forehead, reaching his scalp. He cast a glance on me as if seeing a man to examine, then he looked back quickly at his accounts as if to hide away from the eyes of his guest.

"And peace be upon you, too, and the blessings of God."

He invited me to take my seat with a movement from his right hand. I sat on the left side of the *majlis*. Without uttering a single word, he began to recall his credits and what others were indebted to him for in his acute memory that never makes a mistake. "Three large sacks of Indian rice, a sack of sugar and another one of wheat. Five pounds of oriental spices, three bags of salt, five sacks of wheat bran…"

Then he suddenly stopped and asked me, "Are you ready for the sea? The next pearl fishing season is due shortly."

"I need to know how much I owe you; on the final trip of the last season, I didn't make any *Ashrafiya*."

"Your debts were so large and you could not cover them last season. Work harder this time. The more pearls you fish, the more income you attain."

"And how much are my debts now?"

"I already mentioned that; but there is no harm in reminding."

The *Nukhatha* randomly picked an old ledger with its pages turning yellowish, and he was aware that it was not documented and without witnesses. I found him murmuring or perhaps swearing, or perhaps thanking God in private or public. I think he was thanking God for the absence of any human being. He thought I could not recite the Holy Quran, and I guess he did not want us to read the Holy Book as it is a source of Divine legislation. He wanted to monopolise the authority of knowledge, which is the worst type of injustice. The Ruler hoped that the people of Dilmunia remained without education because it was a weapon raised against him.

"Your debts, man, mmm, yes, five sacks of rice and the same of salt and barley and…"

I interrupted him violently but cautiously, "I never took barley at all. I took three sacks of rice and this list is not like the one you mentioned earlier!"

"Look, you. I do not allow people like you to doubt my integrity. If you repeat that, I shall sell you and your debts to *Nukhatha* Abu Fahad. You know Abu Fahad quite well. You kill, rob and then challenge the integrity of honest men."

I kept quiet and knew that silence may have double meanings. His speech fell on me like a sharp sword and bitter as colocynth. He went on in his insolence. "You have grown old, Abu Rashed, and you must write your testament before the start of the big season. You know that in case of the death of the diver — and death is a leveller — his debts are carried forward to his eldest son. The latter replaces him in his profession. As your son Rashed is still young, may I suggest that you give your daughter, Khowla, in secret marriage to the Merchant? Perhaps he can postpone your debt? When Rashed grows up, he can replace you as a diver and pay all your debts. Then the Merchant divorces her. You know girls get married at the age of nine and never get old except those who …"

"Shut up! The mean is he who relays his meanness and accusations to others. Your likes or those of your master's shall not tarnish our honour and integrity. Your wealth does not permit you to enslave others and challenge their honour. I have no doubt now, that it was you who plotted the death of Nasser. Yes, you benefit from crisis and gain profits."

"Careful what you say; your words are accumulated crimes."

I stood upright, looking down upon him and hated to look at him. I was certain of the necessity of searching for a way out of this inherited law. The rulers use their power to impose ignorance and illiteracy on the people. Education shall expose them. How I wished I did not ask that man about that debt. However, can I remain as a slave owned by his master, the *Nukhatha*, by my own free will? What do you call this kind of trade? A trade where the worker remains a slave from cradle to grave. Some own the land and what is on it, and some own the sea with what is on it and inside it.

I left with a broken heart and a shattered integrity, dehumanised. I recalled my father's amputated leg and my sons and Khowla, who is still waiting for her fortune. I had an awful feeling of depression. It would be the last day in my life if he dared touch my honour and integrity. Nevertheless, what could I do if I died and my sons inherited my debt? Who could ever introduce change when injustice is universal in our society? Some traditions reinforce stupidity in society. That is a sort of communal class penalty. A ruling class that reaps the benefits of taxes and lives by the force of the sword. The trading class, known for its sycophancy, steps on the neck of the working class so that it can remain close to the first class. The working class is the one that tills the earth with its teeth, then chokes with a grain of sand and dies depraved. Hard life is what we live, not what we imagine. There has to be some change led by some who believe in changing life for the betterment of mankind.

(6) The Lady
Second Half of May 1760

The struggler passed away and the human vixen jumped over his property. Everyone behaves in his own way; one of them hoped to purchase. Another person was making up horrible news. Oral armament complements intelligence services. The shortest way to reach the plot of land is that of the heart of its proprietor, the heart of the only woman. Playing with the heart of the woman is the shortest and easiest way to win her holdings and all that she possesses.

Jackson made a bet with his friend and rival, the land broker, for hunting the deceased's farmland, despite how things looked. Jackson was certain of acquiring the land by hook or by crook from the market and by enticing with money at the same time to buy the land. His friend was certain that attaining the land had to be through penetrating the heart of the woman and at a very cheap price. The two both knew that the land could not be taken over in a state ruled by law; and despite the fact that this current law was only made to be broken, it reflects the civilization of society not its anarchy.

At the time, Adam was not bored of talking about political, social and economic changes in European societies. Moreover, through my many and long follow-ups, I was well informed about our history. This information allowed me the ability to read the future and anticipate what it carries, despite a difficult pregnancy. Life is reasons and results, beginnings and endings; all this led me to compete with Adam in posing questions. His nature urged me to do some research and investigation.

One evening, he came to me while I was having coffee in the front garden of the house. It is a brown wooden area separating the house from the turf area. In its surroundings grow many kinds of flowers and jasmine. There is an area covered by tree trunks, and its branches protect from sunrays during the summer and winter. Adam came carrying a small chair made of bamboo sticks. He placed it on the wooden floor, not more than one foot from me. Adam used to sit at a longer distance when he wanted to talk casually, but when he wanted to talk in depth with more detail, he would sit much more closely. That was an innate habit since he was young. His closeness means persistence. I expected a torrent of questions and prolonged discussion. He shared with me a cup of chamomile, then he began his discussion. "Does my mother think that the present situation in towns shall take us to the utopia preached by the famous philosopher, Plato?"

"In short, that shall never happen, my son."

"And why not, momma?"

"A utopia, or societies of virtue that are free from sin, are imaginary places. Man is made of moderation, a mixture of vice and virtue. The utopia is a society made not for man; it is only for angels created only for goodness. Real life is what we are inflicted with, not that one that we dream of. Societies repeat their experiences and generate cumulative knowledge. A society may invent an idea or a way of life; it may succeed or fail. Other societies emulate that. The humanities, my son, are interactive and benefit from each other."

"It seems to me that you are expecting failure for urban

life and the working class."

"My son, communal migration that we see now is not something new. There were other previous migrations, a large exodus from the country and villages; its results were what later were called cities. That was the direct cause for the rise of new economic, social and political systems. Let us go back a little, Adam, and take lessons from the past. European societies suffered many injustices and enslavement of the working classes. The more the pressure and injustice, the sooner the arrival of the eruption."

"As if you are talking about an imminent volcano."

"Yes, indeed, a dormant society is an inactive volcano; it is bound to be active. When you press on it, it becomes liable to erupt, especially with the existence of a nearby flame. This flame is not the cause of revolutionary change, but the spark that fires up the sleeping human cells within us."

"Were there human migrations that led to changes and revolutions?"

"In the fifteenth and sixteenth centuries, similar cases to ours took place. History repeats itself. When the slave class emerged, it became a problem, like a fire that ate everything. This class had no thinkers or philosophers, theorists or ideologists. When their hurricane moved, it had no specific objectives.

"Normally, opposition is born in the womb of the working class under the influence of its leaders. It means refusing the existing system. Once it was buried, it would be transformed into a revolutionary movement. Hence, someone would exploit these revolutions. There had to be a highly crafty person who would theorise and act as a representative for these groups. This type of human, you must have heard of them, are called the "bourgeoisie". They speak about their sense of injustice and being marginalised. They claim that a labourer who flees the countryside has the right to have trade unions that speak on his behalf, about working hours and social insurance. These were their demands and voices."

Adam stood up and asked me to walk with him. He held my hand. A warm friendship covered by the spirit of motherhood. I knew he loved moving around in places and could never stay in one place for a long time. I accompanied him on foot.

"Moreover, what is wrong with all this?"

"This category came to be known as the bourgeoisie. Unproductive. Living on the benefit of the labourers. A domineering and ruling class in western societies. Its theorists managed to put down the principles of life; your father said it was later known as Capitalism and Socialism. The class tumbled down before the noblemen and the clergy."

"An intuitive question that poses itself, mother. What is the difference between the country and town if the man from the country is the one that founded the town?"

"You must know that in olden times, farming was the essence of life where settlers settled, whereas towns are a combination of those without origins, such as nomads or mercenary slaves. They formed the nucleus of the city, where villagers themselves joined them later on."

"You also mean that the migration movement that we live is planned by someone who is steadily exploiting!"

"It is you who has concluded this. As I said earlier, revolutions repeat themselves. They are consecutive human experiences. He who accepts change is saved, and he who refuses, loses a great deal. Change, Adam, has a price, and no change has a greater cost. We also want to migrate to escape from these robbers, traders and clergymen. We are waiting for the right moment."

Without prior arrangement, we approached Carina's house. I interrupted our discussion and asked him how he thought about the girl and her father. He said, "The girl is beautiful; however, I have no emotion for her. Perhaps emotions come at a later stage. You think she will make an excellent wife, and this reassures me. You also confirm that love requires hard work, too. As to her father, he is an honest man. I hope that our property stays with him until the time of our return. I may be betrothed to her until things are clear. We are in need of someone whom we can trust with our property. Let us see if this proposed relationship is sufficient for implanting trust."

(7) Yusif, The Puller
Early June 1760

The role of preparing and rinsing the dead for burial is something that I inherited from my father. The location of our home had a major part to play. The house was built from sea limestone and its utilities built from palm tree trunks and fronds located on the west side of the cemetery. The moment you leave the house and look on your right, you see the rinsing room at the entrance of the yard. A few metres separate us. This neighbouring situation created a kind of intimacy between us and those lying beneath the ground, to the extent that the family and I acted as if we were guardians and auditors of the numbers of the dead.

I realised that death is an unbroken, eternal link as long as people do not stop breeding. It is a world for those coming and departing. The usual frequenters of the cemetery became visitors to our house on Mondays and Thursdays. They come to have tea and coffee and sometimes help themselves to some dates before visiting the graves of their relatives. Some of them became addicted to remaining there for a while, and speaking to them. In its essence, visiting graves reflects our interest in meeting the dead and longing for the next world. However, I see that it is unfair to think of after death and forget about what went before it. After leaving the cemetery, I do have a word with many of them. Visiting the dead defeats human vanity in them and is called modesty.

The people are in the habit of bringing the bodies of their dead for rinsing at any time, even at midnight. They believe that honouring the dead is burying them as soon as possible. Quite often, they lay the corpses on the table while they are still warm, with their blood still hot. At the time, the corpses have the nature of the dead, without a breath and movement. I think the breath does not cease, but we fail to touch it when dead. I normally placed the bodies on the stone table and felt the pulse. At times, I heard a remaining pulse and had to shake the body to double-check that the heart had completely stopped beating. I would then ask those present to recite verses from the Quran near the head of the dead, but they refused to do so. Instead, they would do it outside the rinsing room.

The period when the heart falls into silence casts a shadow over the audience. There is something rising from earth to heaven. It is heavy in its light effect, whether in weight or spread. I cannot surely say it's the spirit they were talking about. I asked a man to put his father's head on his bosom until the heart stopped beating. He then transferred his feelings, saying that the line of memories was renewed unconsciously; even those events we had already forgotten return on their own. We remembered all the events that had passed and linked us to the deceased, as if to indicate that our parts remember all our pasts after leaving our loved ones after death.

I was in this business for eleven years. I charged but meagre sums of money. I never asked for payment for cleansing the dead. However, some people are generous. I was preparing my eldest child to learn the rituals of cleansing the dead. I had to delegate this mission to another person, especially when I had gone diving. Some aides do not want to bear the full responsibility.

Last Friday's event was still vivid in my memory when Abu Rashed, the leader of his people, came early in the morning. With him came a young man in his early twenties. Abu Rashed knocked strongly on the door, shouting at the top of his voice, "Yusif, Yusif, Yusif." My wife woke me up from a nap that overtook me. "Yusif, Abu Rashed is at the door, he wants to see you."

"It must be another funeral."

"We belong to God and unto Him we return."

"This is its habit; people of the cemeteries do not go to sleep, and they stay awake in a perpetual state of expectation."

I went to see the two men and greeted them. I asked them to take the dead to the cleansing room and to recite a few verses from the Holy Quran, and others to dig a grave in a place of their liking. I told them that I would be back after few minutes when the heart of the deceased has stopped beating. Abu Rashed, however, anticipated this and said unhesitatingly, "Yusif, we do not want you to inter a dead body; this time we want you to exhume a dead body from its grave."

"You must be kidding me, Abu Rashed. Exhumation is legally forbidden, and religiously *haram*, and ethically objectionable no matter what reasons are given. It's true that we hear some people exhume the dead and remove their remains to stop people from visiting or praying at them, or even asking for blessing. This has nothing to do with religion; neither Islam nor any other faith allows such a thing. Forgive me, my friend, I would not do such a thing."

"Yusif, hasty decisions normally make a person dubious and thinks evil of others. You would better consider things carefully before you make judgement. The young man shall tell you what he saw in the cemetery this morning."

The young man talked with some doubt clouding his face. "As usual, I returned home after dawn prayers. I remained with my mother, who prepared breakfast for us. Before sunrise, I left for work in the field. I passed by the cemetery. I saw a masked man digging the earth. I hid behind a tree and started observing what he was doing. He held a baby and placed it in the hole that was not prepared as a finished grave. I thought the man was in a hurry and wanted to get rid of the baby, which was newly born as I guessed. The man heaped earth and left in the opposite direction; I still know the location of the grave. I left directly to the house of Abu Rashed and told him what I had seen."

I was very much surprised. I asked Abu Rashed what we should do, and what he wanted me in particular to do. He hesitated a little and then said:

"I think, and God only knows, that the baby was newly born and that it may have been buried alive. We must open the grave and take out the baby, rinse and shroud it the Islamic way, and then rebury it. God questions us."

I expected the baby to be a bastard. Abu Rashed did not answer indignantly. These tales are rare but harmful. Some possible of the impossible. I read that tale on his face. The three of us proceeded to the so-called grave. I asked the young man to start digging with a spade, then by his hands, but he refused. Abu Rashed asked me to do it, but I resisted. Instead of that, Abu Rashed suggested that the three of us exhume the body simultaneously. There was no need to use spades as a black cloth appeared at a depth of one arm. Abu Rashed hesitated a bit as he removed the sand from that piece of cloth, on its ends. He gradually stood as he pulled up the cloth. A rope dangled from the cloth and at its ends were tied papers, candles and some brass jewellery. Abu Rashed gathered everything and then sat beside the hole examining these strange things, trying to decode their mysteries. "I think these are instruments of black magic and charlatanism, locally known as charm."

I suggested to Abu Rashed to take these directly to the sea and throw them on its bed. This is what magic customs do to undo the charm. Abu Rashed objected to this suggestion. He asked us to take all that we found to their house, where the Doyen is, to know what the mind and religion could say. Patience in the face of problems simplifies things.

We moved to the house of the Doyen, Al'amid, where he received us in his *majlis*. Abu Rashed placed what he had in front of the Doyen, who asked the young man to tell the story, and we went to the house of the Doyen, where he welcomed us in his court which is called Majlis.

While the Doyen was listening, he began examining the charm. He saw two parallel lines forming a chain of circles, while on the upper line he saw two pyramids of small circles. On the lower line there were three larger pyramids scattered in different directions. The Doyen scrutinised the geometric design and then looked at the three scraps of paper. The outer form of the inscription seemed to be verses of the Quran, but he could not decipher it. There were other puzzles and five knots closely tied at the end of the piece of the cloth. All these stood as a barrier in front of his imagination and interpretations.

The Doyen moved his lips forward and pressed them. The lower line of his mouth expanded, and he shook his head and said, "I see that we take these to the bottom of the sea in line with our traditions. There is no harm. Do as you like. Rituals do not reflect the extent of our belief."

Abu Rashed then asked him, "We came to ask you what we can do; however, you did not offer us a specific answer. What shall we do now?"

"From my own studies of the Holy Quran and the Traditions of our Prophet, I could not prove anything related to deactivating magic or foiling charms. Reason really refuses that, but stories and repeated news from the trustworthy put us in a real dilemma when they negate and refute those matters. That causes some to be in doubt and bewilderment. I see that doubt, with all the thorns it bears, is a way of life. Throw away these things in any way you like. We shall meet in the evening in two days; our guest will be a young man from the village, and you know him well. His name is Kamel, who may perhaps reveal what is hidden and prove the forbidden.

(8) Carina
Mid-June 1760

For the past few months, I have been feeling the change of words in Adam's mother when she speaks to me. She showed some kindness, full of mothers' cunning. Women have ears different from those of men. Most of the words that pass through the woman's ears run through the direction of her heart. In her talks she used to interpolate the noun "Adam" between the lines. When you get used to something, you become familiar with it. She used to sing the praise of his good qualities to reach her objectives. With our words, we build castles in the minds of the others. The woman found listening ears for her aims and found that Adam was worth the endeavour and trouble. I began watching him writing the lines of his future and building his independent character. Her advances to me were welcome, and my father felt it and turned a blind eye. Some silence is highly praised cowardice. As for me, I wished Adam could build alone our love project and even our marriage. It is a stand-alone relationship while intermediating is a deferred project of failure.

Adam had no past womanising experience, so it seemed. He is still young to violate the world of women. I was forced to practise temptation, as the shortest inherited means to reach the heart of the man is to cross between his thighs. I began the story… I passed him, busy sowing the red soil, waiting for water to cover it, hoping heaven would rain goodness and blessings, after he was commissioned to work in the field and supervise the rest of the labourers. I became like a tortoise in my walk, begged God to settle down when He throws me in Adam's heart. I walked slowly between water wheels and only a few metres separated us. I raised my straw hat in my right hand and untied my hair until I felt it touching my waist, moving left and right with my steps. Dust rose between my feet proceeding me towards him. The man raised his head but took no notice of me. Scandinavian coldness!

Adam was engrossed between tilling and sowing, not heeding passers-by except when he wanted to rest his back and set it upright, or when he wanted to dry his sweat. His brown hat protected his head from a warm sun temperature. I liked this active manhood, as his trousers and shoes were transformed into what looked like mud; an onlooker hardly distinguished between them. He raised his head for a little while, looking far away and measuring what remained of an area awaiting his arms that day. I had to feign exhaustion into reality, as if the trick worked on him. He hurried towards me, offering to lift the big cherry basket that seemed heavy.

"Never mind, I'll carry it myself to the barns, I got used to this every day."

"Let me help you; you look tired. It is heavy, no doubt."

"I can carry it but slowly."

"Leave it."

The man likes to have the last word, qualities of false distinction. Adam knelt without bending his knees, putting his right hand below the basket and his left on the handle. He thought it was heavy but found it on the contrary full of emptiness and air and expressed his wonder.

"Has emptiness a weight?"

"No weight for emptiness, except in the heart of she who is looking for a lover."

He did not seem surprised; half of the surprise is disdain. He dropped the basket carelessly and returned to his work, not saying a word. Ignorance is the enemy of the woman. My eyes were full of anger; a simple trick that did not help me; my efforts went in vain. I sadly called him and he turned his head steadily. He did not want to ignore me. Again, he deplorably said, "What is wrong with you? The basket is empty. It is suffering from emptiness."

"Precisely. The pain of emptiness exhausts the heart."

"Emptiness is heavier than other kind of pains. I think overworking has exhausted you."

He looked at me with a cold, frozen face. The deep eyes were full of curiosity; nothing moved but the balls. His features were neutral and did not reveal what was inside him. Perhaps he looks with his eyes and feels and looks at me with his insight… then forgives. I caught him looking at what I had behind me; he was measuring the distance behind me with his eyes and contemplating the heights and valleys. I dropped a word in the sea of his silence; perhaps his water would move.

"I told you my back is aching and is nearly…"

He never heeded my words. He stretched his neck to my back. It was the beginnings; he examined the slim waist. A woman's waist is her handle. I feared he would devour with his hands so reaching his heart would be easier. Ugh! Man! He did not care for the topography of my body. It was said the man who is in love with a woman because of her body has no real love; in contrast, he who ignores her, she will fight to reach him. I thought that then. He thrilled me with his ignorance of the sciences of woman. At last, he carried the basket on our way to the cabin in the field. He walked next to me, wanting to hurry up and I wanted to slow down. I wished he were a chatterer and he wished me dumb. Aren't humans linguistic creatures? I began with questions, hoping to break the silence barrier.

"When were you born, Adam?"

"1741."

"I think your mother is a Swede, isn't she?"

"My father is British and my mother is a Dane."

"Is there a difference between Britain and Denmark? Do you like life here?"

Terse answers look quickly for a full stop. He did not comment on my question. The flow of questions stopped. Questions do not flow like a torrent unless there is a pool of answers to fill. I asked him to wait outside the store cabin.

"Do not look through the slots of the cabin; I want to take off my shirt and moisten my body with water."

He did not comment; is it a temptation of an adolescent? They say that a woman who begs shyness, has no shyness, and the snare of women is obvious. I repeated, "Do not come closer and peep." I dropped my shirt slowly, purposefully and stooped until my beauties were apparent. Thus, how the trenches are raised and hills are levelled. I put on whatever was available and went out eagerly to him, hoping that his sexual sensors would stand like a lion'.

I went out with great eagerness, hoping that the strongest weapon of woman would win in her battles and differences with the man. An arrow of feminism and a shield of recalcitrance. I came with my gold weapon preceding me. I knew that the man should stand broken in front of the impetuousness of his desire whenever he is provoked.

Nevertheless, I saw nothing but his footsteps in the neighbourhood. This man had made me mad.

"What kind of man are you who is not moved by mature feminism?" A woman, whose sexual attraction fails to attract a man, definitely feels the bitterness of loss and wounded pride. This is what I felt.

At that time, Adam was stretching a rope from the barn to the tallest tree inside the fence tens of metres away. He reverted to his hobby of land surveying, of putting an approximate metric measure in place for adjacent lands. This habit has made him restless whenever he finds a large area of land. He had an obsession with measures and mathematics and the discovery of new lands and its people. He also does not take seriously a body lying at his hands. It seems that being engaged to you is impossible, and it is obvious that marriage is an incomplete sentence if its beginning and end is a man.

(9) The Doyen
July 1760

After the magic incident, I held a lunch party after Friday Prayers, inviting the Imam of the mosque, Yousif, the Puller and the young man who saw the burial act of the charm. I also extended an invitation to Kamel, the man known locally for his amazing abilities. I invited them all to know about the truth of that charm. However, I did not tell them about the purpose of the invitation. I spread the claim that it was a lunch invitation to meet loved ones and close friends to discuss the public affairs looming over the island.

Kamel was the first guest and the last to arrive, they invited only him. The men stood to shake hands with him, and then he came towards me. He was a tall, stout, well-built man. His face was round with small eyes and a short, pointed nose. His hair was bushy and his beard was thick, nearly filling his face, and his eyebrows were connected. I shook hands with him, and my hand was lost in his huge palm. I welcomed him and he reciprocated in a strong, sure voice.

The man sat on my right beside Yusif and began telling jokes and spreading smiles and an atmosphere of happiness and joy. The guests talked about what was going on in Dilmunia. Cases varied between give and take. There, man forgets his reservations, and his soul is elated between his ribs. The tongue is the key of the heart and interpreter of the mind. Discussions went around about the next pearling season and the case of Nasser's death, that was added to the long list of tragedies of Dilmunia. Yusif, the Puller, kept quiet and placed his head between his knees. The young man patted Yusif's shoulder and smiled until his shining teeth were seen. Kamel looked into the face of the young man, forgetting all the discussions and said, "What beautiful teeth, like pomegranate grains."

The Doyen invited them for lunch as they ended their conversation. Local meals are never without rice, fish and dates, followed by some fruits. The young man had some pomegranates and began to chew them. He placed his thumb and index finger at the tip of his lip. With the help of his tongue, he took out something white from his mouth, placed it in his palm, and said, "This is one of my teeth, a grain of pomegranate, Kamel; God protect me from you and your eye."

"Let me see it."

"Here, it is yours."

The *majlis* was over and all were about to depart. I stood outside, leaning on the door, bidding them farewell. Beside us ran our fat cat. Kamel wanted to kick her, but she ran away, staring at him. He talked to her as if she listened to him. "I hate black cats, especially fat ones."

The young man left, followed by Kamel, while Yusuf asked me to wait for Abu Rashed until his return. We went back to the *majlis* to wait for the man. Yusif started emptying the grudges from his heart. "I still do not know, Doyen, why the Merchant is still insisting on accusing me of the death of his son."

"It is an old, waned trick that had lost its lustre. Some used to frame those who demanded their rights, and then they could remove them from their path."

"Is it not stupid to solve a problem by creating a bigger one?"

"It is the top of craftiness and deceit."

The conversation continued for few minutes before Abu Rashed knocked at the door. He greeted them and begged to sit. Yusif welcomed him and before telling Abu Rashed his story, I made it clear that we must differentiate between three things: between magic and envy and the eye.

I explained that magic is a kind of deceit and charlatanism; it is the ability to depict falsehood as if it is the truth. Yusif, the Puller, did not allow me to elaborate and asked, "Do you want to say the magicians of Pharaoh and the rod of Moses are all quacks?"

"No, no, no, Yusif, magic has many forms: one is agility and speed, the other type is fraud, because the fraudulent and the deceitful are pests of all health and sickness of wellness, and a trick. Pharaoh's magicians excelled in optical illusion. They suggested things to people as if they were true. That is why they were the first to believe in the incompatibility of Moses' rod when they realised it was not optical illusion.

The presence of my son, Abu Rashed, was my son, was of great importance. He was a clever man of good learning and conclusion. He explained that the inscription and blowing in the knots are mere lies and nonsense. How can a nation living in the eighteenth century believe in such things? We are definitely at the end of the world. What the Imam saw was nothing but garbage. If we cannot wipe these from the minds of the simple people, do not expect us to move forward and attain progress in life.

The puller expressed his disapproval of what he heard. "If you want to say that magic is false and deception and fraud, do you mean that envy is the same?"

"To start with, let me say that belief in superstitions protects us from worries of the devil. However, envy, as you may know, is wishing the disappearance of fortunes. You know that an envious person feels misery when you are happy. Nevertheless, what is known as 'eye' is something different. This I could not find an interpretation for in the Quran or the Tradition. Thank God for that, some ignorance is a blessing, and lots of learning is dangerous.

Abu Rashed explained that he had an old manuscript by Alshaikh Alraiss, Ibn Sina. In it, he said that the eye hits and affects provided that the soul of its owner conquers all the powers within him, like anger and desire. If the soul is able get rid of all these, it assumes a spiritual power that can affect the others.

Yusif's face lit with happiness. "Here Abu Rashed disagrees with his father and recognises the existence of the 'Eye'."

Abu Rashed replied to him, "The catastrophe is when a man thinks with ears instead of his mind. I never said that I believe in this. I have cited what I read previously. Yusif, I think we are a bit late; I will see you tomorrow evening at the beach. You shall find our fat cat dead outside the house. Take it away before it becomes carrion."

(10) Adam
August 1760

The heart of the mother never goes to sleep until it is relieved. She sent for me. The lady wants to see you immediately in her room. This rarely happens. There is an important, familiar matter. It must be the Church or the brokers again. I knocked at her door. I normally sit on the wood settee where she meets me. Strangely and suddenly, she was waiting for me near the door. She smiled and pointed with her left hand as a gesture of welcome. I followed her to where she made me sit at the edge of her bed.

"Has the Church sent us another agent?"

"No, not really."

"The agents with their foolish acts?"

"No, my son… The matter is about you. It is about Adam alone."

I placed my left hand on her knee, and she took it between her palms and said, "Adam, the law of life necessitates that man should be affianced to a woman. I find that you have become a handsome young man. We shall never let sick minds make up tales about your manhood. Staying without a girlfriend arouses their suspicions, and perhaps they would add a religious touch that could resonate with the clergy. I also absolutely believe that there is someone in your pulsing organ, and that you are in her heart, though you do not feel that. Some love is clouded by recalcitrance and is drowned by secrecy.

You had better not stay lonely. Women are like poplars all around you; have none of them attracted you? Have none of them approached you with kindness and shown you their love?"

I realised then a mother has a bell that she rings in times of happiness and sadness. She makes me feel with what maternal cresset she is endowed. I replied, "Yes, there is Carina, but I paid no attention to her. There is nothing distinctive in her that I like. Perhaps my other interests stand as a barrier that makes me unable to discover her points of strength and beauty. I find myself overworking and focus on my studies. Moreover, our imminent departure makes me think only of the town."

"Adam, there are many who are interested in you; a woman, however, likes him who knocks at her door. Most women want him who penetrates their lives. No woman falls in love with anyone unless he scatters her papers. To tell you the truth, I am trying to search your spectrum in the eyes of close relatives in our family, acquaintances and neighbours, but can find you only in Carina's eyes."

"Carina? The girl who asked me to help her lift her empty basket?"

"Do you need more than that? Illogic is the first sign of love. She is a beautiful and clever girl; why do not you try your luck with her? In addition, she shall remain here with her family after our departure. We can entrust them with our property until we find a solution to our crisis."

After a few discussions I decided, with some explanation from my mother, to enter the world of the women and knock at Carina's door. She suggested I visit her at her home. Penetration is the master of evidence. The science of women is contrary to applied sciences; there is no way out. My mother gave Luke's wise pieces of advice that may be useful in the imminent battle. The next morning, I left the orchard for Carina's family home. I walked between the meadows. I followed the narrow lanes that passers-by's feet dug, randomly becoming a road. It should be nothing but Carina; there was no harm if I guessed the required steps until I reached her. If my intuition was right, it was a good omen. I walked, counting my steps. A few moments later, the girl was out of my mind. Another intentional mistake, Adam. I got near the door. I realised that my estimates were less than I expected by two steps; all was going to be well. I knocked at the door three times, like the postman. Her father opened, welcoming me. I asked if I could see Carina. He suppressed a giggle and said, "She is inside, I will tell your wish." In no time she came.

"Hello, Adam."

"Can we walk far towards that valley? I have a lot to talk about."

She was couldn't say a word. She drew a deep breath and her chest went up.

"Are you Adam, whom I know?"

I held her wrist. Seven steps, then I surrounded her with my right hand. This is how the scene is written. The girl expected a kiss in a minute, perhaps much more later. Her words became heavy. Confusion is the sign of lovers. The man does not recognise any sentimental logic. Her heart spoke before her tongue.

"As if it is not you."

"It is I."

There must be a tumultuous relationship between love and disinterest. We only discover love after it fades away. Every man is an enemy of what is common and only desires what is not available.

"Adam, I promised myself since yesterday to wipe you from my heart, but you returned, as I desire!"

"You are always in the heart; I am in your hands. Go to the cave from this side, and I shall see you from the other side."

Carina went from the hilly side and took the opposite road downwards. She preceded me to the cave and rested there. She laid on her back and the moment I got there, she said she was ready for me.

"How did you manage to get to the cave quicker than I did? The distance I covered was longer, which means that either the body remains in motion in stability, or movement in straight direction, providing there is no power that changes this state."

She quickly put on her clothes, turning her face angrily and… left.

(11) The Merchant
September 1760

I went to the Ruler's Palace to attend his weekly meeting with the appointed Council of Leaders. I asked the *Nukhatha* to accompany me on this visit. I saw in him my right arm that I could count on in time of need.

He had to grow and become stronger and gain experience, by means of communications with the Ruler and the Council on one hand and with the populace on the other. Successful life is a group of selected relations. He welcomed the idea and accompanied me with pleasure. The guards received us and ushered us to where the meeting was usually held. The Ruler arrived and the permanent smile was not on his face. A serious matter confused him despite his high position. Reading his mind through his face was an easy thing. He greeted us all curtly and welcomed the new guest and us. I told him about the *Nukhatha* and his attendance at the meeting as an accompanied visitor, with the possibility of making use of expertise in the future. He did not mind and never cared about our visit. He sat upright and said, "Members of the Appointed Council. We welcome you all to our Council. We will begin with discussing foreign affairs and then move to discuss matters related to the local affairs. We have received a letter from the Ruler of the Persian island of Hurmuz, requesting us to provide him with men to serve under the command of the army in Persia, with the blessings of the commander of the

British forces stationed on the island of Qishm, near it. The Ruler of Hurmuz indicated his desire to build a strong regional Persian army able to spread its influence, consisting of two branches: a Land Force and a Sea Force.

"This army shall be in a position to confront the manoeuvres and quarrelling of armies and other tribes. In his letter, he specified the increasing strength of the Afghan armies and their allies coming from the north and also the Ottoman forces and those of the Mowahidin, in addition to the scattered Gulf tribes. We realise that the British forces in Qashim do not want Hurmuz to be involved in wars with these forces. However, at the same time it believes that building a powerful army will be a deterrent to all these powers attempting to come closer from its frontiers and hit its interests. It also confirms that through various alliances it is the desire of the British Crown to extend its influence and impose security in the Gulf through the islands of Hurmuz and Qishm, to safeguard routes to India and the Asian Orient as a service to the convoys of the British East India Company."

As usual, I was the first to make comments, "We are suffering from an acute deficiency of work-force, and it will be very difficult for us to push tribal men to be enlisted in a foreign army. Then our government shall be without security cover internally against the mobs and saboteurs."

The Ruler answered, turning towards me with his full body.

"I took some time studying and thinking about what I say. We do not know yet what the army will do there for the interests of the island here. Will it maintain our internal security and maintain defence of our borders against any conquering force?"

The members stopped talking. Everyone was talking to himself, building ideas, both positives and counter-positives, until he attained a convincing reality to persuade others. The Ruler spoke in detail, saying that it was possible to send some men from among the men of the sea and some farmers to work there, while we retained our Bedouin fighters. We could not send them so that our bones became weak and easy to break in the face of the wind.

I asked for permission to talk and indicated my concerns about the proposal. The Ruler asked me about the harm of sending people from the villages there.

"Your Highness, there are far-reaching concerns. As Your Highness can see, there are made-up security problems locally on the part of the seamen and farmers. When you send them there, they shall return trained in carrying weapons. This shall naturally be an eminent security risk to the island. We do not trust their affiliation and loyalty to this island and its ruler. On the other hand, sending them to work under the service of the Persian army in Hurmuz with the blessings of the British Crown shall provide them with political cover and an income different from what they get here.

"On the other hand, I see in order to avoid the worst harm, we ask the Governor of Hurmuz to send him some men, on condition that we receive the tax returns from them, and we are the ones who pay the salaries of our men on their return home. The income shall not be different from what they earn here. Thus, we retain the upper hand, and we can strip them of money and arms in case of betrayal and plotting. I repeat, they cannot have an income higher than those working here, as this shall harm national security. We have no need for that."

The Ruler understood what I was aiming at, but he

expressed his fears of the reaction on the part of Hurmuz and the disputes with the British Crown in Qishim before he explained, "We can apologise to them for not having enough men to man that army, and also the British Emissary and their Political Resident can verify that themselves and report that to them. We can also open our lands to maintain an office for the agency of the East India Company on the island. In addition, open doors for the Christian missionaries to perform here. We also agree to pay levies to Hurmuz and open our seaports for their boats. All this in exchange for providing protection to the Ruler and the Appointed Council and to maintain security and stability."

All expressed their agreement to the Ruler's proposals, wishing him long life and happiness, and prosperity to the island and the islanders. It was then suggested that the Ruler send all the decisions to the Political Resident in Qishim and the Persian commander in Hurmuz.

The Ruler then moved on to talk about the internal situation: he permitted the members to inform him about the affairs of the pearling season, farming and trading, and all that concerned local affairs. I spoke, "Your Highness, whenever we meet at your council to facilitate the people's affairs, they usually think we are plotting against them. We want to build the country, and they regard it that we have hidden objectives to dismantle the society and control it. We work at their service and they are certain that we are despots imposing our iron fist on man and land."

"Apparently, it is a question of lack of confidence. We do not want to monitor many instances of lack of confidence, but we want to fill the gaps between them and us. We want to build a strong bridge of confidence and communication. We hope that relations shall be built between people based on love and appreciation. All have duties and obligations. I hope to receive happy news in that context. We want people to coexist far away from differences and to think of similarities and build on them. Thus, a homeland is built for all so that Dilmunia returns a tree for all and a garden that people yearn for from all over the universe. Those from the past saw it as a Garden of Eden, and it must remain as such."

Despite what the Ruler repeats in his councils, it would be better for me to be on his side, giving my verbal agreement, though in fact I do not agree. To swim with the current is easier to reach the bank. Wealth is the art of containing rulers. I asked for permission to say what I wanted.

"Your Highness, there is a plan to initiate a trade business that benefits the whole of Dilmunia. After your approval, I shall import goods from the Asian Orient, from India, Persia and other countries. Then these shall be available for sale in the local markets. For this, I met with an expert coordinator from the East India Company. We have his approval on condition that the company gets a commission in exchange for the facilities and recommendations that help us in our new venture."

"What did they demand?"

"Their demands were easy to apply. These will contribute to building of the quarters of the Christian Mission and give it official approval. Moreover, permit Persian boats and those flying the flag of the British Crown to dock at our ports for lower levies. Your Highness, this no doubt shall help us cater for markets with goods and finance dhows and small boats. Then you can control the market."

"Naturally, there is no harm in importing some new goods

to the market, step by step. However, don't you think that financing the Christian agency might upset the people?"

"The people are good by nature. They do not have any differences when it comes to religion. Their religion is treatment; each has its law and methods. However, I have some conditions for the *Nukhatha*, who wants to work according this agreement. Our guest knows this; the *Nukhatha* must own two dhows at least and must go pearl fishing twice a year. We finance them and they sell us half of their catch of pearls. We can accordingly export it and import those goods. Gulf pearl is known for its high quality on the level of fisheries in the world. As you may know, some of them has eight colours, and its size is the largest in comparison to others and that is why it is easy to export. With that, we safeguard the rights of the seamen and their share and we shall gain the greater benefit."

"You have what you ask for."

The weekly council meeting was over, and on our return, I disclosed to the *Nukhatha* lots of secrets on how to deal with the Ruler, his rivals and the public. To succeed in life, you must know how to deal with every individual alone. The security and stability that the Ruler wants will be in his own interests, as this will ensure easy succession of his throne to his sons. The apex of good luck is to be born with a gold spoon in your mouth; the public interest is when they feel prosperous, but it does not fit within our interests, we the class of merchants and influential politicians. Instability leads the Ruler to depend on us in running the State. Consequently, we gain a lot.

There are many avenues that we tread, and there are many means to achieve these objectives such as financial enticements, intimidation of an imaginary enemy, religious strife and sectarian perils. The objectives are numerous but obliteration is one. By the way, I still do not know how these vocabularies reached them and had a great impact on them. I expect it is the tragedy of communicating with the outside world.

Communication is infidelity and destructive plotting; it is similar to the problem and danger of education. It transports destructive ideas, foreign plans and plots. One of the British soldiers I met on my last journey said that what you practise here is a primitive capitalism that was pressing and became practised without a framework and theorisation. He also said that most of the theories are not innovative, but those who contemplate them, succeed in keeping them in a frame to memorise them and to be attributed to him.

It is a primitive theory of the jungle that enforces the phenomenon of distinction between classes. This leads to the rich becoming richer and the working classes, the builders, being the poorer. Mottos: I can understand nothing from them. They are hollow. That may be suitable for their societies but not ours, which is still primitive and needs more time to determine its fate by itself. I am concerned about these idioms. Many may not understand them, and the spoken word is a slogan and demands a… revolution.

In our last meeting, the Ruler was not in haste to know the trade results, but became concerned about the Persian Hurmuz claims and what may occur as a result. He did not want to go into political and security labyrinths, as he tended to lean towards stability and serenity. The rest of the traders and members of the Appointed Council were planning their objectives on the status quo, without the Ruler losing his grip on power. After all, his existence is guaranteed by theirs too.

All transactions were conducted under his umbrella, even though he was ignorant about what was going on behind his back. Add to that, the story of the death of Nasser seemed effective to scare the people; intimidation is the first step to hegemony. Whenever the people are scared, he who owns power imposes his terms, awaiting obedience and surrender.

(12) The Interpreter
January 1761

After prolonged familial discussions and manoeuvres with the rivals that may not put an end to their wishes, the lady, along with her son, decided to leave for Copenhagen where some of her relatives were and where her hope to live in peace could be realised. Sudden decisions are easier to apply, let alone the sense of belonging to a place of birth is a human instinct that increases with the passage of time and advancement of age. Man longs for that, until his death.

However, the lady was torn between two fires: she was certain that Carina was the ideal wife for her son. She found in her the source of love and kindness that was matchless. Add to that, that her family belonged to the same conservative family as theirs, away from the triangle of fear initiated earlier by King Alfred. She hoped Carina for Adam, because a mother does not offer her son anything except a warm lap that he can trust and confide in. Carina's feminine endeavours did not bear fruit; however, the mother managed to attain the mutual target. Adam began to fall under illusions about his new love, as illusions turn into facts by passage of time.

Love is a mountain of illusions nourished by desires and built up by aspirations. Carina, on the other hand, was torn by two fires: the fire of love, and the fire of the forlorn that seemed to be looming in the dark horizon. Women do not immortalise love, except when it is related to deprivation and desertion. That appears in an inverse relationship that shows the love of control and possession in humans, even in their sentiments.

On his part, Adam did not seem obsessed except by his studies and adventure, even though he appeared to be the opposite. Travelling to Copenhagen achieved that aspiration, as he was fond of studying and the prosperous learning there. Simple scientific steps but gigantic in its objectives. He who can change his innermost sentiments can change and manage the world. News coming from there was hitting him at the core. Carina and he agreed to maintain the line of communication between them. That enriches the bonds between them. Let them find the best means at the time. Postal letters were the most useful. They promised each other to maintain the love bond as long as they are alive. Philosophy of vows may maintain promises.

"Carina!"

"Yes."

"We did not find the time for our love to grow and water from the overflow of our emotions."

"Let our vows be sincere. I shall await you here."

"I shall return when the tempest recedes, within a year or two; we shall build a happy family."

"A promise we shall not break."

The sexual scene prepared by Carina for Adam in the cave was passed and gone during his great departure with his mother to the town. They carried their hopes and were supported by their history. The capital is strength and knowledge is a group of powers. Their route was full of migrating caravans. Their misery was relative, as there were those who perished en route and those who were lost and missed.

They reached Copenhagen after a long ordeal that exhausted the mother and delighted Adam with its bumpiness. He repeated that migrating was a pleasure worthy of the trouble. With difficulty and troubles, the living survive. Fate is written on the side of man, who frequently fails to read it and tries hard with his curiosity to read the fates of others. After search and investigations about a suitable house for settling, Adam decided to leave Carina there. He directly declared his intention to enter the battle of knowledge and to continue studying.

Adam headed towards the town hall in the centre of the town to present his credentials, hoping for endorsement. Before that, he wondered about the benefit of those sciences to travellers who frequent countries of the East. However, people are foes of what they do not know! He found out that recommendations of the German philosopher Emmanuel Kant had the upper hand. Sending a specialist in divinity to the East shall help disengage the relationship between this science and divine books. The people of the East shall help contribute in the concept of this new philosophy because the Arabs are one of the Semitic races in the Middle East. It was a coincidence that accepting Adam came after accepting the other scientists. Among these was a distinguished multi-gifted servant. Is not the servant of the people their master?

The Danish government agreed to sponsor the mission. Those who were selected were sent to Göttingen University for the sake of indoctrination. In the process of admission there was a personal interview for Adam, where details of his life were revealed. The registrar asked him why he wanted to enrol in the University.

"What is the objective of your college studies?"

"To study mathematics, physics and topology."

"According to your results in the preliminary assessment, you can study whatever you want."

"That is a very good thing; I want to specialise in mathematics."

"Listen, my son, you can study whatever you like. Your father is British, and your mother is a Dane; why do you not think of studying at a British university?"

"Science, sir, is like water and both are available to all human beings. One can drink from any source, any time anywhere; as long as the scientific objectives are noble, why should there be no cooperation with the others?"

The registrar was impressed by Adam's personality, promptitude and logic. He was full of hope for his future. He asked him to meet with the rector of the university to coordinate his studies and other matters. Adam had no problem accepting the offer and wanted to know more about university systems and to get closely acquainted with its personalities. All these were matters that clarified his thoughts and scholastic objectives. Two days later, the rector received him at his office. It was full of manuscripts and old books, all arranged on chestnut shelves all over the room. Papers were spread in every corner.

"Good morning!"

"Good morning, sir."

"As I know, you are an Anglo-Danish, ambitious young man, who has the desire and necessary abilities to study mathematics. The university is planning to launch an exploratory expedition to the Middle East. We are looking for young competent men, who have true desire and the required intelligence to meet the Royals and wish to be part of this historic expedition. You have obvious priority, as you know more than one language that would facilitate your mission. Would you accept that the university prepares you academically to acquire general knowledge that would enable you to deal with various kinds of people: Bedouins, urban, Arabs, Persians and diverse religions and sects? Terrains: seas, oceans and deserts?"

Adam's wheel of thinking and decision-making stopped revolving as if the directive came as cold water spilled over him. He requested time to make consultations with his family so that the final decision would be consultative, with all parties concerned taking part. Hesitation is mostly a postponed decline. He was not hesitant, but he was actually facing a difficult decision. He wondered. "What are the declared objectives of exploring those remote lands? We are waging exploration campaigns to areas that do not belong to us, and we do not belong to them."

"My dear, during the industrial revolution that Europe is going through now, competition is increasing between western countries to explore new markets that can absorb its exports. It is a sort of conflict of antagonists. It is the war of dissemination of scientific inventions. It is a dispute between European states, in search of new markets that would establish the basis of industry to invest in and to ensure the sustainability and continuity of their factories. Industry is supply and demand, and demand is the real incentive for industrialisation. This is accompanied by the desire of those countries to acquire raw materials that are under the feet of the Arabs in their regions. Wealth buried below their lands that the whole of humanity has to benefit from. As we have just mentioned that the right to water and learning is available to all, to those we add natural wealth. All this comes contemporaneously with the geographic discoveries to reach remote markets like India and China. The race became heated by sending exploration missions to those lands. Portugal, Spain and Denmark headed for those countries. As for Britain, it surpassed all the others and reached the furthest parts of India and the Sind Valley."

"Is that all?"

"Not really. At the moment, the European countries are suffering from an acute deficit of precious metal bullions. As you know, the industry of ingots is based on gold and silver."

"Aha, so these metal coins are made of silver and gold found there."

"Add to this, the continuous conflict between the Iberians and the Muslims. A conflict based on religious basis. Do you know, Adam, that when the Ottomans dominated Constantinople, strife between peoples was continuous?"

"These are the natural consequences of politics. If the politician wants to establish himself and cling to power without monitoring the corruption files in his government, he has If the politician wants to establish his rule and hang on to play on the strings of religions and sects. There are even governments established by creating disputes between communities of the same religion, and on Divine and Non-divine religions. You have to create an imaginary enemy that represents a ghoul, waiting for them."

"But I am not fond of economic and political studies."

"As I heard from you earlier, in case of your acceptance, you shall be part of a team of five scientists and a servant. Your knowledge and sciences shall be criss-crossing. Study and work complementing each other. You may be assigned drawing mosques and houses of worship and others. As you are studying topology according to mathematics and physics, these sciences are related to religions. Knowledge of religions adds another dimension to you when you start drawing geometric maps. This also applies to drawing general maps of roads and features of every area."

The University of Göttingen proposed an intensified study to the new travellers in preparation for the Middle East campaign, each according to his specialisation. Each one of them takes individual classes in his line, and then he shares them with his colleagues at the end of every month. This type of learning enhances the ability to demonstrate and understand, which is in essence a type of personal assessment. His love for study met with his innate desires. He loved abstract mathematics and became fond of it, because it is a practical study related to reality and life. It has never been a luxury thought.

(13) Abu Rashed
February 1761

The Ruler decided the start of the *Almajni* diving expedition, which is the preliminary dive that precedes the big dive. It is an explorative dive where all concerned make sure of the seaworthiness of the dhows. The Merchant took care of supplies, the *Nukhatha* of management and captainship, while the divers and pullers work on the ability and desire for a good harvest. In *Almajni*, duties and responsibilities are defined. Family spirit dominates; love is the cornerstone in life where selflessness, not I, is the order of the day.

On board the boat there is a cook, an assistant skipper and some hands. There, the pearl fisheries and submarine fresh water sources, *Chawacheb*, are delineated. Everyone works hard and is after pearls, as they are the subsistence of life and the major source of it. Out of it, the Ruler extracts taxes and registers the dhows in a message that reads, "A ruler without subjects is like a farmer without water, as he cannot survive without it." After forty nautical miles and a day's sailing, we defined a number of deep pearl fisheries, *Hayrat,* before we returned home in preparation for the big set-out.

Two months or so from the *Almajni* dive, we proudly embark on the big dive that comes after the burning summer and continues for nearly three months, as if it were the junior brother of the two *Eids*. Its ceremonial rites begin after the Friday prayer, with the Ruler coming in person, followed by the merchants and the commoners. The boats set out in effect after sunset, on the tunes of the sailors performing diviners' folk songs on the tunes of drums and hand clapping, bidding farewell to the men and praying for their safe return.

I found the diving season crippled this year. Fear of the future as warned by the Merchant made the people restless. Mocking up a crime and playing on its tunes made them anticipate his reaction after the death of his son, Nasser. No sleep without security. A question that always imposes itself on me: why is the Ruler's authority helpless when it comes to merchants and men of power? The Ruler is authoritative only when it comes to the powerless. Is the Ruler ordained by Divine order, or is he commissioned by the people to run their affairs and be a despot?

I left the house accompanied by the whole family; the Doyen, supported his wife, Khowla, and her younger sisters. There on the seashore gathered all the families in what seemed like a big festival: women in their best attire and the children well dressed, whether their clothes were new or old. An image that contradicts the expected date of return, when all will be waiting with tears drawing on the pale faces their last touches. The drums had an impact on the ears and hearts, as if it were the beginning of war on the sea and collecting the loot from it. The boats were ready to sail before sunset. Their number reached one hundred and fifty this season. Our dhow set out under the command of the *Nukhatha*, and it is creeping along with its group. She will not lay anchor until reaching the pearl fisheries defined earlier.

I stood contemplating beside the boat. I stood as if pinned to the ground, watching the boats creeping behind their hope. A hope tied to the green waters. I found it this season, pulling the trails of failure and disappointment to the divers and pullers and the rest of the men. The law of life proves that what is baleful to you is beneficial to me. The dhow had provisions on board that would last for one month. Once they have been depleted, she returns for another load of provisions.

Hassan, the Singer, *Alnaham*, stood at the bow of the dhow. He was fair-skinned, handsome and of medium height, unlike the rest of the crew. He was clad in a flowery loincloth and a white T-shirt. He stood at the bow and began to croon the songs of the pearl divers with their tunes and percussion, while the rest were rowing towards the pearl fisheries three nautical miles away.

With the blessings of God we began,
Hi ho, answer our call, thou Master of Messengers,
Hi ho, intercede on our behalf.
With the blessings of God, we began.

At the dawn of the third day, examination of the pearl fishers began in earnest. Divers mention in their tales that pearls propagate only in shallow waters and love the heat of the sun. Accordingly, we prefer the hot season, and rather remain in the three summer months when oysters multiply in waters. Oysters become scarce during the cold season in winter. Very frequently, the sailors repeat their tales and ask the same questions. One of them approached me asking me about the tale of the oysters.

"Oysters live at the bottom of the seabed, but they float at the surface of the sea when it rains. They open their flanks and mix with the rain. If touched by a pure angelic drop of rain, they produce well-rounded pearls. When the rainwater is less in purity, the quality of the pearls, diminish. The most common occurrence is that most oysters produce no pearls. The size of the oyster may reach the size of a plate; add to that, in each ton of oysters we may find three or four well-rounded pearls."

The dhow stopped the first time after sunset and dropped its anchor; tunes began to be heard again after the voice of the *Naham*. The anchor was dropped on the sounds of its tunes. Then the call for prayers was raised. All prepared to pray. Most of them performed the prayer of the evening singularly and the rest in congregation. Then dinner was served, which is one of two main meals consisting of canned fruit, coffee, fish, rice and dates. The meal is full of dried lemon which the sailors use to fight against what they call the scurvy.

My friend the puller and I chose the port side of the boat; a place to sit on a ragged mat leaning on the parapet of the dhow. A marine emptiness bequeathed hollow thought that aroused his appetite, when he saw me unusually frowning. Using a glass eye makes you fall over the feelings of the others. Then, he spoke sadly to me.

"You will return shortly to your folks, old chap?"

"Why do we return?"

"Why this estrangement and weirdness if we do not return to our folks?"

"Do we return to inherit from them the debts, humiliation and humility?"

"Can we change the nature of life?"

"Listen, my friend, it is said, '*Have a good intention*' and, '*According to your intentions you are rewarded*', and the saying, '*As you are, you are governed*'. I do not wish to die satisfied by this life. An animal of burden is mounted. What religion allows a merchant or *Nukhatha* to control our destiny and that of our children? An unjust ruler; what kind of ruler is he who sleeps restfully when injustice is taking place between his hands? How can we live the humility of the debt, and then we bequeath it to our children? We are not men if we do not bequeath good to our children. We are promising evil to them and cannot bring them happiness. I see death as happiness rather than this life.

"However, goodness may come from where we know not. God does not change people until they change their innermost. As you may know, my friend, days are states. They say that the Portuguese are planning to come back and control the land again; so are the British and perhaps the Dutch. In addition, here the Ottomans, the Ya'rubi and the Bedouin tribes, all are trying. They are all, no doubt, the worst occupying forces, perhaps we can start life with them from the cypher, not below it as we are now. Cooperating with the Devil may be comfortable and fruitful. Some nations fight the settlers, and others see them as a lifesaver. When all the wishes meet, then occupation becomes easier. It is said that most occupations are collusions from within."

I heard movement at my side. I turned to him and saw him fast asleep with his snores rising gradually. Some questions are not worth thinking and answering. A kind of non-literal rhetoric. I moved towards the dark horizon where was my father's amputated leg, my young children, and my dear Khowla.

The diving season began promptly in the early morning. Unlike my habit, I had no appetite for breakfast. I felt bitterness and choking. I wanted to plunge in the sea very quickly; ten dives I needed to complete. I was in a hurry as if there were something awaiting me. I felt like I was going to a matter planned for me. I made haste towards it, as it may be the inevitable fate, or I wished it were another type of fate. Both are fates given names and causes to convince ourselves by the hereafter.

I found that my friend, the puller, had prepared the diving kit unlike his usual way. He handed me the nose clip and I tied the stone weight to one of the ropes and held the other. Both of them were heavy this time. I jumped into the water, holding the shell bag for nearly seventy feet. The stone rope started pulling me down to the seabed while the puller was holding the other rope in anticipation of a shake to pull me up to the surface. This is the senor of the diver's call to be pulled up.

Divers were usually light, tiny and lean in body, wearing only white cloth so as not to agitate the sharks. Colours are tantalising to man and animal as well. I descended quickly to the bottom of the sea to my fate. I found myself wearing red trousers. I did not care for the puller's question, "Why do you insist on daring the shark by using red trousers instead of white ones?" I took no notice of him; I began to contemplate the shoals of fish travelling. I moved deeply and deeply and found some stone slabs and next to them small, soft sand dunes.

The stone began to pull me down at an amazing speed. I examined the scattered oysters and realised it was fertile. Ten oysters; so I went back to the top, where I spotted Khowla among these oysters, wearing her wedding white and green dress. She was collecting oysters! I saw her sisters sending her as a bride to the damned Merchant. I wanted to direct myself towards them but... I found a huge shark cutting the path. One of us had fallen into the trap. The red trousers allured it, no doubt; it came to put an end to my life. It stood between them and me. I shook the rope left and right but no response from the puller. It seemed that the puller colluded with the shark, which rushed towards me and plunged its teeth into the trousers. Valleys of blood were spilled, turning the water red. Man's blood is sanctified, but it cares the less. I began to see death. The shark began to move around me, looking into my eye as if talking to me and running the dialogue

"He who gives his honour for money does not deserve living. If the land refuses to keep the body of a man, it declines it all."

"I did not give my honour to anyone."

"Your docility does not give you the right to live. Your land is your honour; preserve it."

"As the sea has a shark, every land has a bigger shark."

The shark did not like my answer; it came closer to me with its saw, a premeditated crime. I thought it was going to slice me; I dropped my gloves but they did not fall. I removed the nose clip. I wanted to shout at the puller so he could pull me. My mouth was full of water. I could not talk with a mouthful of water. I began to shout with all my might, "Hassan, Hassan…"

At last, Hassan, the puller, woke up at the shouting of his friend, Abu Rashed. I woke up from a deep slumber. Sleeping is a move towards discovering the other world. He began to wake me up and comfort me. He put an end to this abominable dream. He brought me a glass of water, and the crew gathered. He raised me and placed my head between his hands, then they carried me to the amber heater to resist the cold of a summer's night at sea. They talked between themselves.

"Chimeras."

"Our dreams reflect our suppressed feelings."

"Drink some water and read the chapter of *Alfateha* before you go back to sleep. Morning is still far away."

"God protect us from the damned Satan."

"He who spreads love dreams of it; he who goes to sleep with a headful of sufferings is haunted by them and they make him restless."

(14) Adam
March 1761

During this period, I read a great deal about the theories of Kant, the famous German Philosopher, who called for subjecting the Torah and the Bible to logical analogy and abolishing anything that was not subjected to mental abilities. His pioneering academic theories were circulating from his collegial lectures. His sayings were the *primum mobile*, main mover, for change movements, or perhaps revolutions were emanating from literary salons and public coffee shops, where his words found a popular echo. As for me, university education continuity, and its links are not complete except through discussions with my mates and beloved mother. My perceptions and knowledge are crystalised through fresh intellectual richness, as if I am implementing the dictum which believes that education begins at home.

"Mother, there are, as you may know, change revolutions and rectification revolutions. There is migration to towns for a better world. All are aware of this and know that man is imperfect and has to be rectified to avoid blunders. There are no infallible politicians or divine prophets who receive instructions from Heaven. Couldn't we perceive that? Couldn't man move in the right direction without blood spilling?"

"Rectification of revolutions starts automatically from inside to enlightening and loving yourself. He who loves himself and conceives his errors, shall try to distance it from falling into sin; and he who can endeavour to change it, shall definitely manage to change his society and perhaps change the whole of humanity. But my son, our age is the age of the machine. Our age urges us to take the machine an ideal, perhaps a god; it is an age based on two machines."

"Two machines?"

"Yes. There is a dumb machine, like the plough and tractor, and there is a speaking machine that embodies a speaking soul. It is the slave and the manual labourer who makes life by his own hands. He ploughs, plants and builds; this is the real cause of revolutions. Man despising his brother and looking down upon him from the top of the pyramid. Man is advised not to be like the top of a mountain so as not to see the small people, and people in return shall not see him small."

"This is the role of the age of enlightenment. It is the age of philosophers and scientists. They say corporal labour is the origin, and the labourer has the stronger role, while the intellectual shall come at a later stage."

"I do not think that will last. Ideology is not absolute. Preference between the scientist and labourer is relative. No one can attain his objectives without relying on the other. It is a complementary process towards a human civilisation."

"Injustice, no matter what kind it is, does not mean social and class stability. It keeps it in a boiling stage that it is always in search for stability. A revolution that does not achieve the lofty goals of humanity is overthrown by a counter-revolution. Achieving justice means stability, but failing to achieve justice is a problem and a continuous crisis."

Talking to her perplexed me. When the obnoxious triangle prospered, the rich became richer and the labourer turned into a hunchbacked machine. When he became a priority, my mother expressed her preservation on the present situation. No one can deny the role of thought and thinkers. How can the workers in a factory carry out their work and produce advanced technology without scientists taking care of the intellectual side? In my trip to the Orient, I hope to find different answers to the coexistence between thought and man power, between theory and practice, and how can man maintain the right of personal ownership without neglecting the commons and the working classes?

Kant was a true believer when he referred the theory of existence to the future. He said that the future is the science that surpasses all possible sciences. He also believed that there is no absolute brain in knowledge. Just as the unseen in itself is not an absolute unseen, rather it is an invisible existence to the human eye. Knowledge, on the other hand, is formed of matter out of which an image is formed inside the human brain; accordingly, the universe is the matter and its image in our mind is knowledge. When that is applied to any world known as love, consequently it becomes an easy thing. Woman in general, and Carina, Women in general, including Karina, are the origin and my love for her is knowledge.

It is a true matter and has a true imagined image in my mind. A knowledge image of the type that I yearn for. Do I consider my love for her not as related to what she carries in herself, but to my mental structure? We see the loved one and form a halo for him according to the image we desire it to be of our partner in life. We cling to that image and think it is love. I imagine Carina as the woman who can provide me with my mother's kindness. She is the one who conceives my needs and requirements. Oh, Carina, is that your love? I find love, like religion in some parts, is not subjected to reason.

"Mother, do you love Carina?"

"Of course I do."

"Do you love her for herself, or find in her what your son needs?"

"I respect her a lot, but she means nothing to me if not engaged to you."

I was certain — in mind and according to the Kantian analogy — that love cannot be measured by reason. It is a kind of future that we build our thought and knowledge on, through a vision that we need and desire. I promised her an eternal love where we could build a family! I think I am deceiving her and myself. Perhaps.

(15) Al Jubur Doyen
May 1761

Towns are normally void of men during the grand pearling season, as nobody remains except the aged, women and children and minor artisans, like farmers and others. Numbers of dhows sailing for pearl fishing are estimated at a hundred and fifty boats.

When the towns are vacant, the Ruler and frequenters of his *majlis*, traders among others, carry out their postponed plans and purposes. They try to restore the idols within them by undermining everyone who stands in the way of achieving their goals. I suppose it is the totalitarian despotic system that aggravates the economic, educational, political and social system. It is all truism that makes the present situation unbearable to all. On Sunday morning, two days after the start of the season, the Merchant's men came knocking continuously at the door. Rashed opened the door for them.

"Yes, what do you want?"

"We want your grandfather, the Doyen of Al Jubur."

They did not wait for Rashed to make way for them and invaded the house, and to the *majlis*, without greetings, said, "Old man, you are wanted to stand for trial."

Their arrival did not give me a shock, nor did their demand, as the unjust never sleep in peace. I was expecting their visits, planned in advance sometimes, but mostly random.

"What am I accused of?"

"We do not know exactly, but we believe there are multiple accusations, amongst which is the accusation of instigation of mutiny against the Ruler and the Appointed Council, and the accusation of breaking into the national security system. We do not have the authority to discuss that. Please come with us to the Council of Justice, where you shall know all the details."

Rashed tried to help me stand up and walk with them but he could not. They were the Merchant's men, or perhaps they were the Ruler's. I could not distinguish between them as they were dressed in local attire. Nothing in them was different except the truncheons and rifles. They carried me to the wooden cart drawn by a donkey. Watched by the neighbours, we walked towards the Merchant's *majlis*. My intuition was correct that time. They took me inside leaning on my walking stick and on one of the stout guards. I found the Merchant sitting on a wide wooden bench. On his right sat the same *Qadi*, judge, while the registrar sat on his left. I greeted him and sat on his left. The Merchant raised his harsh voice.

"As you find the plaintiff standing, you too have to stand in front of the judge as a defendant. The people in Dilmunia are all equal, like the teeth of the comb."

One of the guards came to me and helped me stand, as ordered, then the judge spoke.

"One of the farmers is accusing you of usurping his farm and laying your hand without right. The farmer is standing in front of you with evidence witnesses. If you are convicted, you shall spend the remainder of your life behind bars. As you claim to know the penalty in cases of thefts, that could amount to amputating the hand."

I looked at the plaintiff and found that I did not recall seeing him before. As for the two witnesses, their faces seemed familiar, though I did not remember if I had seen them, nor where. I knew it was an intrigue so that Abu Rashed remained at sea and his father in prison. Thus, the arena would be vacant of any opposing voice to the Merchant. Then the status quo would be imposed. The judge then asked the accuser, "Do you accuse this man, The Doyen of Al Jubur, of usurping your farm?"

"Yes, he stole my farm. I have two witnesses; we shall swear whenever you ask."

"What have you to say, old man?"

"Your Honour, yes, I have laid my hand on one of the farms, but I do not know to whom it belongs. Let us all go — at this point — to the said farm. If it was the farm that I stole, it is theirs. The court gives it back to them and I agree to do so. If it is not theirs, the court bestows it to me immediately."

The judge consulted with the Merchant. I realised then that it was a conspiracy, and that they had fallen into the trap that they had laid for me.

The judge decided to adjourn the case for further investigations. They let me go home. Khowla, Rashed and the others received me with tears. I comforted them. Out of curiosity, they asked me about what had happened at the court. Some aspects of curiosity are acceptable. This is the first step for participation. I preferred not to tell them and dived into another topic that might be beneficial for them in the future. I told them I needed to have some rest and follow it with prayers to thank God.

A few hours later I felt lonely again, so I returned to my solitude to think. I felt the responsibility that history ought to be documented in the sentiments of the family. I have found that documenting events of Dilmunia is an utmost necessity, just in case somebody can publish them for the whole world in the future. I think history can be interpreted differently according to historians. Each claim to know the absolute knowledge and believes that right is on his side. But those who believe in diversity accept conciliation. On the other hand, the moment people disbelieve some aspects of history, you will find some demanding the rewriting of history. There are two types of history. Written history or history books, which can be forged, and the history of earth, like archaeology and repetition, where it cannot be fiddled with. That is why we must transmit it in writing so it can be trustworthy.

Then I asked Rashed to share a conversation with me and document in his blank memory, those catastrophes that drew the events of his country which overflowed with his forefathers' blood. Khowla came along, accompanied by him to my *majlis*. She perceived what I wanted and loved listening and accomplished the art of listening.

"Yes, grandfather."

"Come closer, darling. As you have completed the Quran, you must now be good at reading and writing, exactly as your sister Khowla did earlier. In the large room over there, you shall find lots of manuscripts and books that you have to read in the future and extracts lessons from."

"I shall, grandfather, I shall do what you want."

"I shall disclose the history of your ancestors to you."

"Pardon me, grandfather. I want to know the secret of your amputated leg, and what happened to you this morning."

"Your father will tell you about my leg, and shortly I shall tell you what happened this morning. What is more important is to tell you about my own grandfather."

"Your grandfather?"

I stopped here for a while, wanting to rearrange my thoughts that I knew by heart due to repeating them. Documenting the memory is a very exhausting process, however, and emptying some of it releases some of the overload. I decided to narrate some of it for the first time. I had to be accurate for the sake of preserving the history.

"My grandfather was the actual ruler of the island of Dilmunia before the invasion of the Portuguese. After settling in Hurmus for nearly fifteen years, they were set on invading the island in 1521. Your great grandfather was the leader of the resistance. The real resister is he who does not belittle his weapon, albeit simple. He became a believer in the ability to confront. Their army came on at us with almost four hundred experienced Portuguese soldiers, supported by three thousand trained Hurmuzi men. In the fort, they were confronted by Shaikh Muqren Al Jubur, he was helped by the people estimated at eleven thousand fighters[2]. They all took refuge in the big fort situated at the northern tip of the island. The Portuguese barricaded the fort with their ample modern ammunition, while the local people were using primitive weapons and guns depleted with time. Time was not on their side as it took one week for the arrival of a new consignment.

"What did our great-grandfather Muqren do?"

"When the gunpowder was depleted, our grandfather took refuge in the fort. He refused to give in and surrender his

---

[2] Muqrin Al Jaubur was beheaded, his head was painted, and his picture was sent as a gift to the Queen of Portugal, and the picture is still preserved in a museum there. (The translator)

people to the conquerors. Snipers fired torrents of fire shots. He was hit by three bullets on his shoulder and started bleeding for a long time on the parapets of the fort until his death."

"What did the Portuguese want, Grandfather?"

I slowed down a little, as the question was fundamental. I was afraid Rashed would not comprehend. The dominant system was three-dimensional, difficult to conceive and accept. The Portuguese in Hurmuz represented an old, deep-rooted aristocracy, leading a despotic capitalist system opposed to an existing tribal system led by Muqren Al Jubur. The nomadic Bedouin were anticipating what the confrontation would result in.

"Were the Portuguese Arabs like our ancestors?"

"They were European conquerors. Living in Jamberon and the islands of Hurmuz and Qashm. On that coast, the majority of its inhabitants were Arabs. The Safavid Persians were living on the mainland, while the coast fell in the hands of the Arabs with the help of the conquerors."

"What do the Europeans want from our land?"

"That is, my son, what is called conquest. They wanted to test the power of the of Al Jubur and the extent of their ability to stand and resist. They wanted to enslave the people and acquire their wealth. They imposed taxes on products and crops imported by land and sea. The Portuguese colonisation in that period was considered the worst type among all settlements. They imposed taxes on everything, starting with pearls and passing on to agriculture and livestock, ending in its dung. However, fear had always been their concern. They feared that the Al Jubur would align themselves with the Ottoman Turks and weaken their power, and make them lose their tax revenues or declare agreements with Al Mouahidin and pirates and others."

Here Khowla interjected. "Had our people and ancestors surrendered to the status quo then?"

"The Portuguese were bastioned in the fort out of fear. They never left except for collecting taxes and never mixed with the people. They never interfered in the judiciary system or others, but our people got together eight years later and waged a mutiny on a large scale. The movement was aborted because of treason and internal schemes. Some of the Arabs joined the enemy's ranks for the love of his share and for fear of his people reaching for power. There some cowards who would take advantage of the present situation and think of nothing but their own interests at the expense of their people and nation. These were the Arabs, my daughter; the brother joins an alliance with the foreigner against his own brother. But on the day of reckoning, the losses become serious and apply to all."

"How did the Portuguese withdraw, Grandfather?"

"Counter-revolutions and movements for change that rose on this good earth were hit from within and actual change comes only from without. This status quo is an ultimate result of the population composition and the psychology of the islanders. Hope came from the enemy of yesterday who joined the conquerors, supply came from the land of Persia. The Portuguese killed the brother of the known leader, Rukn Al Din Afali Alhurmuzi. The man demanded vengeance for the blood of his brother. The war broke there with the support of the British and the Persians, and the Portuguese were defeated and declared their final retreat in 1602. It was a deep-rooted history in this bountiful land. The light of Islam was glowing from the Pantheon and Mosque of Dilmunia in what is known today as Masjid Alkhamis."

(16) The Interpreter
September 1761

On a Sunday morning in the first week of September 1761, the boat *Greenland* set out from Copenhagen port on a journey to explore the unknown and disclose the ambiguous. The boat was a kind of galleon of four masts and a square rig; it had two "horses", one in the front and the other one in its rear. The first mast was in the front, followed by the second mast, which was the main; the other two were behind on each side, used only for protection at times of need. The boat had two side coves of forty-five metres and a width of nearly fifteen metres.

The mast occupied the centre of the boat; it was in the middle, like an arrow falling down from the sky on the heart. It carried a gigantic sail of a triangular shape, holding side sails. When it embraced the wind, it sailed in search of new horizons and happy hopes. The presence of the king at the time of setting sail had a great impact on the official and public sides. Political leaders and clergymen representing the government and the church accompanied him.

The campaign had the honour of the presence of the university dons and a large public crowd. An observer felt that it was not an ordinary voyage but an expedition exploring the future. Reading the future and soothsaying are steps opening remote horizons. As if the boat were a sea-horse bringing all goodness, it took the prepared route starting from the North Sea to the English Channel, circumnavigating Spanish and

Portuguese territorial waters on the Atlantic Ocean via Gibraltar, on the way to Marseille for the first stop.

In the port of Marseille overlooking the Mediterranean in the south of France, the boat brought down its sails after two months of sailing. The city was famous for its defensive bastions. The city was also known for its music and revolutionary songs, *La Marseille*. The port was located on half a circular or a crescent ridge. The travellers did not plan to remain in Marseille more than one week, for rest and for some voyagers to disembark and to receive more passengers, and to get a fresh supply of munitions and food. To take advantage of their stay at this port of call, the travellers hoped to visit the basilica of Notre Dame de la Garde, to pray and receive benedictions.

The campaign left Marseille for the Mediterranean that connected the continents of the ancient world. Then it sailed to where two continents meet in one city that is separated by the Phosphorus. It is Istanbul, the capital city of the Ottoman Empire. The campaign stopped there after months of sailing. The travellers were met by an official delegation representing the Ottoman Sultan. Protocols reflected the civilised image of the states.

The travellers were taken to the palace of the Sultan, who promised to lend them a hand to meet their demands. He then ordered his aides to arrange a visit to the landmarks of the city, such as Sultan Ahmad Mosque and Aya Sophia and other locations of interest. This was a plan to transfer the civilised image of the Ottoman State and have it documented in books of history. They stayed in the hospitality of Sultan Mustapha III, titled the Sublime Porte. At the palace they saw the Holy

Mantle, the Sceptre and the Thul'Fiqar Sword[3].

The Sultan invited members of the campaign to lunch at the palace in the presence of senior members of the state and representatives of foreign embassies, among them the ambassadors of Denmark and Norway. Commanders of the army and some notables and merchants were also invited. The travellers left with some guards. One of them went to fetch Adam but could not find him. They thought he had preceded them to the palace.

The ceremony began with a speech on behalf of the palace, welcoming the guests. Then the head of the campaign ascended to the platform and thanked the Sultan and all those who were present. He explained the route and the objectives of the campaign, that would be beneficial to all humanity. His eyes were searching for Adam, who was not among the others. He ended his speech and sat at the side of the table. He could not eat. He sneaked to the Sultan and told him about the disappearance of his colleague.

The Sultan issued an order to the Chief of Staff of the palace to search for the missing man. They closed all the doors of the palace. No one could enter or leave without investigation and search. The dining table was removed one hour later, then the invitees began to leave the palace. They sensed an emergency. It became known that one of the travellers was missing in the palace of the Sultan. A search was carried out. In the evening, the search in every inch of the Palace ended, as no trace was found. Then a search in Istanbul under the slogan "Search for the missing guest of the Sultan".

---

[3] The Holy Mantle is the mantle of the Prophet Muhammad , and is currently in the Topkapı Museum in Istanbul.

An unexpected issue that may lead to the failure of the campaign and disturb its plans and goals.

The news spread all over the city, with days passing with no trace of him at all. It became imperative for those in charge to declare the disappearance of a guest of the Ottoman Sultan after Friday Prayers in all mosques in Istanbul. The travellers were urged not to move without a security escort and permission from the Chief of Guards, to whom the leader of the campaign spoke.

"We wish to attend the Friday Prayers that the Sultan declared."

"You can do that on condition that you should be protected by the guards."

The travellers suggested attending the Friday Prayers in various mosques in order to have an idea of the architecture of mosques and how some were converted from churches. The Chief of Guards took the responsibility to assign the travellers to visit various mosques. The leader of the campaign and the Servant remained, and the chief decided to take them to the mosque of Sultan Ahmad, known as the Blue Mosque.

The leader of the campaign decided to take a tour of the mosque to explore its features, before taking a seat outside during the prayers and drawing it. Meanwhile, the Servant sat in the courtyard. His eyes met the eyes of a giant man wearing a white turban falling on his face and covering his eyebrows. He was wearing a beautiful embroidered Ottoman silk kaftan. The man was carrying his sandals under his armpit. When the Friday sermon began, all attentions were directed towards the speaker of the mosque. Whenever the Servant looked at the man, he found him stealthily looking at him too. He started searching for the Chief of Guards. His heartbeat increased as people lined up for prayers.

"It is a good opportunity while people are all praying. I do not think he shall follow me with his eyes, or come forward to me."

After the start of prayers all worshippers knelt, and the Servant turned to the man and found him standing with his chest towards the *qebla* and his face towards me. His knapsack seemed full. The servant was suspicious of what this man was carrying on his back. "Peace be upon you, and the mercy of God." They concluded their prayer. Finally, the Servant found the Chief of Guards holding the leader of the campaign by the hand, proceeding to the South Gate. The Servant looked behind him and found the man at a distance of thirty metres. They rode the first horse-driven carriage.

All the carriages stood at the palace. They all got off, and so did the man from the second carriage. He neared them and removed his mask and turban and said, "The plan succeeded!"

The three shouted in unison, "Adam, where have you been? Istanbul is looking for you."

"I could not draw this huge mosque except by staying four full days. The stone building is the same in design and structure, but its altar is different at the time of prayers or call for prayers. There is a life throbbing in stone before humans. It was not possible to draw the mosque void of worshippers as it is also empty of soul."

He took out the maps from the knapsack and placed them in front of them.

"Look at the outer wall boundary that surrounds the mosque at three sides. Here are the three outer gates that lead to the courtyard of the mosque. And here are the two inner gates that lead to the mosque itself. In the courtyard, one can note this dome standing on six columns. The mosque itself is covered by a large dome standing on four demi-domes with outlets for light. Here stand the six huge minarets that make the mosque in structure a mixture of bastion and mosque. The altar overlooks the sea, giving it an open area and gives the worshippers a space, making them feel the infinity and that prayers lift them to the universe of heavens."

The leader was impressed by the drawings of Adam and praised him for forgetting to blame his colleague. The Servant praised Adam highly for his disguise in the Ottoman attire. This allowed him to move easily and freely to accomplish the mission. Exhaustion began to take effect on Adam due to extended travelling and the mission he had performed. They suggested that he should take rest in anticipation of departure in two days' time.

Adam did not recover from exhaustion and fell ill as a result. The Sultan sent his own physician to check on him. The young man contracted asthma. The doctor advised him to take rest and continue the treatment. They decided to remain in Istanbul for two months. After being reassured about his health condition, they were about to depart and continue their travel when the Sultan invited them to his palace once again. The Sultan asked Adam about the most important thing that attracted his attention during his four-day stay at the mosque.

"I found the people sincere in their prayers. As in Christianity, I think prayers are the ascension of man to his creator. True prayers are where soul and thought, conscience and heart are joined together. Here I found piety in some worshippers, where they forget their bodies and move a divine world. There they communicate with the sublime meanings in the space of their creator. He rises above mean issues; of matters which provoke the minorities; Man is weakened in the face of pressures and temptations, and then he forgets his Creator and the devil becomes strong. These are the values of all religions, and all people should know that humanity is in every religion."

The Sultan nodded three times and looked into the eyes of his audience. Silence became the master of the place. He placed his two forefingers on his forehead, as if trying to scratch the lamp of his mind. The audience looked attentively to the Sultan as his white turban seemed bigger than his head, where a large peacock feather nearer to gold in colour was placed. His beard tended to be black, of four fingers' length, with a thin moustache. His white *jubba* was embroidered with gold threads, under which was a brown lining up to the wrists. His audience waited for his speech.

"God said, 'And seek help in patience and prayers and truly it is extremely heavy and hard except for true believers. Those who are certain that they are going to meet their Lord, and that to Him they are going to return.' Patience represents the strong stance through which man judges himself stemming from his will and belief; while prayer is a conduct that reminds of God. At prayers, the soul rises to its creator and man lives in its atmosphere."

That was the prayer: Adam felt its meaning without practising its rituals.

"Show us, Adam, your drawings of the mosque."

Adam placed the maps in front of the Sultan, who examined them and asked him if he had instruments of measuring, to which he replied in the negative, explaining that he depended on his insight in estimating distances. The Sultan praised Adam for his abilities, anticipating a bright future and fulfilled dreams.

After that farewell reception and reassurance about Adam's health and the safety of the campaign, the Sultan wished them well and advised them to put on Arabian attire immediately, so they could seek refuge with the representatives and *Walis* of the Ottoman State. The Sultan was extremely generous and warm towards them and felt that he supported the campaign and wished it success.

The campaign proceeded to its next destination by land and sea. One month later, they reached the Aegean Sea and landed on a virgin island, mountainous inside, with sandy shores and crystal waters, called Samos. This island is located in Greece on the coastal stretch, not very far from Istanbul. Then they sailed towards Rhodes. The leader suggested they stay three days in the hospitality of the Ottoman *Wali*. They heard of the Colossus of Apollo, considered one of the Seven Wonders of the World. Its eyes were burning with fire as a lighthouse for ships. The leader of the campaign asked Adam to draw what remained of the Colossus of Rhodes. Early in the morning he went to the Colossus and found many people surrounding it, while other laboured climbing it to change the night flame. He started drawing it and when one of the men descended, he asked him, "What distinguishes this colossus known as one of the Seven Wonders of the World?"

"In general, materials are commonplace, but the way we regard the material gives it an imagined concept. If imagination ceases to expand and feels crippled, then the material becomes one of the wonders."

"Are you a worker or a savant philosopher?"

"A scientist who looks down upon using hands as a fault is an ignoramus."

"Do you mean that during the process of building the colossaus nobody expected it to be one of the wonders of the world?"

"Yes. Before construction, an image is formulated of the imagined thing; if the result is approximate for the previously imagined, then it is normal, but this statue is the end of imagination."

The speech of the philosopher worker took Adam back in time. Carina is an ordinary natural girl; if you imagine her as an image close to fiction, then admiration is generated. That admiration is called love. Perhaps love is the result of two souls meeting. I do not feel that way for her. I feel that my soul is yearning for the Orient. There may be a magic that picks me up. Could that be then the awaited love?

Adam printed the statue in his imagination and continued drawing and outlining it during their long cruise in the Mediterranean towards Alexandria, that port city extending along the coast. The leader reminded his colleagues when they had nearly reached there. "As you know from your studies, this city was called Alexandria after Alexander the Great, who took it as the capital city of Egypt, where he built the famous lighthouse considered one of the Seven Wonders of the World. On it, remains the famous Qaytibay Forts built by the Memluks. The fort was utilised to stand against the extension of the Islamic Ottoman as well as the European expansion known in the Orient as 'The Crusades'. We have to study each according to our specialisation. Then we proceeded towards Mariut Lake before continuing southward to the Gulf of Abu Qir."

Adam managed to visit Abu Qir Fort and drew most of its features. Water surrounds the fort on three sides. Its tower has the ability to identify arriving boats at a far distance. It has two boundary walls and an outer and inner wall for resting soldiers and arsenals. The quadruple-shaped fort is based on three levels, and on each corner, there is a semi-circular tower that allows snipers to shoot their arrows. Level one is used as a mosque, the second as passageways and inner rooms. The third has a large room for the Sultan himself that enables him to spot ships at a one-day distance. Next to the room there is an oven and a mill for preparing bread.

The campaign remained in Egypt for a few months, then sailed on the Nile for The Sinai Peninsula. It was planned for them to visit the Mountain of Moses, which is located on the triangle between the Gulf of Aqaba and Suez. They intended to spend the night at the foot of the mountain. The leader of the campaign began to disclose his knowledge and views.

"Tomorrow we shall proceed to the Mountain of Moses, where he spoke to his God at the tree of Rubus, according to the three divine religions, where he received the Ten Commandments. Near it is Mount Catherine, in the Holy Valley where a church is located, which we will visit. There is also a small mosque, according to historical and religious sources. Opposite this mountain, another mountain was demolished when Moses asked God to reveal Himself. I saw in my sleep last night a new lake where two distant seas converge. I also saw in my sleep the meeting of the mouth of the Arabian Gulf and the North Sea, forming a frozen lake between them."

In the evening, the sailors laid at the foothill of Sinai. They removed some of its stones and slept on the sand of the ground. Lying on your back and looking at the top of the mountain transfers you to the sky. The leader spoke again, and comments began to merge gradually into a warm voice closer to piety and invocation, more of a confession of the soul to the soul.

"A sign precedes every great action; it could be a dream or a vision, it could also be a warning or an event. There are events and signs that make us live life without its details. This great mountain is a sign to all humanity. From here, many prophets passed: Abraham the Patriarch, Ishmael, Isaac, Aaron and Moses lived here. It is a sign of the unity of humanity and the universality of the world, and that peoples are similar brothers. They have the same duties and responsibilities. The unity of prophets means the oneness of the Creator and unity of humanity. Going deep into details leads to difference. We must look for the similar and strengthen the bonds of love with the other. He who does not understand the culture of difference in the world becomes a narrow space and belies the rest of the people. He looks for religious and sectarian differences and never looks for the similar that leads to the diversity of divine religions and the unity of the Creator."

One of his colleagues interrupted his revelations.

"The climate of Sinai has an equilibrious environment; it is the most ideal for living. The height of this mountain is less than three thousand metres, and the triangle of Sinai is the meeting of the continents of Asia and Africa. My studies have shown that the meaning of 'Sinai' in hieroglyphic is 'the barren land', and it was also called Hurib in the Bible, which means 'waste land', while the inscriptions of the temple of Sarabit do not indicate a specific name."

"My God! As if it is the centre of the universe, as if the Creator spreads his teachings to reach the maximum number of people. Death at the foothill is the remaining of the soul at its summit, hovering around it to live in love and peace."

His words were broken and his voice diminished under the tyranny of deep sleep, making him feel an eternal comfort.

(17) Al-Towwash
May 1762

Through my many cruises, I used to sail like Bedouins crossing deserts. I got closer to the *Nukhatha*'s dhow, hoping to be able to buy the pearls they harvested before their return ashore. There, many merchants would try to rub shoulders with other buyers, where bidding and outbidding is the order of the day. I came closer to the boat where I found, unlike usual days, hustle and bustle, an unusual, dramatic scene where the sailors were cordially gathered on board the dhow in the main season. This is how things turned into the past two years, where the usual atmosphere was that of one unified family on board the ship. However, this boat became different; it was aggressive in the conduct of its sailors. I was afraid something might go wrong and the men get hurt. I preferred to stay away, but their Nahham raised his voice suddenly and called me, "Hey, Towwash, Towwash, you are welcome, we badly need you and your assistance, come to us."

I hesitated and waited long. It is not my speciality and my experience to settle differences at sea or on land. The profession I inherited from my father was to buy pearls at sea, to sell on land. In short, it means to search and hunt boats before returning during the pearling season and buy all sorts of pearls. After a long time, I became able to verify all kinds of pearls and knew those who tried to buy. We pearl traders prefer to buy pearls at sea before divers bring them to land.

There, they will accept lower prices and will be forced to pay more tax to the Ruler and the Merchant too. In addition to the bargaining of the local and foreign merchants who depreciated the value of the commodity, I had to sell rice and sugar and other stuff to the divers, after a month-long period of sailing. It seemed I was going to enact the role of the mediator so I would be able to solve the divers' problems aboard the dhow. Again, the voice called out.

"Hey, Towwash, come to us, may God reward you!"

I rarely leave my boat and embark on another one. Selling and buying transactions are carried out aboard my boat, which I prepare for this purpose. I used to invite *Nukhathas*, senior divers and pullers for lunch in my *majlis* here. Truly, this boat is refurbished to be a real Arab hospitality facility. All means of luxury and riches are provided. Appearances are not all deceptive, but all matters of convincing. I placed fine Persian carpets at the back with soft pillows on the side. It is a *majlis* and a marine guesthouse similar to traditional Gulf *majlis*. I know that negotiations with the *Nukhatha* require lots of effort and ability to manoeuvre, and convincing.

The *naham* repeated his invitation for the third time, and I did not want to break inherited traditions, so I invited them to my *majlis*.

"I hereby invite the *Nuhatha*, the chiefs of divers and pullers to have lunch with me. Later on, we can discuss what your problem is, and if we do not conclude the buying and selling transactions here, I shall then come on board your boat."

The two boats got nearer to each other. The *Nukhatha* came with his red cloth bundle of pearls, and two of his men.

"This diver is Abu Rashed, representing all the divers.

This is the Puller Hassan, representing the pullers."

"You are all welcome."

I invited them to have some dried fruit, tea and coffee and to have lunch after doing all the deals.

"We may meet your requests of rice, sugar, salt and other victuals. Workers shall transport these, while we are engaged in conducting the buying transactions. We shall be very happy later to convey your written messages to your relatives."

The *Nukhatha* placed a list of what the sailors required on board the boat. Then they came to me astern. They sat under the canopied part of the boat. The Servant brought the scales and the sieve grader of pearls. The *Nukhatha* placed their harvest on the red carpet. They spread the pearls and began filtering them according to size and quality. All they had tended to be small, of yellow, white and grey colours. Most of them where of the small size known as *sehtit*. Not all their harvest was what they had hoped for as it was of low value due to its quality.

"Gentlemen, I do not think that there is a difficulty in knowing the prices of what you have in order to inflame the dispute between you and disagree with Mr Nukhetha, who works hard to provide you with comfort, and spread the spirit of work and reassurance to you. I shall buy all the pearls you have and shall pay right away, so you can distribute it amongst you, if you wish to do that. I do not think your dispute is on this. Perhaps one of you through the fish rap or wanted to use of modern equipment that the *Nukhatha* was against."

No one took notice of what I had said. The *Nukhatha* took out a bag of his underclothes. He placed it carefully on the carpet and gently opened it. I was shaken by what I saw. Nine reddish pearls called Danat, seven large ones called Hasba. All were of exquisite beauty and clarity. They all knew that this kind of pearl was sought after. It was a great fortune, and I did not have enough money to afford it.

Due to my experience, I can identify any *dana* I see for the first time. *Danat* are like women: even though they are similar, each one has its own qualities. Good qualities are able to conceal bad ones. The beauty of a woman takes men. A skilful and experienced man looks behind what a woman has. As every woman wears clothes that reveal her beauty, so has every pearl a shape and colour that reveals its beauty. For this reason, pearls are kept in kerchiefs normally red in colour, like brides on their wedding nights. Gulf *danat* are of several types and shades. Each shade may reach eight in degrees. Some are placed in yellow or golden kerchiefs or black, and sometimes in red or pink velvet; these are the most famous for their quality.

"I shall pay you one tenth of the price of this treasure, and the *Nukhatha* shall get the remainder of the amount after it has been sold when we return to land."

Abu Rashed spoke in a quiet solemn voice, as if expressing his woes.

"Sir, here lies the problem with your friend the *Nukhatha*. You know, as the others realise, that what you call a treasure is a gift from God almighty. This divine treasure represents a good opportunity for us to get rid of servitude imposed on us by the Merchant. It is a godly sign pushing us to get rid of unjust bondages securely tight around our necks. Heaven does not bestow a feast, but it gives us its components to work hard for this feat."

"As if you talk about an enigma and refuse to disclose it. Where is the problem in that?"

"Hey you, Towwash! We understand and know the whole truth. A truth that makes you lose your friends is better than a lie that makes you win enemies. We know that the *Nukhatha* gets financial credits from the Merchant, and both are the creditors of the seamen all year, waiting for the big season — as you can see — which is apt to settle all the debts incurred on the seamen. The *Nukhatha* has decided to take two fifths. The system of the fifths is unjust to all of us; nevertheless, we are forced to work under it, but we do not accept having our debts forged. Then comes the *Nukhatha,* or the Merchant or the Ruler, with legislation getting hold of the two fifths too. It is a double injustice that we all refuse to accept. You, Towwash, know that all the seamen are indebted to the *Nukhatha* and the Merchant before the diving season, and that the *Nukhatha* is entitled to take one fifth of the harvest. What remains is the rightful property of all. Out of this, two shares are allocated to the divers, while pullers are allocated one share."

"And what would you suggest regarding this situation?"

"We demand that Nukhetha takes his share only and nothing more. One fifth only. We also demand that two among the divers approve the debts as witnesses to prevent forgery and to prove the right for the Ruler and his judges. They want us to remain slaves all our lives because of these debts they offer with all the temptations. The commoners accept this due to their dire need; this is slavery and we utterly refuse. What is worse, the son of the diver unjustly inherits the debt after the diver's death."

I requested to listen to the *Nukhatha* so we could reach a conciliatory solution that satisfied all concerned. It was crucial that all should be at peace with each other, as most fires start with a small spark.

"We do not disagree about the demands of the seamen; I only blame them, and blame is a sign of endearment. I hope that everyone understands that the Merchant supplies the dhow with all its needs. If I fail to settle the debts, the Merchant will take over the dhow. I ask the seamen to appreciate this urgent situation in this season only."

"What are you saying, *Nukhatha*? What innovative story are we hearing? What suits you does not necessarily suit others."

The case was apparently difficult on the surface. I suggested that dividing the shares be done in the presence of the Ruler when they return; I would buy the pearls from those who were willing to sell. Some suggested that the pearls stay in my possession pending the court hearing. None of them were concerned. They knew the pearls that passed their hands even one time, and they trusted me and each other, even their friends without a receipt. They entrusted the pearls with the Towwash; add to that, what if the matter is related to a famous Towwash? It is the good nature and the trust in others. I reached a decision that satisfied all.

"My fellows, devils leave when angels celebrate. Cheer up now, before the whole matter is referred to justice and courts."

(18) The Servant
December 1762

One of my main functions was to make sure that all members of the campaign were comfortable as far as preparing daily meals and cleaning and washing their clothes. Accordingly, I woke up every morning before they did to prepare breakfast. Sleeping at the foothill of the Mountain of Moses was exceptional, as time can never wipe it from the memory.

The sun did not rise when I woke up. One of travellers used his sandals as a pillow; others used a piece of cloth, while the leader used a pile of earth. All their faces were pointing to the sky. I drew back until my back touched a smooth rock; I did not recall who I saw before I went to sleep. I began to examine the sky and wait for the sunrise. Blueness began to push the blackness of the sky. The stars were gradually disappearing, looking pale, until the rays of the sun penetrated the rocks at the top of the mountain.

I went to wake up the leader first. I found his open eyes gazing at the sky, his right hand on his chest and the other at his side. I moved my hand in front of his eyes, but he did not move an eyelash or close or an eyelid. Had he reached the mood of thinking until morning and dived into it? I patted his right shoulder and he did not answer me. I placed his hand at his side and closed his eyes. I felt his forehead, which was still hot. I pulled his robe to cover all of his body. I laid beside him so I could see the dot he was gazing at. Nothing but a white mirage in the shape of a small storm rising to the centre of the sky.

I woke up the rest of the members of the campaign, each separately. The impact of death on the living is crueller, as death spreads serenity around, then the living spoil it with fear. This is how I whispered to each individually. I did not want to wake up the body beside us. I placed my hand on my mouth in a language that makes the awakened know the dire need for looking and silence. They looked at the body of their leader, and then their eyes met. It was the beginning of the gradual fall of life and the campaign.

One of them took the hand of the leader to feel the pulse and could not find it. He checked his wrest, vein and mouth. There was no sign of life. A harmful event that was not part of the plans of the campaign. The stillness of the death began to disperse as voices, groans and cries were heard. "Where can we bury the body? Here or there?" one of them shouted.

"It is the land of Muslims."

"It is the land of Prophets. The land of messages and prophecies. It is God's land for all humanity."

"God granted this to humans, but they tied themselves."

"According to this narrow thought, a Christian should be buried in the nearest cemetery for Christians, the cemetery at St Catherine's Church."

The church was half a mile away. We asked one of the passing Bedouins to lend us a hand by carrying the body in a cart pulled by his camel. One of us hesitated, for fear that a Muslim is prohibited from carrying a dead Christian.

"He is Christian; we want to carry him to the church cemetery."

"Man by nature is pure; he is only contaminated by

vicious acts."

Pascal, the youngest traveller, looked at the grave that we quickly dug. He was inflicted by fear and nearly collapsed. Adam spoke to him.

"When Moses buried his brother Aaron, he was awed by his brother's departure and from the darkness of the grave. God spoke unto him. 'If I permitted the dead to speak, they would have told you about my mercy to them. Your God does not regard the sins of the dead as much as his lack of tricks.'"

After bidding farewell to our leader, Adam had to take over in his capacity as the vice leader. We decided to leave Sinai for Yanbu. Adam was not as cheerful as he used to be. His smile was no more enlightening his face. There was no hidden love between us. Love is something natural that brings together different people and attracts poles. I used to obey his orders like a dumb machine, as lots of discussion is useless. Let us end our trip that shall last for years.

We reached Yanbu ten days later and crossed the sea directly. We encountered no difficulty in transporting us, as gold coins have great impact on the human soul. We reached Jeddah, where we stayed for two months. People in these areas are different in their physical and personal structure. They tend to be relatively short, and their bodies are lean. They are of various races: Bedouin and Urban, Africans and Arab. They were innately generous. We proceeded to the Ruler there, where we informed him about the objectives of the campaign. He was sympathetic and asked us to stay for three days to regain our health. They vacated a house for us, and the servants met all our needs. During one of our sessions with the Ruler, I still recall a situation worth noting. The guards brought in a man said to be a thief.

"Did you steal?"

"A chicken and some pieces of fruit."

"A confession that confirms the crime. God said, 'A male and female thief cut their hands in retribution for what they did, a punishment from God, and God is wise and judicious.' Execute the judgement of God."

They took the man to the front court of the mosque and covered his eyes, tied his hands, and severed his hands by a sword. Awe fell on the onlookers, followed by silence. Some were in favour and others were against the sentence. The leader of the campaign was about to wonder about the legality of the hand severing, but he remembered the advice of the Ottoman Sultan: "Do not argue with anyone about his religion, record only what your eyes see."

On the third day, we headed towards the Red Sea. We embarked with a boat full of goods, on its way to Mocha in the Yemen. A little after sailing, the colour of the sea became different with brilliant shadows. The colour of the water changed as we continued sailing. One of the travellers explained what we saw.

"What you see, fellows, is not optical illusion or mirage; it is the coral reef that grows in the Red Sea."

"Why the Red Sea only?"

"Coral reefs normally grow in shallow, clear waters, with a depth mostly fifty metres, and the temperature of the water is mild to enable its growth. The coral reef that you see is residues of calcium carbonates that feed on algae and carbohydrates, and around them grow coral structures of different types and forms. This how the scientists of the campaign explained it."

Adam stood at the stern of the boat, took a long look then

pointed at a colourful island where there was a lake with light blue waters. I heard him say, "Could this be another sign of a fate roaming in the horizon? As our late leader mentioned, signs are the language of fates."

They decided that the boat approached the island where she moored. The seamen worked as if in a beehive, everyone according to his specialisation: there someone paints, another cuts coral, and one fishes. Everyone finished his assignment, and we decided to leave in the afternoon. We wanted to pull the anchor but could not. All men got together; still we failed. Adam raised his voice; another sign of a coming danger. Two of the seamen went down to the bottom of the sea. The anchor was stuck in the coral reef. We had to stay until the next morning so we could clearly see and untie the rope and the anchor.

The boat was far away from the shores in the direction of Arabia Felicia. I got closer to Adam while he was squatting in the bow of the boat.

"Please, sir, breakfast is served and some hot beverages; perhaps that can change your mood."

He asked me to take a seat with a move from his right hand, then began to look at the distance.

"There is an island waiting for us in the coming days. On our trip it may tempt us from the outside, but we shall be drowned in it. We shall stay for a long time. The heart of the island is difficult to reach; it shall be really difficult to embrace. This is how I found my luck; inevitable road tales."

(19) The Ruler
January 1763

We realise that Dilmunia has no fault due to its geopolitical situation, because it is located between East Hormuz and a western desert of Bedouin. After our declining of the proposal of Hormuz, the ailment of expectation is still stopping the train of our thoughts and vision regarding the investment and progress the people of Dilmunia are expecting. The Hormuz people desire to build a massive land army, parallel to building a giant naval fleet, which rouses our fears of perils surrounding the Gulf from every side. However, this at the same time rouses our suspicions, when declared targets change from defensive to cancerous expansionist. We have expressed our inability to participate by men in the intended army, but their silence has double meanings, and this is what urges us to improve our relations with our neighbouring emirates and kingdoms, let alone Bedouin tribes where city-states are emerging.

Improving relations with all of them and with the Kingdom of Hormuz pours into our security and commercial interests that emanate from the Customs House of Jambrun. Foreign stability, on the other hand, is immune to urge the Ruler to accelerate the speed of change and reforms internally. Therefore, I offered the Merchant, at his own initiative, to manage the internal affairs of the country until I am done with the consequences of foreign commitments. Here we are putting the whole matter to members of the weekly session of the Appointed Council.

"Honourable Members of the Appointed Council, after bilateral discussions the Merchant is suggesting that we entrust him with Dilmunia's internal affairs until we end our security negotiations with Hormuz. Has anyone any suggestions concerning this matter?"

"Initially, we suggest that the Merchant tell us about his weekly plans as well as achievements of the previous week."

Another one suggested that the Ruler appoint a civil judge to settle disputes related to seamen, farmers, and merchants. In addition, there should be another judge to settle Sharia disputes.

"In fact, I am determined to divide Sharia law courts into two divisions: one for pearl fishing and the other for criminal cases. I used to see the law as a lantern which enlightened our path; but which one is more important, the lantern or the path?"

The decision thrilled the Merchant, who swore to serve Dilmunia and its people and work day and night on the comfort of its citizens. The rest of the members were assigned different roles, so they could be a *Shura* council when necessary. They were also charged with following up on rulings issued by the Ruler and judges. After that I asked to discuss expertise and seconded some able clerics to announce some verdicts that complied with Sharia rulings as reported in the Holy Quran and the Traditions of the Prophet, with consideration to expatriates and residents of other faiths, and to settle their disputes according to their creeds. There were some Christian minorities, and it would not be an act of fiction if the island did not welcome families from other religions.

In one of the members' remarks, he explained that the greatest tragedy of the Ruler was to combine government and business. It is something forbidden by Sharia law. He cited the story of the First Caliph, Abu Bakre Al Siddique, who carried his clothes to sell after the Companions elected him. He was asked where he was going, and he answered, "To the marketplace." The Companions asked him to stay at home and a stipend from the Treasury was allotted to him.

The Merchant was not pleased and insisted that his function was an assignment, not honorary. It was a call of duty and service to the country, and after all there was no harm in putting the matter to the Sharia judge to find out if wat is permissible, and whether the Sharia Jjudge was able to issue a verdict. Accordingly, the Merchant suggested Shaikh Saad Albalbul as an official Sharia judge due to his experience and acceptance by the people, and that he should be entrusted with all disputed matters, and that his judgement was irrevocable, provided it was ratified by the Ruler or whoever deputised for him.

I well received the suggestion and so did the Council. Then I suggested that I get news about the country and its affairs; everyone according to his sources. One of them said, "News coming from the sea indicates a good crop; it seems that the sea is opening its arms generously, but there are some hiccups that alter the spirit of love to that of hate between the seamen that could make the sea turn them down and become stingy; then we complain to God of its miserliness."

"Differences between components in the same family are always there, let alone men away from their families in the middle of the sea. I see it not only as a natural thing but inevitable."

"Your Highness, the Ruler, news coming from Al Towwash indicates lots of disputes taking place between the seamen led by Abu Rashed and the *Nukhatha*. It is the second time; we hoped it would not be bloody. There were differences between them about the system of the fifths applied now."

"Dispute about this issue is unacceptable; division by this law is very clear. For the *Nukhatha*, one fifth and the remainder for the seamen. The diver takes two shares and the puller one share. All pay taxes. He who breaks the law is a transgressor; the law shall be applied to him."

Then the Merchant spoke as if revealing what was inside him.

"Your Highness, the Ruler, respected members of the *Majlis*, the case of the so-called Abu Rashed is augmented and spreading. Since the accusation of his friend Yousif, the Puller, in the murder case of my son Nasser, he is instigating problems among public and private people. He is suspecting the civil judiciary, and here we are changing into Sharia, and he has refused to accept the dominant fifths system for many decades. He also refuses the taxes paid by the farmers. It will not be surprising if he challenges the legality of your rule and remaining in power. With your permission, I frankly declare that we should deal firmly with Abu Rashed, so he can be an example for others and put an end to strife. Beautifying oneself with virtues shall take the island to a dark end.

"As I fully, understand internal and external changes create a political message. The root cause of any political crisis is the difference in views in solving a problem, or to make a vision for an existing society. I have ordered a retrial of Puller Yousif at the new Sharia judiciary and to probe into the injustices of the divers and farmers to reach a solution that satisfies the Sharia and all sides, so that Dilmunia remains a land of love and peace."

No sooner had the *Majlis* ended its dealings I followed the news coming from the sea. I received details different from what had happened between the seamen headed by their representative Abu Rashed Al Jubur and the *Nukhatha*. The people felt the injustice inflicted on them; what could I do? I enacted a law that considered the interests of all. The law stipulates that a representative of the Ruler collects taxes from all: the merchants, *Nukhathas*, divers and pullers.

The Merchant started to compensate himself by imposing a tax on the divers and pullers. The *Nukhatha* had no right to violate the law by imposing taxes on the seamen. The law should be respected as it was enacted by the participation of the merchants. One of the articles of this law, stipulates, that seamen on board the boat get one fifth of the pearls. The seamen accused the *Nukhatha* that he had concocted his accounts and the debts of the seamen. He began buying pearls from them before their return, then he sold them at a higher price so he could accumulate higher gains, while the seamen remained in debt that is transferred to their sons when they died. We shall see what Judge Albahlbul can do.

Abu Rashed called his people for a general strike prior to the next grand season of diving. Here, the loss would be greater for all. A peaceful strike that strikers hoped would eliminate injustice. A strike that did not apply violence as an expression, in the hope that the message reached our *Majlis*. Abu Rashed sent his trusted emissaries, as well as his young son, Rashed, accompanying some representatives to coastal villages where farmers were complaining of another injustice, they thought had struck them.

On the other hand, farmers were pay taxes on all their products. The law had it that if the farmer failed to pay his tax, the land was confiscated. I was told that in many cases the land with what is on it is annexed to our properties despite the ability of the farmer to pay, and according to the law, the farmer and his farm are at the disposal of the Ruler, or whoever deputises for him. Truly, I did not know what the farmers and seamen wanted by going on strike! The law was not violated, except partially and through individual violations. We could, by discussion and negotiations, overcome these and find a solution for that.

The promised strike would harm the interests of all concerned, and it was not possible to substitute the seamen and farmers by others from different areas. A situation that placed me between the anvil and the hammer. It was inevitable that I should listen to their complaints on pearl fishing and listen to farmers too. There had to be a reform programme to enlighten their path and make them see a bright future; a programme that all could take part in, put in place and applied by all.

I was resolute and sincerely wished to make a decision that satisfied them all. I first met with the notables, the merchants, *Nukhathas* and decision-makers, who refused to change the existing system because the new suggestions would curtail their power and gains. After a series of meetings, the *Majlis* decided to announce that Abu Rashed and his men were desirous of power. Thus, we could resist change. The *Majlis* sent for aid from neighbouring tribes, tempting them with cash and harvest.

The Bedouin tribes were the quickest in accepting the invitation. They expressed sympathy with us and offered assistance in time of need. We concluded an agreement with them by which they supplied men and arms, if needed, in exchange for providing them with water from seawater sources; in addition to that, their boats would be exempt from taxes for ten years in order to be able to fish for pearls.

These bilateral and multilateral agreements were announced to terrify the public, but anxiety and fear were still dominant as Bedouins could not compensate farmers and seamen. One of the merchants suggested that we import expatriate workers so there would be no more strike ascendancy on farmers and divers again. In his search, he went to the *Ya'arebah*, who came in large numbers, in addition to importing farmers from the Yemen and some Persians and Afghans, with the assistance of the ruler of Persia, Nadir Shah. These hands did not belong to the new country as their spiritual allegiance was to their country of origin.

The situation remained critical and scary. Things had to stabilise. The *Majlis* had found a conciliatory solution that met the approval of all and did not belittle the dignity of the Ruler and the *Majlis*. I sent some aides on special missions to search for minds to help us out of this dilemma and preserve the resilience of the country. A solution may have been nearing

(20) Adam
May 1763

We sailed towards the Straits of Bab Almandab, so we had to pass by the Port of Mocha. Exiting from the bottleneck of the Red Sea to the Arab Sea was not possible without passing by Mocha. The Ottoman State enacted a law imposing taxes on all ships passing both ways. We showed them the letter of recommendation stamped by the Ottoman Sultan as we had in the previous ports. They offered us facilities of passage and three nights to relax before continuing our voyage, but illness refused to depart as fever hit the physicist Pascal. He remained to receive treatment at the port annex; a dispute between the body and soul, ended as usual in the victory of the latter. The man was deceased the following day. I was confused and with some fear and sadness. Sadness is a highly soluble infection. Another death case: what was the move by the Angel of Death? Then another new funeral ritual; where should we bury him?

"Is there a cemetery for Christians?"

"Yes."

"How? Has any traveller passed through here and met his death? In addition, graves are scattered around him by precedence."

"Yes, a European traveller called Lobo. Some of his companions died, so he buried them here, and then the number of the dead increased, as others passed; only few years."

I grew to see premonitions. Prevention of illness is better

than attracting it. How to do that when we were staying for two days in this town? A town that was bounded by lots of archaeological sites that protected its dwellers by a great wall with high towers. Along the sea there were two castles fortified by heavy canons. One of these was called Al Tayyar, and the other called Abd Al Rub. Most of its houses were built with palm fronds; among these stood the stately mosque of Shaikh Al Shathly.

We were urged to follow the dietary and life system of the people of Yemen in order to maintain our health and life. We left Mocha as soon as we could. We sighed a sigh of relief on board the boat. Thank Heavens, we were still alive, but the catastrophe was that we spent one night at sea and then returned. One of the travellers contracted cholera. We were back at Mocha where the disease hits our souls before our bodies. The man passed away slowly, and we buried him in the European Cemetery. A disappointing result; nobody remained with me except the Servant and another colleague.

We repeated the comic scene, and at the first possible opportunity left the Sea of Aden, arriving and escaping to the Arab Sea. The birth from the womb of the Red Sea was very difficult. They say the pain of child-giving is a sign of safety. Safety in this journey became a wish. We were planning to sail to the Indian port of Bombay. During this voyage, calamities and sorrows continued as the last colleague died of cholera too. None remained except my servant and me. After performing funeral rites, we threw our colleague overboard. The white bag floated a few moments before water filled it up, and his soul went to the heavens and the body was left to the bottom of the sea. There is no relationship between light and dust. End of a friendship and beginning of a relation.

I was obsessed by death. My main concern was delivering my diary and what valuable scientific writings my colleagues left, in addition to maps they drew for Denmark. We were on our way to Mumbai, and from there northward to Surat, then to China. I felt the same symptoms of the disease. It must be the end. My fortune said I was going to an island, but we were on the borders of the Indian Ocean only. Perhaps it was one of the islands of the Indian subcontinent. True vision requires no interpreters; it is self-explanatory. One has to fight for life.

I became ill and its symptoms appeared. He who suffers from slow death enters a self-defence battle for life. I followed a strict diet: I ate boiled rice and dried fruits. I drank cold water after boiling it. Perhaps I could not continue writing these diaries; maybe another person would write them according to me, translated or edited in its original. The disease may be hybrid and leave the body, but it never disappears and dies. Impossibility of reaching India and living in it appeared. Only one sailing day remained when a boat coming from India approached us. We received her by the sound known by seamen as emergency shots. She was coming from India in the direction of Hormuz Island on the neck of the Gulf. I did not hesitate; I asked them to transport me and my servant. False choices are those that we adopt from others, but we had what we wished for and it was the right of choice. The Servant asked me, "Why?"

"We must not lose the fruits of this strenuous voyage. I may be robbed or die. What we own is a flame of the beginning of civilisation, a precious treasure."

The new boat headed towards Muscat, then Bandar Abbas, and from there to the island of Hormuz. I read a great deal about its history. I wished I could visit the ruins of

Persepolis, where many of the archaeological secrets were written in cuneiform language. The island of Hormuz fell into the hands of the British and the Persians a few years back. They expelled the Portuguese from it, and their preparations were at maximum to furbish a fleet with a Persian name, to exhibit power to scare pirates and tribes surrounding a nearby island called Dilmunia, or land of eternity. The objective of this was to drive off those who tried to put it under their control after the defeat of the Portuguese. I wished I had taken the opportunity to depart with them; however, honesty had its rules. I had to head north towards Shat Alarab and Basra and receive the amounts sent to the campaign from my country at the Dutch Consulate.

I remained in Hurmuz for nearly two months. I recovered completely and was known to the British commanders, soldiers and their Persian counterparts too. The English language is a velvet magic key. It is one of the aspects of nationalities based on languages. Dilmunia was under their control since they had driven the Portuguese out. That archipelago became the most important point of passage in the trade route between Europe and India. Ther; they established the East India Company by a charter from the queen of Britain in 1600 AD. I asked the consul about the possibility of taking any boat to Iraq as was planned since the beginning of the voyage. There I could send the manuscripts and maps to Göttingen before I died or was robbed or lost.

The consul promised to put me on the ship heading to Iraq that was scheduled to depart in the afternoon within two or three days. When I saw the soldiers on board, I knew it was the expected voyage that took nearly five days. We spent the first night on board. This ship was similar to the galleon that we took the first time in the North Sea. The sea was rough and I gathered it was going to be very difficult. As we passed along in the sea the waves were weltering, and I feared possible disaster. I felt my papers and maps.

After dawn, the waves that normally result from solar storms and natural phenomena had subsided. Nothing of it remained except its ends, dancing on the seashore. Perhaps it still hid a fierce tempest. The winds died out gradually until quietness prevailed. I began to see dawn emerging on the distant horizon. I expected the waters to be dark blue or black, reflecting the depth of natural water here, but it seemed warm and cool. Then the darkness gradually began to disappear. The boat switched off when a low-lying land appeared at three nautical miles' distance. I asked my companion, "Could this be the land of Iraq?"

"Supposedly."

"But the voyage to Iraq lasts nearly five days."

"Perhaps it is a shortcut route! Do not worry, contradictions sometimes push us forward."

"Or perhaps it is the loss at sea. May be the boat lost its direction, or there may be someone pushing us towards a marine battle with the Qawassim Pirates."

"You are rousing my fears."

I went to the captain of the boat, who has just woken up and seemed very happy. He was ordering the crew to stop completely and wait for boats coming from the island. I spoke to him.

"I do not think this is Iraq."

"Iraq was not our destination to reach."

"What is this island?"

"It is the island of Dilmunia, located in the centre of the

Gulf."

The captain waited for the arrival of the small boats, which came in a semi-straight line. On board there was a large number of soldiers. Some of these were sick, and some would be returning to Hormuz to substitute others. Munitions and military equipment were transported on larger sailing boats to the shore of Dilmunia.

"Do you not want to go to the island?"

"But I want to go to the land of Iraq."

"Why? Are you not one of the travellers who wants to discover the Arabian Peninsula?"

"Yes, but I want first to dispatch all the manuscripts and drawings that my colleagues and I paid great efforts to prepare. I want these to be sent to Copenhagen through the Dutch Consul in Baghdad."

I waited on board the ship until the next evening when the time to return to Hormuz has arrived. There I remained for another week, waiting for the voyage to Basra. I was repeating to myself, "Life is but a departure."

(21) Yousif, the Puller
July 1763

When the mock trial came to an end, there was no decisive sentence that I could abide with. That would provoke and comfort me. It is judicial rule; hands are cuffed, and eyelids closed under floors of darkness. It falls on you with its cruelty and bitterness, but its effect disappears when you get used to it. Instead of that, I was diagnosed with Jacob Syndrome. Remoteness of hope enabled Jacob to stay in the neutral area between water and mirage. Falling into misfortunes is undoubtedly better than the impact of waiting for it. I do not know what the situation will be like tomorrow. The Merchant will send his aides to punish me, or will be angry with a member of my family. He will take revenge against all seniors and notables in society, mainly Abu Rashed, and even the civil judge and his assistants, even though they are officially appointed. In those contrasting waves and thoughts, my wife cries out whenever she sees me wandering, helpless.

"Yousif, how did it go with the Merchant?"

"Nothing new; however, I know that he takes pleasure in tormenting me that way. It is just pressure he applies in time of need. The shrewd do not open all their papers. Without an ultimate sentence, they are barred from joining the diving season by an order from the Merchant but ratified by the Ruler. He can make up other accusations, issue verdicts and execute them whenever he wants."

"As you know his aim and can interpret his evil, you should not care."

"They said, that he is accusing me of stirring strife, and that I am one of striking leaders called by Abu Rashed. Perhaps the Ruler and his Appointed Council will confirm the trumped-up charges, and your husband will end up behind bars."

"Yousif, their wolves shall never be innocent of your blood until Doomsday. God shall take revenge for you."

Events were so quick after the announcement of the general strike. Its timing was very affective before the next pearling season. A timing, that places puts the ball in the Ruler's court, to take decisive decisions not to paralyse all but also force them to come up with a solution that satisfies all concerned. They are looking forward to seeing the end of this pearling season and await the crisis the next season. Thus, time passes like a high-speed train.

In these summer nights, I love to lie down up on the roof of the house. I was in the habit of watching the stars illuminating the sky. There, the star of Suhail is lightening on the west side of the sky of Dilmunia[4]. It remains shining until the end of August, when it remains from its rise until midnight, leaning to the south. It is competing with its beauty with the geometrical designs of the group of the Polar Star. I stayed awake observing it, with slumber fleeing away suddenly. I hear noises and knockings on all sides of the house. I am sure they are the Merchant's guards, or what they locally know as bats

---

[4] Suhail (Puppis Star) is a star ten times larger than the sun, and it takes 31 light years for its light to reach Earth. The Arabs called him Suhail. It is promising to see him in the Gulf; Because it is a sign that the peak of summer has passed.

of the darkness.

As is habit, the bats usually come after midnight or just before dawn. This bunch are working under the command of the Merchant and the Ruler. They surrounded our house built of palm branches and trunks known locally as 'Barastey'[5]. My children and their mother woke up and started moving inside the house. On coming down, I saw them all in front of me,pitiful, terrified ghosts. Scared cowards are those wearing masks when asked to implement law and order. The brave rightful perform in broad daylight.

"Yousif, the Puller, you are wanted by the Ruler."

"I shall go to his *majlis* in the morning."

"No, you are coming with us now."

"What am I accused of?"

"Your same previous accusation. Maybe there are other crimes. You know it more than others."

The children gathered crying at the door. They wanted to stop me going out with the bats. My wife stood close to them, full of pride and dignity. She hid her tears and left her lot to the Creator. Her main concern was to comfort the little ones. Her veil accidently fell off her head as the guards stood at the door. One of the legs of their chief was outside. He turned fully inside. He removed his mask, showing the face of the Merchant. Forgetting what he was and what he came for. He began to look at the children and scrutinise their mother. The woman raised her head and their eyes met she got his lascivious look; then she comprehended the meaning in his eyes and the evil of his inner thoughts. He tied his mask and

---

[5] Cottage

133

his looks remained. His men dragged me, and the door closed from inside.

The neighbours crowded around the house and on the road. Some of them wanted to express their objections, even with a word, but they kept silent when they saw guns pointed at their chests and truncheons nearly on their heads. My hands were tied behind my back and my eyes were covered despite me. I knew the way to the court of justice. It is the rituals of arresting individuals. I believe it is the fear that envelops the heart of the despot and strangles his veins. Escape from the eyes of victims is the first indication of innocence, while the unjust are always awake.

The Merchant mounted his horse while his guards rode three donkeys. On the last one, I was tied by a rope on my arm and that made me hurry up so as to avoid falling and be pulled like a slain ewe. I was certain since that moment that the beauty of my wife had killed the Merchant. It was imperative that I had to fight for my innocence, for my family and for my honour.

They detained me in an underground ruined cell. I smelled obnoxious fermentation, the smell of mud, sweat and that of freedom. I found my soul free whenever they locked the doors, but my heart was yearning towards the justice of the heavens. The falcon never leaves its prey until it sees it dead. I found no logical reason for imprisoning me here. Was it instigating people against the regime, or the murder of the son of the Merchant on board the pearl fishing boat? Or was it the beauty of my wife?

One man entered He had a semi-red complexion, strange features not belonging to the dust of this land. The colour of the soil reflects the salinity of the people. The man was very tall, red in the cheeks and had a full beard tending to be brown. He recollected his vocabulary and spoke in a strange foreign accent and with broken Arabic not similar to diverse dialects common here.

"You are Yousif the Puller?"

"Yes."

"Do you know your crime?"

I smiled, thinking he was a Hurmuzian or Persian or perhaps Afghani.

"What is that to you?"

"The Ruler says you must die; this means you are dead."

He closed the door behind him, and the rays of dawn disappeared behind the walls of the so-called prison. I started a new history, whose first page was written at this hour. I began to repeat that the history of imprisoning the oppressed is an honour, but what terrified me was what would become of my family. I remembered a saying of the Doyen: "The woman is like a tree; when it is bare, it catches fire." How is that, Shaikh? My wife was not naked. Every exception has a rule as every rule has exceptions. Would self-flogging solve my problem? I did not think so, I had to fortify myself by faith and patience, as positive patience is the expectation of a happy conclusion.

(22) The Interpreter
July 1763

Contradicting reality is an attempt to mutiny against fate and escape from truth. If a man succeeded in his movement, it is called rectifying revolution, and if he failed, it is called perseverance. Perseverance is an attempt to attain an unknown truth that may succeed or fail. It is the tale of Shaikh Sulieman, the chieftain of the tribe of *Bani Kaab*, that extends its authority in parts of Basra in southern Iraq. This tale also applies to the rest of the tribes, from far or near, old or new. His destiny was to rule Shat Alarab, with its low-lying lands and islands and its muddy islands on the north until the convergence of Euphrates and Tigress where fluvial route to Baghdad and land route to Aleppo.

Neither Shaikh Sulieman, his tribe, nor his ancestors had the right of geographic self-determination, as man does not choose his place of birth nor his mother's milk. The tribe had a position and a contact line and confrontation among two civilisations that may have had political entente or understanding and get united or misunderstood so they fight. And in every case, the tribe became exposed to their disputes and agreements. Tribes like small states fell in the arms of their neighbours for the sake of adoption. And when the imminent danger dispersed, the wish for independence recurred. A kind of political adolescence.

Conflict between the Ottoman and Persian states was at

its height. The former represented in its *Wali* of Baghdad and the latter by its Governor, Karim Khan[6]. The first wanted to extend the control of his empire to neighbouring areas, while the other to lay his hands on disputed areas and rule of jungles.

Concurrently with these disputes and consequences was Adam's wish to reach Baghdad to deliver his precious collections to the Dutch consul representing Danish interests. He had to deliver these or perish. He had also to receive some cash amounts and other aid for the travellers. The captain of the British ship informed him about the dangerous situation. There are two powers: a gigantic Persian power and a huge Ottoman force. Between these two, you find the rightful power of the Arab tribe of *Bani Kaab*.

"Can we reach Baghdad with all the hurdles you mentioned?"

"Our relationship with Shaikh Sulieman is good. He always lets us pass with no quandaries."

"Where is the problem, then?"

"If our arrival coincides with the present military confrontations, we shall not be able to pass."

Last month, the tribe received a high delegation from the Ottoman *Wali* in Baghdad, who threatened to impose tribute: either tribute or confrontation. The tribe was awfully concerned. Shaikh Sulieman stood in his shrewdness and said, "Our tribe appreciates our brothers. Our fate and theirs is one. We never abstained from paying tribute to the Ottoman State. We sent a delegation carrying the tribute to the *Wali* but the Persian force blocked the way and stole the tribute. This is

---

[6] Karim Khan Zand, founder of the Zand state in Persia (1705–1779)

what they do and are always proud of it. We do not have the military ability to stand against the Persians. You have to confront their army and destroy them. Then the route will be clear to receive your rights."

He who came was amazed. By his answer, the Shaikh killed the delegation. "He is dragging us to a war we do not want. Losses of wars are destructions borne by nations with their generations. The delegation preferred to keep silent and slow down to have more details. They have bitten their fingers out of anger. The children of the tribe realise that a successful politician is he who is more able to tell lies and be deceptive."

The British ship neared the north of the Gulf at a distance of one nautical mile. *Bani Kaab* men saw her from the top of the mast of their boat. They sent the common salutation of peace. Canons have one language but various dialects: a religious dialect and another of war and one meaning peace. The visiting ship exchanged salutations and came closer. One of the Arab seamen boarded the other boat.

"Shaikh Sulieman, Chieftain of the *Bani Kaab* tribe, extends his greetings and is pleased to welcome you aboard his boat, *Albasrawiya*."

The captain reciprocated the greetings and ordered two members of his crew to accompany him. He looked at Adam, who stood beside him.

"Come and join us; perhaps your writings will add more information on Arabian tribes. Perhaps later you shall manage to visit the consulate in Baghdad." He did not hesitate to join them as most do, because making a decision is a postponed refusal. On stepping aboard the boat, they found its astern furnished with red carpets and Arabian cushions, indicating the luxuriousness of its proprietor. The Shaikh came forward to shake hands with every one of them. He welcomed them and invited them to his *Majlis*. They sat on his right, facing their ship. Adam was the fourth member of the guests. He gazed at the Shaikh and registered with his memory.

A man, rather tall, stout in a well-built body, with a protruding chest, broad shoulders, rounded face, almond-shaped bright eyes, sharp, long nose, full rounded beard before the cheeks, with some white hairs spread over it. I tried to stare in his eyes that I found like still water; when you ed into them, you only found yourself and read only your thoughts. Water is a deceptive mirror. He was talking in a confident voice that reflected a stable soul that felt security with his companions, as if their haven was in him and to him. I think that a true leader and ruler is the one that the commoners find what they are looking for in. The ruler is not he who is a despot and rules over others but he who represents them as a desire for their happiness.

The Shaikh asked the captain about the purpose of their voyage.

"We are on a noble humanitarian mission in the form of transporting this male traveller to the *Wali* of Baghdad. His mission is to deliver collections of his travels and his colleagues to his country. This is of great importance."

The Shaikh nodded three times in the face of Adam, who received it as a good omen. Then the captain asked for permission to pose a question.

"Sir, are the fees and passage tax in Shat Al Arab fixed?"

"We charge three *Mohammadi* coins on friendly boats such as British and others; seven coins on those who adopt our religion and sect, and twelve *Mohammadi* coins on those who are different from us. Please, please join us; food is here, feel at home among your folks."

Adam took the opportunity of others being busy, went closer to the captain and asked him, "Why are you charged three coins only?"

"Shaikh Sulieman has a far-reaching vision. No shot without a shooter. Beware of your friend and your enemy. Perhaps one day he will ask British boats to lay anchor in one of his ports and have a base in the Gulf."

"What does he gain from that?"

"Small states are cities searching for stability. A tribe in the line of fire between the Persians and the Ottomans, the great nations, more often acts cowardly. It searches for a battle theatre on a land that is not theirs. The Shaikh is expecting a war on his land or dispute between them, where the two adversaries do not lose but the battleground between them is the loser. The Shaikh wants us to take our positions on his land. We are offered faculties in passage between the East and the West, and enrich our trade and power through the East India Trading Company. He wants to augment his power through us, as if we are a scarecrow in the face of those he wants to harm. Defence agreements and hosting military bases do not leave the choice in the hands of the Ruler."

"My God! Why does he then impose different taxes on those identical to him in language and faith?"

"Fear of others. There is an imaginary foe in his mind. He is not asked about him, but the culture he is brought in and grew in develops these fears. Man may fear those similar to him, and may be scared of those he disagrees with."

Shaikh Sulieman interrupted their side dialogue and suddenly asked the captain, "As you may well know, Karim

Khan, the ruler of Persia, is also demanding the tribute and sharing with us a percentage of taxes on ships passing through Shat Alarab. A delegation representing his government shall definitely arrive to negotiate that. From our side, we refuse to have our area annexed to his state, and we also refuse sharing with him tax revenues and paying tribute. We cannot refuse all the demands; either we be part of his state, or pay tribute. We are looking forward to your assistance."

"How can we have a role in helping you and solve the problem?"

Shaikh Sulieman proposed that the meeting with the Persians would be with a third party on a neutral land, through the empire where the sun never sets, on board the *HMS Lupin* that flies its flag. The negotiations should be under the flag of a third party so that the stronger party should defend the weaker party, and the strong should find a peer for him.

The Persian delegation arrived at the north Gulf as expected and boarded the British ship, prepared for the negotiations.

"His Majesty Karim Khan sends his greetings and informs you that paying tribute is an international and human right, because he defends you and your land against covetous states. Without being aware, you are under his protection."

"We did not withhold the tribute, but the Ottoman forces were chasing us from the north and confiscated the tribute sent to you and killed escorting soldiers. You have to cut the Ottoman hand in order to have peace and your rights reach you in full."

The Persian delegation disembarked the ship angrily without saying a word. Shaikh Sulieman sensed the next move; he knew and expected the inevitable result. He reassured his people and companions and asked the captain to return to Hormuz, or stay five nautical miles away. "We know that if the *Khan* sends his boats to us, we shall receive them in Ahwaz. War is not a force only but also a trick. He who plans it, reaps its fruits. You shall hear from me. I trust that I shall transport the travellers to Baghdad if Adam agrees to hand me some or all of it. I have to invite him again. After the end of the crisis with Persia, he can cross Shat Al Arab to Baghdad alone. We shall ask you to take your positions close to Shat Al Arab."

Due to his concerns, Adam became hesitant. Out of his collections he chose his private drawings. These were what he drew himself and could easily redo, depending on memory. He handed them to the Shaikh, pressing his hand to remind him of their spiritual and materialistic value, at which the Shaikh thanked him for his confidence.

One night later, Persian war ships arrived at Ahwaz with their guns firing at nearby coasts. The Shaikh's forces were unable to confront the attack and stood against the conquerors. The gap between guns and canons was vast. He discovered that large boats were three, while the smaller ones were more than ten. He ordered his forces to retreat from the first island which the invaders took control of and marched on to the second and then to the third. As they advanced, he gave orders to the men to pull back and never confront the enemy. Ahwaz waters gradually became shallower and the movement of the ships became less affected as they touched the bottom of the water and stuck in sand and mud.

At night fall, they waited for the low tide which completely paralysed the movement of the boats. He ordered his soldiers to move to the boats in front. They reached slowly, lassoed the canons, pulling them to their boats. Having hold of the canons, Shaikh Sulieman's men confronted the Persians man to man. Here the *Khan's* men pulled back with their large ships retreating and what remained of the smaller ones following them.

After the fiasco of the military solution, the negotiation wheel started turning but with different calculations. The Persians agreed on the independence of the region in exchange for allowing passage of their ships through Shat Alarab and payment of seven *Mohammadi* coins on every ship, provided the boats buy limited quantities of Basra dates on their return. The news reached the *Wali* of Baghdad, who gave up previous claims.

(23) Khowla
July 1763

The wife of Yousif the Puller and her children arrived, crying, to the house where we warmly and heartily welcomed them. The Doyen received them welcomingly. She was in her early twenties with unaffected simple beauty. He ordered taking them to the women's room. It was not possible to take her and her children to the *Majlis t*o avoid possible visits from men. He asked me to stay with her to know the reason for her sudden tragic visit. I comforted her.

"Madam, nothing can stop ill-fate except praying to God."

"God be praised for that."

"Tell us, what is the matter?"

"I think you have not yet heard the news. Perhaps it is good that it was so much delayed because you live on the outskirts of the village."

"What is the matter? My heart is fearful."

She explained that the Merchant with his men had raided the house and took Yousif to a place only God knows where. They said it was an execution of a judicial order with the Ruler's agreement. They did not mention that the accusation was deliberate killing of Nasser, the son of the Merchant. They said there were other cases. They mentioned that Yousif was the right arm of the Abu Rashed, and that he was behind the objection calls everywhere.

They said that he was behind the dispute between the

seamen and the *Nukhatha* at sea, and that he was supporting the intended strike during the next pearl fishing season. He was also behind the anger of some farmers because of the taxes imposed. I felt it was a made-up accusation to create discord.

The Doyen interfered in his paternal style that spreads trust and patience in our hearts.

"My daughter, as it is the case, time is able to find a solution to this matter. I know that confrontation is long lasting with the authority and in most cases ends in favour of the Ruler. We do not opt for violence; we shall throw the arms of love in his heart. Love is the water of life; it is the most effective weapon in confrontations. We must realise that no one enters paradise who has an atom of love for this world. Therefore, any victim should declare his unjust treatment. He must demand his rights providing that his personal interests do not exceed those of the majority. There are those who would like to monopolise power and flirt with authority. There are factors that urge citizens to be convinced by docility and accept dilemmas, and perhaps self-flagellation, because he is looking for stability. Then self-antagonism increases and hope for change diminishes. That is confrontation of power-by-power, violence and counter-violence. The man of authority shall remain higher in position but with love, you can overcome everything. The apex of satisfaction is to be happy in your anger and delight. We can extract reform by pail from the bottom of the dark well, and if it were famine, it would be hit by aridity."

"Grandfather, don't you think that what you say is a sort of world of idealism, and absolute values only?"

"The idealisms you talk about are the world of ecstasy to divine perfection. We shall never reach absolute perfection, but we can ascend some of its steps. That is enough to start with. Walking on this route and believing in it is bound to untie the knot and solve crisis. I lived lots of vicissitudes and pains on this island; force cannot confront force and overcome it. A rule that derives its courage from arms can spill blood and imprison souls, but it can never sleep comfortably. Happiness is as far as two orients; as for the disarmed, confrontation and counter-confrontation with him is a losing phenomenon. However, deep inside her is winning; it will prevail, even after a while. Since 1735, rule has changed ten times and systems of government on this island several times. Bloody confrontations resulted in losses for all sides. The Ruler lost control and the wheel of advancement of the people retreated. Disputing sides have now to extend ties of love and build bridges of confidence and prioritise public interests over that of the personal. There we shall all be happy."

The woman was not convinced with what she had heard; there was no alternative but confronting the murderous Merchant. She held my hand, and we approached the Doyen. She asked for permission to sit beside him and talk with him about something personal. She did not mind my participation in the discussion. She said, "Dear Doyen, you must know from your past experiences and from those who constantly convey news to you, that the Merchant and his aides have lived corruptibly in this land. It is said that this is done without the knowledge of the Ruler, but this does not prevent any evil taking place on the island in the name of the Ruler. Divine and human questioning and even historic shall inevitably fall on him. The Merchant is bent on taking over the farmers' lands by force when they fail to pay taxes due to shortage of crop. He steals the cattle fodder by force. He pushed his calves with the cattle of the citizens to fatten them. Lately, he also ordered the farmers to provide food for any traveller as well as to his men and guards. Yousif told me that he coerced farmers and fishermen to supply the Merchant's and the Ruler's kitchens with fish, dates and vegetables, and he also told me."

The woman stuttered, and husky words stuck in her bosom, and then I asked her, "What next?"

"When they dragged Yousif at dawn, the Merchant scratched my modesty with his sensual looks. This lean hairless man expressed a mean desire that every woman understands easily when she sees herself drawn on the face of any man. This sexual desire and meanness are daring on the face of the man and are drawn on his features."

"Is it not possible that your sense is baseless?"

"When someone is fond of you, something from him is moved to you. You may breathe as long as the silence lasts. Dear Doyen, I fled home and came to you as a refugee. Yousif knew what this mean man wanted, and I was certain of his bestial desire. You must have undoubtedly heard of stealing wives in the country and villages. I do not want to be in the forthcoming series. I hope to be on the list of assassinations that he commits in secret rather than offer him my honour. What can we do to stand against this criminal gang?"

"My daughter, we do not accept injustice and call for resisting it. However, there are matters in Sharia justice that have no apparent judgement."

"I do not understand what you are aiming at."

"You know, Khowla, that there is 'life in punishment'. He who kills shall be killed, and he who steals shall have his hand cut; however, if a man throws a stone at another man on his head and causes mental defect, that is loss of mind. Should the culprit be also hit with a stone on his head? Can we make sure of the loss of his mind then? Is there anyone who can ascertain the idealism of punishment? What would happen if you gave the culprit a jasmine branch? The impact on him then shall be enormous. Payment in goodness defeats evil and punishes the culprit."

I realised what the Doyen was driving at. You may not perceive that with your mind, but you can sense that if light and goodness can find a vent to your heart. It was said in the past that wisdom does not enter an abdomen filled with food. It was also said that he who reads the Quran on an empty stomach, his soul is closer to him. That materialistic meaning is impossible to grasp, but the spiritual meaning is nearer to digest. Those are the cases where man feels satisfaction and content; if you are content with yourself, you feel paradise inside you. Then you feel and enjoy peace. That is the best retribution for the oppressor who wants to usurp the dearer thing you possess. He will not take away the peace and goodness you enjoy; he will be in a limited race with you. He wants to enjoy the paradise you enjoy; therefore, he shall feel the defeat. That is the desired angelic victory.

The lessons that the Doyen preached to his family and community were non-stop torrents of goodness. Some may envy us for that; friends may be delighted for us. Two days after the Doyen's decision that Yousif's woman and her children should stay with us, his generosity continued. Whenever I entered his room, I only found him silent. He who is all alone by himself never feels loneliness. He meets you with his eyes and lineaments, gradually opening up until he returns to the world of the material. He who does not know him thinks he is hiding secrets. It was an exceptional case in his conversation this time. He began to talk to me as a mature woman, with his vocabulary full of wisdom and philosophy. They were rare words when he said, "Welcome, our fabulous beauty." I know that a woman is aware of her femininity when her beauty is admired, and the Doyen never focused except on the beauty of the woman when it came to her religion and soundness of mind.

"My daughter, no doubt you have read the Quran many times!"

"Yes."

"You undoubtedly realise that all divine scriptures elevate the values of man. God has chosen us by giving us the eternal book, as he chose others with His books and messages. The Quran is nearer to us. I have cited a verse; perhaps you can add more of its interpretations to me that I miss. Beautiful Khowla, what do you understand from His saying: 'Do not corrupt in the land after it has been set in order, and invoke Him with fear and hope. Surely, Allah's mercy is near to the good-doers.'"

"Perhaps corruption is cutting trees, paddling in water and withholding livelihood."

"Yes, my daughter. Added to that the importance of God's commandment not to corrupt in the land. God has created the land as a temporary place, not a place of permanent abode. By a creative view, God has improved the conditions of man. Corruption, on the other hand, takes place for not following this principle."

The Doyen spoke in length, elaborating his idea, and the wife of Yousif gained its fruit that was ripening a long time ago.

"Man is a behavioural creature, mentally and non-mentally; that is why there are differences in judging his behaviour as a human being or an animal. They claim that his mind is relative, but it possesses the will and capability. He was bound to take responsibility. There are five matters; if good, the society is good."

He spoke, counting them on his right-hand fingers: reason, religion, money, soul and honour.

"Reason, my dear, is a power that regulates behaviour, and it is the function of the brain. Therefore, the first thing that God created was reason: reason is the core of thinking, the fruit of the existence of man. The universe is changed by minds, not by bodies, and mind is worshipped after God. That is the first creator. He who is addicted to alcohol and hashish for example, wants that brain out of order, consequently, damaging the brain, harming the family and ending up with the community. If we apply reason to one of the laws of marriage for instance, we find that the contract — which is a mental matter — adds holiness to the marital relationship: a husband with one wife, a husband with several wives in exceptional cases like war, sickness, bareness and even disobedience. However, the Oriental family yearned for mutiny in its deviations. There are torrential currents; a current is an imaginary ghost that should be resisted, not obeyed."

"The second?"

"Religion, my dear. Religion is the dealings with its various arts and practices. Religion defines and reforms relationships; religions are perfect while anthropology is deficient. Would you agree with me that I can transform a human being into an animal in just one moment?"

"I think that is difficult and impossible; but how?"

"With one slap on his face, a man loses his mind and turns into an animal. You may hit him in his money and he loses his mind; money is also what is financed with, satisfies the needs and the sane compete on acquiring it. That is the debt that is attained by supplication; it is a sense of inferiority in man juxtaposed with a sense of perfection with man. God said in a divine saying, 'He who wants my mercy, let him have mercy on my creatures.'

"The 'soul', my daughter, appeared as an idiom but in different connotations. It came meaning the body or the creature; 'every soul is tasting death'. It came meaning the *spirit* in his words: 'You, content soul, return unto your God content and blessed.' The idiom 'soul' also means *man*, to whom God made the heavens and earth available. He is the quintessence of existence and its light and the most precious among all creatures. God only received what He offered and He can provide protection for him. He even said, 'Do not slay the soul that God forbade except by lawful means.' The state of defence is only achieved for soul and society."

(24) Abu Rashed
August 1763

On our return from the main pearling season, we headed towards one of the underwater sweet water sources located in the west centre of the mainland. We were a few metres away from a dead coral island known as "Ya'sub", which took the shape of a pear that was ripe and turned into black and was not yet plucked. Some of the sailors dived in the sea with their goat-skin bags to the bottom of the source, where fresh water was gushing up forcibly while their underwear and legs waved up like bees when tempting flowers. All the water sacks were filled at the time of prayers. The *Nukhatha* suggested a break to perform prayers and have a meal before sailing again northward and returning home in the afternoon or before sunset.

During our stop, Ya'sub Island became very close. It is a limestone island rising high, rough in the north and sandy slopes in the south. In the middle, a burial mound seems higher and more distinctive. It was shocking for us to see a lonely man on the island. The man began to wave to us with his hands. I told the *Nukhatha* of our desire to swim to its shore and to know more about this man; perhaps he needed some help. Perhaps he was a fisherman who had lost his boat and took refuge on this island. The *Nukhatha* understood our intention. One of the divers suggested accompanying me, swimming to the spot where the man stood waiting for our arrival.

"Peace be upon you."

"And on you, too."

"What are you doing on this island alone? You must be an angler who has lost his boat. We would welcome you on board our dhow that arrives home this afternoon. We can take you with us."

"I did not lose my small boat; she is tied with oars on the west coast."

He pointed with his right hand and said, "There."

"And what are you doing here?"

He went away a little. He stuttered before he could say a few words. He did not know my companion or me. That made him feel easy. He took me with him bedside the burial mound, nearly in the centre of the island. He asked me to swear that our conversation be regarded as a casual talk, not to ask about his name, family or tribe. He wanted to be incognito before he opened his heart, as if he wanted to say that society imposes certain restrictions that we should adopt ideas and behaviours. When we discard the censorship role of society, personal freedom arises, and an inner censor appears only; then the true metal of man shines. The quinquagenarian spoke as if he were revealing what was inside him.

"I am a farmer living in the countryside of the eastern island, near the main island of Dilmunia. I am married and have seven sons and three daughters, all from the first wife. I also got married thrice but got divorced after one year or two years at most. I wished through my marital life, and polygamy to put a stop to my wild sexual desires that control me every day. I practised licit sex every day, but I was insatiable. On the contrary, I became hungrier and grew more lustful than ever. That outburst led me to seek illicit sex. I began to search for prostitutes both female and male, with the hope that this volcano should subside. It began to eat me up like fire; the more I fed it with wood, the more it produced flames and sparks. I had no choice but to tell my family that I was leaving for pilgrimage. I knew that this sexual condition of mine was a real disease, as one of the clergymen confirmed to me. I preferred to seclude myself on this remote island and live here, so I could re-educate and control myself."

I found myself repeating, "The soul is desirous, if you lure it, but when little is given, it is content."

I asked him about his food and drink and how he could survive on this lost limestone island. He said he was a farmer who knew about tilling the land. Like the majority of the people of Dilmunia, it was not difficult for him to dive and extract water from marine sources. It was not also impossible for him to catch fish that he sold most of to passing boats. In exchange for that, he accepted rice and other victuals. He even built a fish trap from palm fronds to survive on fish.

"And when will you return to your family and people?"

"When the goal that I left this world for is achieved."

I begged to talk to him with absolute transparency and express my views clearly. I believed that what comes out of the heart touches the heart.

"Sir, as you may know, human beings are tempted by the love of lust. Out of these lusts, there is sensual love, social and gluttony, and so on. These lusts are innate and natural. Man was created for it and there is no way he can free himself out of it. All these lusts work on preserving the human genes. Overdoing excessively destroys man himself. The top of manliness is to disobey the temptation of a woman, and the topmost of belief is to disobey the desires of yourself. For example, if balanced love for food turns into material gluttony, that would be a negative, destructive lust. The same thing applies to the love of sex. It is made for certain objectives and once it is overdone, it becomes destructive. The sex liquid is viable for the continuity of the human race. If a man used to masturbate, he will only empty his energy, and he will not feel the overflow of sexual passion."

"Until now, I did not know what you are driving at."

"Man, you can understand sex in its natural situation, if you realise that it is a means, not a human end in itself. The pleasure of sex is momentary; the moment it is over, it becomes a memory. Once you know that man himself is perishable, nothing shall remain of him except memory. It is better for him not to be immersed in sex. Life has materialistic meaning and spiritual. The materialistic is perishable, while the spiritual remains. Keeping away from stimulants is bound to place sex in its natural form. Keep away from materialistic sexual stimulation. By practising spiritual exercises, you shall definitely reach the meaning of human happiness, by forsaking life's materialistic hurdles.

"Here, we have to remember three matters: never deprive yourself of sex at all, remember that sex is a passing moment, and the meaning of happiness is that man lives the care of the human message for life; to live his life with caution, which is the bridle of pleasure. What I say may be a difficult thing, but what is the most complicated matter is to look for something you already have, that is the search for God."

We were in a conversation brief in words but elaborate in meaning when we heard the sound of gunfire coming from the sea. One of the Ruler's boats appeared, heading towards the sleeping island. She came closer to the *Nukhatha*'s boat. A conversation ensued between the skippers of the two bats that we were not able to hear. I thought it was the Ruler and his men sailing to be assured about the condition of the pearling season. The Ruler's boat moved in our direction on the shore of the island. What surprised me was the Merchant standing on the bow holding a rifle. The man and three of his men got down on a small boat, and came ashore.

"I believe you are Abu Rashed?"

"I am Abu Rashed, and this is my colleague, Mohammed, a puller."

"And the third man?"

"He is a fisherman searching for his subsistence on this island. He installed a fish trap there and lives on what it catches and Heaven bestows."

The Merchant went towards the man.

"Did you obtain a permit from the Ruler, or from his deputies to set up your trap here?"

"Yes, I have an oral permission from one of the members of the Appointed Council."

"Listen, you, the father of the Ruler only begot three men: two of them died young and the third is the Ruler. Here, I am representing him; but I do not know that he begot a fourth person known as the Appointed Council, to bestow responsibilities and properties on half and a half basis. Dilmunia, with all its islands and seas, its waters, is all part of the Ruler's properties. You have to remove the fish trap and return with your boat to the mainland before we leave you a lifeless body."

I spoke to the Merchant directly: does not a homeland

mean the land and the people? This man held the right of citizenship in his heart of hearts; he belonged to his people as he belonged to the soil of this land that he lived on. The Merchant could but explain his intention. "You are talking about homeland and we are talking about authority that consists of order, recipient and the relationship between them. The recipient must carry out what the authority orders to guarantee the existence of the relationship in a solid form to protect all parties concerned."

I suggested to the man that we tow his boat and that he boarded our dhow to return with us to Dilmunia. There the sailors welcomed him. I advised him to be happy with the Merchant's decision, as some matters are a blessing, albeit in appearance a mischief.

In a few hours, Dilmunia appeared as a bride welcoming her husband after a long absence. In a few days, the Ruler would announce the end of the season. The coast appeared with mixed bright colours. However, paleness and tears on the faces of women and children during the long period of waiting stole this beauty. They did not know if their loved ones were alive on board the dhow or lying at the bottom of the sea where sharks were competing to devour them.

The dhow moored tens of metres away from the shore and smaller vessels went to meet her. They all gathered around her, and the scene looked like mama duck with her little ones. The small boats were full of sailors and oars were clapping on the seawater, turning it into foam followed by circles of waves.

The dhow lay there empty, like a man deserted by his sons and grandsons after they had shared his inheritance. The women could no longer wait on land and invaded the waters, leaving their children behind on the seashore. Each one began to search for the source of the sound of her husband, to focus on his side. The water reached above the navel. The water did not deter them but added more eagerness to their determination. The arms and bosoms met with each embracing his better half. The waters wet the clothes and the tears on the faces. The smiles of happiness mixed with their tears until the impressive scene was over. Then everyone made haste to their houses. Khowla and her sisters surrounded Abu Rashed. One kissed him and the other embraced him, while another smelled him. Khowla sufficed with a kiss on her father's forehead.

I reached home and found its door ajar. There, the Doyen was trying to stand to receive me, so I hurried to his side. I felt for a moment that I was still a child, eager to the lap of my father. I held him tightly and kissed him on his head and forehead. The house was filled with warmth that touched the heat of the air, the walls and all its contents. I found the wife of Yousif and her children at one corner. I greeted them all. All kept their distances and I remained with the Doyen and Khowla. It was tragic, what I heard.

The next day, I did not have much time to enjoy more with members of my family. There were more responsibilities and more comprehensive. Friends came and invited me to tea on the beach on every afternoon. There the hut or "Baresty", with palm trees on its flanks where the men sat, and everyone came up with what he had and mentioned what he could deduct from the pearling season.

"What is new, men?"

"The Ruler has decided to appoint the Merchant as his right arm with regard to local internal affairs. The Merchant became the tax collector with his guards. He became the one who delineates the areas of farms and orchards, and imposes the amount of tax on crops, or decides the number of trees and palm trees to be leased. The Merchant became the one who issues affirmative and negative orders, after approval by the appointed Council."

"And why is this change?"

"They say until the Ruler has finished solving pending problems with neighbouring states, especially the government of Hormuz."

Another one told me about arresting Yousif and taking him to an unknown destination, and the escape of his wife to the house of the Doyen questing protection, where the Doyen and I were. The story of the desire of the Merchant for the wife of Yousif was widely spreading. The blood is rising, and the heat of forthcoming demands is increasing. These made-up crises need to be confronted. We are working in public and private.

(25) The Servant
September 1763

After our return from our unsuccessful trip to Baghdad, I remained with Adam for nearly two weeks in Hormuz. We got better acquainted with the British soldiers. I began to pose questions to Adam, who became with the passage of time a colleague, a friend, and perhaps a rival. I do not know his exact feelings, but of course, it has changed since the time I was a servant. I began to perform my role not as a servant but as someone who made suggestions, even though I was shy and hesitant when I posed some of them.

Most of Adam's decisions were pre-set for him, but later became of his own mind whenever there was something new or a change of route. He used to say that a leader is he who does not flow with the current, but he who creates an independent current. But later he began to accept my views or began to entertain them. This is because I became a reader of his thoughts, and coexistence is conceived by agreement. I wanted him to treat me as a colleague, not as a servant, as I became acquainted with the secrets of the trip. I knew well what he was aiming at. I sensed that similar friends in a work unit are controlled by jealousy. He should have seen me as a servant, not as a colleague. There were some unsettled matters and most of these were hurdles.

I proposed to him to try to go to Baghdad again. After two weeks the political and military situation would calm down.

We could take the river route to reach Baghdad. He started brooding on the idea; perhaps I read his mind. He did not want his decision on the tongue of others.

"British and Indian soldiers here, talking about Dilmunia, an island close by, as if it is the land of eternity."

"Sir, shall we change our route and head to Dilmunia instead of Baghdad?"

"Here they believe that Dilmunia shall be the headquarters of the East India Agency."

"Will the British ever leave Hormuz?"

"This is expected. Perhaps their headquarters will be in Basra or Dilmunia. It will be great to discover this island described as the Eternal Oasis of the East. All humanity is still looking for the elixir of life. I believe it is one of the three impossibilities. Man does not feel the taste of life if he does not search for the impossible. Attaining an objective in itself provides only momentary ecstasy, but chasing the impossible revitalises desire in life."

"This is marvellous. We shall find the elixir of life in Dilmunia. We can conquer disease and beat nothingness. Death shall be something of the past; perhaps Dilmunia shall be the Promised Land."

Adam gave me a smile that had the taste of abstinence from excessive food. He invited one of the soldiers, who became a semi-friend. Then Adam spoke to us about conquering death.

"Throughout this passage, we crossed several regions: marine, mountainous, desert and others. Every nation is clinging to life and refusing death. They see the cause of death as human. They erect bastions and forts. They build men-of-war and walls. All these means to confront a human enemy they expect carrying death to them. Most humans believe that their existence is never right except by exterminating the other. This is the philosophy of war and its causes. When peace prevails and danger dissipates, man realises that death is not in the hands of humans."

We crossed the land of Egypt. We read and heard the story of the Grand Pharaoh who wanted to build an enormous ladder to reach heaven so he could reach his creator and ask him to grant him eternity.

I was taken by Adam's talk about death and said to him, "Did Pharaoh actually reach his creator?"

He was indifferent to my interjection and continued his talk.

"The Pharaoh reached nothing but air, vacuum and stillness. He realised that his attempt was futile. He built pyramids and ordered people to preserve mummies. Deep inside him he realised the existence of a god who bestows the spirit and reclaims it. He was certain that God shall definitely bring back that soul for a long-lasting life. He was listening to his own voice. To perceive yourself, you must listen more and more. Therefore, he ordered that his body and that of his family and all that he had be preserved."

We heard another interpolation by one of the soldiers.

"This means there is no eternity; isn't there? Why is Dilmunia called the land of eternity?"

It is the human mind that is trying not to keep quiet against death, the impossible. Reality of life is in the heart of man, inside him by contentment with life and with love that offers an elixir. Had it not been for death, eternity would not have been impossible, and man would not have wanted to be alive. Then he would have to search for an elixir that would end life.

Death for him that perceives is happiness. It is discarding of the hurdles of life and its sins. It suffices to say that death, like love, comes only suddenly.

I no longer felt what Adam was saying.

"Sir, would you like some food or drink?"

"Yes, yes, make me the elixir of life with lemon flavour."

The captain of the *Patrick Stewart* came and told us about their next voyage to Dilmunia in three days and another voyage to Basra two weeks later. Adam was very happy.

"I think you will wait two weeks and leave for Baghdad."

"But we'll go to the island of Dilmunia in three days."

I think Dilmunia was an alternative plan but not a priority, as if it were a goal he was running behind for a long time. I asked him, "Sir, do you not want to go to the Consulate; You hand over to them the rest of the collections, and we take the campaign money?"

He spoke in a very soft voice and held a small stick, with which he drew two parallel lines on the soil. I could hardly hear him.

"Since I said farewell to Carina and left Denmark, my steps were preceding me and talking to me whenever I am late communicating with her. There, you shall find your shadow. I did not know that there. And when we were stuck on the coral island in the Red Sea, desire urged me to visit all islands that we passed by. This island we did not pass; it is passing us by now. Man normally does not search for love; it is the other way round."

I packed our luggage easily. He was ready next morning. As for me, I wanted to leave this very moment. How could I wait until tomorrow morning? That night her love deprived Adam's eye of sleep. He laid on his back outside on the cold sand in the evening, as if he were counting glittering stars. My God! It was the same scene that I saw when the leader of the campaign died in Sinai the night of departure; a sky adorned with stars, overflow of emotions. I looked at my companion in anticipation.

"I shall not let death come close to you; you shall not be harmed by it. I shall be vigilant guarding you until morning; no to death." Adam did not go to sleep and I watched him till dawn. My eye may rest in comfort.

The *Patrick Stewart* was moored next to five boats at port. To reach it, one had to use the five boats as steps. The ship was built of Indian timber, which tends to be black in colour. We were told that she was built in the style of the Nao Pkwena ships. They are famous for the height of its bow by seven metres above the water's surface and its stern, five metres; the centre and sides were only two metres highs. It had three masts, the central one was the highest and the first was the largest. There were eight crew on board, some servants and British soldiers with light arms.

The majority of the passengers were crowded at the back while Adam took his position at the front as if urging her to speed up. When I inquired about the position of his sitting, he said, "Innate laziness makes you sit at the back, while hope imposes the front. It is the rule of seating. It seems he is hurrying up the wind to reach his destination." The cruise lasted only few hours until it moored three miles away.

I did not want to intrude on his privacy; I looked at where he was looking. The island seemed low-lying and very long. The waters surrounding it were a calm green. Green trees covered the land and hid it. Another island in the north appeared to look in its roundness like the hunch of a camel. In just few minutes, we found small boats ready to transport us. We examined the people as we got closer. They were in bright white clothes. We boarded a small boat and sat on lateral benches tied to its mast. Then we reached the pier where we docked and the local sailors gave us a welcome reception fit for a guest reflecting their kindness.

We looked into the binoculars to examine the ground we were going to land on and inquired about it. Most of the houses were huts called "barestei". There were also scattered houses built in stone and slabs. These were all either one or two-storey buildings. The lanes were narrow and uneven, with shops on the sides selling local products and some Asian and European products. Fish and meat were sold in open kiosks with nothing to keep the sun's heat off except the shadow. Local vegetables were abundant, like tomatoes, onions and potatoes.

As we came closer, we saw a differently designed building and when we inquired about it, a priest travelling with us said, "This is the British Agency, and next to it are the houses of the missionaries, and not very far from it stand the offices of Mesopotamia of the British India Navigation Company."

A man approached and coming closer said, "I am one of the staff of the missionary agency."

He asked us to go with him. I looked at Adam, who was bewildered and confused. He could not decline the offer but was looking behind the generosity and the constant smile of the people. Among the crew appeared someone, standing behind them on higher ground. When the priest saw the hesitation in Adam, he suggested accompanying the people and that man who was called Abu Rashed, who explained that their homes were not far from the pier. As a compromise, it was decided that I go to the British Agency and to meet in two or three days.

That was the first expected parting between my companion and me since we left home. On the way, the priest said, pointing to one building. "That is the Customs House and around it some rundown buildings which Indian and Asian employees are occupying."

There was also what looked like a hospital; only five beds could be noted from the exterior.

Part 2

(1) Adam
September 1763

The way the people of Dilmunia received us is still vivid in my memory. They were hurrying in a race between them for good, without waiting for any reward. I perceived their emotions and felt them. I found that what leaves the heart is received by another heart. People here are in an innate race with themselves, but they are in a life of anxiety and expectation with the Ruler and his retinue. Each side wants to show his good qualities and both are striving for this; sometimes life imposes on us to play the role of Satan and sometimes takes pride in our good qualities. Between them, the fools take pride in the rudest.

Among this entire multitude and its complex texture, one man, prominent within his people, rose, growing in importance. He received us as the head of a popular delegation welcoming the guests, who was proud of himself to the degree of humility and kindness. He was not hard among his people but was determined. When he talked, they listened and never spoke, except by his tacit consent. He was what many reiterate: people place you where you place yourself.

Abu Rashed was wearing a white shirt and a colourful loincloth where the golden and silver colours intermingled. He placed his head kerchief on his left shoulder that was so narrow and hardly could support that light cloth. I recalled then the folkloric style of the people of Mocha in the Yemen and some of their tribes of Yaariba of Oman. Their styles were similar, but they added to them a belt and a dagger. They wore them out of pride. It seems that the people of the Arabian Peninsula are always on the move. Clothes, styles and dialects are the fastest signs of communication and effects by others. I thought, or rather deducted, that interactions between those peoples and races may lead some to intermarry.

The moment our feet touched the soil of Dilmunia, the people gathered around us in a ring. Everyone was offering to lend a hand with a true pleasure, but they were all observing their leader behind them. They made way for the guests arriving, then for the conversation, to begin welcoming.

"Peace be upon you."

-I mastered the response to it. "And peace be upon you, too, with his mercy and blessings."

The people present were astonished. I read many questions on their faces. How could a red man speak Arabic? It was the basics and elementariness of my learning Arabic since my preparatory stage at Göttingen University, then passing by Istanbul, capital of the Ottoman Empire, then Alexandria, Sinai and Mocha, and here I was in Dilmunia, which is said to be the land of eternity, as reported in Hormuz. I learnt that languages are extracted from their people by practise, covered by dialects, but it can be acquired academically and refined grammatically. Languages are the tongues of communication. It is not letters written on paper; it is said that the language we use to talk about ourselves, not others, is how we are exposed and scandalised.

"Welcome as a dear guest amongst us. We hope to offer you all we have for the sake of achieving the goals of your trip."

I heard his confident voice

"Thank you for your good welcome. I must introduce my colleague. He was the savant for the campaign, but he became an effective member in it. He masters the art of cooking and has a sixth sense regarding delicious kinds of food. He says that every table in the world has a taste of its soil and a flavour of its people. He always repeats that the taste of the table reflects the colour of the soil of the people and flavour of their taste."

We all laughed happily and exchanged courtesies which were characterised by spontaneity, as smiles break the wall of silence and shyness of strangeness. I extended my hand to shake that of Abu Rashed. I relaxed it in his dark, smooth but rigid palm. Can hands reflect some of our personalities too? I think so.

The man knelt to raise our luggage, but they all raced without his asking. The situation pleased me, and I placed my hand, patting his shoulder. He should feel the value of this luggage; what it contains of experience is bigger than its weight. He may think that all is plentiful is inexpensive. Then I told him about the Servant's wish to visit the missionary agency at the request of the priest who was aboard the boat. As for me, "I shall accompany you with gratitude."

We all walked a few metres then we reached the donkey stable. The largest of the donkeys was brown in colour, pulling a wooden cart. Its wheels seemed smooth and worn out. We were invited to place the luggage and pile it on the cart and mount the accompanying donkeys. The luggage was placed there, but I carried the maps and drawings in front of me while on the donkey's back. They looked at each other and their smiles met until they burst out laughing in surprise at what I did.

Some men preceded the caravan while others mounted their beasts, as if it were a merry group wedding, whereas Abu Rashed rode his donkey at my side.

"We shall take you to stay at our place. There you can keep your luggage in a safe place. There you can bathe, relax and regain your strength before you attend to your business again."

"Thank you for your generosity, Abu Rashed. I think I shall be an unwanted guest."

He smiled and replied, "The miser is he who sees generosity spendthrift."

The caravan passed by the houses in the north of the mainland. It was one of the scattered and similar villages on the coast of the island. Each village was in the shape of a group of houses embracing each other, and there were farms with hedges of dates, palms fronds and a few mosques. Unplanned scattering resulting in geometrical beauty.

Accidents and spreads also have their magic. Incidence and scattering have their own magic too. It was said that beauty was not in itself but from the angle of viewing it. This how the country seemed. We passed through lanes and the narrow, serpentine passages of those quarters or blocks. After a few minutes, the crowd stopped at the house of Abu Rashed. A mud house, some of its façade was painted with lime and white gypsum. The rear part of the house was built of palm trees and fronds. I knew later that the front room was known as *majlis*, where guests were received, but the inner rooms were the living rooms. There was also a top room known as an *alarish*, which was for women gathering in the morning before noon.

Abu Rashed asked me to dismount. Men lined up to greet me, being bid farewell before leaving their abodes. Abu Rashed began introducing them to me personally. It seemed they were the closest to him, or relatives. Then, he opened the door of his house and ushered me through a cove in the large door that led to a long, uncovered passage that took you inside the house. On the right of the passage was another small outlet that ended at the *majlis*.

Despite the simplicity of the building, it was fascinating. The wooden door of the *majlis* was short and double-sided. It was in the centre of the long wall. The room had three windows on two opposite walls. I saw there an old man with no distinguishable features except his leanness and wrangled face. Years had drawn lines and shapes on his face. A body that really depressed you. I got closer to him and found a young, merry soul hiding behind these wrinkles and behind that figure. The old man smiled, revealing the beauty of his soul and frailness of his body.

"Welcome, Adam," murmured the old man.

"How did you know my name?"

"Goodness precedes the horse. Welcome amidst us an honoured guest. I hope you feel at home with your family."

Abu Rashed came closer to introduce him.

"My father, the doyen of the Al Jubur family, our reference for all. He is the backbone; we sit in his shade at times of crisis."

Then the man went on to introduce me to his family.

"These are my young children, Rashed and his brothers."

"It is my honour to know you, Shaikh." Turning to the children I said, "and you heroes."

I was I was totally shocked and kept silent when I saw a

young woman behind the children, hiding half of her face. She had a spectrum that robbed vision. I stared, and my mouth was half open but no words came out. I still remember her first looks. She had almond eyes, wide like the sea. She had a moon face and was full-cheeked. Her upper lip was like an eagle hovering over her lower lip. She was medium height that I did not see anything of its forms and lines. She was hiding her body and part of her face with a cloth, like an Indian sari, that she wore from the top of her head to the bottom of her feet. Staring at the woman exhausted me. Woman is a liquid difficult to anticipate when its shape freezes.

Abu Rashed realised the situation.

"This is my daughter, Khowla."

I nodded my head and she replied with half a wink, reassured. I swallowed my saliva and wetted my lip with my tongue. Then I felt thirsty. The Doyen invited me to sit on his right, facing Abu Rashed. I hurried to thank them for their kindness and hospitality. The Doyen smiled again, and said some lines that I wrote later.

"O, Mawi, richness is useless to the man, if the soul is stuck in the bosom,

If my loved ones showed me a beautiful slippery-sided wool

And went quickly clapping their palms saying that beating wounded our fingers.

O, Mawi, I do not say to beggar one day that our money is scarce,

O, Mawi, money comes and goes, and what remains of money is saying and remembrance."

No sooner had he finished then Khowla and Rashed were listening and putting down in writing what he had said. I felt that what he had said was like jewels that had to be documented. I did not understand what the shaikh said. Khowla, however, asked him to explain those lines. The lass spoke my mind and I added my admiration to it and to her. It seems that first love is to look into the eyes of a person you feel that you saw earlier, but I shall slow down and keep away the devil's temptation. Love is a bilateral partnership; the woman is the first and last partner.

The Doyen explained in detail.

"My daughter mentioned that Hatem Altaei was so remounted for his Arabian generosity in pre-Islamic times. It is also reported a splendid tale about his wife, Mawieh, that went like this. "They were in a very severe winter night, with cold wind blowing. Their children were hungry, groaning without food. The woman took charge of the situation by lighting fire under an empty pot so they would go to sleep, hoping for food to be cooked for them. Then, a woman arrived at the tent with eight children, asking Hatem to feed them.

"'O, Abu Ady, these youngsters are howling like wolves of hunger; we have no one but you to help us.'

"Hatem said to his wife:

'I know now that the vicissitude of life is important for renewal. Hurry up; may God fill you and them.'

"The wife came to whisper in his ear.

'We have no food; you know that our children went to sleep groaning of hunger.'

"Hatem asked her to give him a knife. He went to his horse, which was all he had. He cut its neck and put its flesh on the fire. When the meat was cooked, he asked her to feed the woman and her children until they were full, then to wake up their children to eat. Then he took the remainder of the food, searching for the hungry in the desert. He only returned at dawn."

(2) The Merchant
Early October 1763

Concurrently with the fabricated national crisis that was created and executed by Abu Rashed and his gang, I came to know about the arrival of European travellers to our land. They set foot on Dilmunia, the land of eternity. The sailors were spending the evening as usual on the shore adjoining the wharf. Most people used to spend summer nights by the shores in search of sea breeze. During following months, they stayed at their detached homes in neighbourhoods. I thought Carsten Niebuhr, who used to travel the region, may have arrived at Dilmunia again[7].

It was imperative that the Ruler and the National Council meet the travellers to stop Abu Rashed supplying false and misleading news to the guests. It would be a fatal mistake to let the opposition deliver their voices and demands abroad. Then the voices of the opposition would turn into revolution, and consequently the reputation of the regime and its relationships would be in permanent danger and their demands for change and reforms would assume the nature of right and duty. Then only, the inevitable would occur and investigations with prisoners, Yousif amongst them, would be opened. It was a series of expected and unexpected events that should have

---

[7] Carsten Niebuhr, a famous Danish traveller who visited India and the Arabian Gulf.

been killed from the beginning.

The next morning, I hurriedly paid a visit with some merchants and clergymen to the Ruler at his palace. To give credibility to any action in a conservative society, you must give it a religious quality. Many of the silent majority are not scared except by the voice of religion. We were in need of a counter popular base. To put an end to infant differences is lawful. The Ruler welcomed us at his palace. We were met at his office. We managed to depict the truth and the imminent danger coming as a ghoul that wants to destroy the seat of his government. I, therefore, saw fear gradually increasing in his soul. Scared souls are shivering and the word is coming out hesitantly. I said, "It is reported that Abu Rashed and his people received the travellers without prior permission from Your Highness."

He answered me after he had relaxed in his seat.

"I came to know that was at the request of the traveller himself; as for his servant, he had gone to the Missionary Agency at the invitation of the priest who accompanied him on the trip."

"After Your Highness's permission, we all believe that the traveller should leave Abu Rashed's house. It is also illogical that an alien visits our country without the approval of the Ruler himself, as he may impart some fake news, and in turn the traveller transfers to his country. Then this news falls in the hands of foreign powers and this may enable Ottoman and British interference. Powers aiming at stability in the region to preserve their own interests and our problems shall never come to an end. As the proverb goes, Your Highness, the people of Mecca know its alleys better. Problems should be solved internally with all our consent. We utterly refuse foreign dictations. How can a traveller intrude on our privacy?"

The Ruler placed his left hand behind his head, near his ear. Playing with his hair and said, "Yes, our internal affairs should remain between us. Problems of the same house should be solved within its walls. We strongly object to foreign interference, but we must define the problems facing our society, and fear that others should know them."

His denunciation of the existing crisis put me at stake.

"There are the demands of the seamen and farmers too, for evaluation and reducing of taxes. I propose that we extend an invitation to the man and his servant. We can tell them about the Ruler's peaceful plans, and his sincere intention in maintaining the honour of all the citizens. Half-sycophancy may attain happiness, but one quarter of truth attains sadness."

The Ruler reiterated his permanent adage like a parrot: all citizens are equals, like the teeth of a comb.

The weekly meeting was over, after which I returned home without achieving anything. I began to recall the chain of events. Abu Rashed received the travellers for three days at his home. The duration may increase according to the desire of the traveller himself. We could expect what that invitation would lead to. As you know, empty minds are easy to fill; they will overflow with what they are filled with.

I sent one of my Private Eyes to find out what was going on there and to sense the pulse of the street and to know what the man and his host were planning to do. If the guest was not working in the interests of our country, then we could ask him to leave the country. Perhaps he was in contact with foreign bodies that wanted to harm our country and plan to change its stability and security. Incoming news was not reassuring, as the guest expressed excessive happiness with the hospitality of

Abu Rashed and his *Majlis*. It became imperative to move before the Ruler himself. Racing for good deeds is a human and a social duty. The racers, the racers.

On the same day, I sent two representatives to the house of Abu Rashed and the Christian Agency to invite the honourable guests to accept a dinner party in their honour. Neither Abu Rashed nor others had the ability to prevent the invitation. It is said that the guest declined it before consulting Abu Rashed, who gave him the green light. The guest, however, insisted that the visit should be short and that he return to the house of Abu Rashed after that. The traveller accepted the invitation unwillingly, but the Servant accepted it happily. At last, they accepted the invitation and went to the bureau of the Ruler in the afternoon. The first came, accompanied by Abu Rashed, and the other one in the company of one of the priests. The priest and Abu Rashed pulled back to the end of the *majlis*, while the two guests sat in the forefront.

"In my name and the name of the Ruler, it is our honour to welcome you to our country and wish you a happy stay."

"We highly appreciate this honourable invitation."

"You can visit the Ruler's palace soon to explain to him the purposes of your visit, so we can offer you required services and facilities to attain the goals of the trip."

"Our trip, sir, aims at visiting archaeological sites and studying the sources of income and the riches expected underground to help you benefit from the natural riches you have. We shall also transfer experiences of our governments and countries to help you. As you may be aware, Oriental societies are considered closed when compared with vivid European societies. There you find scientific revolution and here deep-rooted traditions. Civilisations may benefit from each other."

"We do not want science or knowledge that opens hearts and minds and that also corrupts and spoils our people. Our sciences are Quranic; we derive them from the Book of God and the Tradition of his Prophet. We love those who revive the *sunna* and kill *bid'a*."

"All divine religions are designed for the service of humanity; they call for knowledge and work. In general, they all concur with virtues. They uphold reason and prohibit demeaning it. The educated man is better than the illiterate. I do not think that differences between humans are religious; these are pure human, made by man himself. Therefore, all can return to the principles of religions to overcome the inhumane qualities in man, these qualities that advocate hatred and seclude others. All this is for maintaining an honourable life for all humans."

At the far end of the *majlis*, Abu Rashed stood and requested to be heard. He was allowed. He then said that there were some misunderstandings between himself and the travellers on the importance or necessity of knowledge. He mentioned a verse, or *ayah,* in the Quran that created an uproar between the *jahilya* of Quraish and the preaching of the Prophet of Islam.

"God said in his holy book, Al-Rahman, who taught the Quran, created man and taught him eloquence, one of the attributes of the Creator that nobody shares with Him is the *Merciful,* because His Mercy is omnipresent. All His offerings are for the compassion of His creatures. One of His attributes that manifests his mercy is knowledge. The knowledge by which man perceives the universe. There are some theories that claim that the number of prophets reach more than twenty-four million. Only five of those are entrusted with Divine messages. They are all preachers of love and goodwill between all humans; they also preach science and knowledge.

"The method of the Quran and other divine books encourages learning and compassion between peoples. Some of the followers of the prophets disobeyed them and preached enmity between religions because they ignored true learning. We find the Glorious Quran saying, 'We have honoured the Son of Adam' and also says, 'You shall find those most compassionate to the believers those who said we are Nasserites.' Undoubtedly, there is a difference between religion and its followers, between thought and conduct. Every educated person knows that not every Muslim carries Islam in his heart. For all this, sir, we can say that sciences that open hearts and minds keep us away from all kinds of corruptions. I call on you lovingly to keep fear away from your heart; fear turns obsession into disease. I also call on you to stop marginalising others and excluding them."

"We never marginalise anyone."

"You do. Marginalising is robbing the right to choose from others. This also applies to the right to education. Some say that education makes people easy to lead, difficult to run. It is easy to govern him but impossible to enslave him."

That was the intervention of Abu Rashed and his sharp retorts that abounded lots of challenges to the Ruler and all members of the *Majlis*. There had to be a way to get rid of him physically and mentally.

(3) Abu Rashed
November 1763

One evening, I met Adam and we had an interesting discussion with the Doyen, a quiet dialogue adorned with science. I returned from the mosque after Maghreb Prayers and found them like whispering doves. I had no idea about their dialogue, and I could not overhear it. They did not hear my greeting despite my loud voice. As soon as the Doyen saw me standing before him, he invited me to take part in their discussion.

The Doyen told me that Adam was engulfed in lots of miasmas that prevented him from knowing what was going on in Dilmunia. He wanted to study the archaeology of the island but preferred to know more about its inhabitants first. The deplorable events drove him mad. Happiness deserted him that was supposed to be permanent in the land of eternity. There were lots of questions that resulted from the loss of confidence between the Ruler and his retinue on the one hand, and the majority of the people on the other.

I answered him that we did not understand anything in the affairs of government except the weighing scale of right and injustice,]; this scale was obvious and clear. If what is going on here, you call a political affair, then we must talk about it. Political maturity of the ruler is not by the quantity of spilled blood or by filling prisons; maturity is by decreasing discrepancies between components of society itself, between authority and society.

In his interpolation, Adam brought a beautiful definition of this science known as politics, saying that he knew how rulers dealt with the local affairs, socially and economically, and others. If the people are economically satisfied, you shall not find anybody interested in the rulers' affairs, even in the case of luxury. If the economic and living situation is bad, the public is waiting for the straw to break their backs and open their mouths. After that, they demand just distribution of wealth and a share in government and elections to secure the promised justice. There is another cause called the social dimension. If distinction is based on religious and family basis, it breaks the base of social justice, which is sufficient reason for destabilising security and arousing the public. Private property, for example, is social utilisation, not ownership. As man has no right to cut his hand, he has no absolute freedom over his private property; he only spends it in good deeds.

The Doyen made it clear that one of the basic reasons of the crisis in Dilmunia was the result of the control of the tribal system on the political system. A system cannot coexist with the present time in an epoch where people see political activity either declared publicly, or crippled, handicapped depending on privacy in its silence. This is something that is refused by many people.

Adam, biting his lips as if there were something on his mind, aroused me. I asked him:

"Due to your many travels and your experiences, Adam, can some societies solely be distinguished for these movements? Can we consider some societies to be incapable of demanding their right of determination? Have they not the right of choice?"

"Human experiences, my dear, move from one place to

another and are not restricted to just one type of people."

"Then why marginalisation? Is not that the worst type of will deprivation?"

Adam sat right as if he were forced to disclose what was on his mind. He explained that people are similar when it comes to rights and obligations. There are data that indicate expected trends between peoples and their rulers, and cases of instability in existing relations. Someone says that I have been made *Wali* over you to give you orders, as one judge in the peninsula in the case of amputating a robber's hand. It is better to apply the reasonable style in solving disputes and to reach solutions that satisfy all sides. But as you may be aware, the ruler is always scared that the pillars of his rule may shake, so he fights others. The good ruler is he who plants love in the heart of his people and makes them build his edifice by their hands. But if the ruler built his edifice on their blood, it shall disappear. There are in Europe now, and in previous years, unnatural migration movements. People escape in group migrations from the country to towns; there is demographic change that reflects a state of instability.

"But we do not have those towns in Dilmunia that you talk about."

"Not necessarily that demographic change is related to movement to the town, movement to outside town, and sometimes by changing the structure of the population in the society in general. These changes mean instability that is the existence of a state of popular turmoil."

The Doyen had a Quranic interpolation that struck his mind. He cited the story of the Pharaoh of Egypt and his conflict with Moses. He explained that the sublime responsibility of man is to stand against the despot and the demi-god. It is the beautiful aspect of man. Then he came up with a bit of his literary sense that characterised him.

"Beauty from god is an honour for those who seek purity and peace."

He did not finish all that he wanted to say and said, "When we passed Sinai, we saw that history preserved in the place. Places retain events and document them. When you visit any location, events are engraved in the depository of memory. You shall find it in your thought and feel it by your soul; history cannot be seen by the naked eye. The thought and the soul are two eyes by which we read accumulations of historical events. In Sinai, for example, if you sense Moses, you can see him in every atom of dust, and if you perceive the power and injustice of Pharaoh, you shall see his marks in every step you take. Pharaoh, who did not believe in any god, ordered his people to build him a ladder to the sky so he could see the God of Moses because of that human tyranny. In exchange of that tyranny, we find that weakness and human docility, he orders his people to build the pyramids to be buried in them with his property and dreams.

"At one stage, he did not believe in a god, but he believed that he should be resurrected. Who is going to resurrect him then? In Dilmunia, I found you, but there is anxiety. There is a crisis of confidence and a missing link. Expectations and worry from the other. I read this in the eyes of the people and saw it more in the eye of the Ruler. It is natural that there should be a view and a counter-view. In our country, we see this juxtaposition as a life necessity, a divine law. Here, I saw the opposition view besieged and prohibited too."

The Doyen spoke in a tone of satisfaction and content.

"We, dear sir, are a people small in number but big in

expectations and ambitions. We rule the way we are. We tend to be more peaceful and secure, but man is a stance by which he is immortalised. What do we leave for our children and what do they inherit? Let us be more truthful and honest. The Ruler has a law in place for the distribution of pearls; it was approved by the merchants, *Nukhethas* and seamen. It is an unsuccessful system and unjust to the seamen. However, it was legal according to the initial agreement. The system determines that seamen get one fifth of the catch only, and the *Nukhetha,* the Merchant and the Ruler get the rest. It was really expected that the seamen would grumble and after a while they would demand changing it. Look what happened: the Ruler ordered by the authority invested in him to impose a tax on the catch, and from the Merchant, the *Nukhetha* and the seamen themselves.

"Then the Merchant, to compensate the taxes he paid to the Ruler, imposed another tax on the *Nukhetha* and the seamen, that is on one hand, but on the other hand, the Merchant undertakes to make provision during the season on condition that he buys the pearls from the *Nukhetha* at the price he sets."

"It is a lie and excessive injustice."

"I have not ended the story yet."

"The Merchant finances all the divers with food and provisions for the whole year. In exchange, the seamen sell him their catch after the pearling season."

"Nothing wrong, nor harm."

"The whole harm, as most of the seamen are illiterate, the Merchant documents the debts, and the seamen print their thumbs as a proof. If the one fifth of the crop exceeds the debt, the Merchant raises the debt, so the Merchant is always the creditor and the diver is debtor all his life. Here, you realise the benefit of ignorance."

"My good god!"

"That is not all. The Merchant, at the recommendation of the Ruler, in order to get his share, decided to transfer the debt to the most senior of the sons of the diver after his death. So, the death becomes eternally familial. It becomes a totem hung on their chests."

These details amazed Adam. He felt great resentment and pain for this inhuman behaviour. Then he remembered what was going on in his own country. There, my family and I used to live under another kind of despotism. Human methods vary, but the satanic authoritative conditions remain the same. There, you do not find pearl fishing industry, but the basic profession is agriculture and industry. There, taxes are imposed on farmers, on all crops and all kinds, even fruit-bearing trees. When there is famine, disease, and even snow, if anyone harms the crop, then the farmer had to bestow his farm to the governor or the Church, on condition that he and his family work on it. So, the farmer and his family work on his property without owning except his daily subsistence. He owns no wages nor land, nor anything. Philosophers and theorisations gave that kind of injustice the name of slavery.

The Doyen smiled, looking at his son.

"This condition is repeated here in a different manner with the farmers. The farmer who is unable to pay taxes, and is insolvent, then all his land is owned by one of the merchants or the Ruler. Debts are one of the successful ways of remaining in humiliation."

"We call that feudalism. The Church moved and took advantage of that, where it made alliances with the feudalist lords so as to reap one tenth of the income or give the farmer a document of indulgence that guarantees heaven after death. If he refuses, it gives him a document of excommunication. That unjust stupid movement led farmers to escape to towns before another class exploited them; this class is known as the bourgeoisie.

"Human concerns seem to be the same all over the world. There may be many faces, but the abominable face of injustice is common between them all. The wiser is he who makes use of the brains of others and puts them on his side and perceives the errors committed in other people's experiences, so that goodness is a blessing for all.

The Merchant did not have enough of his flattery but raised his staff in the face of those who raise their eyes to his face. His son was drowned in an attempt to learn diving. It was accidental; however, the Merchant is insisting it was a premeditated murder. Yousif, the Puller, is behind bars and no news is known about him. The Merchant and his retinue are playing a tune in the face of those who are demanding their rights. I do not rule out another trial, along with Yousif, accused of plotting the murder of the Merchant's son. People are standing on moving sands and asking for safety. However, between this and that, life must go on. Man, as Adam says, is an incomplete art painting and needs to be completed.

(4) Adam
Third Week of November 1763

After the first meeting we had together at the Merchant's house, I was supposed to meet my servant again in two days' time as was requested, to pay a visit to the Ruler. I began to feel that the Servant had become a colleague, or perhaps a rival with the eliminations of barriers and overcome roles. There was an obstacle separating us as long as there were places between us. Abu Rashed and I, accompanied by two of his men, went to the Missionary Agency in the area close to the port. I met my colleague but was received with obvious lack of warmth; I read in his eyes a non-welcoming attitude. I intended to take him along with me. The protocol mission that I should leave him at the agency was over. However, the British major at the agency invited both of us to visit the Ruler with him. I realised the presence of Abu Rashed, so I asked him, "Would you agree to accompany me to the Ruler?"

Abu Rashed smiled and came closer to my ear. He whispered in Arabic not similar to that currently in circulation; A murmur which was a blend of dialects and languages, but I managed to grasp its content.

"You have to ask them for prior permission, in order to know if my visit is welcomed or not."

"You tell me first about your desire." With a silent smile he said, "Yes, I would like to visit him."

The major said, "Britain conferred legality on the ruler of

Dilmunia to settle disputes. There is no harm in Abu Rashed or others coming along."

With the consent of the major, we headed out of the agency. We crossed roads covered by sand and pebbles on the sides. The roads and lanes were more of a desert. Most of the buildings were of mud and lime, all attached, but had their character and privacy. As to what is known as 'Barastiy', these were built with palm tree trunks. They are perforated to allow the passage of air from all directions. When looking at these remote houses in neighbouring villages, it would be difficult to distinguish them from the colour of the soil. These formed the inhabited areas in the north of the mainland. These are a group of districts or villages, such as Ras Alruman, Albilad Alqadim and Alkhamis, where the Dilmunia mosque is located. These areas were amenable to expansion and uniting. A kind of geographic expansion appeared after some time as green areas densely planted with palm trees that turn more of a green cloud.

We took the route through the orchards, where there were different types of fruit-bearing trees such as local lemon, 'Lause', papaya and others. Most of these were either flowering or fruitful. Amid these trees, I found vast grounds covered by green plants and vegetation. I also saw a stream overflowing on both banks. We were told that it originated from a source known as a virgin pool that was pure and never touched. The water moved northward and eastward and diverged into brooks and rivulets that flooded the area with its sweet waters before it met the sea. These two bodies of sweet and salt-water formed two seas, or Bahrain, with distinctive flavour that is unique in the whole world. After these green gardens appeared, the features of the desert that we were used to in the Arabian Peninsula were conquering us again. We passed a long a chain of small mounds that looked natural in formation and creation.

"Fabulous, after these vast green areas. Here we are in an area full of natural mounds, after which it is mountainous and again sandy desert."

"These mounds, Mr. Traveller, are in fact, burial mounds, locally called 'tuús'."

"My god! Are these not natural mounds? Are they really graves?"

"Yes, burials and very ancient graves."

I crossed geographical areas, from Europe to Africa and Asia, and I did not find anything like these burial mounds. One of my traveller colleagues surprised me with his vision. He was an archaeologist, talented in deciphering symbols. Interested in discovering history, on the other hand, I have learnt a lot from him. I wished I had the time to draw and examine these. They are treasures preserving history beneath the sands and undoubtedly want to disclose its secrets. I posed a question to Abu Rashed and the major.

"Will the Ruler allow us to dig one of them and discover its contents?"

The major answered, "They were exposed to robbery. However, we need to have permission when we pay him a visit."

I anxiously asked, "To whom do these graves belong?"

The major was not interested in these matters. Objectives of his presence were limited; they were political and military objectives for the purpose of maintaining the British interests and defending those he represented on these islands. The major raised his shoulders as a sign of his bewilderment. He was silent and looked to Abu Rashed, like me, waiting for a convincing answer.

"Dilmunia is considered the land located in the centre of several civilisations, such as those in Mesopotamia, the Yemen, Persia and the Arabian Peninsula. As man desires what he does not have. The peoples of these regions imagine this island as the promised paradise because of the natural water pools and wells, in addition to the greenness that distinguishes it from other arid desert areas. It is a green spot between seas and deserts, graded in its geographical variety between north, centre and south.

"This land is considered the melting pot of all those peoples who wanted to be immortalised in the Garden of Eden, who came with their treasures to be buried on its land after his death. For those who wanted to do business, Dilmunia is a gateway between East and West. Those who escaped oppression of rulers also migrated to this island, where it was difficult to get at them because of the sea. Many Bedouin tribes moved to the island and became its guardian. All this was due to the nature of the people of this land. Since time immemorial, they were known for their tolerance and love of others and most of all preferring guests to themselves."

I interrupted him and patted his shoulder. I looked at him and read him. You can read everyone when their eyes are clear to penetrate their hearts without effort. I praised the man and thanked him as he elaborated on narrating his talk.

"This land is also considered a haven and land of safety for those victimised by political, religious and sectarian oppression, due to its insular nature. Whenever a family is afflicted by oppression, it flees to Dilmunia. Here, races and nationalities are multiple, with diverse dialects. Most of these reflect the areas of their origins. They formed the textual population of the island by the passage of years."

We were all impressed by Abu Rashed's talk, even the major, who had reservations about his coming along with us. He liked that enormous detailed knowledge. The chain of the burial mounds did not come to its end before two hours, when a black cloud sprang upon the ground. I thought I would add this phenomenon to the wonders I witnessed on route to my visit to the Orient. Abu Rashed rushed to me once again with his explanation: it is the biggest mountain on the island located in its centre, called the Mountain of Smoke.

The more we approached, the more we began to distinguish the dividing line between the mountain and the sky. Smoke was engulfing it at a distance, raising it higher. We went to the foot where no greenery was found, and no glimpse of hope for life. Stones of various sizes were spread here and there and keeping its distance to form what is called a road. At the end of the desert road, I saw a solitary building, a building different from what I had seen in the northern villages. Its colour was sandy and could not be distinguished except by coming closer to it. They told me it was the palace of the Ruler.

I wondered why the Ruler lived far away from his people. It was another sign that may explain the existing relationship between the two sides. We came closer and found a man spreading his arms like a white bird, a sign of peace and affection. The major said, "Look at that man; he is the Ruler, welcoming you."

I wondered again about his servants and retinue. They told me that the Arabian Ruler welcomes his guests outside his palace and greets them outside. This is the nature of great men. We came closer to him, having left his servants and family inside, as is the custom of Arabian originality when receiving guests. He was dressed in white clothes, and on top of that wore a white robe of wool called a 'bisht' locally. On his head, he was wearing a head kerchief made of cashmere; the headgear was woven of gold threads. He had a dagger around his waist with a leather sheath. I also noticed a ring on his right little finger.

He took us welcomingly to his *majlis* covered by red carpet; I estimated its size at a hundred and twenty square feet. Its walls were decorated and engraved in gypsum plaster, and above this there were shapes and Arabic calligraphy of verses from the Quran. The doors and windows made of Indian teak wood were numerous; I saw nothing similar in the villages or the country that we passed. The ceiling was made of wood planks, on top of which mat mesh was placed under dry mud to absorb drops of rain. I saw some people place something from this temporal world in their homes, but I found the Ruler putting the whole world in his home.

The Ruler sat on a large wooden chair with many engraved geometrical shapes. Its front legs were open, and the seat narrowed at the end, with two poles on its back base. The seat and its back were cushioned with red velvet. Solemn silence overfell the place as no one could speak without permission from His Highness. He welcomed us again and a black man served tea from a long-spouted pot. This was followed by coffee from a smaller pot. Abu Rashed told me that we were waiting for lunch that was brought few minutes later in brass trays placed on a mat on the floor. I hurried to extend my hand to the food, but Abu Rashed punched me, saying, "The Ruler must first taste the food and then invite us; that is ancient Bedouin protocol." The carcass was on the middle of the tray. That meal was called *ghouzi* that abounded with nuts. I expressed my admiration at the aroma of the food, while talking to the Servant. Abu Rashed punched me again.

"Speaking during eating is not permitted."

As the Ruler began opening the ritual of eating, he also ended it. When he raised his hand, he dropped the grains of rice sticking in his hand, then came the servants, or the boys, with a water container to wash the hands again. This time we were perfumed with rose water. Then the boys came to serve tea and coffee from the brass pot that was always placed on the lighted charcoal burner.

The Ruler sat right on his seat. He had a long face with a sharp, long nose, and a light, fully-rounded black beard. He had a fair complexion like the Arabs of the Arabian Peninsula. He spoke in a soft voice, greeting us all, then he accorded me and the Servant with a stronger greeting.

"Similar travellers come to our country and have scientific and commercial objectives. We welcome you and bless your efforts, wishing you good a stay amongst us and we will provide you with aid to achieve your objectives. We are aware that this Danish campaign, like other campaigns, is aiming at spreading goodness and benefit among all."

"Thank you, Your Highness. he government of my country appreciates your generosity, and we would like to convey to you the greetings of the Ottoman Sultan, who paid a lot for the success of this campaign."

"You shall have the free choice of choosing the place of your residence; we shall provide you with hands whenever necessary."

"Your Highness, I chose to stay with the common people, and enjoy the hospitality of Abu Rashed. As there are studies on archaeology, there are also studies on humanities and botany and others. We are hoping to acquire your generous approval."

Then, the Servant spoke for the first time, thanking the Ruler for his generosity and asked to stay at the kitchen of the palace to offer his expertise that may add to the variety of cooking and to know new methods."

The Ruler approved our demands and promised to extend help as much as possible. The Servant went along with the boys to the large kitchen. Then Abu Rashed requested permission to speak to the Ruler, who nodded approval.

"I shall be very honest with you, Your Highness. There is a number of cases that should be in the hands of Your Highness, as you are the most responsible to take the most appropriate action for the public. There is the incident of locking Yousif, the Puller, behind bars, without any definite evidence of his role in the drowning of the Merchant's son. There are also the extra taxes imposed by the Merchant on the *Nukhatha*, the divers and the pullers. These are all matters that require reconsideration by Your Highness, to judge their legality."

The Ruler promised us to look into all the demands and to be truthful, too.

"Do not worry; most convictions are the result of a simple misunderstanding. Here is the Servant working in our kitchen. Moreover, here we are extending a hand to the traveller. We shall discuss with the judges the question of Yousif, the Puller. We shall meet with the Council of Notables to discuss all matters about the taxes."

We left, and Abu Rashed was murmuring in my ear: "Truth is the greatest means of deception."

(5) The Servant
December 1763

The Ruler passed his orders that I should be among the workers in his palace and given the responsibility to supervise the affairs of His Highness's main kitchen. His family and the workers at the palace warmly welcomed me. I even thought I was not a mere servant and a cook. Their way of treatment was full of appreciation and respect. They allocated a room for me previously used by one of the Ruler's sons. They showered me with their humility, altruism and generosity, until I almost forgot that I was a servant in His Highness's palace.

The next day, I asked the cooks to help me prepare a new, different meal for His Highness. They began to work at my service like a beehive. I obtained petty details from the cook about the flavour that the Ruler preferred in his food. I found that he preferred Indian and Persian cuisine where the flavour tends to be spicy. I maintained that flavour and used it in one of the Ottoman dishes. We waited until lunch and I set the table myself and placed the main dish at the centre. I personally invited the Ruler to the table. Then he asked members of his family to say grace. He smiled and nodded with satisfaction. That made me happy. Later I remembered what Adam said, that praise makes a successful nation, whereas blame destroys it, let alone a commendation from His Highness, the Ruler.

"It seems you are an expert in your field."

I answered him with pride and confidence.

"Anyone who loves his work can excel in it."

"Where did you get this magic recipe?"

"From travelling and moving around countries that offer people more knowledge. I found that tables change according to the change of countries. For example, there are countries famous for spices, others for salad dishes, and others for potatoes and rice. If cooks visit other countries, they will be able to blend all this and create new, delicious dishes."

The Ruler surprised me by his spontaneous decision, ordering the director of his *Majlis* to highly reward me. He invited me to remain at the palace until departure from Dilmunia. I expressed great pleasure and consent. The man came and placed a little bag of coins in my hand.

The Ruler retired to the room of one of his wives and asked me to wait for him until he woke up from his siesta. It is one of the dominant habits in the Arabian Peninsula. Perhaps the heat of the sun has a role in this. The Ruler left to a room of one of his wives. People, there, hide from the sun's power and cruelty when it is vertical in the sky.

After nearly one hour, the boy came, hurriedly calling me.

"His Highness, the Ruler, wants you inside."

The boy left me no time to ask. I expected him to be ill. Perhaps he would accuse me of attempting to intoxicate him. Worries began to chase me while hurrying behind the boy. He knocked on the door of the main room and ushered me in. He invited me to enter, closed the door behind me and left me alone to my fates. I found the Ruler sitting on the edge of his bed. He was bareheaded with untidy hair, his head between his palms and fingers in his hair. His eyes were red. I was awestruck. He asked me to sit in the chair close to him and said, "There is a serious matter I need to know your views about."

I was bewildered. "Yes, Your Highness."

The Ruler began strolling in the wide area between the fixtures in the room. I thought the matter was serious and the Ruler was looking for a way to dive in. A few moments later, he spoke.

"As you are a European traveller you must have crossed many countries and lands and sailed seas and crossed rivers. Those travels made you a good servant and cook. It must have taught you a lot about other cultures. For all this, I have no doubt, you have acquired many talents, perhaps, and one of these is the interpretation of dreams."

"Dreams? I?"

"Yes, you, and you shall tell me about interpreting the heavyweight or nightmare that sits on my chest when I go to sleep. It deprives me of movement; I become awake in my sleep. It passes through my head like a dream."

I looked at the pillow. I was told that the pillows of ostrich feather do not counter nightmares... I asked him, "And what do you see, Your Highness?"

"Did I not tell you that you know that? Yes, it is like a vision. I see a slain person swimming in his blood on the ground, and I see a young man coming out from the head of the murdered while saying, 'Give me a drink, I am thirsty.' This nightmare is continuous; I could not find an interpretation for it. Thank God who sent you to me to tell me about its elucidation."

The Ruler left me no room to retreat. He would have received and accepted any word from me willingly as if it were a fact. I said, "Somebody is after your life, Your Highness."

He retreated three steps and sat at the edge of the bed

again.

"That is it exactly. There is the danger of the army being put up in Hormuz, that I may be a victim of; there are also the demands and local objections lead by Abu Rashed. I think both are imminent dangers. I need you with me to search for a solution to these two dangers."

I found myself amid endless tales and illusions. How can a man in power at the top of the pyramid on the island build his policies with his subjects not on dreams and expectations but on fears and superstitions? The Ruler offered me a hasty status. I did not find anything wrong with benefitting wealth and prestige from it.

The Ruler moved to another subject. He asked me directly about what Abu Rashed and his group were planning and about the role Adam was possibly able to play in all this. Signs of concern were clear on his face, even though he was feigning comfort. It was an opportunity to dwarf Adam in exchange for obtaining the prize of the Ruler's trust. There is, sometimes, no harm in attaining benefits and mutual objectives.

I made it clear to him that Adam welcomed the demands of Abu Rashed and his group. He had explained to them that their demands were just, as there were many examples of this in western countries; these would have various resonances if transferred outside the borders. These movements were known as the rights of labourers and workers. There were revolutions and movements demanding reforms in places that we passed through. These interests normally opposed existing systems and threatened their being. If the Ruler ignored these demands, these would add more discontent to the public. If he promised reforms, he would find welcoming sentiments.

The Ruler explained that the situation was different and

there was no way to make a comparison between them. The European countries became industrially productive, but countries of the East were still consumers. They knew nothing but agriculture, fishing and primitive handicrafts.

I conveyed to him what the British were saying in Hormuz Island. They confirmed that the causes of the durability of the tribal situation on Dilmunia Island were due to the downfall of the Portuguese power that was active and penetrated the Gulf. Added to that the occupation of the Ottomans fighting the Safavids; that situation led to establishing the patriarchal system. Adam concluded from all this the growing desire of the British to spread on land and sea.

The Ruler suddenly rose and said, "That is what you want to interpret? Who is the murdered that comes in my vision? What does Britain want exactly? Does she want mandatories or mandate?"

The Ruler left me no room to think again. He leapt over me with his talk, and I said, "I think the murdered in your vision is one of the victims of the Portuguese colonialism, and perhaps one of the victims of the present crisis on the island, as to what Britain wants."

"The present crisis? What would you suggest for a solution to this sudden crisis?"

"They say change is the nature of life. He who declines it wants to destroy it. That destruction will sweep him before others. You must find a way out of this crisis, by either oppressing the people or responding to their demands."

I found the Ruler powerless, very polite; perhaps he did not know what was going on in his country. He leaned more towards a peaceful solution. This might satisfy all, but his clique, the Merchant amongst them, described the situation as the ghoul that shall destroy everything. They imposed on him adopting much of what they were planning or hiding in their minds. The Ruler was up to his neck in the mud of accumulating crises. As a result, he became a believer in visions and their interpretations. He was looking for a hand that could pull him out of his dilemma.

I told him, "You can solve the present crisis and get rid of its consequences by many ways. Firstly, and easily, meet the demands of the people and satisfy them. The noble is he who is just to his enemy. That, however, as you say shall definitely contradict the wish of the members of the Appointed Council such as the Merchant and the retinue. You can banish Abu Rashed or imprison him and expel Adam to Hormuz or Baghdad. He should proceed to Copenhagen as a persona non grata. This shall rouse the suspicion of neighbouring countries and governments as to what is going on here. The British want a foothold, a solid, safe land so that your island becomes headquarters of the East India Company. It is an important economic factor for you. As to the Ottomans and the Persians, they are waiting to see what is going on here. If you cannot find solutions for this crisis, it will be easier for them to cross the borders and reach the seat of government due to the legality of the people's demands. Do not forget, Your Highness, the tribes settling nearby regions, let alone the pirates who are sailing on the Gulf waters. Instability shall urge these powers to vie for this land and its wealth."

He placed his head, as it was his habit, between his hands and said, "One of the learned men told me that, 'The top of stupidity is to leave your reality with all its bitterness to a sweet future with its illusions.' Dilmunia's affairs are complicated."

The next day, the Ruler asked for a meeting with the

Merchant, *the Noukhathas* and the nobility as soon as possible. In particular, he asked for the active presence of the clergy, and he strongly asked for my personal attendance for offering advice, and to be aware of what was going on here and there. He began to repeat, "The top of courage is to confront."

(6) Khowla
Early January 1764

Family hospitality for the European traveller continued at our home. With the passage of time, we became more familiar with him and our affection increased for him. Gradually, he came to occupy a space in our hearts. His kindness and his ever-smiling distinguished him. He was very learned and knowledgeable, constantly searching for anything ambiguous to him or new. Moreover, I found him unpretentious and modest. The more he learnt, the more he felt the need to know more and the necessity for research.

One day, after his return from a visit to the Ruler after the afternoon prayers, people gathered around our house. They came from distant places and the hubbub reached the neighbourhood before the return of my father with his guest, an extraordinary guest! In the past, the guests were Arabs, sailors and travellers of the same race and skin. This man was different from them.

I wondered if there were people of different shapes and colours over these wide seas and oceans that we heard of. I knew that God's land is vast and has many peoples and tribes, but I never thought that I was going to see a man arriving to our house from those countries. Normally, people here see the land levelled ending at the end of land beyond our sea. However, we hear about remote lands and gigantic oceans; what do its people look like? How can the levelled land be infinite? Conflicting questions preceded every new matter. Abu Rashed told us that according to his guest, Earth is not levelled as we think, but a globe that revolves around itself, and the moon is part of its system and turns in its orbit. This theory contradicted previous beliefs. Here it was said that the moon never drops on the earth because she is hung over the horn of a huge bull that stops her from moving or slipping down. I thought Adam could explain these theories. It was necessary to know from his knowledge to make facts clear, and real science is clear.

Since the arrival of this foreigner, activity gradually increased in our house, and the tempo of life was enhanced. There were always those who cleaned and those who cooked and prepared the food. There were those who rearranged the *majlis* and another who made leeway for places of relaxation and sleeping. My father, like most men, did not care for interior decoration. He was content with what God had bequeathed to him.

My mother was a diligent housewife, an ideal mother who provided comfort and safety for us and our guests, a responsible mother and a first-class housewife; the mother is nest, and the father is might. I had never seen a European man before. How did they speak, eat, and what did they wear? Did they have many things in common with us? Imagining became impossible. As they said, if the guest was near, my heartbeat increased, and my confusion was on the rise. What is the matter, Khowla?

At last, I heard noise outside. All were on the sandy road in front of our house. The sand did not rouse its dust as usual, as it was moistened by water. They placed green palm tree fronds on the sides of the outer door, and rice grains were thrown on the soil. I went upstairs, and took a window out of the alcove on the roof. I saw the guest dismounting a reddish mule. His shoulder was next to my father's shoulder. I could only see his back. Unlike our first meeting, I found him tall and lean, perhaps artificial leanness, showing a structure that was stout and robust. He was dressed in Arabian attire, perhaps presented to him by someone before he came here. He was received at our door and began to shake hands with all those around him, as if it were a small festive season that had befallen our village.

Now that I could distinguish him clearly, I saw a man in Arabian dress but definitely not Arab. The attire does not alter the essence. A long face with an eagle eye in its lustre. A not well-trimmed beard tending to be red and a long sharp nose. He was wearing a turban, but it sloped on one of his ears, revealing the non-professionalism of its owner. He smiled to all when shaking hands.

Abu Rashed took the responsibility of introducing this person arriving from other regions. He introduced them to him and described them, which was a kind of bringing strangers together and creating acquaintance. What was the mother tongue of this man? How was my father able to understand him and speak to him? There was a strange tradition and sad thing. Something very surprising was pushing me to him with some sort of curiosity.

Suddenly, the sound of fire shot was heard. Light smoke was flying from the top of one of the nearby houses. It was the source of the shot. The guest fell down, his face covered with blood. There was a fuss around him. Noise and expectations increased. People moved away from the man and my father came closer. He moved what looked like a turban from his head, and dark red blood was spilt on the ground. The source of the bleeding was not known yet. Expectation and waiting for to what Abu Rashed was going to reveal.

Four men carried Adam quickly inside the *majlis* that was prepared for him as a reception and bedroom. Rashed and I thrust ourselves to the *majlis* in anticipation. My father cleansed the wound with water and disinfected and bandaged it.

"It is a fire shot from a shotgun that hit the skin of the right side of the head above the ear."

I asked him if Adam was all right.

"The wound, my daughter, is superficial and not deep. Blood will soon stop. The man needs more time to recover and for the wound to heal up and to absorb the shock of the incident. We must help him recuperate."

A few minutes later, the bleeding stopped and there was no trace except some red drops on the bandage. One hour later, a cold, water bag was placed on Adam's face. The man woke up slowly from the shock. He opened his eyes gently, as if things seemed foggy to him because of the shock, but with time his vision cleared, and he felt the spot of the pain and directly asked about the cause.

"Has a stone fallen on my head, or have I suddenly stumbled?"

"It was not a stone but a bullet from a gun; it did not hit but the skin of your head, thank God a lot. Perhaps he missed his target and touched your head only; he did not hit you directly. The wound is not deep. Perhaps the target was either of us. We did not know the perpetrator; the men are tracing the source of the gunpowder. They shall definitely find him. We all apologise to you. The guest has the right of protection."

Abu Rashed went out to the front ground outside our

house. Three barefooted men came, pulling a young man wearing a loincloth and underwear only. One of them held the gun. He asked them, "How and where did you find him?"

One of them said, "We went to the source of the shooting. We found the trace of the culprit on the wall after his fall. He has hurt himself, and due to his fear took off his sandals and ran barefooted. One of us followed his footsteps until we found him in one of the farms. We caught him with this gun. It is empty of shots."

The accused confessed that he was one of the aides and workers of the Merchant. Abu Rashed ordered his men to tie him up in one of the nearby farms until it was decided what was to be done about him. Then he asked all to leave the house and its front.

"Pray for Adam for a speedy recovery. He must stay in bed until he gains his strength and health and then understands the incident."

All the people left lightly. My father commended me to visit the wounded and be reassured about his condition.

"Frequent the *majlis* with Rashed; perhaps the patient needs food or drink. I have lots of commitments morning and evening. You can be as expected from you. I trust you. Let your grandfather inside and I shall commend your mother to take care of him."

The lunch and dinner meals became implicitly my responsibility, but my father could not stay during the day beside his guest, due to the duties of his business at the farm, in addition to the affairs of the sea. I was charged with offering food and drink and delivering these at specific times. Rashed accompanied me when I delivered the first meal. Adam was lying on his left side at the forefront of the *majlis*, placing his head on a woollen pillow. His leather bag that never left him was behind his head. Adam placed the palm of his hand under his cheek. He was quiet in his sleep. He snored softly in tune with his inhales and exhales. His body was exceedingly tall, with weak legs and wide shoulders.

Rashed asked me where to place the meal. I suggested the middle of the *majlis*. Then Adam opened his eyes at the sound of movement, and his eyes widened. I thought he was seeing unclearly, as if looking at ghosts. He spoke as if moaning. It was the first time Ihad heard his voice since he was wounded.

"Are you Abu Rahed's children?"

His words were Arabic but not like our language; like water topped with foam. Water does not seem to be water but a mixture of both.

"I am Khowla, and this is my brother, Rashed, the children... do not you remember us?"

"Children... Abu... Abu... Rashed."

"Yes, Abu Rashed's children. We brought you some food; you must be hungry. We are outside; all you have to do is knock on the door if you need anything."

"Do not go. Please stay."

He tried to get up and sit down but felt the pain in his head.

"I feel dizzy."

Rashed hurried to help him while I came closer with the water. He sat right but was like a bent frond yearning for the ground. He placed his head between his hands, feeling the place of pain. I gave him the water and Rashed helped him drink his fill.

When he raised his head, I noticed he was watching us with a scrutinising eye. He examined the corners and dimensions of the *majlis*. He was not only looking, but as if photographing everything in it. There was something mysterious about this man. He asked me, "Does your father have enemies to the point that they fire at him or one of his guests?"

"This is the first time that shots were fired here. People do not have guns. Guns and rifles are only distributed when the island is under conquest; then the people are trained to fight the conquerors. No one has guns except the Ruler and the Merchant and those working for him. Perhaps the fire was aimed at you, not at my father. You must be cautious and take care of yourself."

I offered him two dried dates when my hand was squeezed in his palm. His grip was big. I pulled my hand when he held the dates. This was the first time ever when my flesh had touched the body of a man not from our family. He was an alien, a stranger… and maybe more!

My father returned in the evening and went into the *majlis*. He wanted to see how Adam was faring. The Doyen was also brought to the *majlis*. Then some men also came with the defendant. Rashed and I stood behind the door, listening to what was going on inside. After few words inquiring about Adam, Abu Rashed asked the defendant, "We know you are one of the Merchant's men. Did he himself send you to fire at the guest or on any one else?"

"The Merchant did not send me to kill anybody. I wanted to disperse the crowd only, not to aim at you. I fired in the air and do not know how your guest was hit."

The Doyen spoke as usual in detail so that the guests might learn something important. Evil as well as good is an inflection for people to learn from.

"Once upon a time, there was an Arab, sitting far away from his nomadic people. Close to him, he placed a casserole of water and wet crumbs of bread. A pigeon came near him to eat the crumbs when she felt safe. One of the passers-by hit her with a stone and killed her. The Arab was infuriated and swore to kill the man, or his tribe would raid his tribe, because the pigeon was safe in his hospitality. Protecting it and the guest was one of the Arabian virtues. He threatened him with a long-lasting war like that of Al Bassus War. The crisis was aggravated, and the chieftains of the tribes met and decided that the man must pay blood money, or a ransom, in exchange for that pigeon. The phenomenon of safe borders is one of the basic principles that all religions preach; note that if anyone takes refuge in the Kaaba, he is punished even if he is a criminal, except if he is outside the sanctuary. People can ban the supply of food and water without infringing on his security."

One of the guests wondered if the neighbour and neighbourhood had all those rights.

"Yes, the guest is like the neighbour; if you have any of them, he has rights and obligations both moral and practical. The Arabs in the past found it shameful to eat while their neighbour was starving. On that issue, Hatem Alta'i said:

'My fire and the fire of my neighbour is the same

And he puts up his cauldron before mine.'"

Adam added, "Should we not forgive this ignorant for his misdeed?"

The Doyen replied, "Modesty in the presence of the rich is a humiliation. Bearing fear in your heart with the criminal is better than bearing mercy. I commend you to forgive at the time of ability when you confront the Merchant with his crime."

Adam said, "Perhaps I disagree with you, Doyen. Man is the brother of man whether he loves him or hates him. Release him, that is the best judgement."

(7) The Doyen
January 1764

Abu Rashed came to the courtyard where I sat every day. It was on Friday, the weekly holiday. During this day, all business closed down in preparation for the Friday prayers. People here delayed their work obligations from morning until after prayers. These times were utilised for family and social visits. That is why they say Friday is the best of all days.

Abu Rashed asked me to accompany him during his visit to our convalescing guest.

"We must spend more time with Adam as a gesture of hospitality and politeness, and we can listen to his talk and benefit from his views. What do you think, Doyen?"

I said nothing. Silence was more eloquent. He came to help me rise, and when his sons saw him help me, they all came. Doing good or being charitable to the parents makes me happy. A human habit elates people. This is implanted from childhood and not acquired later. They all extended their hands so that I could rise to the *majlis* where Adam was. No sooner had the guest heard the greeting than he responded with a better one. He tried to stand when we entered. He was too fragile to rise. I asked him to sit.

"The ill are not to be blamed."

It seems that travelling is the best teacher. All cultures of the world are stored in one soul from which we know the best qualities and values. I noticed that his health condition was gradually improving, though slowly. Better slow than never.

Adam did not stop confirming his thanks and gratitude for what he had received. I answered him that what we were doing for him was really nothing in the sea of virtues. Audy bin Hatem Alta'i used to crumb bread for ants at the door of their house so that they could find food every day.

Abu Rashed preceded all by touching on the present situation with an obvious bitterness. He spoke in the presence of the guest of the plans of bartering that were reported by the Merchant, as said by the *Nukhatha*. Those barters that show the meanness of their perpetrator.

The Merchant said in his letter addressed to me, "I can write off your accumulated debts all these years if you agree to marry off your daughter, Khowla, to me." Thus, with all meanness he was trying blackmailing. A demonic provocation meant for enforced marriage! I really do not know the concept of marriage and polygamy. This led me to discuss polygamy and underage marriage. I was watching with a smile, signs of astonishment and anger on Adam's face, as if he were concerned and that the issue was touching him personally. He overcame his pains until he uttered a few angry sentences, then spoke without permission.

"Dear Doyen, through my travels I saw and knew many peoples. I lived with various tribes in different countries. There are Indian tribes that prohibit polygamy for one man as permitted in Islam, but allow polygamy for one woman; thus, brothers can marry one woman and copulate with her all together, or designate a night for each of them. There are also tribes that permit absolute polygamy for wives, without terms and conditions. Then the woman chooses the best of them to be the father of her baby. Despite all this, I did not find a legal marriage based on enforcement. Enforcement is a debasement of humanity, moral poverty against all principles and values."

"Our honoured guest, we must refer this in the context that Islam does not permit polygamy on its wide-open doors without rules. It was permitted in particular cases, such as in the case of an ill wife, or non-children-bearing or barren, or non-loving. God has left this restriction to us; polygamy solves a problem and hides a thousand problems."

Abu Rashed asked, "Has this anything to do with burying girls alive in their infancy; which was common in *jahiliya* or Pre-Islam?"

"A man in *jahiliya,* when a girl was born to him, he became a recluse; that was considered a moderate attitude. In his mind, he refused burying his daughter alive, but he was influenced by society's outlook. He was torn between his mind and heart, while the extremist would bury his daughter for fear of scandal and shame expected from her. He expected that perhaps one day she would fall into vice, or marry someone not worthy of her, or she may be taken captive in war and be dishonoured. Black thoughts and imaginations overcame him and made him believe that the top of manhood was to bury his daughter in infancy. This has become the case that influenced their literature and poets. One of them, a poetess said:

'Why Abu Hamza does not come to us
And remains at the neighbouring house
He is angry that we do not give birth to males
By God! This is not in our power
We are like the soil to our farmers
We only grow what they cultivate in us.'

"Another poetess responded to her:
'I do not care if she becomes a maid

Rinses and cleans my hair
And picks up my veil
When I am eight
I enshroud her in a Yemeni veil
I marry her off to Marwan or Mu'awiya.'"

Adam expressed his views with regard to Christianity.

"Our religion as you may know, prohibits polygamy for both sexes as a radical solution. It also prohibits burying females in infancy and the law punishes its perpetrator. I do not know if Islam has put a solution to this awful phenomenon that was very common."

"Yes, yes. God said, 'He bestows to whomever he wants females and bestows to whomever the males.' Accordingly, God's bequest is a grant from God, and humans have no right to intervene in it. One of what is reported about the Prophet is that he said, 'If anyone of you brings home food let him begin with the females.' It is an act, as I think, that falls under classification, not belittling; both sexes are similar; none of them is better except by piety. Misfortune may be the opposite. God may love a man and inflict him with children, or give him a good progeny. We may inflict you with evil and good and both to your liking."

Abu Rashed clapped, smiling. "Copyright of magic is not reserved for women."

Our talk at the most made Adam lose his mind and go to a remote distance, as if remembering a woman clinging to his memory, perhaps connected with events and the turmoil of society, or perhaps he was thinking of another woman. Absent-mindedness of the man in its most is towards his heart. His heart makes him heavy and wounds him more, but a woman playing on his cords revives him when he loves her.

I redirected the helm of the conversation towards the Merchant and his desire for bartering between the debts of her father and winning Khowla. Abu Rashed did not care for the hallucinations of the Merchant. He saw it as mere words to kindle the atmosphere with mines. It was a kind of self-admiration, said Abu Rashed.

"Admiration is a fleeting symptom and lust is movable, that Merchant is expressing what he feels. It is excessive compensation, a kind of disease. When a man feels his sense of inferiority and impairment, he exhibits pride, greatness and tyranny, too."

The surprise was the reaction of Adam.

"I think this scoundrel should be resisted; most fires and disputes start only with a small spark."

Abu Rashed commented on him with a clear calmness.

"It is the devil playing with the minds of the humans."

Adam answered him back quickly.

"The Doyen previously said, some ideas have multiple meanings; therefore, the idea that Satan lures us comforts the humans, but it is also multi-faceted. Is it not?"

I smiled because I found my thoughts spoken by others.

(8) Adam
February 1764

Khowla knocked on the door for permission to enter. It was lunchtime. Her father was still out as his habit and returned only in the evening, while the Doyen was in the *barastiy*. If he was not lying down, he must be performing his prayers. She entered, carrying the prepared lunch. In hot regions, the main dish is rice with either meat or fish. She walked slowly with locks of her hair falling on her forehead, with her smile turning her face to a full-rounded moon. She placed the tray on the eating mat. She asked me if I wanted anything else. She proved her kindness and generosity. She left the room with her head down out of shyness.

Carina was showing her temperament out of allurement and for beautifying, while Khowla was out of modesty and shyness. Covering is more arousing and affecting on man than nakedness. The sexual eye is searching for ambiguity and can only see in the darkness, while over make-up is an exposed weapon. I, sometimes, still miss the odour of women despite my being away from them. I know keeping away from them is bound to put up a stone barrier on the heart of man, but without a natural law, he misses them every time wherever he escapes.

Khowla entered the *majlis* again. She held a beaker of water and was about to place it next to the eating mat when she found me where I was previously. I did not move.

"What is the matter with you?"

"I want to talk about the benefit of the headscarf that you put around your head."

She touched what was on her head. "They call it here a veil, *hijab* or *khimar*. What is wrong with it? Don't you like it?"

"What is the purpose of putting it on your head: to hide yourself?"

Khowla quickly provided the answer already ready in her mind.

"The woman's veil is inside her; the veil itself is something symbolic in itself. As the body of the woman infatuates some men, the veil is the voice of the woman that makes them feel that there is a human being behind this body. The woman is not a refuge for lust to wipe off her humanity, and looks are shed on her from all sides. We realise that woman in nudity is like a bare tree without green leaves to protect her; then she becomes an easy prey for burning and penetration."

Carina's vision crossed my memory. Then I realised.

"Isn't it? What you call a veil is the opposite of nudity; which is the closest human image to nature? Nudity annuls apparent differences between people and makes us equal, doesn't it?"

She added, "Haven't you heard what he said? 'And their genitals appeared to them, and they started covering them with leaves from Paradise.'"

She said, "That is, that Adam, father of humans, hated his and his wife's genitals to be exposed, so they decided to cover themselves. Their act was natural and the opposite of what you said, Adam."

"That is Adam, the father of all human beings after he was expelled from Paradise."

"Yes; don't you know that a man who does not search for a woman's body gains an angel?"

Khowla elaborated on her speech. She was fervent in her defence of her convictions. There I was mesmerised, enjoying listening to her. I began to monitor how she spoke and search for what was behind her words. I compared between the fascination of nudity and cover-up, between Carina and Khowla...

The girl realised after few moments that silence is a kind of utterance; her voice decreased, and her beauty increased with more lustre. Tongues are more capable of building in the mind of others. I felt a desire that I forgot a long time ago. Her words and convictions tantalised my affections, pulling me to her. I suddenly asked to go to the toilet.

"Can you help me stand up? I want to go to the toilet."

She opened her eyes wide, and then her mouth increased in width until reaching the width of her eyes. I signalled to her and she came closer. She placed her veil in her palm. I recalled my mother's black gloves that fell in the hands of that greedy man. Khowla extended her right hand, and I dropped my hand on it. I tried to rise, and she placed her left hand under the elbow of my other arm. My legs did not support me, and I felt a severe dizziness. I thought I was going to fall on the floor. She prepared her body as a resting place, and I could not resist. My body fell on her. I fell on her back; I became, I, over her.

Moments later, I was conscious. She was trying to move me with her hands. I opened my eyes and began to regain my balance. The smell of her body began to invade all my cells. The seventh sense is the ability to sense the desires of the woman. The power of her hands was subdued. I met the pupils of her eyes and penetrated them and cringed to her lips, and they were inflamed.

I dallied and was lost in her. She was silent for moments, but her tears were flowing profoundly and were about to drown both of us. The bitterest cry is the one that its weeping is silent. I praised her beauty, and her tears were more profuse. I raised my head, asking, "Why sobbing, Khowla? We do not harm anybody."

"I love myself excessively!"

Her response killed me. True words are those uttered by tearful eyes. I regained my strength and was able to move lightly and gracefully, as if a positive innate energy fell on me. I withdrew from her. She gathered herself and covered what was naked of her body, then left with her head down but with high spirit. I had mixed, contradicting feelings. This girl loved herself; and she who loves herself is wished well. Loving oneself keeps us away from falling into sins. He or she who does not love themselves, and cares for it, shall not love others, and shall not love their Creator, and shall not fear Him.

Something urged me to take my feather and reveal myself on the whiteness of my paper. I interpreted my ego and experiences in words and sentences. From here, my love for writing and documenting started. I wrote notes about the trip since we had set out from Copenhagen, but this different moment pushed me to write on scientific reality, mixed with feelings and human sentiments. Perhaps I shall not be able to publish all that I wrote; however, I am certain that there will be someone who shall come across me and my writing in his life and convert it into a human literature to be read by hearts before eyes.

All I wrote shall be converted into a world of literature, liked by many souls. No wonder I had many difficulties in expressing some thoughts. Some may have been unattainable, but I keep thinking of the thought until it was within my reach. I do not know exactly the cause of the change that overcame me in writing; however, I am certain that a good translator can be creative when he is in love. That is Khowla's wind. I shall ask all whom I encounter in my life to write his tale and mine in his own style, no matter the quality of expression and the language used. The translator in my mind shall have absolute freedom to translate the thought and envisage it. I have no doubt that wedding the language produces literature; lulling it gives you a story and a novel.

Thus, I began my writing and my scripts are waiting for a narrator.

"I am a human being and more entitled than others to love and appreciate myself. Fear of punishment is a futile reason to keep away from sins, while man's love for himself and adoring it is what elevates him to the level of purity of angels. I have more right to love myself, and take care of it. Love of good deeds is more effective than the fear of punishment..."

The love of Khowla for herself filled her with spiritual energy that kept harm away. This kind of love adds beauty to the face and strength to the body and determination to challenge difficulties and overcome them... I do not find justification for the energy gained by my body except this "Love" energy. Here, I am narrating my experiences in more detail. I am trying to interpret my alter ego and offer myself for love, to be a human. With love, I decided to fight myself and make others happy.

After that acquired energy, compunction had no impact on me. I can exalt myself from my faults. I returned the generosity of Abu Rashed by betraying him and the knowledge of the

Doyen with ingratitude, but I trusted Khowla's tolerance; the girl who stores positive energy within her must be above blame. You must know that all humans are fallible, but the gap between the classes of the angelic and humans makes man falter in thought and emotions. There is a power pulling us up to the highest, opposed by a power of meanness and lowliness. He who loves his ego must not escape from this world or gives it up for piety, but he should elevate himself from its ignobleness. Love of God is easier than the love of humans because by nature we love perfection rather than imperfection.

(9) Yousif, The Puller
March 1764

Nearly nine months had elapsed since I was thrown in jail in the case of the death of Nasser. Mine was a mock trial; I stood against my opponent, the accuser. On the surface, it seems a fair trial, with a judge sitting between the accuser and the accused. The judicial system is independent; I was happy that the opponent was not the judge. Good omen. However, the opponent did not care for the judiciary. He had a more influential authority than the judge himself. Traditions and legal codes demand the separation of authorities. The executive authority separated until it became more powerful than the judiciary.

In my isolation and separation from the world, the strip of events was repeated in my mind. He who is cut off from the present world stays with the living through memories and relives the past moment. The scene of Nasser's insistence on diving and going down forcibly, and then the sea turned him into floating foam to depart from this life.

The image of taking me away from my family at one dawn; I did not recall its heat. It makes me wonder why the arrest took place at dawn. Why the law enforcer is always masked? Why this many guards and security men to arrest just one unarmed man? Why did they blindfold me before going into this dark tunnel? Why, why, why? No specific answers. Just deductions. Perhaps it was the fear of the despot of the victim; the despot who cannot sleep and the victim who sleeps is fearless.

My children's cries and screams still resonated in my ears and their images roamed in front of me. Anxiety was filling my wife's eyes. Fear of their oppression and the anticipation of an unknown future and a dark fate. Neighbours gathered on the event. Heavy security was spreading throughout the alleys, and in every corner, there were sticks, batons and even gunpowder. I thought for a while that it was not about me; then I started to suspect that I was a criminal, and I thought I was a gang leader. The horror of the security scene empties you of what you are in and then pours its aims into you. That crucial moment defines your determination and strength; either you give up to what they are aiming for or you realise the truth, and you refuse to embrace falsehood.

This loathsome cellar — cell or prison — had many names and one meaning. It was an enforced separation of the body from the world, but it was a spiritual exile from life. Man is a sociable creature by nature, The best way to torture him is by isolating him from others. Torture is extreme moral bankruptcy; here I could not distinguish day from night except when they opened the outside door. A ray of light by which I could tell the time, whether it was day or night. When slumber overtook me, I realised it was night. I woke on hearing voices coming from far away.

I began to know the contents of the cell by sensing and touching. The sense of touch became stronger and more effective. I touched the walls and the protruding stones. Here was a smooth stone, and there a pointed one. This plaster was dry and hard, and there was soft and wet. The height of the ceiling was not level. One of its corners is tilted, the trunks of its roof almost touching my head when standing. I bend right and stand left. I levelled the floor and softened one of its sides. It became a place for my sleep. I became aware of every spot there, but I could not get the points of direction yet. As the sun rises from the east, I pinpointed the east. I cited the east side; it was the spot from where the light came at the side of the external door.

Since the dawn of the first day, I have been immune to rising from the reaction. They came, calling me names hardly ever heard except between children who were not linguistically refined. I should not recall these vile words. The meanness of these is an indication of moral desertification. You son of a… you brother of… you… are all pathetic filthiness.

That pride made them turn to physical punishment, a kind of primitive castigation. They made me lay down and tied my legs with cane sticks. I screamed out of pain and the more they hurt, the less was my voice. I lost the sense of feeling pain. It comes when our bodies invite it. A tumour turned my foot into what looked like a wooden board. An adverse relationship between intensity of pain and feeling it. They made me stand up but I could not. They tied my hands to the ceiling of the cell. The punishment moved to the knees, hitting from the side and behind them. I felt that my foot was amputated. I became limbless; one tied and one severed. I feigned unconsciousness so they would leave me.

The first one said, "He is unconscious."

The second one said, "Use cold water."

The third said, "Do not let him close his eyes, and do not ease his eyelids."

I woke up from unconsciousness forcibly. You son of…

This is when they extinguished cigarettes on my back and bottom. I screamed with the remainder of my voice, "What do you want?"

"Shut up."

They threw me on the wet floor, and I do not recall those seasons of punishment. I woke up from a deep slumber, feeling and examining parts of my body. I gathered myself at one time and scattered at another. I crept to where the imaginary place of sleeping was, the remains of earth and soft mud. I felt thirsty and hungry. Death was approaching. I saw the angel of death hovering in the darkness. I addressed him.

"Come to me, relieve me."

"Your death shall transport the corporal punishment to your fellow beings, your family and even children. You have to resist; a believer makes his cell a mosque the same way the wine merchant makes his tavern."

For a moment, I thought the angel of death was working under their command too. There was no hope in him. I screamed as high as I could. I needed some water, some water.

I heard the squeak of the door. Rays of light poured in and I closed my eyes to its evil. I opened them slowly. They placed something in the remote corner near the door. They closed it, and darkness fell on the place and vision returned. Silence fell again. To hear the sound of silence, you have to stop the function of all the five senses together. Then only you shall hear the silence. A sound that drowns you in fear, then only you can hear the sound of your conscience or inner soul, and if you disobey, it shall be immediately severed. I did not want to speak with him; no, not now. My abdomen first. I crept towards that thing, on my belly like a snake, and on my limbs, like a tortoise. They gave me some water in a small container the size of the palm of a man, and another container of bran, and nothing else.

I got used to the food that came to me every day. I think it only came in the morning. It only filled me but not to the fullest. The food became a great problem and torment. Despite its meagreness, it imposed on me the need to get rid of its excrements. I chose the opposite corner to relieve myself. Sometimes I missed the direction, as the intensity of darkness was the same, and I did not overbear myself searching for the spot. The odour of stool recedes, unlike that of urine. I fell sick of familiarity, and the smell was no more obnoxious. It seems that the sense of smell reflects the psychological state of the individual. It is like the smell of the desert when imprisoned, and the smell of sea sweat when it is missed, and the odour of heaven when buried.

The jailors took rounds in delivering the so-called food and water. Because of the shift, sometimes I was discounted, either by mistake or deliberately. Then, I found no harm in drinking that yellow liquid called urine. I contracted skin disease because of mosquitos and bugs gathering, that built farms on my back where I could not reach with my hands. Scratching the wall with my skin was an ideal solution. The wall became clean and my back soft and bloody.

I did not feel the days and their counts, but in less than a year, as they claimed, change began to occur gradually. Fate threw two new inmates in my cell. My God! It was no longer a solitary confinement. One of them asked me after a long scrutiny, "Are you Yousif, the Puller?"

"I am not so sure, but it seems so."

"They say that Yousif, the Puller, has been thrown into jail for nearly a year or more. We think it is you, or his remains!"

The other man said, "We are farmers working in the Merchant's farm. The Merchant accuses us of selling part of his crop to our own account. When we denied that, he ordered his men to throw us in prison. We did not know about your presence here. It is rumoured that you are in one of the Ruler's prisons."

Since they were brought in, the system of feeding had changed. We were offered two meals a day: white rice at noon and bran and dates in the evening. The dosages of water were also increased. After three days or so, they blindfolded us and told us of their intention to change our cell. At the time, I was unable either to walk or to comprehend.

One of them threatened me. "If you do not walk with your colleagues, you will remain here."

My colleagues volunteered to carry me, out of pity. They were terrified; I became a group of connected bones, but on the brink of dismantling and keeping apart and even dissolving. I was a light weight for them. They took us to another mud cell with two coves allowing light to filter through and change the air. My two inmates asked to go to the toilet three times a day and to let them occasionally have a bath.

Amazing changes had happened lately. At last, there was a sudden matter, as they allowed for the passage of light, air and water and human beings, too. They told us of a new date for a retrial of all prisoners. Judge Al Balbul would listen to all opinions in the presence of the Ruler himself. The verdicts would be final and irrevocable. My colleagues said that I had spent nearly one year in prison on a false accusation. This time the verdict that I expected was a death sentence, due to premeditated killing.

Those days were kind to me. I was able at last to know what was going on outside; news about my family and village, my relatives and tribe. I asked them about what was going on there.

"Tell me in detail about what is going on outside, stories fictional and actual."

"Do not worry about what is going on outside. Stick to the inside; they say the Ruler wants to empty the prisons and cleanse them."

"Why? It is turning the world inside out."

"He wants to initiate a reform programme whereby the laws of diving and agriculture and others are neutralised. The Merchant's men moved us from his private prison to the state prison so that responsibility would be direct for the Ruler."

"Why were you sent to prison?"

"Theft is the official accusation, but what Abu Rashed told us is that his men would be thrown into jail one after the other. They started with us and perhaps would end up with Abu Rashed himself. The matter is related to the demands of the sailors and farmers. We did not commit a crime; we are punished for our opinions only. We are prisoners of conscience."

The day of arraignment had arrived. A security man held every prisoner by the arm, and two men held me to stand on my feet. The Ruler was sitting opposite the three judges, surrounded by security men and his guards. Nasser's case was the first. The judge spoke.

"Are you Yousif, the Puller, the accused in the killing case of Nasser the son of the Merchant?"

"Yes."

"The case is clear. Not all the accusations against you are

without evidence. We would like to pose all the questions to you about the objective of killing that young man. In case of confessing, the court shall indict you. It shall confirm all the charges against you. However, due to the wish of the Ruler, he shall declare an amnesty general to all prisoners so that there can be a new blessed page in the life of Dilmunia."

I was certain that the trial was nothing but a mock trial, with confessions that put you in line with the mean. I decided to raise the flag of madness, which is the apex of sanity, and with which you comprehend the world. According to agreement with the people's demands, the Ruler would release all prisoners as a gesture of kindness and generosity on his part. In case talks failed, I should no doubt remain in prison. I ignored all judges as they had only a dramatic, absurd role. I went directly to the Ruler, remembering lessons of dignity from the Doyen.

"Your Highness, I have nothing but to remind you that a day of affliction does not pass from the oppressed without a day of prosperity passed from the king of the oppressor. My imprisonment or your reign has durability. I shall only make an invocation to God to please you with what was given to you and to raise your heel high. You have ruled and were just."

The Ruler did not wait to hear the verdict of the judges. He ignored tradition and gave his judgement of imprisonment of ten years with immediate effect. He gave his orders to his men to send me back to the Merchant's prison, where isolator jail is. I expected nothing but that. The judges and audience were surprised. Al Balbul, the judge, spoke to the Ruler.

"May you live longer by the grace of God. What made you angry with the invocation of this man?"

"It is a pun he learnt from Abu Rashed and the Doyen; I

cannot be deceived by this. This damned uses an invocation addressed by someone to Harun Arrashid. His saying, may God make you pleased, is a derivation of His saying, 'We opened for them the gates of every pleasant thing, until in the midst of their enjoyment in that which they were given, all of a sudden, we took them in punishment! They were plunged into destruction with deep regrets and sorrows.' He is also praying to God to raise my heel; that is to say I should die hanged. He who is hanged is the one whose heel is raised above the ground.

(10) The Servant
April 1764

The Ruler was upset and refused taking his food regularly. His meals had certain rituals covered by sanctity. At most of these meals, he met with all his wives and sons and looked for them all at his table. The late comer leaves first. He remained at the table, which was rich with all kinds of food. He spoke a little with his imposing presence. After the meal, talks began, as words and food do not come together in one place. His table had funeral rituals; no sooner he finished, then the mouths open but within family propriety; low voices in his presence.

During the last few months, his abstention from food became obvious. His habits were upside down and his conditions changed. When the soul is terrified, its body surrenders. Even in his sleep, he became austere, attacked by confused dreams. The imaginary enemy visits you in your sleep. Blackness conquered the beauty of his face and signs of old age arrived prematurely. Unchanged conditions are impossible. He who is acquainted with him knows that anxiety fiercely attacks him. He rose above showing pain and hid his real agonies, seeming disdainful for self-preservation and emitting reassurance to relatives before non-relatives. However, he was solely responsible. There was always a hidden voice asking and surprising him, "You are the main one responsible for what is going on in your country. Your duty is to maintain the humanity of your people and to use the riches for their benefits." The Ruler was naturally noble and sensitive, always asking for advice. If he liked an idea, he made the choice. When the revolutionary anarchic conditions spread, and the public demands intensified, he became apprehensive and fearful. It is said that man has multiple facets and characters and is never with a specific character and between these, he searches for himself.

After the Monday meal, no one spoke at all. Only the sounds and dishes and chewing of food was heard. We returned to the kitchen, and the voice of the boy came. "The Ruler wants you." I went hurriedly. He ushered to me with his right index finger to come closer to him.

"Come here. In your capacity as my special adviser, and as a traveller who crossed vast areas of land and studied peoples and many tribes, you possess ample experience and knowledge to be consulted and we will act upon your advice when we like it. You personally receive the news and hear it from various sources. Demands made by the people have two facets; some like and others dislike. Between the two, I find myself dispersed, mentally torn and indecisive. It is said that the people's demands are legal, and that they should have them. When I think of it, I find it justified. However, the appointed council of traders, some close friends and clerics all think that this is the first nail driven in the throne — as they claim — the first step towards weakening the responsibilities of ruling and the liberties of the giant class of officials. How can we find a solution that satisfies all parties concerned, maintain authority and raise its dignity above everyone?"

"Your Highness, these demands do not differ in essence from what I found in our country and in various places in the east and the west. Conflict of interests of peoples creates crisis, and it is difficult to solve a political problem without going deep into the causes of the rise and fall of civilisations. You shall find that things flow in their stream by politics. There is no problem without a hidden solution, and the sane have to find it. There are several solutions to come out of this abnormal crisis, solutions I found in many countries: the first and easiest is to tyrannise the opposition movement by killing or throwing them into jails and terrorise their families and deprive them of a permanent income."

"Stability is not fed by blood; the same as he who is stiff is easily broken. You are talking about someone who cannot be me."

"There is another unique, easy solution; this can be represented in meeting their demands."

"These demands are opposed by another group; most merchants absolutely decline, and the Appointed Council as well who fervently oppose opening a dialogue with those opposing the current law."

I found the Ruler liking the word "opposing". He began repeating it as if implicitly agreeing to the other view. This had an existence and an echo in himself, and here, according to data, there has to be a change in the language of communication. I suggested to him to search for a group of people who opposed the protesters themselves. It was not wise at all that the Ruler should be against his people; there should be another stream opposing the stream that demands changes on the temporal law, and reforms that included the systems of pearl fishing, agriculture and taxations. Two opposing streams where the Ruler was the dividing judge between them and not a party in the crisis. I suggested to him to be a rider when life is a horse, and to use his influence and that of traders in forming that group and showering them with cash. Inciting hospitality and threatening them whenever necessary. Then he had to leave the matter in the hands of the leaders of the two groups, provided he remained as mediator between them and endorsed proposals of the majority.

It was during the day of mid-week when the Ruler made up his mind and decided to act. He continued discussing things with me until he decided on its epitome. I thought it was not a successful plan, depending most on the ability and creativity of implementation. It was an adventure in the shape of manoeuvring, followed by the downfall of one of the parties. Plans remaining on paper are purely theoretical. The ability to manoeuvre during implementation is the decisive matter. He asked his supporters to form a group to oppose the demands of the first group. He gave them a month to enlist the public prior to notifying him of their readiness.

At the beginning of the last week of that spring month, the Ruler ordered a proclamation be made in all villages, mosques and markets to attend a Friday mass prayer at the largest mosque. Dilmunia Mosque was the best choice[8]. This was located to the south of Bejoueya village and the Bustan Palace. This had political and religious significance. It was the assembly point for trading, particularly agricultural crops brought from neighbouring fields. The desire of the Ruler to meet the two disputing groups was announced.

Men and children from all areas crowded at the mosque. People from remote coastal villages arrived one day earlier and stayed at the courtyard of the mosque, while the rest came in the morning. Those present were nearly two thousand: that

[8] It is called Al Khamis Mosque nowadays.

was nearly half of the population of the island; they were all hopeful. They gathered in all parts and in the courtyard of the mosque, until coming closer to the ancient graves. The platform was set up over the edge of the mosque at the south. A canopy of date palm fronds with a wooden chair below it was covered by a velvet cloth. After the Friday prayers, the people simultaneously sat in two groups. To the left were Abu Rashed's supporters, and to the right, fewer in number, with the Merchant at the centre. From his chair, the Ruler spoke.

"Fellow Dilmunians, our country is passing through a chaotic discord blowing on us from every side. Foreign powers stand behind these causes of discord; they are alien to us in nature and character. There may be some infiltrators on both sides, and perhaps there are some unfriendly neighbouring states that stand behind these saboteurs, who aim at destabilising security and stability.

"Dear citizens, out of our national, legal and moral responsibilities, we must stand in the face of this wind and face the problem together. Without any exception, we are all responsible. A positive and active ruler in his country must look for an agreeable solution to all problems. He must look for means of prosperity and security for his people. For this purpose, I asked for this assembly with the conflicting groups to reach a concession. Here, we are looking for a solution agreeable to all of us. With your help, we shall reach a solution that will save our boat from this tempestuous sea. This group on my left, represented by Abu Rashed and his companions, has a justified case. I believe no reasonable man can stand against it. As that group has just demands, so has the group on my right parallel demands worthy of consideration. No group should be marginalised at the expense of the other.

"Dear Believers, people in our country differ on issues relating to their livelihood. They disagree on the rate of taxes imposed on pearl diving boats, on the crops of pearls, fish and others. They disagree on the value of boat provisions provided by merchants. They also disagree on taxes imposed on agricultural products and methods of selling and investing in them. Some believe that taxes and current laws are unjust; on the other hand, there are those who see them justified in view of increasing prices at the place of origin. In view of our position responsible to God, His Messenger and people, we are going to choose two individuals representing both groups to discuss with them in your presence, and the outcome shall be binding to all concerned."

The Ruler turned left, addressing the group.

"Fellow Dilmunians, you can choose one among you to represent your interests, without fear and hesitation."

Immediately, they all upheld Abu Rashed, saying, "We choose this man, and agree to what God determines."

Then the Ruler turned right, pointing to the Merchant to sit in his place. No one raised his hand to nominate himself. The Ruler decided to choose one of the simple peasants who worked for the Merchant.

The Ruler invited the two men to where he was standing; in turn they ascended the stairs and joined him. He addressed the multitude

"People of Dilmunia, these are your choices: Abu Rashed on my right and this simple farmer on my left."

The uproar rose, the majority agreeing to oppose a reserved minority. The Ruler raised his voice.

"Do you agree on the ruling issued in your presence and approve of it after consulting with your representatives?"

The crowd shouted three times "yes" in unison.

The Ruler repeated to the crowd in other words, so the meaning became clear and unambiguous.

"People of Dilmunia, I see that these two men are the best representatives of the neediest class and the most deserving for protecting their rights. If you agree to this judgement and its results, I shall adopt it immediately after this meeting. Abu Rashed is a public figure who needs no introduction. He came because of your nomination. As to this illiterate poor farmer, he works at the farm owned by one of the merchants. He who chooses Abu Rashed again, let him raise his left hand, and he who chooses this farmer, let him raise his right hand."

The people realised that the result was decisively known beforehand, as there was no comparison between the wisdom and experience of the two men. Voices rose in approval by applauding. However, I heard the Doyen whispering to one of relatives, "Beware of the evil of death; do not forget that despots sometimes beautify themselves with the colour of butterflies."

Abu Rashed and his opponent came close to the platform, surrounded by guards and secret eyes, and then the Ruler spoke.

"People of Dilmunia, this is Abu Rashed, your representative, and this is the simple illiterate farmer who represents the other group. We shall ask both of them the same question and then let all those present here choose the most correct answer and the most beneficial for the people. We shall act on the view of the majority. Do you agree?"

Voices rose from the side of Abu Rashed's crowd, approving and recognising appreciation, while approval came shyly from the other side.

"Now, we shall let you choose one representative. I shall agree to what he says and we put an end to this dispute. Prosperity and peace shall prevail in the land of Dilmunia."

The Ruler asked the two to write the words "Date Palm Tree" or "*nakhla*". "He who has the ability to answer correctly is capable of convincing the people and is the worthiest of representing them. Do you approve?"

"Yes, yes, yes."

"People of Dilmunia, I asked the two men to write '*nakhla*'; if either of them fails to write it, we shall not take his opinion; you all have to be the judges. Do you agree?"

Abu Rashed's supporters expressed their confidence in their man limitlessly. The Ruler gave two papyrus leaves. Abu Rashed wrote "*nakhla*", and the illiterate farmer drew the shape of the tree. The Ruler held Abu Rashed's paper in his left hand.

"People of Dilmunia who can know what either wrote, let him raise his left hand." Only six persons were able to read it.

Then he raised the second paper.

"Dilmunians who can know what the farmer wrote, let him raise his right hand."

All people who found the drawing of the *nakhla* clear raised their left and right hands... A discussion, a unanimous solution.

(11) Adam
May 1764

After dinner I used to meet Abu Rashed and his father, who had some ideas that we discussed. I refused to have the dinner meal because I, as Abu Rashed noticed several times, lost my appetite when I was not happy. I am certain that most of these discussions added to my knowledge in life. Their talk this evening had a different nature. I was concerned that Khowla may have revealed her secrets about what had happened between us. We know that vice is either to satisfy an instinct or to satisfy a stomach, but neither of them was a motive for that slip. But neither of them is a motive for that stray. Disobedience is always a dark spot in the page of sin. I thought her father was going to scandalise me whenever our eyes met. I turned away from him in avoidance and shame, until my head turned constantly like a pigeon's head in vigilance and agility. I shunned from him whenever he arrived, until the Doyen's sharpness of mind was in place, and he said in surprise, "I can see that you intend to carry out an exceptional, unique experiment."

"That is the nature of my profession that made me cross the deserts and oceans for it."

I felt that that evening was not like others, as it carried invisible messages. There was an invisible movement rather than what we three were doing. As if it carried future signs. I was not aware whether it read the fortune of the humans, or the humans were those who read it. Some of the signs indicated forecasts of many future events, events waiting to be transformed into reality. Temporising, then, becomes a great wisdom.

The Doyen was as usual the first to anticipate what should be discussed. He asked me without introduction about the essence of death and its quintessence. The place dividing me from them became empty. There was a shadow of movement accompanying it. I answered him.

"I was planning to conduct a survey of Dilmunia graveyard and study its burials. Perhaps then, I can find there a meaning for death that is different from annihilation."

Abu Rashed asked, "Do you really want to make a survey of the tumuli of Dilmunia grave field?"

The man was astonished about my wish and decision and began again to look into my face; perhaps he could read something that was unknown to him. Implied silence reflects true friendship. However, I wished that would not be interpreted as an escape. The Doyen interfered with his kindness to lift the blockade. He began to address the inactive side of my head with those words that glow the mind.

"I see that you are a traveller who bears the knowledge of man first, the successor of his Creator and his inheritor. The knowledge of solid matter like land and sea, with what is on and in them, comes next, created for him, and he can adapt it for his service. That proud man begins as a sperm and eventually ends up in a hole in the ground."

"That is the crux of the matter; that hole which embeds the dead is exactly what I want to study on the land of Dilmunia. I know the difficulty of the task. Success is a wish dropped in a sea of decisions."

Abu Rashed expressed his view by asking about the benefit of studying human beings after their death. He mentioned, that there were some discouraging, destructive people who did not see the greatness of man except after his death. They did not see the true value of man as long as he was with them. Then the Doyen had a wonderful interpolation about death.

"By nature, man is afraid of death because he is not familiar with it. He sees it as part of others and does not see it as part of his own self. If we only think of it, we know that death can hit us any moment. There are some parts that die with us, like the skin and nails and others. A substitution is born every time. Death hits us continuously, but we do not feel it except when it hits all of the human body at once. We know that every soul shall taste death and this 'every' applies to all living things. We must realise that death is the greatest thing that man fears. But when it is familiar, he gets used to it. He who pronounces death excessively is the one who fights for life."

I added, asking, "Should people get used to death in order to remain alive?"

"Even if man gets used to death, he still feels the dread, which is necessary for the survival of humanity. Death is an invisible preacher. It is worthy of being a law in itself that prevents many repeated crimes. Those criminals, the moment the culprit is set free, they recommit crimes again. When the prison is spacious, it becomes a luxurious home. If life was an absolute open space without death, it would be a spacious home too. Life, Adam, is a flowing river; one should enjoy it and its tempo, because death wishes those who refuse to sing."

"But how can death affect human conduct and reform it?"

"People talk about life while death reminds us of truth. Should not man decrease his zeal, and prefer the morality? Life is not a forest where we fight with talon, the tooth and the strong bite the weak. Are man's claws not stronger than animals' claws? Should not death suffice as a preacher? In actual essence, we are biting each other. In addition, in materialistic reality we eat each other when bodies dissolve in the earth."

I asked him again about the nature of death, about this ambiguity that we are ignorant of, despite all its definition. He said, "I earlier said that every soul is dying, that is, every soul feels abandoning the body and departing from it. No doubt then that after a while it yearns for the body that it embedded for years; therefore, the soul hovers over the grave. It is said that the souls meet and feels what is going on. The soul remains not out of that whole because it is not a dying genre. The single soul that comes in the sense of spirit is immortal, while the body is attacked by the meanest creatures, as worms and the like."

"What is after death?"

"All humanity unanimously agrees that if there were no God, it would be imperative to create one. All divine religions concur that man is rewarded after death. This logical principle was deduced by the ancients naturally by their thinking. There you see pharaonic burial grounds and here the cemeteries of Dilmunia and its mysteries. Religions did not differ with ancient beliefs and folklore that this life is not the end of man. Ancient religions do not disagree with beliefs and folklore that life is not the end of humanity."

The talk with the Doyen made me more interested and boosted my decision to invade the burial mounds of Dilmunia and its graveyards. The discussion urged me to intrude on the world of the dead, the death that orphaned me, the death that disturbed our mission starting with the leader in Sinai and the rest of the members in the Arabian Sea. I wanted to touch the idea of death; perhaps I could coexist with it and describe it. I expressed my intention to go to the nearby burial grounds with whomever was interested among Abu Rashed's men.

Abu Rashed said, "We must inform the Ruler about the area where we shall dig and explore."

I said, "He gave us an implied agreement. I do not think he is going to restrict us with one specific area. It is all up to us."

"However, he told you he was going to provide you with assistants."

"We shall inform your men about the matter; you shall find many who would like to volunteer. If the Ruler wants to send some of his men, they are most welcome; however, I can work on my own!"

"You, work on your own! In an ancient, deserted cemetery in a desert area?"

"I do not think the cemeteries are not inhabited."

I looked long at the man. I looked carefully at his entity; the shape is that of Abu Rashed, but it is not him. He began to elaborate in his speech.

"I think that love utilises death for life. We shall break into Dilmunia's graves with you tomorrow morning."

Abu Rashed told some friends of ours. Four of them agreed to lend a hand. We left early to the area known as Hilat Assif bordering the northern coast with its yellow, soft sands. It was an area full of fresh water bursting from sea and land. There, seamen dived into a spot called Alqassassir; they remained in the salt water, filling their sheepskins with fresh water from the source. These formed two contrasting bodies of sea. In the south, water flowed from natural pools flowing into rivers and streams to irrigate gardens of date palms, pomegranate, citrus and others.

We left that area through its green soil towards the south. The land gradually rose, revealing its angry features; a stony, arid area. The burial mounds appeared at a distance as a raised high dome when compared with the long chains of graves that we passed by on the desert road to the palace of the Ruler. Desert sands began to revolve. Sands reveal their secrets when moving. The whole area appeared to be virginal, as if nature itself built these burial mounds. A terrifying area hard- hitting the soul. We proceeded to the western side, where I chose the smallest burial mound.

I decided to build a resting hut from date palms fronds, to have sunshade during work that began in earnest in the early morning. The first task was removing spread grass and small stones. Then slow digging operations began from the top going downwards. We removed grass and small stones and sand to a spot three metres away from the site. The most important feature was defining the entrance of the mount that was on the northern side of it, from where we proceeded inward. The work was continuous, and the men never stopped except for lunch and prayers, in addition to resting for siestas.

After three days of non-stop work, news of death was announced. Crisis comes only suddenly. News, like a thunderbolt, fell on us. He who knocks at the door of death is swallowed by it. A messenger came to us from the neighbourhood, looked pale, and spoke in a hoarse voice. He started with the usual salutation, then recalled, "We belong to

God and to Him we return."

"Who is it?"

"The Doyen passed away last night. Mourners at the funeral are waiting for Abu Rashed to conclude the funeral rites."

Thus, disasters come unannounced. The death of the Doyen was considered a great catastrophe, with many people around him, both dead and alive. Those bidding you farewell are readers of your life; however, I preferred to stay as I have lived with numerous deaths. There was still danger of leaving, as Abu Rashed really read expressions on my face. What cannot be expressed by words can only be read in silence. The message reached him. He understood my dire desire to accomplish the mission. Before he left, Abu Rashed reiterated some verses of elegy that his late father used to repeat in the recent few days, confirming that fine poetry refines the soul.

"Life is but the beauty of a tree

If one side of it is green, it became dry on the other

Do not let your eyes weep

On those who have gone, you are going too."

I remained alone with the dead; it was a decision I imagined on my part, and then my soul became blind. Some decisions are dictated to us, making us believe that they were. By passage of time, we realise these have nothing to do with us. This island abounded with tens of thousands of burial mounds. I had no idea why I chose this high area in particular. Perhaps because of its burials high and far from the coast for fear of being swept away. In the past few days, friends had helped me excavate these burial mounds, and I had to complete this task all alone.

This mound told the story of the remaining mounds,

estimated at a hundred and fifty thousand in number. It was singled out for its height of nearly twenty metres and a depth of seven metres underground. The opening of the mound and its entrance were on the north-western side. I used the method followed by the grave builders, because I began from where they ended. They started the task by choosing a dry, stone site; they removed soil shell until the red shell appeared, then the ground was dug to build burial rooms. The foundation was laid in a round shape where stones were lined accurately and carefully. As the outer wall rose, the area separating it from the burial chambers was filled until it took the shape of a huge dome.

Before night fell, I sat on another mound, contemplating the mound we had excavated, and its shape appeared. An architectural design could be entered through a T-shaped channel where the burial chamber was on the southern side where the dead were placed in a squatting position, as if in the womb of their mothers. The north chamber, where the dead were facing, was more of a depot containing pottery utensils, shells, beads and even metal coins and spears.

I was examining these finds when I recalled what the late Doyen said about death. Visiting cemeteries soften the heart and provide lots of energy; therefore, we feel the value of life after a visit. An idea crossed my mind; perhaps it was a crazy thought. I decided to enter the tomb and return all possessions to their former place, and then lie down in the tomb in the same place as that of the skeleton. I had mixed feelings as to whether the soul of the dead was still hovering around his skeleton, as it did over his body? Could these souls speak to me? I wanted to touch death.

I lay down in the tomb in a squatting position, closed my

eyes, expelled all thoughts and then tried to slow down my breathing. I nearly... I did not know my feelings at the time, but a line of madness overcame me. I listened to a sort of dialogue between SHE, who was within me, and HE, who was addressing her.

HE: What are your wishes now?

SHE: To return to Life.

HE: Return to *Life why*?

SHE: I felt the necessity of atoning for my sins; the debts of humans are troubling me the most. This is what agonises man until his death. God may forgive you for your sins and errors, but those debts remain with you. Punishment will not harm you, and non-punishment troubles you more.

HE: Why do you carry your possessions with you?

SHE: Man does not carry anything with him after death except good deeds. These are materialistic, representing obsessions and worldly filthiness; our desire to immortalise ourselves. The spear that you can see has referred me to the animal world. With it, I think that others and I shall fight wrong and I fight him; I did not believe in diversity between people as a complementing act.

HE: Do you carry funds and jewellery?

SHE: We, human beings, assign to everything a vanishing material value and forget the eternal spiritual value; the value of love; the value of boosting similarities between us and dwarfing dissimilarities, even obliterating them.

HE: If you return to the worldly life, what would you insist on carrying with you?

SHE: Spread love between all the people. By love, Khowla maintained her chastity and was above punishment. By love, the Doyen was familiar with annihilation and loved it; someone will come here in the future and read your books with love.

Suddenly, I screamed loudly, shaking the darkness and the cord of silence was broken. I opened my left palm and found an intangible worm; I hardly felt it. What a man! A mountain of air.

I retained my usual human nature. I doubt that I will accept many theories later on. Some say that man is compelled in his conduct with himself and with others. We blame Satan for our mistakes to ease our conscience. I found this an incomplete human interpretation to lift responsibility from his burden. I realised, now, that the soul is the one who sees, feels and hears. The tongue, the eye, and the ear are nothing but instruments for it. Death is separation between these means and the soul. I can confirm that the idea of touching death leads to the meaning of life. With love we can defeat our foes, and with love we can be familiar with Death; perhaps we can defeat and overcome him.

(12) Adam
June 1764

I was received by the locals and their folkloric songs; it seemed that after only few weeks they forgot the departure of the Doyen. They celebrated my arrival similar to a popular wedding celebration, with songs and folkloric dances. They gathered outside the boundaries of the village near its southern entrance where two sandy roads intersect with each other. I did not know how they expected me to come back on that particular day. I did not tell anyone about that decision, even the man who worked as a messenger and whom I'd entrusted with the responsibility of delivering food and water. I did not inform him of my intention of returning.

The irony was that I was not aware of this step. Something urged me to pack and return that morning. I dismounted my donkey to shake hands with them one after another. Some of them insisted on kissing my cheek until the turn came for Abu Rashed. He took me with some joy and some sorrow. I think that joy of the reception made him forget the sadness due to the death of the Doyen. I asked him, "Who told you about the timing of my return this evening?"

"I knew you would be back forty nights since you first left."

"Did I spend forty nights at the burials mounds?"

"Yes. The rank of happiness is accomplished at the age of forty."

"Really?"

He suppressed a giggle and his smile appeared different. Whenever I sat with Abu Rashed, a harmonious feeling of love led to knowing my intention and expecting the time of my return. He invited me to mount one of the mules while the donkey was loaded with my luggage. They began to walk around, reminding me of the burial mound; a high dome surrounded by three small hills. I told Abu Rashed about the necessity of modesty and of being among the people, just like them, to be closer to them. "I want to dismount and walk."

"Do not worry; you are just one of us. We appreciate your fatigue and weakness now."

We reached Abu Rashed's *majlis* where I took my place in the forefront, there, between the red cushions with black lines. After a few minutes, the men disbanded and returned home. I did recall the Doyen but could not see his vision. I remembered his presence, but his absence seemed normal. Light and darkness are opposites, one of which is known as the other.

I recalled some of what the Doyen said: everything is known by its contrasting epithet with the exception of God Almighty. He is unknown by his opposite, as He has no opposite. We only know Him by His qualities. His greatness is that He created all creatures in his own image, despite its variance. Here, I am adding: death is not the opposite of life too. He who does not experience death and absorb it, feels its unfriendliness.

Khowla and her sisters came to greet me and welcome me in their midst. This young woman was sublime because she felt that human beings were fallible, and he who sheds the dust off his mistakes without reversion is the real human. Strength of will and steadfastness create an angelic human being. This Khowla was an extension to the school of her grandfather and father. She offered love to reap virtues. I remembered when my father departed in Copenhagen. The mourners were greedy wolves and hungry dogs. However, comparison is unfair. I spoke to her.

"May I present my heartfelt condolences for the departure of the Doyen of Al Jubur. The deceased was a school. His virtues shall remain with us for a long time to come."

The young Rashed interpolated by saying that his virtues were everlasting; that is, he did not die. Khowla nodded her head and smiled shyly and retreated, with the children following her. I certainly realised that fear of death of a man may diminish when we realise that there is no fear of death. The fear is that of concern on the self. The love of the ego indicates that departure is responsible for the agony of the self and creates a sense of dreariness.

After dinner, I felt the warmth of the place close to Abu Rashed. Intimacy comes when a man understands your sentence after one word. I had no need to go into details. He became content with the headlines, and soon he came up with the idea. He began to ask me about benefits and lessons learnt from my seclusions at the burial mounds.

I said, "Death, my friend, is not annihilation but the distancing of the soul from materialism and the removal of its physical dress; that is why I find the Doyen present. We, as human beings, can triumph over the darker side of ourselves, to love ourselves and keep it away from vices and errors. He who loves himself shall definitely love others. Behind every black cloud, we must reach a light. Domination of evil does not mean that good is not there. Earlier, I said that there is no problem without a solution. The problem is that when man feels that this is an infinite problem. Self-love is selfish and scares others. He is born not knowing evil thinking. Then, that other feels that there is someone who wants to oust him and bring his downfall. Good can prevail; however, cowards refuse to spread goodness."

Abu Rashed asked me about my next moves. As a traveller, I had to attain the objectives of the trip that I made. I pointed out that the declared objectives were purely explorative; however, I had found objectives that were more noble. Geographic and economic discoveries are really important for the prosperity of humankind, but exploring or discovering man by himself is a more sublime objective. This is what I discovered and wanted to achieve on the land of Dilmunia, then convey this experience to my country. Perhaps scientific and economic development, even military and political are more advanced there than here; however, science that does not benefit its owner is pure ignorance. Here, simplicity brought man down to earth and to the nature he was born in. I found man abounds with high ethics. Some overpasses can be rectified if we spread well to all people and make them perceive that the source of light and life is close and not impossible.

He asked me, "Do you want to deal with social issues by revealing love?"

"Yes. Love is an easy, applicable principle. If the unjust and despot feels the love of the oppressed for him, he is bound to change and become closer to him. He feels and fraternises him, and when the oppressed feels the love of the oppressor, he must overcome his mistakes. Then, he would say I have forgiven my oppressor for oppressing me. We want, Abu

Rashed, to go to the commoners to coexist with the poor, and sit with the rich, and feel for the needy and the sick, and urge the opulent to have a feeling for others. Love is a creed that revives life.

"Tomorrow, we shall set out for the lanes, mosques, open spaces; then we go to the *Nukhatha*, the Merchant and even the Ruler. Every heart, no matter how hard it is, can never be void of its good nature. The eye illuminates the way to the foot, and the light of knowledge illuminates the path of the soul. He who is content with good deeds feels paradise inside him, and he who is not content with himself — fire of all kinds, fire of envy, anger and misdoubt burn him. This fire hits the inside, affects the outside. You can see anxiety and sadness on his face."

Abu Rashed was, as we knew him, believing in right even when it was against himself. He suggested we go to the largest marketplace in Dilmunia, the one held in the courtyard of its mosque. There, people from all walks of life gathered. We would not wait for anyone to come to us, but rather we would invade people's lives to know their concerns then try to offer them help and guide them to the right path.

We headed towards the ancient mosque one day mid-week. The outer courtyard of the mosque turned into an open space, where transactions of selling and buying took place. A continuous action. Our entry was from the southern end of the court. Abu Rashed was a public figure, and my accompanying him made things worse. Those we met were easy-going and at ease. They approached, greeting us attired in the best of clothes. Man is humble with his peers and tries to be nice with others. Most of them came to salute us, except one young man who was tied to a trunk of a tree like an ewe. The youth was in shabby white clothes, but time had painted him with its tragedies. The rope was tied to his right arm. His head was shaven, he was beardless and skinny with an obnoxious smell. We stood a few metres at his side. I spoke to Abu Rashed.

"Why is this young man tight like a stray animal?"

"He has been waiting for his turn to be tight inside the mosque for a few hours."

"Why people are tight there?"

"It is said that he is infected with an 'eye". His condition of losing his mind worsened. This eye is similar to a spell of magic."

"It is an opportunity for us to relieve him from his agonies and extend him a helping hand. First, we need to know the causes of his ailment. Knowing the causes of the problem helps in reaching half of the solution."

Abu Rashed elaborated from his own knowledge of sorcery. "My father mentioned that there are several kinds of magic: some is like the quick, light hand that spellbinds the eye and makes believe what is not real. The effect of this type is extended to the body; this is what is known as imagining the esoteric. I find all this nothing but quackery and charlatanry; it is depiction of the false as true. These are all acts of deception and men of reason do not believe in it."

"I still recall my discussion with the Doyen about magic. He mentioned that some think that the judgement on a magician is by death sentence. It is an implied admission that magicians have the upper hand over their victims."

"The Sharia verdict is on the magician, not on the effect of magic, because the magician denies a necessity of his being religious. He denies that God has all the universe. This divine ownership is a divine right to God alone. Man's ownership is temporal and vanishing. The magician's contending with God is a denial of one of the religious necessities that is extended to curing, even at the hand of a physician."

We went closer to the spellbound young man. His clothes seemed filthy. I found red, black and green threads around his wrist, neck and leg. As we came closer, he began to beg, asking for benefaction and help. People, in turn see that helping the spellbound and possessed keeps evil away. I asked Abu Rashed again, "Could he not be inflicted by the eye? Let us look for evidence."

We spoke to the young man about his name, family and village; he shook his head. He did not answer or make a comment. I told him that his name was Ali and that he was from Addayre. He answered negatively. His answer was proof of his ability of comprehension. A good sign of hope.

"If your name is not Ali, what is it?"

He spoke to us gradually and began to familiarise us. We sat with him on a mat and invited him to eat with us. He told us in broken sentences that he had a family. Someone tried to create discord between him and his wife, who hated him and asked to leave him and eventually divorced him.

I always repeated that there is no problem without a solution hidden beside it. A discerning individual is he who delays patiently and explores that solution. A family problem; the man thought it was the end of his life and the whole world. This young man was unable to find that solution. The problem became complicated and hit him psychologically, hard. He wanted to leave life. He threw himself in the sea several times, but the sea refused to swallow him. He was hopeless of life. He imagined sickness and discarded this world. The simplest form of sympathising is to assume lunacy and be spellbound.

There is the reassured, the blaming, the sick, and the evil inspiring. When we distinguished between psyche and its suffering and treated it by love, then his psychological condition could be controlled. Jasmine could be planted in his heart so he could love life and remove thorns from his path.

(13) Al Nukhetha
August 1764

The relationship between the sailors and me began to deteriorate and became dry in a way. The souls started to undress and the hidden became apparent. On my side, I had always tried to satisfy the sailors materially and morally. I was fair to them, looking for financial stability throughout the year. I tried to make them content during the pearling season. The Merchant was putting on pressure, by all his means, refusing to see any of the sailors were better off. He was insisting that all should be in need of him and the Ruler. He thought that the class system was a way of life based on differences or inequality between people. The Merchant was sending his messages directly: I shall buy all the crop of pearls on condition that the sailors take less than the previous year.

After that famous voyage, discord increased with the sailors, as the Tawwash, at sea, failed to find a solution or a way out that met demands of all parties. Despite the reasonable and human nature of the demands, I became torn between two adversaries. I became worried and that affected my family relationships. Psychological stability is a necessity for harmony within the family and society.

Abu Rashed and Adam, the traveller, knocked at our door. By the testament of all, they became close friends; each was pushing the other. The latter came to study what is beneath the land of Dilmunia but changed to examining what was above it with great interest. Spreading good and happiness to the people of Dilmunia became a mutual target for both of them. They adopted diffusing happiness wherever they went. They perceived that conquering darkness was a means of conveying light and beauty. One evening, they came and Abu Rashed spoke.

"We came wishing for your generosity and hoping for your kindness."

"What is on your mind?"

Abu Rashed begged his companion to speak.

"We clearly know the future objectives of the Merchant. Undoubtedly, he does not want to see prosperous people and welfare offered to the whole community. This matter is no concern of his. He sees that God created men in categories and classes. This class system is essential for continuity of life."

Adam commented on this.

"The class theory is not a child of the imagination of Dilmunia and the Dilmunians. Perhaps the Merchant is not aware that it is ancient and widespread, like cancer in western industrial societies. There, some philosophers are publicly advocating this; it reflects what is known as cultural illiteracy. There, the ambitious individual wishes to move from the atom to the galaxy, but he remains brutal and uncivil in his behaviour. Aristotle said that the class system is a human necessity. He who buys slaves is not equal to them. This is the same principle that St Augustine preached when he said that he who calls for abolishing slavery is calling for, not worshipping God. Europe is treating its simple people with the same treatment as that of the master to the slave. It is the worst of philosophical authorities."

I did not know the names that Adam mentioned, but it

seemed these were great names for nation makers. Abu Rashed continued the conversation in a parallel line but from a different angle

"The Prophet, PBH, kissed the hand of a worker saying, 'It is the hand of God on His land.' One of the companions said in this context, 'Farmers are the treasures of God on the land.'"

I expressed my amazement at what the two men wanted. I asked them about what they meant. Abu Rashed expressed his dire desire to resist the class system, and what the Merchant was aiming at, solidifying its principles on the land of Dilmunia.

"What can I do? How can a simple individual resist huge waves?"

"We can by joining hands and acting in solidarity to help the poor and the needy. When we help them, the Merchant shall not stand against love and good. God commended his Prophet to pay alms when He said, 'Take alms from their wealth in order to purify and sanctify them.' To sanctify the soul and the wealth, no one can reap without society. You cannot gain wealth without working for it in a communal environment. The Prophet had many times urged giving to charity during one's lifetime; it is better than after his death. Alms giving or *Zakat is* due for the unemployed and the needy."

"Isn't that a tax like what we pay on our crops to the Ruler and his followers, and what the Ruler pays to Britain and before that to Portugal?"

Abu Rashed explained that the term "from" means part of the possession, while others said that it was partial; some of the wealth. In both cases, it purified and sanctified the soul. Revenues, *Zakat,* Ruler's dues, tenths, and there is also the tithe or the fifth according to what God says: "Know that what you gain, to God one fifth." They, however, disagreed on the conception and its public and private context. Some saw that gain included all that man possessed while others saw it as a gain of war only.

I said, "I find you, Abu Rashed, comprehensively competent."

Adam said, "Not really, *Nukhetha*. Man should represent one whole unit. Literature, politics, religion and others are horizons that complement each other. For instance, how can a religious individual comprehend the rhetoric of the Quran without loving literature? This is what you see in this man, Abu Rashed."

I found that the conversation had greatly diversified and become profound. I recalled an incident that I live with every day. I told them about a young man whom I had been observing placing hurdles in front of my house every morning. He put stones, tree trunks and other trash to the extent that the whole family was hurt. I wondered how I could help him; he was healthy, robust and able to work and earn a living.

Abu Rashed pointed out that the Prophet believed in work and found it shameful that an individual extended his hand to the "sweat" of another. Then he said, "It is better to confront that young man to know what his grievance is and what makes him angry. Most people's actions are based on reactions. You must look for the deed that made him end up doing such a shameful act."

The two men left my *majlis*, and I spent the night brooding on their conversation. Would simple acts illuminate the path of good and spread roses in front of those who chose the path of power and tyranny? Would the impact of love and virtue be stronger that baton gunpowder? I spent the night thinking of choosing those goodwill acts. I decided to confront the anger of the sailors and farmers and others with the weapon of love.

I woke up early, waiting for that young man who was in the habit of placing stones, tree trunks and litter at the entrance of our house. He stood opposite the door of the house, placing stones slowly. I slipped out from the other side. I was behind him from the opposite direction. I placed my hand on his shoulder, patting him. I greeted him smilingly.

"Peace be upon you and the mercy of God."

The young man uttered no words. He looked into my eyes angrily. He breathed deeply and his chest fully inhaled. I was afraid of his corporal might but I gathered my strength. I waited for him to say something. He was utterly silent. I said, "Come closer to us. If there is a need, we may help you. Peoples help each other. He who helps is helped."

The young man removed my hand from his shoulder and left silently. His face was a blank page. The condition that puts man in a state between sadness and joy. That state that makes a person in between happiness and sadness. I went inside the house and waited for my breakfast before my daily duties. I left after more than an hour. The surprise was that the entry to the house was completely clean, without any obstructions.

(14) The Foundling
February 1765

People have always been despised me with haughtiness, starting with the young and old, the literate and educated, the poor even before the rich, from all spectrums of society. Society disagrees on many issues; it agrees on when it comes to what concerns me. A mountain of sadness fell on me, making me suffocate with tears.

All realised that Dilmunians disagreed on most marginal and essential issues. They disputed on matters of religion, sect and politics, but they agreed that I was a foundling, or a whoreson. I found people calling me in Arabic, *malqutt*. I could not find a synonym or meaning for it. My name became my address that I carried, with all its cares on my shoulder.

I worked as a farmer and servant for one of the proprietors of a field for three years. Those were years of bounty and prosperity, of increased crop production crop. With our sweat and hard work his capital was boosted, and he purchased another farm. He praised my colleagues and me. His words became like medals on our chests. He confessed with gratitude that God bestowed him with abundant wealth in return for his kindness. He constantly used to say that where there is water, there is wealth. Moreover, with wealth comes discord. The sky was not generous during last year as it was a dry year. As a result, all sources were dry too and production dwindled. He tried to find a way out to protect him from a forthcoming crisis.

He met with us to discuss the situation.

"Rains were scarce, as a result some pools dried up."

"That will influence the crops, especially those that must be embedded in water."

"What would you suggest, folks?"

"Pools became scarce and semi-dry; as a result, rivers and streams were affected. I suggest we dig a well to compensate for the deficiency of water."

The proprietor liked the suggestion but saw the difficulty of applying it. Digging without heavy equipment is very exhausting. I expressed my willingness and eagerness for manual digging. We were trying and begging God for success. My colleagues saw that task and were convinced and adopted the idea. The proprietor expressed his content with me and promised to provide me with a hut as a residence in the farm itself, as a kind of gratitude. Then he spoke to all of us.

"You know, men, if we fail in farming this season, matters will be very complicated. Things do not start with digging the well then harvesting only. If we are unable to pay taxes to the Ruler, he shall give a pretext to the Merchant to buy the farm at a very low price imposed on us. No doubt, the Ruler wants the revenues, and the Merchant wants to invest opportunities before they slip through his fingers as clouds. He hunts and catches."

"Do not worry; once the means are there, problems can be solved. We shall find a way out to compensate for the deficiency of water."

We dug the soil and a rich pool gushed out from the crust layer of the ground, waiting for a chance to liberate It overflowed, flooding the farm and neighbouring lands. Water was no longer the problem; the affluence of water made the proprietor very happy and So he could fly with joy. We tilled and sowed the land, waiting for the forthcoming harvest season. One month or so later, the crops were more than expected. Devastating news came with the advent of the worms and the rot following on all the products. Consequently, we were disappointed, and the proprietor was dismayed and scared. He began to look for causes. He tried in vain. A great loss that would force him to give up his farm after a long wait. He decided to meet all his farmers and declare his decisions.

"After depending on God, we tackled the problem of scarcity of water; we drilled pools. We followed all usual steps; however, the results were disappointingly adverse. Until I was certain of the cause."

"What was the cause? What went wrong?"

The proprietor pointed at me and said, "He is the bastard. The foundling sitting in your midst. He works hard and is no doubt loyal. However, divine blessing is withheld from him and from anything that he touches. He cannot tread on any land without bounties fleeing. Accordingly, brothers, we decided to get rid of him and expel him from the farm and its abodes."

I was broken-hearted; nevertheless, I decided to hold to the string of life. I approached some *Nukhethas* to work for them as a sailor, an assistant puller or a cook. The answer came quickly from the *Nukhetha*.

"There is no place for a foundling among us. No origin of yours is known. God will not bless our work; perhaps you shall bring us a lot of problems. It is in the interest of all that you should keep away, to immigrate, or disappear, so that God may find a way out for you and us."

I looked for other jobs; however, the result was the same. A group decision expelled me from society. An agreement that the foundling had no place amongst the others, And that there was no blessing behind it.

I felt that there was no refuge for me except with my creator. Poverty is solace; that is why most people turn to God at times of distress. Since I was a child, I loved praying. I listened when the Imam was preaching. I joined several Quran teaching houses, but as soon as they knew that I was the foundling, then…

I learnt reading but after this labyrinth and empty circle, I went to the grand mosque seeking asylum. I had a dire need to complain to my last resort, to my God, who is the omnipotent. The caretaker of the mosque decided to take me and provide accommodation for me in one of the side rooms in return for cleaning the mosque every day. I earned my living from alms given by worshippers. Praised be God who is at the side of his creature at times of distress. I made friends with worshippers and alms-givers until I began to find myself. I thanked God for His bounty. One Friday that I cannot wipe from my memory, came the Friday prayers with its faith impact. The Imam delivered the ceremony before prayers.

"O, Believers. God said, 'In the name of God, the Compassionate, the Merciful: the adulteress and the adulterer — flog each of them a hundred lashes and have no pity on them, in a punishment prescribed by God, if you believe in God and the Last Day. Let some believers witness their punishment.' Creatures of God, out of my responsibility to God and society, I commend you to do well. God's judgement is obvious regarding high sin and adulterers who are squalor and produce squalor. I came to know that there is a filthy person within the walls of this mosque. There is a foundling desecrating this House of God. The caretaker had a role in this.

He tried his best but erred. He must repent. You Believers must oust that foundling from this mosque to secure its sanctity. I say this and ask for forgiveness to me and unto you."

A sick cleric is he who pursues the mistakes committed by others. Thus, the result was inevitable. The worshippers threw me out, showering me with curses and smacking. Now, I was a fugitive of a society that I was thrown in against my will. I thought of staying away in a wasteland farm on the outskirts of Ajajaj village to the south of fort. There the gays, thieves and highwaymen met. I was not one of them. They found their refuge in me. They made me a guardian of the wasteland and their possessions in return for food and accommodation. I was not at all happy with my lot. I left as a fugitive from a social jail and was caught in a criminal prison. I found myself thrown in a valley I morally did not belong to.

The bandits came one night carrying a stone tablet with lots of inscriptions. It was a stone but not like other stones. It was milky in colour, like a sea stone or slab called locally *firsh*, with an inscription in Arabic, as if it were a direct epistle from its writer. They deposited the stone with me and left for a few days. They disappeared for unknown reasons. They returned to find me hunger-stricken without leaving the place for three full nights. I told him about my hunger and how I was about to perish. They asked me to work and make lots of money.

"Take this tablet and sell it in the local market held every Friday morning."

"I do not think there is anyone who would buy a hard stone."

"It seems this is a precious stone. Some appreciate relics and antiques. It has many ancient inscriptions. You had better look for British soldiers, or Europeans and travellers. Someone must know the real or symbolic value of this stone. They shall pay a lot for it."

"Where did you get it from?"

"Never mind. Just look for someone to buy it. We shall keep an eye on you during the selling transaction. When you receive the price, we shall split it with you."

As docility is to give forcibly, the agreement was convincing and worth trying. It was an agreement that would provide me with food for the forthcoming period, perhaps days, months or years.

I waited for the promised Friday. I carried the stone on my back. It was heavy and I carried it for metres and then lay it down. I suffered from it. I came nearer to the gardens adjoining the market. I spent the night near one of the fountains. I chose the entrance to the market and sat near the vegetable vendors. Many showed interest in what I intended to sell. Some derided, while others frowned. The heat of the sun increased and none of the promised buyers turned up. Friday prayers were approaching, and vendors packed their wares and left, as it is forbidden to do business when the call for Friday prayers is made. I was afraid of carrying it lest I break my back. Some of the Ruler's men and his secret agents ordered vendors to pack until after the prayers. They came towards me.

"Is this hard stone for sale?"

"Yes."

"How much do you want for it?"

"What your generosity offers."

"Because it is precious relic, we shall only buy it from its owner."

"I am the owner."

My tongue dropped me in a pitfall that was called later a

crime. I indirectly confessed to security men that I was the robber of this stone. They hurled me quickly into jail in anticipation of the trial that was held every Monday morning. There at the court sat three judges, with a notary public on their right. Courts have their ceremonial rites too. These normally start with sipping three cups of coffee. Then the cases are investigated that the interpreter passes, and the witnesses' sayings are recorded. I was the first defendant, and the witnesses were two police officers. The judges heard my story, followed by questioning the witnesses, and finally, they issued their verdict. "The court, in presence, orders imprisoning the accused for three years in jail with immediate effect and confiscating the antique stone."

I still remember details of that unjust trial. I told them the truth about that stone and how it came to me. The judge was not convinced with what I said and was even not prepared to listen to me after he had asked me about my name: *almalqut*. My name was in itself an indictment. He confronted me with the security officers who arrested me. I did not want to beat around the bush. Then I confessed and now I denied. The judge told me that this stone belonged to a mosque in one of the villages that was looted a week ago. It was strong evidence about my involvement in the looting. I confirmed to him the presence of the bandits in the said farm. He asked for them to be summoned; however, nobody was there. It seemed that they had changed their abode. The European man, who later I knew was the servant and advisor to the Ruler, came closer to the stone, felt and smelt it. He knocked on it with his right hand.

"It seems this is an antique treasure. It had better be referred to Adam, who undoubtedly shall discover many mysteries about the civilisation of Dilmunia and about the religions practised there before the advent of Islam."

The judge sentenced me to three years. This could be repealed if one of the alleged bandits was arrested. There shall always be a way out at times of difficulty. This three-year sentence was a blessing for me. I secured a place of accommodation. There I was no longer a vagabond and was not exposed to a wild animal or a human demon. In prison, I could obtain my daily food without interruption. I thanked God immensely. In prison, I was happy to be acquainted with the doyen of prisoners: Yusef, the Puller.

(15) Yusef's Wife
March 1765

Since the accusation of my husband for the killing of Nasser and his apprehension at dawn, terrifying our children, Yusef was thrown in prison before the trial. He was forcibly held, then framed him for the murder. We waited for a long time and had not lost hope yet. I took my four children to live in the grand family house, the "big house" as it was called. Then I went to the Doyen's house to tell him about the crisis. I found manhood in him as a precious metal, though melted by life. He expressed his concern and sympathy with us. He confirmed that time is capable of finding an answer to any unresolved crisis.

It was very difficult for me to live alone without a family. Here, people observe and oversee each other until you are made sick with made up tales. This became a rooted habit to kill time, pushing people to commit suicide. Those who kill themselves are a failure in life. To put an end to this and cut tongues, I moved to live at my family's home with its extended family system. Every son getting married builds a family within the same house. This was more of a group of families and generations living together. For months, we were not able to visit Yusef; mixed contradictory news did not give clear evidence of his whereabouts. There were discrepancies in the news coming from the Ruler's prison and those from his retinues, like the Merchant. The children were about to get used to his absence, equivalent to death. There had to be a way out of this crisis, to conquer fear.

I managed, accompanied by one of the brothers, to reach the men of the village and neighbouring areas, to no avail. They told me that I was searching for a mirage and most wishes were illusions. The people were living in a state of anticipation and communal fear, urging them to think of the future of their families and to keep away from the source of fire. You find them glorifying occasions of grief because collective grief brings happiness.

Everybody was afraid of dealing with the issue of Yusef's imprisonment. To them, there were more important, vital matters than that, such as the questions of naval and agricultural taxes and the attempt to stage a coup d'état, and plotting with foreign powers. Various issues that kept people uninterested in private matters and rather focused on greater issues. I knew that Abu Rashed would do his best for the release of Yusef. They told me that he had lately paid a visit to the Ruler; but the case had changed from a criminal case, as they claimed, into a political opinion case related to national security.

My brother and I decided to approach the Merchant himself. He was the most influential man in Dilmunia, but he hated to announce that in public. In fact, he was the accuser, and the case was his. I decided to talk to him and explain the condition of my children so that his heart may move and forgive Yusef, the innocent. Confronting him had double danger. On one hand, it made an attempt to know the fate of Yusef, and on the other, resisting the demonic inclination of his. I still recall his sexual looks.

The Merchant lived in Abu Jarjur, situated on the top of a rocky hell on the south-east coast, close to the affluent class. We took the rocky, narrow lane, one passage only that led to the house, that white castle when the sun shone on it. Kind of pride and distinction. White is the source of all colours while black is its grave. At the beginning of the long road, the guards stopped us, asking about our destination.

"Why are you here; what do you want?"

"We are visiting the Merchant."

"Is he waiting for you according to a prior appointment?"

"We do not have a prior appointment; it is an important meeting. We hope to see him just for a few minutes."

The Chief of Guards ordered one of his men to escort us to the White House. Other guards stopped us at the second entrance. The man left us and went to talk to them. One of them entered, closing the giant wooden door behind him. The guard told us to sit at a distance until the guard returned. He quickly returned. He closely body-searched my brother. He asked me if I was carrying a white weapon or guns. I answered in the negative. The world outside the door was the opposite to what was inside; a desert-like, rocky passage contrasting with a lawn passage with tall palm trees lined up on both sides and fresh flowing water. They led us to the Merchant's *majlis*. I let down the *abaya* on my face, covering it tightly. I still recall those ugly looks. I came to know that some men like a woman and they desire her.

We found the Merchant sitting at the centre of the *majlis,* with all the pride, in a wide velvet chair. On each side stood a man holding a large falcon, in addition to swords and shining spears hanging behind him. He pointed disdainfully for us to stand at a distance.

"You asked to visit me. You are welcome. What can I do for you?"

"Peace be upon you."

"And on you. What next?"

"We are looking for Yusef, the Puller."

"How do I know what you are talking about, woman? Who is that Yusef, and what can I do?"

I told him that we represented the family of Yusef, the Puller, and that he had been in jail for nearly two years. His family had the right to visit him and be reassured about him. There are children and a wife without a supporter.

"I do not recall that we have a prisoner with these descriptions; whose Yusef are you talking about?"

"That defendant accused of killing your son, Nasser, at sea."

The man realised that the woman's tongue was her spear. He was dismayed and frowned his forehead. Then he placed his right hand on the lines and wiped them to separate them, until the forehead became smooth.

"I remember now. Are you his wife or one of his sisters?"

I covered myself tightly with the *abaya*.

"His wife refuses to meet you; I am his sister and this is his brother, too."

"That woman refuses to see me, then. Yusef was convicted for killing my son, Nasser, on purpose and with predetermination. Punishment was clear since that trial."

"That trial was not ordered by the Ruler. It was a mock trial."

"The result in short is that your Yusef killed my son, Nasser, and his wife, because of her pride, adamantly refuses to meet me. There is no harm in that. Tell her of my decision:

I shall reconsider the case of Yusef. You know that in Hell there are several levels and the most burning one is the abyss. I promise you to throw your Yusef in this abyss so that the fire in my heart is put off."

The Merchant stood, fuming with anger and pronouncing the vilest epithets.

Then he ordered four of his men to tie us up.

"Guards! Remove their Yusef from his prison and place him into a harsher and darker cell. Tie him up in solitary prison where he cannot see the light of the day. Let him drink only to quench his thirst and feed him only to sustain his life."

"O, Merchant! Be a dealer in the market of principles just once in your life."

The Merchant ordered his men to place us in one of the rooms at his farm as a temporary detention until he was done with the case of Yusef. We spent a horrible night. In the morning, they took us back to his *majlis*. The man was so proud of himself, walking like a peacock.

"We found that your prisoner was moved to one of the Ruler's official detention centres. Unfortunately, there he is served with three meals and is permitted to have a walk in the prison courtyard. He is allowed to have a bath every day. He, however, committed another crime that deprived him of privileges bestowed by the Ruler. He was moved from solitary to communal prison. There, he became acquainted with the foundling, who trained and enlisted him to assassinate the Ruler himself and overthrow the system of government. A plot against the state. Life imprisonment shall not be the punishment this time; it shall be execution in the yard of the grand mosque after Friday Prayers."

The style of the Merchant was not deplorable or awful. A

slain sheep is hurt when skinned. We would not be surprised if he did not make up fictional tales. However, smiling in the face of the despot insults him. He was furious and ordered his guards to throw us out of his castle.

In the evening, I headed to Abu Rashed's house. He was conversing with Adam. A woman was safe in his presence. The man found me about to weep.

"What is the matter?"

"We visited the Merchant to inquire about Yusef. He added plotting to overthrow the system to confirm the accusations of killing Nasser. He was moved to the Merchant's prison last night. He threatened to kill him in revenge."

"My daughter, a man's belly is only filled with dust. Do not worry; I have visited your husband at one of the Ruler's prisons. He is well. The Ruler shall agree shortly on your visit to him. He is not under the influence of the Merchant now."

After that, Abu Rashed spoke about his present plans. He mentioned that Adam intended to send him a letter informing him about the Dilmun burial mounds. We would attach to that letter information about a new plot planned by the Merchant. We would try to reach the Ruler first; however, I expected that the Merchant would precede us with his cunning and come up with a new tale of a plot. Do not worry; we were not in want of a strategy. We would find a way out.

(16) Adam
April 1765

In accordance with the social treatment, by love and noble values that we put in place and adopted, Abu Rashed was able to see light through sombre darkness. Punishment by love is the worst agony. Enlightenment is the best vision to resist dark, demonic powers within the soul. I suggested to Abu Rashed to pay a visit to the Ruler and try to find the best possible means to his heart. From his side, he suggested, parallel to this, to seize the opportunity to request a visit to Yusef in his prison. The idea was good and logical but perilous and may have led unjustly to throwing us behind bars.

We did not care about risks, but we were searching for the source of light in the heart of the Ruler. There was definitely a human sense deep inside him that may have been affected by what was filling his mind with true and false news. A man, no matter who he is, is a container who holds what he is fed and filled with. There are the sycophants, social climbers and drummers; each one provides a piece of news or an idea of interest to him. We planned the visit to the Ruler without the knowledge of the Merchant and members of his council. Sometimes, deceit is transported and removed by the effect of places.

We took the desert route that both of us knew well. We took the shortest cut, away from the eyes as much as possible. The reception we had from the Ruler was full of welcome and happiness. This meeting was quite different. His smile was yellow and affected, as if it were not from his heart. He made us sit on his right. The boy came as usual, serving Arabic coffee, a tradition that reflects hospitality. Our intention was not to discuss essential cases that developed from the crisis of confidence between his supporters and opponents. We did not want to talk about taxes imposed on divers, agriculture and fishing. The first step was to stir still waters and reinstall the human aspect to the government.

"Your Highness, we know as well as all people that you are the father of all. All come under your flag when they are in trouble. You are the safe haven for all of them. A ruler bears a great responsibility to himself, the people and God. He wishes them well and all are responsible, and when is applicable to all, they all feel secure and stable."

The Ruler was very pleased on hearing this. He relaxed in his velvet chair and tossed his string of beads around his index and middle fingers. The kind word is charity by which bridges of love are built. He answered, "We pray to God to be up to the responsibility in the service to the people with the satisfaction of God Almighty."

"Your Highness knows a human and religious right of a prisoner is to communicate with the outside world, and should not be thrown in prison deprived of these rights. It is necessary that prisoners communicate with their families and society until the end of their term. Your Highness undoubtedly is aware of this more than we are."

"Is there anybody in the prison of Dilmunia who is deprived of this right?"

"The Ruler's question is a clear indication of a human's natural feeling."

"Although this man swore at me, and wished me death, and was according to the judge's verdict directly responsible for the death of Nasser, the son of the Merchant, I never ordered that he should be deprived of visitors nor that he should be ill-treated."

It was not reasonable to talk about Yusef's innocence. A nation that wants to leave its crisis behind its back should not dive into the past. The ability to empty the memory offers enormous energy. We should forget negative memory and look for the rays of the sun in a cloudy future. He who eternalises memory is never cured of catastrophes and tragedies of time. Sailing to safety is on the surface of water, not into its depths.

We seized the opportunity when we thought the time was right. We requested the Ruler to issue an order permitting Yusef's family to visit him after all these unfruitful months. We also asked about the possibility of visiting him that day. We did not know where the central prison was. He ordered one of his men to take us to visit Yusef, and said, "O, Traveller, I need to know in detail the results of your excavations in the Dilmunia burial mounds today. Written by you."

"It is difficult, Your Highness; it is impossible to do that today. The route from the northern coastal part of the island to reach your palace in the south is too long. It takes time and effort. It is impossible."

To Abu Rashed the Ruler said, "Your friend can help you and guide you on how to use pigeons. An easy way that saves lots of time."

"Your Highness, you shall have what you requested."

We left the *majlis* of the Ruler feeling his good intentions. One of the security officers, who did not speak Arabic fluently, accompanied us. After few minutes, I asked my friend, Abu

Rashed, "What pigeons was the Ruler talking about?"

"Time shall come to talk about those pigeons. Now, we have to proceed to Quzquz village, located north-east of Dilmunia. It overlooks the east coast of the island that looks like a pear in its rounding." ·

We managed to reach Qazqaz, taking the east route of the mounds and headed northward, a level sandy area. There, you could see lots of rundown buildings and you were awe-struck by its untrimmed palm trees. People only lived on its outskirts. In the heart of Gazgaz, the prison was set up. We were unable to enter the area by night. We waited at the hospitality of one of the farmers until the morning of the next day. The security man and a farmer were our guides. The farmer left us when the marks of the frond prison wall appeared. Our companion spoke to the sentinel. They led us to the area. We were not allowed to enter the prison, which apparently was underground. They asked us to wait in a hut overlooking a pen for breeding fowls. The guard entered behind the room of cow fodder. We heard the squeak of a heavy door. Minutes later, the guard returned and sat beside us on the trunk of a date palm.

A robust man of a medium height, of white complexion, was supporting a man absolutely fatigued, more of a skeleton than anything else. Wrinkles covered his cheeks and forehead; he had an obtruding lower jaw. Abu Rashed quickly stood up and went to them shouting, "Yusef, Yusef", embracing him and kissing his head. Tears did not take long to drop. Abu Rashed received that skeleton. He took him beside him on the tree trunk and introduced us. I greatly welcomed him and was sad for what had become of him. I felt implicitly their wish to be left alone. I pulled the hand of the young man accompanying us to the wall of the cowshed. I asked him about the reason for being in prison. He was as transparent as truth is the soul of love. He told me about his imprisonment and the story of the antique stone that came his way. Incidents change the life of man; however, what he chooses purposely remains of little impact. I asked him, "What made you go to the waste farm? Why did you pull out of society and prefer seclusion? Isn't he stupid who breaks his door?"

"Whoever I meet say I am a foundling. My origin is not known; I have no roots. I am banned from entering mosques, and my presence in any work is harmful to the proprietor and prevents blessings to his business. This is what I was told when I was at the grand mosque and a worker at one of the farms. They did not accept me to work at sea for fear of their catch and safety. I preferred to withdraw. Here, I am in prison, a place I did not choose, but it is the best place for me. It is my safe haven and where I go to sleep with a filled stomach. I enjoy talking to Yusef."

"And where is the ancient stone?"

"The Ruler's police retained it."

When Abu Rashed and I returned to the village, our hopes grew, and the list of tasks grew longer and compressed. There had to be a solution to Yusef's problem, and what would come out of it in terms of a political opening, as his case was that of a prisoner of opinion, not a crime. God does not question us for our ideas but our deeds. Then we had to examine the stone tablet, and to reinvigorate the foundling, then the smitten or bewitched. Then search for the problem of the Merchant, the judge and the *Noukhatha* ending up to the Ruler himself. Human tasks leading to a happy life. Living in ivory towers does aid life, but drawing a smile on the face of the deprived is absolute happiness.

I spoke to Abu Rashed about the terrible state of that foundling. He said people described him as a son of adultery and cursed him as a bastard. I know and am certain that Islam, as well as most religions, preaches love and compassion. It sees human values as a method yielding happiness and unity between the people, but I did not know yet how it regarded, with a religious eye, that foundling or a son of adultery.

For his part, Abu Rashed cited a Quranic verse. "The fornicatoress and the fornicator flog each one of them a hundred lashes and have no mercy on them, when it comes to the matter of God's religion, if you believe in God and the Last Day; and let a party of believers witness their chastisement." (Al Nur, 2.) This verse is clear when it comes to the punishment of adulterers in order to protect a society of sinners and ill-doers. On the other hand, bastards have no sin of their own and may not carry the sin of their parents.

Morally and ethically, we must not implant these values in society. A foundling, though he may be a child of adultery, nobody has the right to banish him from society. Then, he may be transformed from a useful instrument into a harmful one.

I suggested to Abu Rashed that we pay a visit to the Imam of the Friday Mosque in Dilmunia. I found the idea was on his mind before I completed what I wanted to say. How could the Imam devote the Friday sermon to the rights of the foundling, the son of a doubt and that of fornication? He said it was worth that the said young man be present during the sermon, then he could listen directly to it. I realised that this required a new meeting with the Ruler to release him from prison. I asked Abu Rashed, "Shall we proceed to the Imam or to the Ruler?"

"The Ruler needs to listen to the Imam to realise that his decision is in accordance with Sharia before the foundling is set free."

"The young man known as *malqut*, or foundling, needs to listen to the sermon too, so his life can change."

"We are moving in vicious circle, not knowing from where to begin."

"Do not worry. Good intentions find good signals that move them. These generate a hidden energy that can solve the ambiguity and spread flowers on rough soil. You should be hopeful, my friend; there is someone who will open doors and facilitate matters for you."

Things were over regarding my friend. He left for home to his family. I was, however, obsessed with another issue: that of the ancient stone. Perhaps it was an extension to the Dilmunic excavations, which I had lately conducted. I thought it was another signal that would lead me to another obscure matter that might solve the Dilmunic enigma.

(17) Adam
May 1765

In accordance with the wilful wish of the Ruler to know the outcome of my visit and experiments at the Dilmunia burial mounds, he commended Abu Rashed to show me the famous towers of pigeons found all over the island. He commended him, in a manner akin to an order, to acquaint me with the means of carrier pigeons to communicate and correspond with him. In his last audience with him, he unequivocally said, "I want you to take Adam to the nearest tower of pigeons. I wish to know closely and accurately the results of Adam with regard to those historical burials."

The recommendation was clear. As a result, I compiled general details and detailed graphs of the mound accidentally chosen. In the first letter, I specified the location of the mounds and the position of that particular mound in it. Then, I clearly explained the method and technique of excavation. I mentioned some of the collectables discovered inside there. However, I deliberately did not mention the funeral ritual simulation inside the grave and the visionary dialogue with supposed spirits.

Abu Rashed and I went then to the nearby area to the west of Barbura village. We reached the mud tower on its outskirts in a rocky, arid, relatively high ground. There, we found bird cages distinguished by the beautiful carrier pigeons, which were considered the fastest and the most accurate in postal communication between the Ruler and other areas of his country and other places. Despite its different genesis, the carrier pigeons were known for their love and clinging to the soil of their country[9]. This instinct was boosted when they had chicks left behind; then their speed was increased. We were told that the position of the sun was used to define the directions. It was also said that they had a strong sense of smell that enabled them to distinguish the soil of their country.

As the time became fit to open the door for demands, I postscripted the letter with a small demand on this occasion. I expressed the dire need for the foundling to help locate the place from where the antique stone was stolen. I also explained the need for him to carry the stone, as he was strongly built and was able to perform lots of hard work. The Ruler did not dally to reply and comment. The response was positive and quick, as expected. He mentioned his wish for me to visit his palace the next Wednesday.

I promptly headed to the palace of the Ruler as he ordered. He sent his men to fetch the ancient stone. Barely one hour later the stone was carefully placed between his hands. At the time, the Servant was there and expressed his wish to be heard first

"I am the first to suggest to the Ruler the scientific necessity for him to examine the stone. I expect there are many mysteries to be unfolded."

I told, without showing gratitude, that all pertaining to the signs on the back of the stone was my main occupation and specialisation, and I was the most capable at assessing the

---

[9] Letters were tied to the legs of the carrier pigeon, to check on their arrival; they used mothers' pigeon.

expected value. I did not go any further in this to cut down his further thoughts. I told him of some urgent business that needed no further elaboration to go through right now.

They brought the stone and placed it in the centre of the Ruler's palace. That stone was one metre high. It had an inscription similar to a will in Arabic. Someone had placed cold water as a charitable donation for worshippers in the mosques of the area, provided they read *Surat Alfatiha* and some verses from the holy Quran for the soul of his parents.

The Ruler had the true intention of preserving the history of his country and confirming its Arab identity. He tried to document its civilisation and bring it out in the best possible image. He preferred to spend strenuous efforts for that noble target. Through all that, I was certain that luck comes only suddenly. I insisted on reminding him of the necessity of visiting the foundling in his jail, in order to obtain his assistance outside the prison even for a short period.

"Your Highness, I would like to see the *malqut* in his jail and obtain some information about the area where the antique stone was found; perhaps there may be some stones and other relics that maybe useful for documenting the civilisation of Dilmunia."

"The guard shall take you to the jail of the foundling. He shall be released for a limited time, provided you can guarantee his return next Friday evening, where I shall be at Dilmunia mosque for the Friday Prayers. I hope the *malqut* will return to his prison while I return to my palace. One of the palace guards can be your escort."

I quickly agreed, and the escort brought in the *malqut* as if he were expecting this all. He stood kneeling in front of the Ruler.

"How did you find your colleague, Yusef?"

"He is a quiet man, amiable, but his health condition is deteriorating and may end his life. His health condition is not encouraging."

I said, "But your sentiments, Your Highness, are clear to your subjects. This indicates the extent of his sense of responsibility that all can bear witness to."

The *malqut* added, "Yes, as you have moved Yusef from his prison two days ago, to a more comfortable and cleaner prison. Now, you are allowing a temporary release for me from prison. Thank God and to you as much as the heavens are big."

The Ruler rose, shaking in his *majlis*.

"I did not allow Yusef to leave his prison; his term of imprisonment has not expired yet."

The Servant interpolated while listening with malice to the tense conversation at the Ruler's palace. I realised that treachery begins with an idea when he said, "The prisoner Yusef must have been forced to break away. He cannot be alone by himself or walk right; how could he open the doors of the jail and break the locks and climb walls and run? I said this several times, that Yusef is nothing but an instrument used by the opposition to exert pressure on the existing system. He no doubt represents them from his prison. I do not rule out that this *laqit* is nothing but hired, like him, so he can make him break away. He should not be transferred from his isolated confinement. He is a murderer and a dangerous criminal."

The Servant's speech found an echo in the heart of the Ruler, who stumbled back four steps. He felt the throne behind him. He was assured and threw himself in it. He shouted to his guards in a hoarse sound like thunder.

"Take back *almaqut* to his jail immediately. I want to

287

know who ordered the removal of Yusef to another prison. Find out. Bring them both to me before the end of next Friday's prayer."

I preferred to stay away and accept the Ruler's sudden decision. I thought I had knocked the light side of his heart, and with it matters would be facilitated. However, as it is said, if people knew what was in the heart of others, they would only shake hands with swords. It is back to the shocking truth. Man has no control of his fate. He is a blend of deterrents and encouragements. Do not discuss matters with someone furious; results could be fatal then.

The foundling was sent back to his prison. The Servant's eyes smiled with a shake of his head as an expression of a winning round. The guard assigned to help me carried the stone on his donkey. We left the Ruler's *majlis*, thinking of the state of utmost emergency for the search of the criminal agent, Yusef. This is what became of the man.

I headed to Abu Rashed's *majlis* in the evening. As usual, the man received me with a smiling face. Beauty is a half-wish and the other half is determination. He availed his *majlis* for three visitors: the stone, the guard and me. He read sadness on my face. I had no need to tell him about my feelings whenever a matter popped up. He went on in detail, giving me no opportunity to speak up. He informed me that there was a person waiting for me with Khowla inside the house, anxiously awaiting my return. I said, "Is it Yusef's wife waiting for me inside?"

"Yes."

I was more certain that a helping hand doing well should find who will aid it and facilitate life for it. Then self-satisfaction and love for charity generates happiness. We can be happy with our determination, not stopping at the blunders of others to create hills difficult to mount. He who has a pure soul can interpret slips of others as a bad work for a good intention. Then we can forgive those who err and throw goodness in their hearts.

Khowla entered the *majlis* with a shining face, reflecting her purity. She was leading Yusef's wife, holding her by her left wrist. The woman, in her forties, seemed ageing, with her beauty leaving her, despite her. Long years had fatigued her with her agonies. Long wrinkles covered her oval face. Her upper jaw obtruded due to her paleness. Her back was arched; her leanness transformed her into more of a scarecrow. Khowla greeted all who welcomed her in return.

"This is Yusef's wife. She hopes that his jail term shall not be identical to that of Yusef the Prophet, so he will not be away from his family for forty years. She came with the hope of finding her husband. She saw you during the visit to the Ruler; she stayed awake all night in agony for his absence and the impact on her children. She hopes to find good news from you to bring life to them."

The woman spoke blurredly and confusedly. Her words came out contradicting and expressing unconnected ideas.

"Yusef is sick. I visited the Merchant. Where is the Ruler? Four children, how…"

I found in her crossed words what she meant; she was asking about her sick husband.

"Yusef, and your concern about your children; then you mentioned the Merchant…"

"Yes. Two days ago, I visited the Merchant, begging clemency on our family. He was furious and threatened to punish him harshly. He said he had undisputed evidence that he was the murderer of Nasser and that he is plotting to overthrow the system of government."

Despite the cruelty of the news that was reported by her husband, I was optimistic and hoped for the best. I went to Abu Rashed.

"Did I not tell you that beauty reforms itself and that darkness leads to light? Good will leads to success. The puzzle of Yusef's disappearance solves itself. I have just come from the Ruler's palace by a prearranged visit. I was supposed to meet Yusef in his jail to be reassured about his health and request visits for his family. The catastrophe came when we discovered that Yusef left his jail without the knowledge of the Ruler."

"This explains the obscure truth that there are hidden hands operating under the umbrella of the Ruler, using his confidence without his knowledge. They are waiting for the moment to attain their objectives and interests."

"If what you say is true, it is the mother of all catastrophes. The state is like a boat at sea. No two skippers or more can sail a boat; it will be tragic if there were someone using his influence without the Ruler's knowledge."

Khowla clearly expressed her view.

"If you knew, that would be a catastrophe, but if you did not, the catastrophe would be greater."

I told them that the Merchant was accused of kidnapping Yusef from his prison, and that the guards and the police were working day and night to find his whereabouts. "Do not worry; Yusef is under the mercy of all vigil eyes. Now we must prepare for the sermon of next Friday prayers. It is going to be a turning point for future life."

Khowla opined, "If the next steps are linked to religion, it will have major or fatal consequences. Religion has bearing on the heart of man. Even he who has no faith implores a deity that he ignores when he is in trouble."

Abu Rashed was enthusiastic about going to Friday Imam to discuss with him explaining the general concept of the foundling, the suspected, and the son of fornication, and what were their rights. What were their civil duties? The Imam should be convinced to deal with this issue in his sermon. It was a difficult task. Khowla listened and added:

"Determination to do good eases tasks and solves problems before tackling them. With determination, we exalt man, which is a shame to value him at any price."

We headed to the Imam on his farm after the evening prayers. He received us with open arms and a smiling face. A good omen and a signal of good hope. He ushered us to his *majlis*. He did not even ask us about the nature of the issue intended for discussion. He knew that there was something about the visit. In all tactfulness, it is better to let your guest say whatever he wants. I felt then that I should leave the *majlis* and wait outside to save embarrassment. Abu Rashed glanced from the corner of his eye and took over the task.

I waited outside the *majlis*, moving between palm trees and listening to sounds of insects and animals that keep quiet the moment they feel a movement. Another indication that it is necessary that there is a reaction for any action; some acts disappear because there is no reaction to it. Should the Imam talk about *Al Malqout* on Friday?

Abu Rashed came out with an equal feeling and facial expression. It was difficult for him. I had to guess about how the meeting ended. He was silent to the degree of making insects and animals speak up; however, I recalled that some acts hide behind the magic of silence. We walked towards his house, listening to nothing but our footsteps.

Time was running very quickly until we reached midnight. An idea suddenly occurred to me. I put on my jacket. As usual, Abu Rashed nodded and said, "It is necessary that *almalqut* should be released, even for one day."

I headed towards the nearest tower of carrier pigeons. I sent a message hoping it would get to the palace of the Ruler.

"Your Highness, Yusef is at the Merchant's prison. I badly need *almalqut* just for one day. I shall be most grateful as long as I live. Adam."

(18) Khowla
May 1765

Abu Rashed came looking for me, calling with a soft, gentle voice, "Khowla, Khowla." At the time I was, as usual, helping my mother in the kitchen. He came with open- armed greetings. We stood up in appreciation for his advent. He held me by my wrist, saying to my mother, "I need to have a word with Khowla."

I read content and a smile on my mother's face. He asked me to put on my shawl and accompany him on to the Beach Road. After passing through lanes, we took the road adjacent to a little stream called al-saab. We walked along one of its banks that flowed into the sea. The sunrays were not burning; that is why we decided to keep away from the shade of the trees. We walked on the soft sand next to the running water. He was talking about public matters that Dilmunia lives on, but I was expecting what was behind that.

We reached the sea and my father took the left side of the shore towards the south. We came closer to one of the fishing boats moored on the shallow waters, anchored for fear of drifting away. We moved to the derelict wooden boat where my father helped me sit on board. He boarded from the other side, facing me.

"Khowla, my daughter. The boat, Khowla, is similar to a human being in its natural life cycle. It is built on land, which is similar to the bosom of the mother, and when it is carefully built and able to cope with life and be able to float, it is launched onto the sea. Man, in his life cycle, does not differ much from the boat. He is brought up by a family on land on solid soil. When he is fully built, he is thrown into the sea of life. Man is weaned twice: the first time when his mother stopped wet-nursing him; then his father weans him after few years."

"How can a father wean his son, Father?"

"He weans him by throwing him in the wide sea, in life where he can depend on himself."

"Father, do you want to throw me in the sea of life? To wean me, marry me off, for example?"

"What a natural intuition! This is the nature of life."

Abu Rashed then spoke about his life experience and how he was prepared by the Doyen to fight the war of life. It was a long period of preparation. Good up-bringing has an impact on children. I shyly started looking at the bottom of the boat. He placed his hand under my chin and raised my head. He told me to look at the wide horizon of the sea, to the future and life. I became eager to know the man who convinced my father.

He said, "He is definitely not the Merchant."

I asked by hand gesture, "…?"

"He is the traveller, the young Adam."

I turned aside, away from the face of Abu Rashed, towards the horizon that became unusually closer. I found the line separating the sea and the sky so close. I recalled that abominable incident. My father wiped my head.

"Take your time in making a life decision for you. Your mother and I can help and explain some matters that you may miss."

The conversation did not last longer than that, so we

returned quickly. We took the same route and that became too short. Moments later, we were at the door of the house.

"My daughter, take your time. I shall listen to you when you ask."

I asked for permission to meet Adam in a short dialogue, a dialogue similar to that of previous ones. That was not the custom and tradition of Dilmunia, but I wanted to know his real sentiments and some other delicate matters. My father agreed that I visit him in his *majlis* the next evening, away from the treatment task. The taste of life had completely changed since that moment; I found it really different. As if I have grown up two decades. My silence increased and so did my seclusion, adding to my bewilderment and shock. My mother talked to me about the same issue. I repeated my desire to meet Adam. I went to the *majlis*; knocked on the door. The answer came after a while.

"Who is it?"

"Khowla."

The response was delayed for moments; I thought he was sitting right and fixing his attire before he allowed me to enter. I thought he would stand and welcome me. He remained in a corner in the *majlis*, immersed in his thoughts before raising his eyes. He invited me to sit on his right and then continued in his thoughts. He said, "I was thinking of spending some nights all by myself, but I do not know where to find that."

"I suggest you go to one of the remote orchards for few hours or nights. You shall find what you are looking for. The eye of love beautifies creatures."

I knew he was still looking for himself. He was hoping to be liberated from his fetters. He who feels the beauty of nature and its creativity, his human spirit is not subjected to the traditions; his being can never imprison him. When he recalled that satanic incident between us, I found in him insistence on recovery from that miserable moment, from that black scene. I found a new human being created inside him. The creative is he who is not frozen in his tragedy but he who extracts happiness and the bright side. I said, "Why do you want to be all alone? Are you in love?"

Without looking at me he said, "True love, Khowla, represents the renewable vitality of man, opens your humanity and speaks to your mind before your heart; it is represented by purity, where man lives his humanity to its full. A love that pushes you to open on the universe without touching the instinct. The woman you truly love is not a creature that intuits sex only. Love is to read a woman as a novel and write it as a tale; love pushes you to be by yourself and by others, it may push you to think in the infinity and nowhere. This love pushes you to achieve your single and social aspirations; it pushes you to confront the death of life."

Meeting Adam was an advanced step in my life. I used to breathe knowledge from my grandfather's manuscripts and my father's readings, added to this my knowledge of the Quran and its oral interpretations. I learnt reading at the traditional schools, or *katatib*. He who does not read, cannot see life. However, the kind of knowledge I saw at Adam's was different in sources and origins. Man is a container you fill and taste its liquid. At his hour of serenity and hallucination, he talked about Christians, Jews, Mandanians, Muslims and others; several discrepancies became apparent to him. He told me once in the context of his speech about Christians who believe in the tenet of coerciveness and their choices, explaining, paradoxically, the principle of choice that he found among

Muslims, then he found its restriction here with the theory of God and the divine text.

A man who stopped at green lands, oasis and deserts, talked to me several times about its inhabitants, about the tragedy of distance between theory and practice, about man's ideas and how these are not the fruit of his mind only. It is a fruit influenced by society. He also said in the context of comparative religion that humanity did not have an idea about the unity of the deity as the Greeks and Romans had; the Arabs had three hundred and sixty-five idols, which is proof that not all who came later took from the earlier.

In his elaborations, he also mentioned that social environment begins with the family, then the society where he is influenced by his behaviour. He cited an example of the natural environment and its effect on humans. He said that man who lives in the desert differs from he who lives in green areas. He met a Bedouin and asked him about his name; he said it was Jazi' (Afraid) bin Thalim (Unfair) bin Ghawi (Misleading). This was his name that came as a result. He used to talk about idioms that we do not know and expected to be used. He mentioned the ancient Arab proverb, the hair denotes the male camel, and lots of injustice that led to explosion. Then he explained the philosophical dimension of the proverbs.

About the wonders of the human race, he said, "In Persia, I found three levels or classes of people: the class of slaves; the class of writers and thinkers and the class of princes and clergy. They placed a way and tradition like obligatory law in life. Nobody from the lower class had the right to study and learn to move into another class. This came parallel to a line found in the ancient Roman society: the class of women and slaves was of inferior, modest intellect and should be kept at a distance from leading and noble classes. Various societies may be geographically apart, but they are liable to easily accepted intellectual marriage."

Adam's experiences made me fall in love with him. The most beautiful type of love is that experimentally set on woman's beginnings and man's ending. In his hallucinations, Adam was representing a documented history of some of the world's civilisations. That is why many admired him. He was reading the past and the present and deducing future reality. That discussion aroused me to ask him, "Do you expect changes in the constituents of this western society of yours?"

"Did not the Arabs say, Khowla, that the hair indicates the male camel? There are introductions indicating future change."

"What could change or happen?"

"Societies based on class and distinction between humans are living an infinite crisis; those classes that discriminate between people based on race, religion and sect make of the situation a time bomb. I expect those oppressed classes to revolt against the ruling minority that has full control of everything in its countries. This situation applies to many societies. Ruling systems must realise that ability to comprehend the meaning of change. They must realise that strengthening similarities is better than searching for differences. The Ruler is not a divine representative, like messengers; he is human, placed for the service of his people. He who does not believe in the end of oppression does not believe in the justice of the heavens."

I was listening to him with all my senses. I learnt that the art of listening is more effective than oration and stalking. I realised that he felt that his words touched and shook me. With the passage of time that changed into mutual admiration. Neither of us had the ability to reveal, but I comprehended it with my heart and felt it. Perhaps that was the reason why he asked me to marry him. Could this man really be my fate?

After that fiery meeting with Adam, I asked to meet my father the next evening. My mother prepared the setting for that meeting. I had the same target that Adam held in his heart; then I spoke.

"Father, I accept Adam as a husband for me, after he has listened to my conditions and is able to meet them."

"Changing love relations could be aborted, Khowla; we must love the other as he is. What are these conditions?"

"I shall not mention these unless Adam proposes to me directly; I must talk to him, in your presence, face to face."

One evening later, my father invited me to see Adam in the *majlis*. He was sitting in his corner. He stood up and came forward in our direction when he heard my father producing a sound announcing our arrival. He approached us with his head lowered. The man seemed really different. His body was full. He turned his head, becoming more shining. I glanced at its modesty and kindness. My father asked us to sit down, and said, "My daughter, Adam is asking your hand in marriage; what do you say?"

"I wish Adam to forgive me in advance and to remind him of the fear we live in, in Dilmunia. Events occurred quickly with conflicting worries of life here and there. There are social shake-ups storming us. There are demands for the right to live and self-determination. There are hurdles for improving social conditions and abolishing discrimination between classes. There is a wish to clean up prisons and reform the system of government and living conditions of the poor class. In the midst of all this, Adam wants to hold marriage ceremonies."

"What has your marriage to do with the events in Dilmunia? Should we stop the wheel of life until we attend to all reforms?"

"It is not all that, Father. We still have the wish and ability to reform. I agree to marrying Adam after he meets four conditions for me."

"What are these four conditions?"

"I shall tell you each condition separately; if the previous is met, I shall tell you the next one."

"What is your first condition?"

"You know that I am Khowla, daughter of Abu Rashed, and you know my grandfather, the Doyen of Al Aljubur. He is one of the prominent personalities in Dilmunia; everyone knows that. If you are asking my hand in marriage, you must invite the men of Dilmunia for this occasion. Proclamation of the marriage should be at the same level as she you are going to wed, Adam."

"And what is your second condition?"

"I shall tell you when the first condition is met. Our meeting shall be next Friday or later."

My father nodded in consent and I left his *majlis*, with the voice of the female talking to me.

"She who gives in to the desires of a man for his satisfaction gets angry with herself."

(19) *The Foundling*
Mid-June 1765

I was really shocked when the prison warden came with a sudden order from the Ruler. The matter was quite clear with no ambivalence, a planned order. The instructions had to be carried out in full.

"His Highness orders you to leave the prison and proceed to Abu Rashed's house where Adam, the Danish traveller, is waiting for you. One of our guards shall escort you. You must be up to the nobility of the situation and appreciate the responsibility. You will have to return at the end of your assignment with Adam. You should not create problems or try to escape. That will harm Adam himself, as he shall be thrown into prison instead of you. That was his guarantee for releasing you for two days. You shall be on an official mission and return to prison, escorted by the same guard, on Friday evening."

The message was quite clear with its instructions that roused lots of fear. I did not know the latest development that made life turn upside down with such decisions. If the matter was related to Adam and his friend, then a solution was at hand. It was coming from God, whom we see as we see ourselves. My right hand was cuffed to the guard's left hand. We left, mounting two mules, to Abu Rashed's house. The scene was exceptional; it roused the curiosity of passers-by more than seated ones. Some of them came asking out of natural human inquisitiveness about this unusual scene.

As the guard knocked at the door, the voice of Abu Rashed came behind it. "Welcome, *Almalqut*." How did he know I was at the door? How and why did he expect me? As if everything was facile and blessed, and a hand was pulling the strings of life. The two men received me welcomingly at the *majlis*. They told me about the moral responsibility. "We do not expect you to run away; we trust your honesty. You are a man on a human mission that you would benefit from." I asked, "How?"

Abu Rashed said:

"Let it be known, man, that he who conceals evil in his heart may be touched by the flame of its treason, and he who conceals goodwill shall benefit from its goodness. Matter may be precipitated, or it may be delayed; however, fate is inevitable. Fate that urges us to do well makes religion mature and beautiful. We would like to ask the guard who took the trouble of escorting you to release you and untie your cuffs, and ask him to leave you alone to the open space of Dilmunia mosque to enjoy the Friday sermon and prayers. Stay unnoticed and masked so no one can recognise you."

The two men left me no room for manoeuvring, as if they were commanding angels and all the rest should obey them. That night I closed my eyes but stayed awake. On the designated Friday morning, I left early before anyone was up. I left masked and disguised, closely following the instructions. I went to the mosque by winding roads, getting closer to the edges of Albajwiya village, which is an area that abounds with date palm tree groves. I followed the route of one of the streams until I reached the mosque courtyard from the northern side, where some worshippers passed through to go to the mosque or to flock on the south yard to conduct business in the open air.

A beautiful idea that achieves the goal crossed my mind, in which I would be out of sight soon to hear the sermon. I climbed up one of the scattered almond trees, and lay down among its upper branches. It was set in the form of the symbol five (V). The place above the branches was prepared for lying down and sleeping as well. There I listened to the sermon and joined the worshippers after the first kneel, where they could not turn or talk.

I noticed an unusual movement hovering around the tree. The Ruler's guards arrived; I could recognise them from their faces and attire. I eavesdropped on their chief giving instructions.

"The Ruler shall disguise himself as beggar and lie here under the shadow of this tree. We shall secure the place and watch at a distance without being noticed."

"What does the Ruler want from this scene?"

I heard murmurs and other questions, until I knew that he wanted to inspect the condition of his subjects and listen to the Imam without his knowledge, so he could speak freely. He wanted to be closer to the needy and poor. I heard Adam say to him once, "An official with a sense of responsibility is he who moves around in society to examine negative and positive aspects of life. You must be active to know the spirit of life, to read your society with its challenges and changes. Then the stage of challenge begins, the stage of change of quantitative transfer."

"It is a human gesture on the part the Ruler."

After preparing the location, the guards vacated their places and went away. The Ruler then arrived incognito in the attire of a pauper. He sat on the ground prepared for him and leaned on the trunk of the same tree. I saw him adjusting his mask and clothes. I had some thoughts, perhaps satanic: the Ruler, without retinue and guards, was just a human being no different from any other man. Only God could distinguish us by piety.

If I jumped over this relaxed man and strangled him by my own hands, would I put an end to all our problems? Would the curtain not fall on the drama of the so-called opposition to the rule of the despot and his loyal subjects? Would it not be possible to put an end to all injustices inflicted upon all divers, farmers, fishermen and others? Would not his death empty and clean prisons? However, there were counter-questions that forcibly imposed their views: would the killing of the Ruler and his departure put the country in the eye of the storm and render it a lawless country, where the rule would be for the powerful? Is not the powerful he who has the power of finance? Would the vacuum of power be more beneficial than the injustice of the Ruler? Then, power would end in the hands of the influentially corrupt, if there was a loophole in the system. The dual wish in reform and change was bound to initiate a quantum leap. I became torn between two fires: cease the opportunity or accept the fate of God who will decide what will be. I recalled Abu Rashed when he said, "The Prophet, PBH, was so kind and loving with his worst enemies. By love, he was strong. Tolerance is stronger than violence."

It was only few minutes when the sound for prayers woke me up. The movement of worshippers gradually increased. They came from all directions to occupy the shaded area, then covered the unshaded one. The Imam went up the pulpit that was placed in the cavity of the minaret. There, the sound was contained before it erupted through the ventilation outlets where it was amplified towards the sky. He began his sermon by thanking God, and then focused in his speech on two issues. The first was financial and administrative corruption; the second was the phenomenon of widespread prisons.

"In the name of God, the Merciful, the Compassionate, dear Believers, through our moral commitment, it is worthy of us to learn lessons of past nations. It is not more appropriate for us to follow the example of the Prophets who only speak of what they do. You do not see contradictions between their words and their deeds. They represent responsible people who do not think about the absolute, and do not live in the hermitage of learning. He is a man of responsibility in college life.

"On this blessed Friday, we recall a stance of the Messenger of God, Yusef, PBH. It was reported that he had said to the pharaoh of Egypt, 'Make me in charge of the treasures of the land; I am all-knowing and honest.' Despite the fact that Yusef was a messenger, he did not second himself, but asked to be responsible for the treasury of Egypt, because he found himself competent to control the finances of the country and distribute it justly between the subjects.

"As a man he wanted to implement justice. He thought if it was given to someone else, it should be marred. He said about himself that he was a good keeper and knew well what to do; that is to say he was careful on public wealth and knew how to dispense it. His words were reflected in his actions. He began with himself. In the seven years of scarcity, Yusef refused to eat until satiety. He used to leave the food though he desired more. And when some of his close followers were surprised at his behaviour, he said, 'The ruler must empathise with others, even if he owns all the treasures of the whole world. He should not be self-opinionated, as bigots are fools.

A ruler who aims at justice should taste the hunger of the hungry and feel the misery of the miserable and be with the depraved.' That was the principle of Yusef when he accepted his commission in Egypt. We have a good example of the Prophets and Messengers of God.

"Dear Believers, there is another issue worth mentioning and paying attention to due to its importance. The youth of Yusef was unjustly wasted in the well and his prison, and his energy was wasted for forty years. The spread of prisons in our country became a cause exoterically good but esoterically bad. It was rightly or not rightly filled, until a poet said:

'A hand was fettered though some scarify themselves for it.

And another hand is kissed though it should be amputated
To claim innocence for despots is a humiliation
A meanness is committed by the justifier,
Someone is sanctified because he is related to a family
And someone is unjustly treated because he does not kneel.'

"Let us remember, dear brothers, that prison is a form of criminal punishment. Its aim is to punish the culprit and be a deterrent for future crime, so that it is not repeated to harm society and individuals. The noble aim of jail is to reform the prisoner and to prepare a solid ground for him to be a productive element in his environment. Nobody knows what is right except those who committed wrongs. Yusef, peace be upon him, was unjustly imprisoned. Moral values and human principles strongly object to send a prisoner of thought to jail. Freedom of thought is a human right and should be guaranteed to all. We would like to shed more light on jails. These are the graveyards for the living. Humanely speaking, no one should be placed under solitary confinement, even if he is a criminal, as this is considered as depriving him of his social freedom. We have no right to deprive him of his right to communicate with his familial and social environment. Cleaning prisons is a necessity to endow humanity with happiness. If jail has an advantage, it has something with testing friends and knowing rejoicing of enemies.

"Dear fellows. Jail may be materialistic or spiritual. The latter is not less dangerous than the materialistic jail. Man may be free in his movement but jailed in his society and this is a tragedy. When we decide to expel an individual from his society as a result committed by others, this is a double black injustice. In all societies there are sins; man is a sinner. All sinners are repentant. Man should not pay for the sins of others. A child should not be responsible for his parents' errors. His rights should be safeguarded."

I was listening to the Imam, relaxed on the branch of the tree, with my eyes focused on the disguised Ruler. At the time when I thought the sermon was addressed to me, I saw the Ruler talking to himself, as if what he heard was addressed to him too. I saw the talk about the jail was meant for me and described my case. I had no fault in what others committed. I was unjustly imprisoned and expelled from society. As for the Ruler, it seemed he was responsible for public wealth and corruption and jails. It was the same responsibility that the Prophet Yusef accepted. The only difference was that Yusef promised to sincerely apply his convictions. This Ruler, deep inside him, believed he was pure and white as snow. Light leads to benevolence, while the black side was imposed by his retinue. Between this and that, between difficulties and success, we are waiting for an openness.

(20) The Interpreter[10]
The Third Week of June 1765

According to the sincere desire and the conditions stipulated by Khowla on accepting to marry Adam and concurrent with his effective steps that he made with Abu Rashed for a way out of the tunnel of existing cases in Dilmunia, Adam met with the Ruler through natural channels. He came to know about the wish of the Ruler, who was very keen to know about minute details of the Dilmunia burials and their historical and mysterious contents.

For the first time, Adam went to the official *majlis* of the Ruler at the fort, located tens of metres to the south of the offices of the missionary in the north of the mainland. The fort consisted of four connected round towers, where training of the Ruler's local and expatriate police officers took place[11]. The Ruler made one of the rooms overlooking the sea on the north side a centre for running the business of the island and a meeting place for official receptions.

An arranged invitation to meet Adam took place there. The young man made detailed a presentation of the burials, explaining the design of the construction, its contents and

---

[10] I was unable to obtain a complete manuscript for translation or transmission of this chapter. It is the product of scattered snippets and conclusions in the same vein as previous events. (The Interpreter).

[11] The Fort was first built in 1750 AD by the ruler of Persia, Nader Shah.

finally its closing and filling it up. Then he went on to talk about flaring issues of destiny such as public debt, Yusef, the Puller, *Almalqut* and the firing incident, but all these were put aside.

The star of Khowla, who strongly imposed herself on Adam's thoughts, shone, and he started to praise her in the presence of the Ruler. Among those present at the Ruler's court were some important persons like the Merchant, the Judge Albalbul, the Servant Advisor and some *Noukhathas*, in addition to the major, the British political agent. Adam told the Ruler about his wish to have a private audience with him. The Ruler expected the talk would be about the investigation into the gun shooting, or the imprisonment of Yusef, the Puller. Therefore, he reluctantly gave him an audience.

"Your Highness, Dilmunia is a very tiny island in this universe; however, it is not different when it comes to its humanity. Like other nations, it has a natural human and class conflict. Some pull it towards the heavenly world of perfection, and others pull it towards the earthly world of meanness. The weak cling to the great values, and the powerful are ascribed the descriptions of despots, while the powerful show strength and knowledge for the welfare of all. It is the nature of life; but I, exceptionally, found on its soil the place that spreads happiness in the hearts. This island has begotten pure hearts and live conscience. For all this, Your Highness, I found on its soil the woman I would love to marry."

"The woman you wish to marry! It is said that the man wants the woman; then he desires her... Are...?"

The Ruler stood up and started moving in full circles around Adam. He began to look at him from a remote distance. He placed his hand on his beard as if trimming it. He recalled a situation.

"A few years ago, there was a Christian lady among the Missionary Agency. Her brother was helping her with medical and teaching. When the lady got closely acquainted with many Dilmunian women, she wanted her brother to marry one of them. Albalbul, the judge, explained that a Muslim woman cannot marry but a Muslim man. After all, Adam, let us summon Shaikh Albabul to know the opinion of *Sharia'* about the question you intend to ask. I think he has the ability to deduce judgements and change them according to public interest."

The Ruler called for Shaikh Albalbul, who came attired in a brown robe and a white turban. He was very tall and slim, with a long face and a thick white beard. The Ruler welcomed him and asked him to take a seat.

"Reverend Shaikh. Our guest, the traveller Adam, wants to marry one of the daughters of Dilmunia, and I gave my blessings to this marriage as long as it is within the bounds of the *Shara'*."

"The first principle of the Islamic Law is that a Muslim woman should not marry a man from the People of the Book; while on the other hand, a Muslim man may marry a woman from the People of the Book. However, as the Ruler gave his blessings to this marriage, then it is possible for a man from the People of the Book to marry a Muslim woman, according to the secondary principle that maintains the necessary individual and public interests."

That religious fact did not frustrate Adam. On the contrary, its details made him rejoice; he knew from experience and what was fixed in his mind that there is no problem without a solution beside it. A problem may be described as complicated, not in itself, but because we do not search for the key that takes us to that solution. Here was the Shaikh putting the right solution as he saw it. Adam asked the Shaikh, "Is the marriage of a Muslim woman to a man from the People of the Book considered a punishable sin?"

"God said, 'Allah forgiveth not (The sin of) joining other gods with Him; but He forgiveth whom He pleaseth other sins than this: one who joins other gods with Allah, Hath strayed far, far away' The Holy Quran can interpret itself in many instances. There is no doubt that the major sin that God Almighty does not forgive is polytheism."

The Ruler laughed and directed his attention to Adam and patted his shoulder.

"And who is this woman who stole your heart and made you decide to marry her? Do not you find yourself from a class different from others in Dilmunia?"

"There is a black person, a coloured person, and a blond person. The same theory describes the blond mainly, while the other is a metaphor for the coloured one

While the scientific explanation insists on unity of origin, the cells of the brain are all the same; the differences are acquired by the environment and education. For all this, and away from all theories, I found some inspirations and some signals urging me to get married in Dilmunia."

"Inspiration is an adjusted intuition; sometimes it lies. Who is she?"

"Khowla, the daughter of Abu Rashed, granddaughter of the Doyen of Aljubur."

The Ruler moved to the throne as if he were shocked.

"Do not forget that signals of love are deceptive."

"Do not forget that the woman is the greatest creation; I

hope to be honoured by the Ruler and the Chief Justice to be present when I propose to the daughter of Abu Rashed next Friday evening."

The Ruler apologised for not being able to attend due to prior engagements on that Friday; instead, he promised to delegate one member from the Appointed Council and Shaikh Abalbul as his representatives. Adam excused himself from the Ruler and invited the *Nukhatha* and the *Tawwash*, who both gladly accepted the invitation. As for his servant friend, who with time became an advisor; He understood the reasons for the ruler's refusal and the effect of staying next to him.

The promised Friday arrived, and Khowla's first condition was met. The elders of society met Abu Rashed in his *majlis*. Shaikh Albalbul was the first to speak, reciting a verse from the Holy Quran saying, "God said: 'And among His signs is that He created from among yourself spouses that you may find repose in them, and He has put between you affection and mercy.'"

The Judge Shaikh showed enthusiasm when he found Adam to be weltering about the interpretation of the *Aya*. He explained that creation is of two kinds: the simple creation, that is the first creation, and the compound creation, that is transformation. It is said that God created Eve from dust as He created Adam not from his rib. That is to say that the soul is one in creation and origin. He made the human soul marry from its own kind so they may find repose in each other. God assigned man to settle on earth…" According to the wish of the Ruler and Adam, I hereby come forward asking the hand of your daughter in marriage with the guest of Dilmunia, the traveller, Adam."

Then, all talked about a lot of public affairs, among which

was the legality of the marriage. Abu Rashed expressed his initial agreement; however, unlike the social norm in society, said that absolute freedom of decision lay with his daughter. He knew she was able to solve the legal problem of marriage with a member of the People of the Book in her own way, in accordance with the confidence and knowledge deep-rooted in her mind and heart,

The meeting ended after nearly one hour, while Adam remained at the *Majlis*. Abu Rashed went in to tell Khowla about the details of what had happened.

"Last week, Adam extended an invitation to senior notables in Dilmunia to attend the ritual of proposing to you. A member of the Appointed Council representing the Ruler, some *Nukhathas*, Tawwash and some clergy asked me if you would agree or not."

Khowla asked to go in to the *Majlis* to see Adam, and gratifyingly, "The first condition is met, and the notables of Dilmunia to our place, are you still on your wish and love?"

"He who has no eyes of a crazy man will never love."

"I know that the woman is a repulsive female, Adam, but you know the size of tragedies Dilmunia is going through. Discord and disorder are continuing with some supporting and others protesting. Victims are imprisoned. Problems of divers and farmers and others are looking for radical solutions to spread security and peace in the hearts of all citizens."

"Adam, you have with the help of good people to throw love and goodwill in the hearts of others. When matters stabilise and their affairs are rectified, we shall be at the doors of joy. Now we cannot get married and play the harp of happiness unless all people share with us our happiness. Then we can help people get rid of their grievance; then only we can play the tune of happiness for life. The second condition lies in the ability of eliminating injustice from the backs of the Dilmunians."

Adam was not surprised at Khowla's demands, but was more attached to her as he shared her and her father's human care and responsibility. She had a sacred objective. He expressed his readiness and accepted the challenge, believing in the nobleness of the aim and his ability to attain success.

Khowla greeted him on leaving and said, "Then only I shall tell you the third and fourth conditions."

(21) Adam
The First Week of July 1765

The Ruler summoned me to the fort, his official headquarters. I had got used to the corridors of the huge citadel as it was my second visit. As usual, I asked Abu Rashed to accompany me. The guards let us into the Ruler's quarters after a routine check, then asked us to wait in the waiting hall until the arrival of other invitees taking part in the meeting. Minutes later, members of the Appointed Council arrived, headed by the Merchant, who did not greet us, even out of courtesy. The Political Agent was among the attendees. We were then asked to proceed to the meeting room, and when all were there and each one of us took his seat in the place previously arranged, the Ruler arrived with his private bodyguard behind him. Unlike the Merchant, a smile was carefully drawn on his face. All rose out of respect and appreciation at his arrival. He took his seat and the Servant Advisor on his right, after greeting all, invited us to take our seats and said, "Honourable audience, the Appointed Council welcomes you all to this extraordinary session. We also welcome the British Political Agent, Adam, the traveller, and Abu Rashed, the representative of the divers and farmers. I am pleased to inform you, on this happy occasion, about the decision of the command of Hormuz Island and the leaders of the two powers, the British and Persians there, about exempting Dilmunia from sending some of its men to serve under the command of the army of Hormuz.

The agent who was present with us here, said that Great Britain wishes in parallel to that, that we find a political solution to take the island out from its crisis, and to deal with the schism of its components, and satisfy all and have goodwill and stability prevail. After a lengthy discussion with the agent and the special adviser to the Ruler, we are happy to inform you about our future expectations, and we allow the honourable audience to have the power to make proposals and reservations for the benefit of Dilmunia."

Afterwards, the Ruler expressed a true desire and away from the devious ways, and with the principle of transparency. He wished first to put an end to the financial crisis; the crisis that ruins man wherever he is. He officially appointed the Judge Albalbul as head of the Public Debt Tribune. He also ordered the cancellation of the Pearl Dicing Court, where judges used to take the side of the financing *Nukhetha*. He stipulated, that debts of the divers should be registered in the presence of three divers as witnesses, and that debt settlement be through the court and in the presence of all witnesses so that divers would not dive with their debts and sell their possessions of farms and private acquisitions. He also issued an edict by which half of the debts were to be eliminated and the debt would be automatically written off at the time of death of the sailors. The law also annulled the transfer of the debt from the divers onto their children. These historic decisions were to be declared prior to the next Friday prayers.

Abu Rashed asked to be permitted to propose that the Ruler order the cleaning up of prisons and proclaim an amnesty general, and that Yusef be the first to be set free, as he was the longest serving prisoner without a truly fair trial. He also expressed his wish that the system of *salafia* be replaced by the one fifth system, whereby profits would be distributed on a one fifth basis and the Merchant received one fifth only. It was unfair that the *nukhetha* gave loans of sugar and rice in return for what they gained from diving, especially that the divers gained in fact more than their debt and remained slaves forever to their creditors.

The Servant Advisor suggested that next Saturday be proclaimed a public holiday and a national day commemorating this happy occasion, where food would be served in public and meals would be offered in appreciation to the Ruler for adopting this gigantic event. I did not want to tell him that love of events was hypocrisy, but I read what was beyond that. So I wished him a pleasant stay with the ruler, where he finds his ultimate paradise.

It was the Political Agent's turn. He conveyed the greetings of the British government and expressed its desire to move some of its naval vessels to be stationed at Mina' Aldar on the east coast of Dilmunia. That port would be a base to ensure the growing passage of boats of the British East India Company. He wanted battleships to be a fortified shield against threats to the security and stability of Great Britain, according to the desire of the British monarch, who was proud of the consequences of the golden seventeenth century. That historical epoch that led Britain to be set free from the hegemony of the Church to inherit world dominance from the Arabs and Ottomans, and led a literary and artistic renaissance after the old age of the Moguls and Turks through the giant enterprise of the British East India Company. Later he praised the effective steps taken by the Ruler, and expressed his happiness at the presence of Abu Rashed and he explained that modern nationalism is accompanied by opposition. As an inseparable phenomenon and a necessity for the correction of the tribal system of government.

After that, the judge spoke and expressed his readiness to hold sessions of the court in accordance with the future vision of the Ruler. He said he was content about the awareness of the discussants and their knowledge of the difference between discussing and arguing. Then, he swore in the presence of the Ruler to follow *sharia'* cases in deducing judgements on various cases and to brief the Ruler on the process of justice whenever he wanted.

The meeting came to an end and all lined up behind the Merchant to greet His Highness, the Ruler and bless that historic move. Some kissed the Ruler on his forehead, others on his shoulder or his right hand, but Abu Rashed and I and the Political A only shook hands, blessed his steps, then wished Dilmunia all the best.

The meeting was over and Khowla returned, leaping between my mind and heart. I held Abu Rashed by his left wrist. He asked me, "What is wrong with you, man?"

"You always repeat, 'According to your intentions, you are given.' I thought I should not meet Khowla's second condition due to its greatness and complexity. Here is the heaven shaking my hands me and bringing the answer to the second condition without realising it. I hope to see Khowla this evening to tell her about the Ruler's decisions and ask her about her third condition."

As usual, Abu Rashed did not answer my question except by shaking his shoulders and the look in his eyes; then he prayed to God to bless our moves. In the evening, I went and asked to see Khowla, who entered the *majlis* and greeted me. I told her, "The second condition is met, Khowla; the Ruler promised to whiten the jails and wrote off some of the debts, and start a reformed age to build the future of Dilmunia and take her in the direction of the sun, on the road to development and happiness."

"How did it all happen with such speed?"

"That was the outcome of the meeting held at the fort."

Khowla was adorned by her shyness and then showed a suppressed joy and said, "According to that pledge that we hope will come true, the third condition shall be easier, Adam."

"What is it?"

"You have to bring your family to propose to me. My children shall carry the name of your family, and I shall live in their midst. They have the right to know where you will put your semen, and how your children will be brought up."

Khowla was unique; she grew and was elated in my eyes when she announced one of the conditions. The woman who contemplates the end bestows happiness of the beginnings and joy of continuity. I confirmed my initial acceptance and added that I would work hard to close the Dilmunia files and then head to Copenhagen, but she said, "Keeping away is the vexation of love, Adam. Distances may lead you to search for other women."

"Is it not insanity to ignore true love and search for an unknown one?"

Two days after the fort meeting, after the Merchant sensed the inclination of the Ruler to come out of the crisis and come to terms with the whole people, he proclaimed his wish to help out of true patriotic responsibility. He expressed his dire wish to stand against injustice inflicted on the needy classes. He offered the divers and the farmers to buy all their debts and settle them all. To pay all their debts they would have to work for him the next season only. He also offered to buy the whole crop from all *Nukhethas* and resell it to Indian traders. He mentioned that these Indians were skilled artisans and made pearl necklaces to sell at double prices in world markets. Then, he promised to import goods and distribute them in local markets at low prices after paying taxes at ten per cent to the Ruler, bearing that only by him. The Merchant convinced all by his plan that placed the ideal solution in the hand of the people and uplifted the economy of Dilmunia.

The people liked the Merchant's promises and his idea of eliminating the debts, more than the Ruler's idea of writing off only fifty per cent of the debt. The *Nukhethas* and followers of the Merchant worked hard to fix the idea in the mind of the people by getting rid of the debt for good instead of retaining only half of it. Joy spread and optimism increased between the people, as they had two choices bringing the whole prosperity to them.

The promised Saturday arrived and large crowds of divers and farmers gathered at the new court of justice. They expressed their wish to write off the whole debt parallel to the generous offer by the Merchant, but the judge refused that and upheld the decree issued by the Ruler. This led to the rise of another crisis amid the heated race of apparent goodness between the Ruler and the Merchant.

I found that these measures taken by the Merchant were in fact a stark challenge to the Ruler and his Council, while Abu Rashed was looking at the distant future when he said, "Dilmunia seemed like a pregnant woman with her embryo calcified in her womb and is waiting for a British midwife to find a suitable method to deliver her baby. The future is capable of separating just from the unjust."

Within this joyful atmosphere that Dilmunia had been enjoying for years, and on this happy occasion resulting from the fort meeting. The British Political Agent held a party the following Sunday evening at the British Agency the Political Agent held a reception the following Sunday at the British agency, attended by the Ruler and the members of the Appointed Council and leading dignitaries, as well as foreign communities. The only one absent was the Merchant on the pretext of not feeling well and being fatigued. The agent invited them to dinner at the Missionary Agency, ending it with a musical show similar to Christmas evenings. Just before the end of the event, some of the private guards of the Ruler came to the scene. They were worried and whispered in his ears. He went with them to a private room, then quickly returned, asking the audience to keep silence before speaking.

"Respected audience, we have just received confirmed news about a group of saboteurs connected to a foreign power. They looted shops and damaged dhows and went to detention centres and jails. They shot at guards, broke doors and smuggled prisoners. For this, we are declaring maximum alert to face these outlaws and present them to justice and reveal their relationship with foreign enemies."

A few days later, the arrest of the heads of the riots was announced and the type of bullet used and its similarity to the ones used in the shooting incident on Adam nearly a year ago. It was a licenced weapon belonging to the Merchant, which he claimed was stolen long time ago. The defendants were tried then flogged, twenty lashes after Friday Prayers and taken to prison to write Dilmunia a new page of its bloody history.

(22) The Interpreter
Mid-July 1765

The Ruler invited Adam and Abu Rashed for a consulting meeting at the fort, which became the centre for issuing important and vital decisions. He appeared to be willing to listen to the voice of the people of Dilmunia, and to be enlightened by Adam's view because of his long experience. The Ruler did not want to let the Merchant and members of the council know about that meeting because he was so certain of the existence of someone who reported the news of the fort and the palace in detail to the Merchant.

The two arrived and were warmly received by the Ruler at the tower and moved with to the meeting room, which was separated by a wooden divider from his private office. The Ruler, after welcoming them, spoke about the declared aim of that meeting.

"As you are aware, I have adopted a reform system for Dilmunia, to elevate its people and alleviate their suffering. As Adam has lots of experience that has polished his mentality, and as Abu Rashed is well read on previous experiments, I have invited them to this meeting; perhaps we can reach together to what we are hoping and aiming at. We do not want to delve into the darkness of the past; we must look at the light of the sun coming from the sky.

Abu Rashed said clarifying, "Before we go into the mechanism of Your Highness' programme of reform, we must get rid of ills of the past that led to discord among the people of Dilmunia. We must unify the people so all can work together."

"What are you trying to affirm?"

"Your Highness, you undoubtedly recall the tragedy of the problem of arbitration that documented the future of Dilmunia in detail, on the drawing of a palm tree and writing its pronunciation. I think it is a brand of shame in our history. How can an epoch of reformation include such an incident? He who brandishes an olive branch and spreads love between his people must establish its pillars. One of these is to help them acquire the right to education. As Adam mentioned, education in his country was the effective instrument of change and reformation. If the people here are unable to read, they are kept in darkness. They cannot communicate in the correct language that helps them maintain contacts. Education helps us preserve our scientific history; with our heritage we do not start from scratch. Many houses abound with enormous amounts of reference books and scientific resources."

Adam asked to take part in the discussion out of his love for all.

"In this context, I must recall a famous saying of one of the philosophers of the west. 'Education can make any people easy to lead, difficult to steer, easy to govern, but difficult to enslave.; I find this a correct dictum; therefore, I find it very important to transform the people of Dilmunia from the era of dominance of illiteracy to the era of enlightenment. We must eliminate the hurdles to education. That shall be by your will, as one of the principles of your reform programme."

At that moment that witnessed a serious discussion and fruitful ideas, the Advisor to the Ruler, the servant of the travellers, knocked at the door, requesting permission to enter. The Ruler gave him permission without hesitation. He sat at the other end, facing the Ruler, who continued his speech. He explained that the question of arbitration was a past era, and then he said:

"The spread of love between people is liable to strengthen all human values. I see no harm to see all pass the illiteracy stage; then the individual shall be aware of his duties and rights. Nobody will be able to fiddle with debts of the divers and others because that individual realises the role of public auditing of the people. Theorists will not be able to spread their intellectual venoms in those minds."

He explained that sincere work for Dilmunia was centred on several topics, and that he would try with the help of sincere individuals to gradually climb that ladder that achieved prosperity for the people of Dilmunia. The advisor, or servant, was attentively listening and nodding as an expression of his satisfaction in front of the interlocutors.

Adam spoke again about what is known as epidemic of fatal illiteracy. He explained that some philosophical theories that survive only in illiterate society are looking for an ignorant soil to grow on. One of the philosophers, in his reference to the East, said that combatting these ideas could only be possible by education. Due to my travels, I found the broad difference between a rural society closed on itself and an active European world; between an Oriental illiterate world and a European educated world that is easy to deal with. That is one of the responsibilities that rulers should bear within the existing contract between the ruler and the ruled.

In another issue parallel to this, the Ruler mentioned that there was an inherited social contract, an unwritten contract between the Ruler and the people of Dilmunia. It was a contract based on providing the basic services of security and other requirements, in exchange for the people relinquishing their political rights and accepting an autocratic system of government that did not have a popular representation. Therefore, the failure of the Ruler weakened his legality, and he absolutely refused the description of the programme for change and reform as failure. He realised that there was an opposing opinion, and he realised also what Adam had mentioned, that the opposition accepted the dominant patriarchal system but demanded wider freedom of decision making.

The discussion between the Ruler and the two men in the presence of his advisor was endless, as they put off a candle, then another was lit. Adam spoke of reasons for change and the transformation that led to the rise of the Industrial Revolution in the West. He said, "It was the product of various causes, among which was the spread of theoretical philosophy, the presence of minorities that enriched society with various cultures and the continuous search for natural resources that feed the industrial sector."

The western society turned into an industrial society and forgot at the apex of its prosperity lots of human values. Therefore, it confirmed that disobeying the machine was permissible. That industrial revolution that upheld human theories and hollow slogans, an industrial revolution with its waste could feed all hungry Africans! A revolution that made the poor poorer and the rich richer. The age of the machine had the upper hand in solidifying the abominable class system. Then he turned to the Ruler. "Your Highness, if you want to know your value in the hearts of your lovers, take your whip and sword from their necks."

Abu Rashed looked at the Servant, adding to what Adam has just said.

"Islamic rituals are based on elimination of classes and bringing peoples together. Cannot you see that at pilgrimage and Friday Prayers and group prayers and other rites, all are equal and classless? These are the tasks waiting for the Ruler and his advisor in the Change and Reform Programme that he has adopted."

The Servant added in turn, "I think you had better suggest to the Ruler that he generously sets free Yusef, the Puller, accused of killing and attempting a coup d'état."

The Ruler wanted to end this prolonged discussion.

"At the end, I said I had confidence in your cooperation in achieving those great human values. However, I have a little request to make of you, Abu Rashed."

"Yes, Your Highness."

"As you are in the footsteps of your late father, may his soul rest in peace, you do not stop to teach whoever wants, and as you are holding your classes at your *majlis*, I would like you to give lessons to my three sons, provided this is done in private so that they can benefit more."

"Dear sir, Your Highness. Two women came to Ali bin Abi Taleb, asking for their stipend from the treasury of the Muslims. He gave them what they asked for. The first of them said she was Arab, while her colleague was non-Arab. Ali picked up a handful of earth and asked her if she found any difference between this and that. The woman said no. He said to her:

'You are all from Adam and Adam from dust.' Your Highness, how can you eliminate discrimination and sectarianism between the people? How can we spread love in their hearts, and you are professing class division? We must first get rid of theories and hollow slogans. We must start change first with ourselves."

The Ruler did not like what Abu Rashed had said.

"The Programem of Change and Reform is on and shall achieve all its goals. We cannot put all our eggs in one basket. Sons of the Ruler cannot meet with others in the same educational environment offering similar products."

(23) Khowla
Third Week of July 1765

Up till writing this, which came at the desire of Adam to document his travel and visit to Dilmunia, he did not finish his research and his objectives. He once said that studies in the humanities are endless, and that history is an eternal tail and an everlasting head. Possessing one side only loses the past and hinders the future. In his recommendations, he focused on various matters, among that documenting what goes on in the soil of Dilmunia, then preserving or exchanging those manuscripts that he hoped would be timeless, as there would come someone who would document our writings.

Adam mentioned that a true language is the language that conveys emotions and thoughts. That is why man is familiar with the race that speaks his own language. He mentioned that the language that does not make us feel this is considered untrue. He affirmed that it was the ideal method to transfer experiments between generations. Accordingly, it was necessary to document history to learn lessons from. As life is able to arrange you according to its priorities, he decided to cut his trip short and return home to bring his family and relatives to my engagement. He was full of desire and enthusiasm to achieve his declared objective that was spread in Dilmunia like a drop of ink in a running river.

I asked him if the love of desires was what moved him, the way it moves man and makes him lean to the other sex. He asked first to define desire and know the nature. To specify is to frame elastic concepts and define them. I elaborated.

"Desires are the pleasures of life and include women, children and funds."

"I, like all humans, love all that you mentioned. It is a divine order thrown in the heart of man, and man has no choice in what the heavens bestow. What man must realizs is that it is not by necessity that those desires are utilised for the love of the world alone. Then desire becomes an ultimate aim, and it controls him and dominates his behavior, while desires are ultimately legislated for the sake of rectifying the human behavior in its way to acquire these desires and enjoy them."

"Do you think that religion is a dire need for preserving the human race?"

"That is a dire need and absolute for organising life and worshipping the Creator. Many philosophers, theoreticians and politicians advocated the existence and its domination to the extent of authority, and that an unreligious society has no authoritative reference and is liable to extermination[12]."

Discussions with my father or Adam and the Doyen before them did not end except to begin another more exciting and interesting tale. It was rumoured that Adam expressed his desire to leave Dilmunia; this reached the Political Agent like lightening. It was announced that a reception in his honor would be held in few days' time. He also expressed his wish to hold a farewell reception in Adam's honor. Invitations were sent and the boisterous party was held at the fort; a number of

---

[12] He said later, the famous French leader Napoleon Bonaparte (1769–1821): If the papacy had not existed, I would have created it because it overcomes obstacles. (The Interpreter)

Dilmunia's notables were in attendance. Invitations were also extended to the public who were sympathetic and loved Adam, the man. After the party, the guests highly praised the honourable guest and his noble manners. Then, the Ruler presented him with his robe and a rosary, or beads, as a gratifying sentiment and honouring him for his fruitful efforts during the excavation on the burial mounds of Dilmunia. The Political Agent promised to arrange for a private boat to transport him to Shat Alarab in the northern Arabian Gulf and to be safely delivered to the Dutch Consul in Baghdad.

It was necessary for Adam to place the Servant among his plan and to inform him of the end of his mission in Dilmunia and the start of the return line to Copenhagen. Adam came closer to the Ruler and requested the Servant in a private word. He extended a direct invitation to return home; however, the advisor declined that invitation, preferring to stay in the company of the Ruler, saying, "I wished to return with you, but I was told that you would be returning to Dilmunia."

"I hope so."

"You shall return, because you left your heart here; only then I shall accompany you on your final journey back home."

Adam retreated and left the fort, just waiting for time. He waited until the promised day arrived; there was no way out. Then, he decided to take a final tour in the neighbourhoods and lanes in the area he was familiar with, around the house of Abu Rashed. Normally, neighbourhoods draw themselves deep inside us and make us yearn for them. Buildings often bestow some of their secrets and make you feel a constant or intermittent separation. My father accompanied him, passing by popular markets. There was herb seller; another vendor of vegetables and local fruits; another was displaying his meats on the trunks of trees in the open air. Adam was pleased when he saw the spellbound among the vendors, who was brought by another vagabond to sell next to him. The man apparently became a productive element in society. He spoke, congratulating himself: mission accomplished.

The scene made Adam stop, and he was mesmerised in his place, happy with how the spellbound story ended. As usual, he took out his watch tied it to a silver chain from his left pocket. The spellbound and his friend came closer to Adam and stared at the watch. The spellbound wanted to see the watch, and Adam was scared of them. Suddenly, his friend snatched it and began to look at this strange thing and saw what it was inside dancing in a round circle. He placed it near his ear and listened to it. His pulse began to increase. He was afraid and became suspicious. He retreated and Adam was pursuing him. The vagabond shook and placed the watch in a pot full of water. Adam got closer to him, upset with what he did. But the vagabond pointed to him not to come much closer. Adam asked him, "Why did you drown the watch?"

"I want to drown the animal inside it and kill it."

"It is a dumb machine; there is no animal inside it."

"Oh yes, there is an animal working under magic by the order of Satan."

"Now, I know that the treason of the machine is an industrial nature."

The watch continued in its stubborn turning. The vagabond threw it on the floor, breaking it into pieces and crashing it with his feet and was hit by madness. He was not quiet and started collecting the pieces in a dirty piece of cloth and started running away until he vanished. Abu Rashed asked one of the famous tracers to trace the footpath of the vagabond.

The man came asking, "How can I help you?"

"We want you to trace the footpath of the vagabond and know his destination."

The man examined the footpath of the vagabond, then explained. "It seems the man trembled and ran quickly. I dare say from his traces that he was very afraid. His footprints are apart and do not touch the soil; from his speed we can tell it is small and hardly visible except for his fingers and the toe of his feet. We shall trace him easily."

The three reached the sides of the cemetery and found the vagabond inside; they stood behind the tree of the west gate near the house of Yusef, the Puller, watching what he was doing. Another young man came and stood watching. They were four now. The vagabond took charge of burying the fragments of the watch. He dug what looked like a grave and placed the spell in it.

The young man addressed Abu Rashed. "He is the same man who buried a spell before. The spell that Yusef, the Puller and I took to you and then to the Doyen. However, what is he carrying in the bundle this time?"

"Fragments of the watch and a piece of cloth; he is trying to bury it and save the world from its evils."

"What is a watch?"

"It is a small instrument to know the hour and measure the time."

The tale of the magic watch came to an end, and Abu Rashed and Adam returned after having grasped the common concept of magic and spells. They came and my relationship with Adam assumed a new nature of connection. Where everyone talks about the possible and awaited marriage under the name of Khowla for Adam. There were lots of hiccups that forced some people to expect the failure of the project, among which was the difference in religion that forced one of the partners to convert to the religion of the other partner. I recalled what God Almighty says: "Oh people, We created from one male and one female and made you peoples and tribes, the most honourable among you in the eyes of God is the most pious; God is most omniscient." I was comforted when I recalled that the Quran fights the class system of all kinds, whether based on sex or wealth or social, and the Prophet went to on say that, "you are all from Adam and Adam is from dust." I wished success and found that legality of intermarriage was an act of melting the class system.

The two men came together and began telling the story of the spellbound, the vagabond and the trace finder who took them to the cemetery. I then asked them to bring me the trace finder on the appointed date, the day of departure for Adam. The wheel of time turned quickly and the last day for Adam in Dilmunia had arrived. Adam spent more time with Abu Rashed, who invited me to share with them the last discussion... My father asked me, "Adam wants to know your fourth condition before his departure."

"I mentioned that earlier, Father. I shall not mention the fourth condition before the previous condition is met; that is to bring some of his family members and relatives."

It was really a short night. Nobody when to sleep before dawn, then saying farewell began. Some of the people gathered with an official delegation representing the Political Agent and the Ruler, to accompany Adam to embark the British ship. I asked the spellbound, after asking for permission from my father, to ask Adam to walk barefooted towards the ship. The trace finder followed him so he could read his fortune when he saw his traces. I did not believe in fortune reading nor traces; however, some forbidden is desired, and at time of necessity logic and veracities are annulled.

After the official and popular farewell for Adam, the trace finder came along with my father. I asked him, "What did the trace tell you?"

"I cannot read his trace before reading yours, too."

I walked in front of him barefooted a few steps. He went to Abu Rashed and whispered to him something and left quickly.

"What did he tell you? How did he read the trace?"

"He said, 'If we consider the woman a partner, and life extends from her, I read in Khowla's trace, that she tends to be individualised in her depths. As to Adam's trace, he tends to be multiplexed in his depths. Between individuality and multiplicity, a distance makes matters difficult.'"

Part 3

(1) Adam
Last Week July 1765

HMS Patrick Stewart arrived from Hormuz, a boat similar to me in its travels. She moored about two miles to the north of Dilmunia Island. She had been waiting for long hours to transfer passengers and cargo by local boats and sailors. The boats unloaded their cargo of humans but loaded cargo and various goods, mail bags, food and some necessary medical equipment. The ship still maintained its military character and hosted the Union Jack, emphatically announcing the will of the Royal Crown to dominate the land and sea from west to east Asia.

I was warmly welcomed by the captain of the ship, who allocated a comfortable place where I could relax, meditate and sleep and feel independent. I emptied my bag and laid manuscripts and maps in my possession. My eyes fell on the manuscript of the plan of the burial mounds of Dilmunia. I went through it again and looked longer, moving from the island and the sketches. Dilmunia looked like the foot of a mountain raising high to its top. I wondered if a man could add the burial mounds to the Seven Wonders of the World. I felt the pangs of loneliness with memories unfolding in front of me: Khowla, the graves, pearls and more and more. Memories cannot start unless the place is out of sight.

On sailing, I became like someone pulling a thread from a delicious dough called Dilmunia. The route of the *Patrick*

Stewart was different from those commonly well known in the Arabian Gulf. Those boats, if not met by pirates, were closer to the lovesick pirates. Quite often these boats were attacked by pirates, and on other occasions some skippers concluded prior agreements with pirates and announced their lost at sea and losing their route. Then the pirates came and imposed levies on passengers and goods. The endless fables of the Gulf are legends mostly made by man and allied with nature to a little extent.

The voyage did not last long until features of Bubian Island appeared in the north of the Gulf. The island was rich with all types of migrating birds. It was a white, level island in the summer and turned green in the spring. It lay on the left of the *Patrick Stewart*, which continued sailing towards Shat Alarab. Some bids could be spotted through binoculars. A small dhow came closer to the British ship to receive the mail coming from the Far East and paid the agreed-upon fees.

The *Patrick Stewart* proceeded towards Shat Alarab. We were sailing in the same area where political arbitration was concluded between the Persians and *Shaikh* Sulieman, whom I look forward to meeting again in Southern Iraq. Waters can, at times, maintain events on its surface; politics, on the other hand, can supersede military solutions, provided negotiators possess the ability of deterrence. However, I do not think there is a compromise that satisfies adversaries if the balance of power is in favour of one of them. Shaikh Sulieman managed to dominate the area competing with regional rival powers, delineating the borders between the Persians and the Turks. He was hitting the roots on a burning line; therefore, I did not expect his emerging state to resist for long decades.

The *Patrick Stewart* began to approach shallow waters

and tried not to touch the bottom of the sea. The colour of the water gradually changed from black to dark blue, ending in green that revealed the beauty of the bottom of the Gulf. It became difficult for her to continue; here, small boats played their designated roles. They transported passengers and cargo to ports and piers spread on both banks of Shat Alarab and its marshes. Among all these boats I managed to identify the ones owned by Shaikh Sulieman. I asked to visit him before continuing to Baghdad. The commander of the boat welcomed the idea, knowing that I was not an Arab, and that I wanted to thank the Shaikh for his generosity and hospitality nearly two years ago, and to check on the deposits I left with him for his care.

The voyage on the rowing dhow took only an hour when we reached the marshes, the shallow waters covered by papyrus and sugar canes. It is difficult to distinguish between land and water plants. The two environments are different though similar. The people of the marshes know better its water and land. A little later, I was told to disembark and carry my luggage to mount a donkey to take me to the *majlis* of the Shaikh, which we reached after few minutes.

Shaikh Sulieman warmly received and embraced me in the Arab manner of greetings. This was natural, with kisses on both cheeks and hugging that makes you feel the warmth of the soul before that of the body. As usual he invited me to sit on his right. His boys came with the tea and coffee and some of the dates, famous in this region, and then spoke.

"You look happy despite the discomfort of travelling, Adam."

"Happiness at meeting you again, your Honour."

"How did you find Dilmunia, and were you happy there?"

"I found her like an extremely beautiful woman, that beauty nearing perfection, urging man to cry."

The Shaikh smiled, repeating, "That is Dilmunia, land of eternity, extension of the land of Sumar, where we are now."

I asked him to excuse me to open my sack. I took out the Arabian robe, *bisht*, that the ruler of Dilmunia gave me, a thick woollen *bisht*, hand-embroidered in the Persian style. I moved closer to him and said, "I hope you accept this little gift as a token of gratitude for all your previous services rendered to us."

"Adam, I believe that the stronger relations are those resulting accidently. That is why our relations are true and have no interest that blemishes it."

Our discussion continued about the plan that enabled me to reach Baghdad safely, where the Dutch consul representing Danish interests in the region was. The Shaikh expressed his wish to accompany me until I reached Baghdad to avoid possible risks. I suggested that some of his men be assigned instead of himself. He insisted on adopting this mission in appreciation for the human role that the campaign was charged with. After two days of staying at Alhammar, where the tribe of the Shaikh took it as its centre, we set off on a small boat built of papyrus canes in the early morning of a cool Saturday in the company of two of the Shaikh's men. His relationships with the Shaikhs of the tribes were strong and the distance was extending for a hundred and twenty kilometres until the Alqurna area, where the two rivers of Tigress and Euphrates converged, and that would make our mission easier.

We met many of the local inhabitants of the marshes, known as *Almi'dan*, who earned their living by fishing, rice planting and buffalo grazing. After spending most of the time on the boat, one of the Shaikhs of the tribes invited us for dinner and to stay the night at guest hut located on an islet of its size. These huts were spread on many islets formed by the flow of the two rivers. After accepting the invitation, a simple meal was held in honour of the Shaikh but was rich with the presence of the people of the area. They were very pleasant and smiles never deserted their faces. After performing our evening prayers, we had dinner consisting of lots of rice, sweetened fish and some dates. Then, we moved to the hospitality hut standing on seven bundles of papyrus canes covered by date palm leaves. The roof of the hut took the shape of an arch. There was a pot of water and a coffee pot on a charcoal stove.

The two escort guards lay at the two opposite corners adjacent to the small entrance of the hut. I chose the further corner facing the corner of the Shaikh. Remaining on the sides allows you to think and read the space more comprehensively. I placed my luggage as a pillow, wanting to have some sleep that I missed so much. Just before midnight we all woke up on a rustling sound coming from outside the hut. One of the guards said, "It must be one of the stray buffalos; I shall keep it away, do not worry. The marsh people are used to these animals."

The other man asked to accompany him, but he refused. The man went out without returning. The Shaikh carried his sword, accompanied by the other man with his truncheon. They searched for the man without finding him. Suddenly, four masked men jumped over them, killing the guard. The Shaikh drew his sword and the four men engaged with him. Two of them came closer and fought with him. His sword broke and its grip remained in his hand. They surrounded him in a tight circle. One of them stabbed him in his side. At the time, I was watching what was going on. I pulled the sword of the first slayed guard from his possessions and went behind the hut and stabbed one of them with all my might in his chest. He screamed and fell on the ground while the other three managed to flee. The Shaikh went bleeding to his men. The first was wounded and the second lost his life.

The people of the area woke up at the bloody incident. They quickly carried us to the chieftain's hut. They treated the Shaikh and his companion received first aid; then the news of the passing away of the wounded guard. The Shaikh was angered and spoke in a sad tone.

"After this sad incident, you can, Adam, continue your passage towards Alqurna, while we, we shall go back to our tribe."

"I shall accompany you, you are both wounded."

"You did very well, Adam. Had it not been for the mercy of God and your valour, you could have been among the dead at the hand of these cowards."

The Shaikh remained for another night at the hut of the chieftain, who bore the responsibility of protecting his guest after the sad incident. He pledged to God and in the presence of the Shaikh to punish the culprits and to protect us with his men on the way back.

The wound of the Shaikh was deep, as he had bled so much. He realised that his body was becoming frail, and he could not last long. He decided to go back despite perils and fatigue. The men secured his passage, but it seemed that this was an isolated incident. Looting crimes were rare in this part, except with strangers who refused to pay highway tax.

Two days later, we reached the Shaikh's tribe. His condition deteriorated. I read signs of death on the face of the men before reaching Dilmunia. I began to notice signs of death in his voice and fluctuation of his vision. The Shaikh realised that his end was nearing, and he wanted to make his testament. He made an order to meet with his men in the evening. Before the gathered men spoke, a young man raised his voice.

"Don't we have the right to declare war on those who killed the Shaikh of our tribe?"

The Shaikh spoke in a sad voice and moans of him who was about to depart.

"My people, war is an endless battle, and a burning fire in the soul of some men; this is what I do not want or love."

"But the history of our tribe and its independence urges us to fight."

"He who is proud of his past loses his future; this treacherous stab was very successful. I feel that my end is not very far. I know that death is inevitable. The sick who does not know his malady lives longer; however, I know that my fate is near. This is the nature of life. There is someone who wants to revive hope in you. I perceive a lot from life's experience. My people, you know that God Almighty has not endowed me with a son who will carry my name. He has given me five daughters and they are fit to lead our large tribe. Therefore, I commend you knowing well your interests after God Himself; my will is that Adam marries one of my daughters in recognition of his valour in defending me. I also commend him to be your chief. May God Almighty grant him a son so I am his grandfather, and he in turn is your chief in the future. I know how much we love to immortalise our names for fear of death. I want my name to remain so you can terrify your enemies."

Shaikh Sulieman left me room to voice my view in a fateful case of a tribe I did not belong to except in belonging to the same creation of humanity. I only knew its people recently. The Shaikh has burdened me with an onus of responsibility; how would things go? How could I marry anyone other than Khowla? It was a great high treason. The worst type of injustice is to yearn for a woman, and you are at the side of another one.

Shaikh Sulieman's will became a tangible reality within only one month. Death, like love, hits us unexpectedly; there are always exceptions. The man departed and his beloved met to execute his will. I was appointed chief to a tribe I did not belong to. It was the law of inheritance and mandatory. I met with the elders and men of this large tribe and said, "My brothers, you are all aware that I would not have become a chieftain, had it not been for the will of Shaikh Sulieman. I did not have any desire to be your chief. If anyone among you has such a desire let him come forward."

No one came forward and raised his hand. Their elder spoke.

"We are aware that you are a traveller; however, we are certain that Shaikh Sulieman was more capable to rule the tribe from his grave. What he commended regarding ruling is due to his ability to communicate with you from the other world."

The Arabs, when talking about the mind, mean the heart. That is why it is said that they have hearts that they do not perceive with and they have eyes that they do not see with. I was certain that a successful ruler was like a successful husband in his ability to manoeuvre. That is why I had to put on the dress of the Shaikh. Hence, the first link began when I said, "Dear brothers, the Shaikh willed that I marry one of his daughters, but I want to delay this step until the right time. During the period I am spending with you, I want to have a general framework of government in place. A framework that we abide with, and future generations shall follow, provided they have the right to make amendments on laws that we enact now, so these can be compatible with their time and interests. Our laws are manmade or conventional, not divine laws. You gentlemen can go back to your natural life and practise your activities the way they were. Taxes on transit boats in our region shall remain as they were. All shall produce in the area of their work, as life does not stop with the death of one of us."

One week later, I met with the men of the tribe to announce binding decisions. I stood to deliver a speech.

"Brothers, due to my urgent desire to return to my homeland, I shall leave tomorrow for Alqurna and from there to Baghdad. Ten men shall accompany me for protection purposes. For the public interests of the tribe, I decided in this meeting to elect a temporary Shaikh for the tribe. The vote shall be on the basis of one man, one vote. Some shall stand for election. He who gets more votes shall be the chieftain; so, you shall be your own ruler. As to my marriage to the daughter of Shaikh Sulieman, I shall declare it after my return when members of my family shall be with me."

Uproar broke, then their elder spoke.

"Shaikh Adam, the Traveller. The decision is not ours; Shaikh Sulieman decided that you shall be our absolute chief of the tribe. You have full freedom to enact laws and we shall abide by these. This is his wish as he willed, and we shall abide by his will."

Men of the tribe refused the law of election, and the land Mi'dan, like Dilmunia, remained as it was. As they were brought to love the most powerful tyrant.

I recommended that one of them be the vice chieftain until my return. I set off to Baghdad hoping to reach there in one piece.

(2) Khowla
August 1765

This was the first time that I held a pen to write since Adam's departure. I found that a true pen could only be fluent at times of catastrophes. I was so fatigued in choosing the first word to blast off. The beginnings and ends were similar as far as the degree of blackness. I learnt that writing a novel is a retribution against despots in the shadow. I knew that the hesitant pen does not know how to put a full stop at the end of the line.

Since the first meeting called by the Ruler, attended by his followers and the Political Agent, Adam, the Merchant and members of the Appointed Council, there were no voices louder than the voice and wish of the Ruler. People were optimistic about the pure intention that would bring about the expected reforms that would change the system known as *khamamis*, the fifths by all divers. This was accompanied by looking into the grievances that broke the back of farmers due to taxes imposed on their crops. This came along with the beginning of the opening of the markets for local products such as pottery, yarning and weaving.

After the departure of Adam, the Merchant asked for an emergency meeting with the Ruler, his advisor and the Appointed Council at the fort. The Ruler asked if the presence of Abu Rashed was necessary as he represented the people and the other public opinion. The Merchant adamantly refused the presence of what could be an opposition voice.

Abu Rashed informed me after he had received an emissary of the Ruler. "The Ruler informs you of his desire to attend the next meeting at the fort, but as an observer, not a participant."

"Observer?"

"Yes. As you represent the working sector that demands radical change in the present system, the Ruler wishes your presence while the Merchant is opposing it. Therefore, the Ruler decided you come to the fort secretly from the back door. You can listen to what goes on in the emergency meeting, then leave even more secretly."

"What is the benefit of my presence if it is secret, inactive and ineffective?"

"The Ruler wants you to be informed about the conducted style of leadership in Dilmunia, and to realise the many difficulties he is confronting to get out to safety. These crises related to human beings are more complicated."

Abu Rashed went to the fort what looked like stealthily. The emissary ushered him to a side room to the conference hall. He was able to listen to all that was going on in the main room that was separated by a wooden screen. He could have participated; however, he decided to remain silent until the end, according to the wish of the Ruler, and respecting the word he kept.

The Merchant entered first, followed by the members of the Appointed Council, then the Political Agent. There were side discussions in the audience before the voices receded and went off with the arrival of the Ruler and his advisor, who walked on his right. The Ruler headed the meeting as usual, beginning with welcoming the audience. He praised the constructive measures taken by the Merchant and the

Appointed Council. Then he went on talking about the priority of security and stability spreading over the island, thanks to the British presence and the link of contact with its Crown through the good offices of the Political Agent. Then he went on to explain. "This meeting was called as an emergency at the request of the Merchant. Let us listen, gentlemen, and see what he hoping for Dilmunia and its people."

"Yes, after the announcement of the reform programme Your Highness advocates. We highly praise it for its noble aims. Our faithful men, who are trying with their efforts to maintain the security of our country, are working round the clock for the comfort of the people of Dilmunia. In their weekly reports, they have unanimously mentioned that there are some lawless groups who are trying to undermine the stability of our peaceful island with the aid of some foreign powers. These evil forces do not care for the welfare of Dilmunia and its people."

The advisor interrupted the speech of the Merchant and addressed the audience.

"For all this, and the security issues, we highly appreciate the Ruler's reform measures; however, at the same time we hoped he would delay the implementation of the reform programme."

The Ruler wondered. "Why should we postpone or delay it, if it is for the benefit and prosperity of the people of Dilmunia?"

"Your Highness, the people of Dilmunia are not mature enough to determine its future. They, just like the people of the peninsula, are unable to manage their lives. For this, we plead to His Highness to delay the first step to start the reform programme."

My father mentioned later that he tried to change his position so he could read the faces and see what they did not utter. The eye when scrutinising is more eloquent than the tongue. He moved two steps to be closer to the wooden wall separating the two rooms. He heard the advisor's voice rising gradually, more daring than usual.

"Your Highness, we should not disagree with the logic when it comes to what the secret agents report about the misleading group that aims at destroying Dilmunia. Some are trying hard to assassinate Your Highness and kill all your efforts. Is not that enough?"

The Merchant praised what the advisor said, and Abu Rashed inferred that there was a common line of intrigue between the Merchant and the Servant. They were both wrought of the same metal. Then they addressed themselves to the Political Agent, who expressed the true wish of the British Crown that security and peace would prevail over Dilmunia and its trade would prosper.

The Ruler asked for some time to make his decisive decision before the end of the meeting. The Political Agent left, followed by members of the Appointed Council, which was a consultative council with no powers. The Ruler remained in his chair with the Merchant near him. The Servant was hovering around then, saying, "Does Your Highness remember the troublesome nightmare that you had for some time?"

"Of course, I still do remember, but its episodes stopped the moment I told you about its details."

"That nightmare that suffocates you and lies heavy on your chest at the time of going to bed is still persistent. In it, you were seeing the murdered swimming in his blood, and there was a handsome young man coming out of his head crying for blood to quench his thirst; do you still remember that nightmare, Your Highness?"

"Yes, I still see him in front of me the moment you told me about it."

Abu Rashed was stealthily looking through the cracks in the wooden barrier without being seen. The Ruler placed his head between his palms and closed his eyes. The Servant, who was carrying a thin line, turned around him. He began to tap the Ruler with his left hand and turned a thin line round his neck. With his light two hands he pulled the line, saying, "This is the interpretation of your vision."

The Ruler tried to resist and clench to life to stop his strangling. The Merchant held his truncheon and with all his might hit the Ruler's head, who stumbled and fell to the floor. With his string, the Servant tightened just below the jaw. He lost his power and his soul departed from his body. The Merchant praised the Servant's action and joyfully said, "Well done, man. You shall be highly rewarded. As we agreed, you shall remain the advisor to Dilmunia."

"How can we get rid of the Ruler's body, now?"

"We shall carry it to the inner room behind the wooden barrier so we can take it out at night."

Abu Rashed heard what the two men intended to do in carrying out the fatal bloody plan. He was unarmed and would be suspected if found here, so he decided to escape from the way he came in. He opened the door, wanting to get away, but the two men spotted him. The Merchant shouted loudly at the security men, "Apprehend the killer."

This was followed by the voice of the advisor.

"Catch the killer, this thief."

The security men gathered round the accused and began beating him nearly to death when the advisor interfered to stop them.

"Abu Rashed should not be killed here; he must be taken to court where Judge Albalbul will listen to witnesses before pronouncing his judgement, and so that he can see his family before that, and that the Political Agent be invited to the open trial as a neutral international party. That is the same reform program that the Ruler was leading and what should remain as a dominant light in Dilmunia."

The next day, the Merchant announced the wish of Dilmunia to hold the court next Friday in the presence of three judges and several witnesses and the public. The deliberate armed killing accusation would be made against Abu Rashed, who had nothing to say in his first defence except saying to the Merchant, "If you kill me, God shall kill you too. Neither the Carmathians, nor the conquerors or colonising countries like Portugal were able to make Dilmunia kneel and subjugate its people."

The Merchant spoke to Abu Rashed and to his security men and those present from the public.

"Justice of the Heavens shall prevail. No man or devil can break the balance of its justice. Here is Heaven bestowing right on the people of Dilmunia. It shall punish him who instigated the killing of my son Nasser by drowning and roused disputes between the people. Then he looted the fort and deliberately killed the Ruler and tried hard to subjugate Dilmunia that the Heavens protects to remain eternal."

I, Khowla, after my last encounter with my father, hereby document this crime in full for history to preserve and be proud of the future of Dilmunia. It was said that he who writes history is called victorious. I wrote this entry with my blood, tears and ink. This manuscript entry will not be completed due to tears spilled on it. However, it shall definitely find someone to unearth it and place it in the hands of the people after centuries. It is a big trust placed in your hands, for you as a writer. You have to translate the events and emotions on paper. You have to transfer meanings and thoughts and to rewrite in a style appropriate and closer to your age, because I find in you the hope with which Dilmunia shall remain forever in the hearts of those who inhale its breeze.

(3) Adam
Mid-August 1765

The men of the tribe of the late Shaikh Sulieman made a promise to deliver me safely to beyond the town of Alqurna on the outskirts of Basra. During that trip, I was the uncrowned chieftain of a tribe that I never belonged to; I never felt proud as much as I felt pity towards the deep-rooted spirit of servitude with most of the people of the East, a sense of inferiority and an innate aptitude for being led. However, no wonder that some leaders, despite their status, worshipped a cow. On the contrary, I felt safe because of what the men did in terms of security duty in protecting their non-elected chieftain. I began to document what I missed beside my luggage. I began pouring from memory storage and put it down on paper, being comfortable. Sleep only attended me when I needed it, with no trouble.

Basra was then officially under British sovereignty that was responsible for safeguarding trade and mail routes. This sovereignty was understood to mean the urgent need for the empire to stay there for a long time. However, it never ventured to get involved in the daily life of the people. Theirs was an experienced management that maintained the interests of the empire that the sun never sat on. One policy and various results. That administration was similar to the style remaining in Dilmunia, without slipping into local ditches. One policy and various results.

The men handed me a precious trust for one of the leaders of the scattered tribes, who promised to secure the passage to Baghdad. When he found my Arabic was fluent, he asked me to change my name until the objective was met. He chose for me the name of Jaafar. I did not know the wisdom behind that. Then he offered me Basrian clothes so that I do not rouse avarice. I asked him, "What is the amount you want when the mission is accomplished?"

"I do not want any cash amounts; moreover, money does not last."

"I do not own any jewellery or precious stones that you may ask about… I have but my luggage and this is not for sale."

"I just want to accompany you alone, provided that you secure a visit for me to the mausoleum *of Imam Hussain* and his brother Abbas in Karbala."

This man made me angry with his exceptional demand, as if the East ended without its discrepancies. He was talking with much pride about these characters. High spirits and values seem absolute for those who leave this world. I promised him to meet his demand as soon as I received aid sent from Copenhagen to the Dutch consul in Baghdad, provided that I had the choice of accompanying him to those places. Perhaps I could paint them and add them to my collection of treasures of the East. Perhaps they would be added to the Seven Wonders of the World.

That man assumed the character of a wise peasant that I loved so much. He was pleasant and always honest. He disclosed many personal and social matters. I felt safe with his clarity that that I would leave him in few days. With him, I felt like someone being alone with himself. I found nothing wrong with answering him openly. I would change him with another one, due to the route's requirement. No harm. He who changes colours is always happier, but he surprised me and shocked me when he asked, "I feel that there is love in your eyes dissimilar to the love of others."

The wise man stunned me with the physiognomy other than that which I saw in Dilmunia. There, you find who reads the individual and knows to what tribe he belongs, and reads his features, the way he walks and his voice, and returns the branches of his family to its history and early soil. There is also the one who reads the trace and knows the fortune and here is he who knows love and draws the future.

I asked him, "And how is the love of others?"

"It is easy for me to perceive that you are in love; love is something natural, as it is the double of singularity and selfishness. As for you, your love is human and generous. Therefore, you did not hold anything from me when I asked you. I realised the heavenly love inside you when I asked you."

"Did you know that I am in love when I agreed to meet your condition?"

"Not all that, man. I see your hunger for love stronger than your thirst for sex; this stage came over to you after many experiments. Your love is immortal. Therefore, mature love is the one that comes late. In the law of human life, love does not stay after connection, but I see your love, beautiful and fresh in your soul. Cannot you see that lovers are the living? Your love, my friend, is for every human being."

My companion, the wise man, stunned me while listening to him and looking into his face. He nearly drove me mad and erased whatever reason remained in my mind. As if love was a divine order, ordained to some and could not be restricted.

His talk took me back to the land of Carina and the oasis of Khowla; love of the beginnings without experiments, and love of endings and misleading. A love based on the foundations of sex, and a love ascending the throne of reason; between these two is a vast gap. The more delicious of the two does not come through the organ of vision. The lover is definitely he who does not see with his eyes.

Wow to that beautiful Khowla; I never sang her beauty in public. They certainly said that a woman who does not bewilder you, never touches you. I was afraid that love not based on connection was not capable of lasting as it is staggering on the line of extermination. The first vision of meeting her was still attacking me. She was hiding behind children and covering half of her face. I do recall the almond eye and features of her mouth. At the time I stuttered, and her father brought me back to my reality. I greeted her and she responded with a shy nod, that fascinating beauty. As for Carina, I surrounded her waist with my arm, and wished for a kiss that broke emotional barriers and beyond. It is an unjust comparison.

The wise man broke the chain of my thoughts again, as if he were reading my mind.

"He who does not praise a belle will never reach her; she shall remain fixed in his mind and apparent in his heart only. This love raises him up, but the bottom of the heart pushes you, man, downwards. The difference between these two loves is like the difference of the heat of the surface of the sea and its depth; one of them is near and tepid, yearning for the sky and the other is cold, dragging you to the earth."

His talk made me relate him to one of the greatest contemporary philosophers; I preferred to tell the story and quote it to emphasise what the man said.

"It seems what you are saying is true; in Germany the star was one of the philosophers, called Goethe, who frequented a bar in his early days. There, he fell in love with the barwoman and wanted to marry her. He lauded her in his poems and called his collection *Annette*, as a token of good luck. The girl did not reciprocate his love. He won her over and in time left her and looked for another one. Two years later, he fell in love with another girl, called Werther, and wished to marry her. That was not possible, because she was the wife of his friend. He wrote his famous novel, *The Sorrows of Young Werther*. At the end of it, its hero committed suicide as a reflection of the impossibility of Goethe's marrying that woman to prove that addiction to wishful thinking is similar to that of killing. The first is of the soul and the second is of human beings."

The wise man answered me with a smile.

"That is the love of sexual intercourse, or earthly love, Jaafar; it is a love for all humans. It is the platonic love where you wish dead in the arms of your beloved to enjoy the warmth of his tears. The love that cures the malady of hatred. The love that the ruler maintains for the comfort of his people; he closes no eye if there is anyone moaning of hunger."

I asked him about the lover who seeks love and wants to keep away from sex. He quickly answered from where I did not expect.

"It is like him who wants to retreat to the desert and devote his time for worship. This is the abrupt worship, the worship based on rituals without getting involved in its essential meanings."

We arrived, without being aware, at the trade road that led to Baghdad that was under Ottoman domination. On our way, from time to time, we came across some scattered villages, considered as a rest area. Sometimes, the local people asked for some money, or received you as a guest and showed their hospitality and generosity. We passed by one of the remote villages where people were gathering around a sandy hill, apparently celebrating a swimming contest on the river. The elder promised the winner a silver coin. The losers would be charged with preparing the food.

The loser grumbled and went away from his folks. He saw that we were travellers and approached us, complaining about the injustice of his people. The wise man revealed to him a novel way of cooking meat that might do him justice. According to the advice, the contestant placed the black pot on the top of the palm tree. They all laughed at his action and stupidity. The head of the judging panel wanted to see him and asked him, "Is it not foolish of you to light the fire below the palm tree and place the meat up there to be cooked?"

"Is it not a foolish thing for my mother to light the fire on the other bank of the river and I win the race because she had warmed me up?"

The wisdom of the contestant scared the judging panel. They took back the symbolic prize from its owner to give it to the contestant who deserved it. He asked them to wait a minute and came to us and asked, "Come with me to receive the prize. Had it not been for you, I would not have gotten it back."

"You are the only winner, and no one deserves to share the championship with you. That was your achievement; take it alone."

We declined to stand beside him as that was his chance to distinguish himself. Our presence beside him, at the time of honouring him, would steal the limelight. It was another signal that came to me as lightning, when something unexpected happens but in a spot and another place. A vision saying that something serious was blowing up Dilmunia.

They took back the prize and the contestant came to thank us, and then asked me, "What is your name, honourable guest?"

"I am Jaafar, and this is my friend and companion, the Wise Man."

"And where are you heading to?"

"Baghdad."

"I belong to this area, know the easy and less dangerous routes to that destination. I can join you and protect you, I can be of help and do lots of things. Then I shall return when the mission is accomplished as a sign of gratitude for your noble attitude towards me."

"Excessive manhood is just like none; take it easy, and do not be misled by your youth."

After we became three, I, Jaafar, and my friend the wise man, I felt very safe and in a relaxed situation that took me back to Dilmunia and made me unconscious about the place. The wise man asked me, "Did you find an evil signal of what is going on in Dilmunia?"

"There is someone who wants to steal the right from its people, and perhaps it coincides and hastes the tempi of events and evils."

I could not reach that wisdom and read the future using the imaginative power, had it not been for the events and paradoxes of Dilmunia, and the companionship and existing with the Wise Man. It is described as a natural wisdom, and I say it is acquired learning, that arrives as a result of experiencing the ability to manoeuvre. The closest example of the ability to manoeuvre is represented in the famous incident of arbitration in Dilmunia, when the Ruler asked the two parties to define the meaning of "palm tree". Abu Rashed wrote it, "*Nakhla*", while his friend drew the shape of it. Those tricks clearly showed that a successful ruler is he who is more able to manoeuvre, even if it was a loser.

Here we were, approaching Baghdad after two days of riding. A group of equestrians stopped us. It seemed they worked as watchtower and security patrol. They led us to one of the camps belonging to the main tribe. There, they posed some questions that the Wise Man advised me not to speak unless he nodded to me.

"Where are you coming from, and where is your destination?"

"From Shat Alarab. As to our friend, he is coming from Dilmunia, the land of eternity."

"What is the name of your companion?"

"Jaafar."

The tribesmen began to look at each other before one of them said:

"As you were coming from Dilmunia and your name is Jaafar, they must have asked you to pay extra passage tax, and a tax for using their area in Shat Alarab; how much did you pay them?"

I recalled my first meeting with Shaikh Sulieman, the chieftain of Bani Ka'b Tribe, who bequeathed me his position. I remembered that taxes on anchoring of British and friendly ships were three *Muhammadi* coins. Other ships, whose owners were different from the religion and sect of the tribe, paid seven *Muhammadi* coins; here the commercial operation was the opposite. The Wise Man chose the name of Jaafar for me and crossed the transit area without paying any amount. Here I was, after some years, finding the solution to one of the mysteries of the Arabian Peninsula and its dependencies.

(4) Abu Rashed
September 1765

The authorities were propagating from its platforms and the minarets of Dilmunia the incident of arresting Abu Rashed, while the public preferred to call it apprehension. That incident represented an important turn in the history of the "Land of Eternity". It represented a dramatic film of past events. The more I closed my eyes, the more it took me ahead to the future. The truth that embodies advice is the continuous attempt to escape from a passing tragedy by forgetting it is a flopped attempt. Forgetting is in fact a strengthening of memory; you shall never forget a painful incident unless you manage to reach a solution or cure to overcome it. From the first moment of leading me and tying my hands, I was looking beyond the event. I was not moved by the inelegant, malicious manner of framing me up with various accusations, as I was searching in the dark corridors of the future for the worst scenario that may befall on Dilmunia. Prisons shall never be a successful style to inhibit people from their rightful demands. It was a motive that makes the truth upright and worthy to be followed.

After this malicious apprehension, I was led to one of the cells that I did not know the whereabouts of. I only remember its odour. They blindfolded me and handcuffed me behind my back and started beating me with a truncheon. I was jogging between their hands. Gun stubs fell on my head and canes on my back and buttocks. I did not know whether I was going or coming when someone kicked me in the chest and forced me to sit on the ground, motionless.

"You murderous criminal, you shall remain here until the Merchant decides the time of your trial. It shall be public as assurance of absolute divine justice on the land of Dilmunia, in accordance with the legislation and justice laid down by Heaven."

I answered that loud voice.

"Never mind; but who are you?"

"I am the detention warden and charged with your temporary imprisonment, the servant of the Merchant and the whole of Dilmunia. Are you not afraid of punishment?"

"They plot and God decides; He is the best of deciders."

"Therefore, and according to approval of the advisor and the Council, His Highness, the Merchant decided that the court hold its sessions in public at the courtyard of Dilmunia Mosque. Judge Albalbul will hear your plea and the pleas of defence and witnesses. It shall be an open trial, where right will be revealed and falsehood will be defeated."

"The false shall die."

I remained alone in the cell prior to the trial. The prison, with its walls and ceiling, were emitting warmth and comfort, while the warden was foul and rude with no sense of humaneness. The task of food and water and even cursing was assigned to the prison guard.

He left me blindfolded with tied hands at the back and said, "You shall remain here until next Friday; I shall be your mate in this cell. I shall feed you whatever you like and dislike."

"This is God's will."

I felt very thirsty and asked for a drink of water. He said,

"You shall only have a drink four times a day."

"I want to have the first drink. I am very thirsty."

He asked me to wait. I heard the squeak of the door when it opened. A few minutes later he returned, saying that he had brought the water.

"Please untie me so I can drink."

He laughed loud, hitting my face with the hot water. I could not perceive the shock until he said, "That was your first drink; three more remain."

I took out my tongue, hoping to get the few drops that fell from my head and forehead, I reclined on my back with my hands tied at my back and said, "May I have the second drink?"

"Open your mouth."

I opened my mouth for him to throw the water on my face. I swallowed a little and most of it was spilled. I said, "May God Almighty reward you. You have saved a soul. He who saves a soul is like him who saves the whole world."

The guard was silent and approached me. He made me sit, made my back lean on the wall, and said, "Why do you wish me well?"

"Because I love myself so much."

"I do not understand you!"

"By making me drink, you have done lots of good. I do feel happy for you; because I love myself so much, I wanted some of the goodness that I have to befall on you, too. I could not but wish you well."

The guard left the cell and returned a few moments later. He got closer to me and said, "Listen, you murderous criminal, I shall tie your legs."

"The sheep shall not be harmed by skinning when

slaughtered."

"I shall tie your legs but un-blindfold your eyes and untie your hands. I shall place the third glass of water as your third drink and some dates. This is your meal for the day."

While he was at his work finishing his tasks, he heard the voice of the Merchant coming closer. He left hurriedly, leaving the water, food and his heavy club. I had some dates and drank water and thanked God so much. The guard came back hastily, breathing heavily. I left the heavy club and said, "This is your club; do not leave it in the hands of your foe. Your enemy can only hurt you with your help. I didn't drink your water and didn't touch your food."

"Why didn't you untie your legs; why are you never angry with me?"

"I did not untie my legs, as that will expose you to the wrath of your master. And your negligence shall harm the security of Dilmunia. Is this not what the Merchant and his advisor claim? As for my anger, you must know that calm is the spice of life."

The guard asked me to untie my legs by myself; that I did. He asked me if I wanted something else, and I asked him, "I cannot read but love in you; why do you perform your work and you do not love it?"

"It is my livelihood and instinct satisfaction. With the requirements of this job, I can meet the needs of life."

"Man is bigger than instinct. He whose only concern is to fill his stomach, his value becomes what is excreted from it."

After all this, I thanked him, and he left the cell, locking it securely from outside.

Early next morning, the warden came to me with what I expected and needed, then he asked me if I wanted to perform my prayers; I asked for water for ablution, which he instantly brought. He sat in front of me and watched me praying. When I finished he asked me:

"Could it be you, Abu Rashed, who killed the Ruler and stole the fort?"

"If I stole, show me what I have stolen, and if I killed, I would be punished."

The warden kept quiet, then lowered his eyes to the floor and asked me, "Do you want to escape the cell the day of your trial just before Friday prayers in the courtyard of Dilmunia Mosque?"

"I do not want to do that. I am not afraid of the path of rightness even though few are following it. Being here is an imprisonment for my body; my escape is an imprisonment of my soul. Shackling the soul is more dangerous than shackling the body. My release to safety would be cutting your throat."

I really realised the role of the energy of love that I talked long with Adam about. That energy shows you the full part of life, that does not let you lean to the negative side of life but urges you to take the path of goodness and hope. This is a positive energy that moves rocks and melts iron; no wonder that the heart of a simple man is affected.

Time passed quickly and the appointed time arrived. The Merchant and his secret service men to dragged me in the markets. The guard refused to escort me, pretending that he was not well due to an illness. I realised what the man was aiming at. I was dragged in the roads. On both sides of the roads, bystanders lined up. I read sympathy in their eyes. I responded with a smile, hiding behind it the spirit of triumph; whenever my eyes met anyone, he started clapping, happy as an eagle.

Afterwards, the crowds turned into what looked like a popular participation in a peaceful march. The Merchant was displeased. He ordered his men to cover my head with a black kerchief. The people jeered at the move and became prouder and more supportive of their leader.

The tribune was held in the courtyard of the Dilmunia Mosque. The platform was set up in front of the hall that witnessed the famous arbitration event. The judge, Shaikh Albalbul, sat between two judges, one on his right and the other on his left. I was tied like a sheep to the trunk of a palm tree on the right of the judges. The Merchant, the Adviser and members of the Council sat on the opposite side. Albablbul spoke.

"Abu Rashed, you are accused of breaking into the fort and stealing its contents and deliberately killing the Ruler. What do you say, and how you defend yourself against these accusations?"

"You are accusing me as if you know everything; assuming monopoly of knowledge is an endemic disease. I did not break into the fort but was invited by the Ruler. If I stole the contents, where are the stolen things? I did not kill the Ruler and did not intend to do that."

"Many witnesses saw you running from the fort."

"I wanted to be away from a crime that the Merchant and his advisor were about to commit."

"The Merchant and his advisor are accusing you of murdering the Ruler; the secret service men are accusing you of breaking into the fort. Let us hear the witnesses."

Two secret service members came forward. They swore and said that they had arrested Abu Rashed during his attempt to flee from the fort. The Merchant and his advisor swore that they saw me in the Ruler's inner room with a club in my hand which was the instrument of the crime. The judge deliberated with his advisors and quickly said, "God said, 'In retribution there is a life, O people of discerning, so you may become pious.' The court is passing the judgement in presence by confirming the crime waged against the defendant, Abu Rashed, by life imprisonment. The court is dismissed."

I asked to have a word with the Merchant and his advisor, but the latter redressed by saying, "In view of the public interest of Dilmunia and the prosperity of its people, the Appointed Council refuses to talk with the defendant. He is very dangerous and is refused to communicate with the people and public as a precaution for maintaining public security and unity of the people, Therefore, in the name of the law, he shall be taken to the prison of the fort."

I was led on foot from the ad hoc tribune in the courtyard of Dilmunia Mosque to the prison at the fort. I was taken and pulled through the markets and yards where children's playgrounds were located. I was tightly tied on my wrists and around my neck, and an iron chain was put around my legs. A security man held each rope at an end, and both walked around me in a semi-circle. Most of them did not speak Arabic. The guard who feigned illness came along with them and was without a rope but walked beside the ring. He looked towards me, but looked to the ground when our eyes met. The heavy gate of the fort slowly opened, and I was pulled up to the upper floor on a stair built from mud and palm tree trunks. Everybody stood there waiting for the advisor and the Merchant, who asked, "Shall we place him in the solitary jail or with the rest of prisoners?"

The advisor said, "Place him in the solitary cell. Don't you see his negative impact on the guard who sympathised with the man? Had he stayed longer, he would have been one of his men. This criminal called Abu Rashed has an enormous energy, I know not from where he got it; however, it is able to move hearts and minds. I see that you throw him in the upper cell and bring his companion Yusef, the Puller."

I stood with security men to examine the cell. It was really an upright, totally quiet room; you heard nothing but the whizzing of mosquitoes. Its only entrance was from the ceiling. It was square-shaped with a distance of nearly two metres from each corner. Its depth by descending from the ceiling was four metres. They dropped me down by a wooden ladder, then they pulled it up and tightly closed the ceiling of the cell and it became sombrely dark. No one could climb the smooth, high walls. Added to that, the cover could only be moved by four strong men. Three meals were brought in with some water at a specific time by lowering them by rope to the sandy floor on the bottom of the cell. I asked them where the toilets were.

"You can dig at one of the corners and use it as a latrine."

This awful, filthy situation lasted for more than a week until the warden came.

"Mr Abu Rashed?"

"Yes."

"There is a guest who would like to visit you and spend the remainder of his life in your company, in your cell."

"Who is that guest? Yusef, the Puller. We suggested to him to join you in your jail, and he was very happy."

They lowered the ladder and a ghost of a man descended, a skeleton. They said it was Yusef, the Puller. They left part of the opening in the ceiling. I recognised what remained of his features. He was thin, like a feather in the wind. I thought he was a bag holding bones and remains of flesh. His eyes were protruding like a mature frog. His hair and beard were akin to those of a nomad. No sooner was he descended and touched the floor of the cell, he fell down. I reached this strange creature and realised some of his features; I found difficulty in tracing the place where I could touch him. I raised him in one mass, the way he used to pull me up in one mass from the bottom of the sea.

When he settled down and overcame his fear, each of us listened to each other. Our parting was so long, and I was so happy for our reunion. Our conversation turned most of it into what looked like hallucinations. At times, he directed the dialogue and I discussed with him his affair. I asked him about the secret that kept him alive, and he said it was, "The patience of Job and Jacob; their patience was beautiful and fruitful."

I said, "Patience, Yusef, is an inspirational spiritual power, a power that urges you to overcome all your desires and whims. The patient character can control his point's strength and weakness. He is stable when confronting challenges with his mind and wisdom. This is what I found in you, Yusef, you focus on your patience and will on endurance and do not kneel in front of crisis and disasters."

The puller wanted to sit leaning on his hands and then emitted a long groan. I hurried towards him, but he said, "Never mind, my friend, but what is wrong with the warden, of whom I felt his love towards you?"

"He is like all human beings. They are all equal in humanity. You can, in your confrontations, triumph over stone before men. You have to be competent in carrying arms of human values. Be soft-tongued with your enemy before your friend and be kind-hearted with whoever disagrees with you in opinion. Open your heart for love of people and all their hearts shall open for you. Lower your voice and refine it, their feelings shall soften for you. Be peaceful in your approach and demands. Have you not seen that the term 'peace' occurred more in the Quran than 'war'?"

Talking took us back to the memories of the sea and pearls. False crimes meet unity of fate. An accusation of killing Nasser was made up against him and I was accused of killing the Ruler; between them the dreams of the people of Dilmunia of getting a just system of government were aborted. Throwing us in prison was the tax of just demands, that all without exception know the governor and the governed in Dilmunia. A just divine system of government where people rule themselves is a strong system because it is a moral system, a collective system. The group is stronger and more able to survive. That kind of government is based on respect of sovereignty and peculiarity of society and individual. A strong law is the one derived from strong people and it is not beyond their aspirations and will. It is a system that allows participation and refuses tyranny and the convention based on the power of coercion. Opposite to that is a system that does not see the changes in society as a natural, dire necessity.

Yusef, the Puller said, "Stop that, man. Don't you see that with freedom we lay in prisons? The existence of the oppressed and the right for jail is the harshest punishment for the oppressor."

"Yes, Yusef. God created man and extracted him from nothingness to existence, and this existence has the right to freedom; otherwise, you punish the wisdom of God and negate His creatures for your nothingness. With your foolishness also, you think you could frame God. Man has the freedom of movement and transporting, his tongue has the freedom of conversing, and his eye enjoys seeing the creatures of God, and the mind and thinking freedom of thought. How did the Merchant allow himself to banish those who disagree with him? I may disagree with you, but I must retain my human relationships within the limits of love instead of following the philosophy of prisons to punish differences of thought."

"What is the shortest and easiest route to come out of this dilemma that threw us in prison to remain behind the walls of an impregnable fort?"

"It is the ability to discuss. I asked the Merchant and the advisor for a discussion after the judge of Dilmunia issued his verdict, but both refused. True discussion is related to the human composition of the individual. He who searches for discussion is bigger than he who hopes to transform thoughts into tangible reality. He who refuses, excludes the other. With discussion, we connect the heart and mind of the other instead of exclusion. With purposeful and constructive discussion, all parties feel reassured instead of adopting an aggressive, destructive spirit. Most political and sectarian wars are products of language misunderstanding, opposed to accidental and an individual, movable desire."

That was the kind of discussion with Yusef, who felt the warmth of prison life. He repeated what the Arabs said, that reason is the guide of the soul, knowledge is the guide of reason, and eloquence is the interpreter of knowledge. Yusef began to sleep in peace until he woke up one cold night, upset by a nightmare. I asked him, "What is the matter? I see that you are highly upset."

"This is the second time, Abu Rashed, that I see this

dream, just mere chimeras, or fantasies, no more."

"Remember God from Satan; tell me what you see."

"I see you, Abu Rashed, in a dark, deep sea, carrying two candles that do not light your way. The sky with its clouds and rains gets closer to one of them and puts it off. One candle remains to light our way. The waves rise higher, coming closer to it, trying to swallow it and drown you. You try to protect it with all your body and power until you are about to fall in the sea and the only candle will be distinguished."

"The vision, Yusef, has its own interpretations, but the fantasies of dreams are just like foams. If the vision is true, it is an indication of something coming that will explain it. Do not worry except by content, and work for a brighter future."

Two nights later, Yusef, the Puller, woke up terrified. He followed the same rituals before talking, describing his vision.

"The vision came back, Abu Rashed, but with a little difference. What I saw was you carrying two candles in the same terrifying sea. One of the candles went out while you were protecting the other candle. Your father, the Doyen, came and took the extinguished candle and placed a lightened lantern. The lantern began to glow until a little baby appeared saying, that he was your son, Rashed, and still…

Yusef, the Puller continued describing his vision when the warden opened part of the ceiling of the cell to allow the light of the sun to warm us and…

Both said, "The sun of Dilmunia is still the most beautiful."

(5) The Interpreter
November 1765

The Dutch consul in Baghdad welcomed Adam and his two companions, the wise farmer, and the strong young man, at his residence at the centre of the historical capital. The residence was distinguished for its beauty of design. This led Adam to spend more than three days to draw the external façade of the building with all its details. Then he spent another day to know more about the internal details and its secrets. The building was constructed on Abbasids architecture and it amazed Adam. The buildings in that quarter were close to each other, forming lanes with mostly red bricks. Adam was crazed by the architecture based on wooden windows known *Shanashil* or *Mashrabiyat*. They were adjacent to each other and allowed light and air to flow easily and at the same time maintain the privacy of the house. That is why Adam asked for his short meeting with the consul at one of the *Mashrabiyat*. The consul welcomed the idea and met with Adam and his two companions. Then he bombarded him with questions which he was looking for answers to for a long time.

"I was so much looking to your meeting for a long time, due to what was rumoured about the goals of this exploratory trip to the Orient and its expected results. I really hoped to be the first to congratulate you for this achievement after the goals of this historic trip had apparently been achieved."

Adam spoke in detail while his two companions sat at the

far end of *majlis*, knowing that the pride of the silent is more important than the pride of the speaker. He said, "The exploratory trip that the Danish monarch, Fredrick V, adopted had specific declared goals and a clear route. These goals may be listed under various subjects, the first of which was to research and investigate answers that would satisfy academics who were looking for other avenues, each in his own field and scientific specialisation. Accordingly, it was expected and hoped from the traveller to draw many maps that showed features of the Orient, and the best ways to land over its treasures. Those features that could raise the importance of the various human civilisations. Added to these tasks was to copy a document and decipher cuneiform and Syriac scripts that would be counted on later. These treasures of the past monitor the future. Geologists had many hopes that the traveller would provide laboratories with natural materials as samples of minerals and rare fauna and flora that would help them in their research. Academics recommended that the traveller make efforts to collect as many historic manuscripts as possible, whether scientific or religious, related to ancient civilisations. That is why the campaign focused on providing accurate geographical and historical data that would help commercial and military passages expected to accomplish their missions. Orientalists and those interested in the world of the East, especially in the field of anthropology that depended later on the recommendations of the historic campaign. All these noble objectives put together were not expected to start with six scientists and quickly end with only one!"

The consul was so happy to know about those objectives and wondered if all or some of them were met. Adam explained that from the first step the Scandinavian campaign set out towards the light emanating from the East. It was going on with determination behind declared pivotal goals. Those in charge were not aware of the risks involved with their trip. Astrology was a desperate attempt to decipher the mysteries of the sky, despite the attempts of the astrolabe and other instruments. There were goals set by theoreticians and academics for this campaign, but the achieved results were higher than expected from the humanistic point of view.

Accidents were golden keys of success. The proposed route of the trip was to discover the features of Istanbul and Cairo and decode their historical enigmas, then move to Sinai Peninsula and the Arabian Peninsula that were both considered sacred lands touched by the feet of prophets. Arabia Felicia would have been a pivotal point in that trip had it not been for diseases and communicable illnesses. This was given up and sufficed by touching its coasts. The route of the voyage was diverted to the Indian Mumbai Port. This led us to deal with Jewish and Indian traders, who allowed us to use their routes within their trade network and provided houses for our accommodation. However, the will of love on the island of Dilmunia had cut short the route, and the passage was altered. Fate had hastened its will that Dilmunia become the jewel of the East, that would remain eternal in the diaries of the Scandinavian campaign.

Then Adam went on to add about the difficulties that the campaign encountered. After the scientists broke through the lands of the East, they began to fall one after the other like autumn leaves. The beginning was in Sinai Peninsula, on route to the Arabian Sea. Bodies were scattered on the sands, mountains and seas. No one could stand against the black face of fate except Adam and the servant of the campaign. Since the start of the return from Dilmunia, Adam made it a point to compile all his drafts and began to empty the crop of his memory on paper, until he was overburdened, as these were loaded on three beasts of burden. Then came the tragic scene that epitomised the difficulties suffered by those who touch the soil of the East and then try to get away. Adam decided to leave Dilmunia, where he left his heart with his female, Khowla; and as he promised to communicate, he began to send mail pigeons to Barbura in the Land of Eternity whenever he came closer to Baghdad. I hope the pigeons maintain the line of emotions strong.

Adam proceeded forward after his only companion left him alone; his servant, who became the advisor to the Ruler of Dilmunia and then to its merchant and powerful master. The Servant remained in Dilmunia and the scientist returned with his books. The *H.M.S. Patrick Stewart* transported him to the northern neck of the Arabian Gulf where he stopped at Shat Alabrab, then the Ahwaz then moved to Basra, which was under the domination of the British where the Crown protected the desert route leading to Aleppo. A route that cut short the distance between Europe and the East to five months instead of eleven. This was traced across the horn of Africa at the Cape of Good Hope.

After Adam and his companions stayed with the Dutch consul and received his dues sent from Copenhagen, the wise man reminded him of the end of his mission.

"I promised to accompany you until arriving safely to Bagdad, and that was accomplished.

"I shall keep my promise. Tomorrow morning, I shall bequeath you what suffices you to accomplish your task hereafter, but I want you to tell me about your emotions towards that eternal martyr that you want to visit his mausoleum, and then give me your fortune-reading and what fate has in store for me.

"As for my visit to Karbella, I found that you have carried its contents and values within yourself. Through your exploratory travel, you have added many noble values to your heart and mind. Those absolute human values you would find when man transcends with his mind and soul. However, it is very difficult to have these combined in one man, except when these are transformed into absolute behaviour. That behaviour is translated when man is convinced into reality; then only man is called great and deserves to remain eternal."

"I have perceived your idea and what you are aiming at, but how the wise man does find my future and how can he read my fortune?"

"Your love, Adam, for Khowla, is never unique or new but can be classified under wider concepts. Digesting those mundane concepts enables the reading of fortune-telling quite easily. If we speak about divine religions for instance, we shall find their origins one and the same. Prophets and messengers preach the same principles in this life and the hereafter; however, these represent the differences in practical application. This led to human disputes and wars due to misunderstanding and misconception. These differences are natural, and the Creator allowed them for the sake of integration between the human race. Then the only connection between them shall be based on love and mutual respect."

Adam expressed his inability to understand what the wise man was aiming at. He requested him to be direct and clearer. "Human civilisations differ from each other in language, location, time, and wealth. Also, other causes believe that religious differences are urgent civilised necessity. Divine religions are not a human specialty for one nation exclusively. At the time of difference in thought, we must resort to positive dialogue focusing on similarities and belittling differences. This is in general, and when you can read it thoughtfully, you shall be able to read your personal fortune in its close environment. Your love for Khowla is a divine love unparalleled, a love of angelic giving that exults man but cannot survive on earth. The woman is similar to the apple that we desire whenever we remember our first sin. That is why most love comes in the shape of sin. God gave us freedom in love and the ability to choose, but the humans make it difficult for themselves when putting it into practice. Your love cannot withstand the wind that is controlled by religious shackles. Some restrictions prevent your engagement. Read this particular fortune by understanding the general situation."

Adam knew what the wise man was aiming at and became depressed all over. His colour changed as he was preparing for a long trip. The wise man advised him to avoid the desert route as much as possible on his way to Mosul. He said that water has the ability to quench the thirst of the body and has great energy to cure psychological depression provided that you are aware of the benefit of thinking about it, and that you understand the other meaning of water. Then he sang what the Arabs said. "I saw that still water is rotting, but when it flows; it is good and if it is not running, it is not liked."

***

It is the second stage. Adam set out to his home via the risky land route from Baghdad to Lathika on the Mediterranean. The route to Mosul, parallel to the Tigress and the Zaab Rivers, as the Wise Man advised Adam. He preferred the country lanes instead of the rough desert route with highwaymen and professional robbers. The two men crossed the Tigress at any possible opportunity.

The waters contained Adam and its impact flowed inside him. The encounter with the Wise Man that took place by accident made other meanings for the water after urging him to think about it. Water is undoubtedly a vital element for the continuity of life and for the origin of existence. However, Adam knew that if psychological streamlining agreed with the line of flow of water, it allowed for spiritual relaxation and helped to perceive and consider the inevitability of creation and existence. Then only man surrenders his fate where his soul lands. It is a stage few can attain, as it requires steps of spiritual advancement and intellectual clarity. Those were the lessons that Adam gained in the East.

Adam realised then that time has cooled down his love and did not want to kill it off. Behind every great man is a woman that he runs away from. Night had fallen and his young guide suggested that they spend the night at Diyar Bakre. Adam and his guide rented an old shabby hut. Adam lay down to relieve his body while his companion went into sound, deep sleep. The series of rapid, terrific events was repeated. The squeak of the door was heard opening slowly; he thought the visitor must have been a burglar. He closed his eyes but left his vision ajar through his eyelids that were semi-closed.

Without introduction, he saw a mule entering slowly. Adam did not budge and was the least scared. He was patient to give time for the event to act, something that made the mule lose his temper. It stood to be the body of a man and the head of a mule. Adam jumped from his sleeping spot and what stood in front of him let his legs race the winds, making the head of the mule fall and roll on the ground. His companion woke up to find the head beside him. Adam approached, lifting the head and throwing it towards the guide asking him, "What is this?"

He picked it and examined it.

"It is the head of a young mule. Robbers slaughter these animals and retain their heads. They dry and salt them in the sun until they are ready for usage. When the victim is stunned, he runs away and the robbers storm the place and get away with the property. It is one of the primitive means of robbery."

Adam laughed and bit his lips, saying, "I'm amazed at the world of mules."

In the morning, they proceeded to Aleppo via Latakia. They found the fluvial route very tiring and risky. He changed his mind, recalling Abu Rashed's saying: "Do not let life arrange yours according to its priorities, but rearrange its chapters as you wish to be happy."

They moved to the desert road after consulting with his companion. His guide was that strong young man, who was pleasant and always smiled to those he met. He knew how to deal with the chiefs of tribes and clans. They were received as guests by one of the chieftains of scattered tribes, who welcomed them but allocated bad and dried food and promised them of the arrival of horses in the morning. The Shaikh was checking carefully on Adam's belongings, and he was afraid of him. He perceived that there was a thin thread between being candid and rude. He asked his companion to take turn in vigilance. Afterwards, he went into a deep sleep. Adam felt that a hand was stretching to snatch his inkpot and box from behind the wall of the hut. Adam gave a resonant loud cry: a thief.

Only moments later, at the speed of light, the Shaikh and his men entered the hut. The Shaikh asked Adam, "What is the matter, man?"

"There is a thief in this area who wants to steal my belongings. He intended to take my inkpot."

The Shaikh ordered his men to search for the assumed thief, but they returned moments later with an expected answer.

"We did not find the thief."

Adam placed his hand on the shoulder of the Shaikh, patting him.

"Sometimes, man can see remote things in front of him but cannot see things close to him behind his back!"

Adam paid the Shaikh the price of the horses, and the two companions headed towards Bilan. There, he found unlike what he used to, the houses of the area empty and vacant. He saw, in a shocking thunder bolt, rotten corpses spread all over the place. Morning wind was blowing from the east with its polluted breeze. Winds either come with good tidings or eulogising. He heard its moaning and it innately guided him to keep away from the area that was haunted by beasts of death that fed on the bodies of the dead. He found many hyenas. Wolves. Foxes and mad dogs. His companion was dismayed at the presence of these animals, and Adam answered him:

"These beasts feed on carrion and enjoy human dead bodies. Have you not seen what the plague has done with the people of this area and killed them all?"

Adam did not like to remain in Bilan, so he proceeded to his final Asian stop. The route to Lathakia on the coasts of the Mediterranean was more moderate and less dangerous. He joined a trade caravan after travelling alone. He was grateful to the master of the caravan, but he was dismayed when he found that it was carrying a sick European man. The man was ailing and constantly in pain and moaning. Adam was scared that he might transmit his infection after he had fled the disastrous plagued village. He expected lots of difficulties because of the presence of the sick man. He wanted to pay the caravan master extra kroners so they would leave the man and his illness behind. However, he was concerned that the other travellers might disagree and accuse him of being selfish.

Two nights before the arrival to *Lathakia*, the caravan stopped for resting and the moaning of the man increased and his voice was higher. The caravan stopped, and just before dawn the robbers arrived to attack the caravan. Adam was half-asleep. The robbers were confused on hearing the moaning of the ailing man. They thought they were going to be attacked, so they left the task for which they came for. The man in his illness was bringing delayed goodness to the caravan.

After more than a month and a half since leaving Dilmunia, here he was, saying farewell to his strong, young guide. He reminded him of the river race and advised him to be wise when making a decision. He presented him with some metal currencies as gratitude for his services and the role he had performed. Then the young man asked him, "Will you return to Dilmunia and cross our lands?"

"You are asking me about Dilmunia, where I found the world epitomised in it with its good and evil; with its past, present and future. With its love in the heart of its people, that of Khowla, her father, the Doyen. With its ruler, who admits his deficiency, and was looking for someone to guide him to the right path; about the Merchant, who laid ambushes with an evil intent to dominate his power; with the Servant, who represented the thorn that the Scandinavian exploratory mission left on its side to be ready whenever the ambushers wanted. I was and still am fond of love of Khowla of Dilmunia; with love that exalts all humanity by positive talk engulfed in love to surpass all hurdles and difficulties. The love of Khowla, despite its impossibility, imposes on us to rewrite history by the eye of the future and not to remain hostages of the past in those ages. We must start a dialogue in the spirit of wisdom, as it is really stupid to speak while you are captivated by rage."

His guide was listening silently and falling outside the circle of his words. He did not comprehend many of his unconnected talks that amounted to hallucinations sometimes. He wished him well and success, then he joined the first trade caravan returning to Baghdad.

Adam left Lathakia, heading by sea to Larnaca. He left the East with its magic, and here he was after long misery, embracing the West in the age of industry and the rise of the machine. He boarded a merchant navy vessel that sailed the route protected by some naval vessels. He crossed the Danube, breaking into Europe, and from there, he headed towards Bucharest, then to Warsaw and Hanover, and finally he landed in Copenhagen. Eagerness was carrying him more than vessels and horses did. It is the emotional unsettled state of the traveller. In his travels, he does not feel estrangement, but the moment he starts the return route, then he realises that he does not belong to the same place. Eagerness moves his emotions and inflames his anticipations with images of memories.

***

Adam had an official reception hosted by the University of Göttingen, from where the cradle of the idea for the exploration campaign had started. The reception was well attended by academics, politicians, diplomats and an audience of followers. The audience lined up in front of the ancient academic building with an entrance in the middle of a square-shaped building with a triangle top, with three upper windows and two others on both sides of the main entrance. The main academic hall behind that entrance had a conical shape with a tail at the farthest end. Adam began shaking hands with the audience before proceeding in the company of his teachers to the main hall to give a brief report about the results of his trip.

"Honourable audience. The results of the campaign were different and completely varied between the expected and the hoped for. It added a lot to the declared aims, and other aims were imposed due to unexpected events. Time is not appropriate to narrate them all. I promise you to issue volumes that document its stops, to be lessons for future explorers. However, in passing, I must stop at one aim that was beyond all expectations and hopes, related to an island called Dilmunia. Through several studies and investigations, I found that the civilisation of Dilmunia is deep-rooted in history that goes back three thousand years or more before Christ. It was part and an important corner of the first civilisation known by man; that is the Sumerian Civilisation. That was the pioneering mark known as the civilisation of Mesopotamia where the invention of cuneiform writing originated. It was used as a land of eternity. The word 'Dilmunia' means 'eternity and continuity'; if anyone dies and is buried there, he lives immortally, between death and life."

Adam left the campus of Göttingen University to meet his family. He longed for the lap of his mother, as if he were just born. He met her and his soul was revived and was cured by her warmth and kindness. He asked her about Carina and she told him, "Carina married Jackson, the realtor. Both got hold of our properties in the country; we have nothing left but what we have in this town."

"Where is the supposed love of Carina, that she sang?"

"Love that freezes outside the bed never becomes hot after warming up but is rendered as vapour. The more lovers quarrel, the more their souls are closer."

(6) Khowla
December 1765

The Doyen departed, and Adam left my shores; Abu Rashed was unjustly to remain behind bars. Tragedies of life do not end except by the extermination of man. I learnt that extermination comes by steps and on amassed stages. O, Man, you have to be content with your fate to be happy. The best of fate is what appears to you and the worst is what is absent and unknown to you. As the Arabs said, "People do not bear the flow of bounties, and when the earth exposes its flower, corruption rises, while with contentedness we enjoy life and life is satisfied with us."

The departure of the Doyen meant the annihilation of the body alone; his intellectual and humanitarian works were deep-rooted in the soil and its branches in the sky. He planted many values and moral principles and lighted a lantern for life, illuminating allies of darkness. His traces never ceased, as he thought that the handicapped is he who walks ceaselessly in the desert.

When it came to my father, Abu Rashed, the plot was harder than throwing him behind bars in a repeated and open policy that expressed the inability of the fake leadership of the Merchant, who was afraid of the nature of change and resisted change and reform since he had invaded Dilmunia by force and deception. He wished for stagnation and status quo. He believed that human beings were only created in various static classes. The class system was a natural life that maintained its heritage. A way of life with which authority was secured and public capital was violated.

The Merchant may have allowed the public freedom of criticism and of scolding members of his Appointed Council, but would never condone touching his sacred self; he would not allow for a legislation that allowed for opportunities for the people. He would allow conditional discussion under absolute freedom in name and actually restricted. Authority is an ailment: it is difficult to live without it for he who is brought up since childhood. He was domineering and a sadist at an early age. In his dictionary, change was synonymous with death, and death in our belief always misses us to inflict others; let him sing the praise of our dead folks.

The power that the Merchant restricted to himself was the hidden restraint that moved his desires. Likewise, the sexual instinct for the despot is never free from his perversions and avariciousness; you in find him a sadist's temper, appearing only frowning due to a fatigue somehow inside him. The despot drifts in his luxury to where his testicles desire; that is why I perceived his sexual wishes when he coveted the wife of Yusef, the Puller, when her beauty infatuated him. As if he wanted to repeat the slip of our black history, the history that allowed those in power to combine blood and vulva, and that produced a forbidden alliance or incest, and that in turn produced sick, hybrid posterity. The Merchant used to spread between the people that Yusef, the Puller, wasted the blood of his son, Nasser. He waved this flag like the shirt of Othman wherever he went. He threw Yusef in a bottomless prison. He framed him with pure criminal accusation and another public opinion offence, and the result was the legality of the right of adultery in Dilmunia, and the right of copulating with the wife of Yusef, or rather, raping her.

His seductions were endless to start another link. He wanted to have an affinity with my father and to marry me in the hope that this affinity would thaw the ice between the people of Dilmunia and its leadership. I still recall the whole events when he sent his emissary to my father.

"The Merchant conveys his greetings and requests marriage to your daughter, Khowla. Her dowry shall be relieving your debts and one of the orchards in Barbura, the fruitful."

My father answered him with the pride of a mountain that withstands the wind.

"We do not make money from our women and daughters; our dignified selves refuse that. God has bestowed on us from his generosity and bounty; we refuse the marriage of he who has no values of his religion that uplifts him from the lowliness of this world and its evils. You desire to marry blood and relations; we like human affinity approved the Heavens to be blessed and Earth is happy to bear the fruit of beauty. People like us do not marry people like you."

The Merchant was charged with internal affairs, but he was angered when he disagreed with the Ruler and his intention. Revenues were distributed between the rulers, their governors and the public affairs. In addition, when he deposed his master, he took control of everything. He was cruel to Yusef and that made his wife more adamant and stronger. He wanted to tighten his fist on Dilmunia and that made it an ember burning in his fist, to slip through his fingers.

I, with all that I promised Adam to be loyal to document, stood unable in front of the pen with its feather and its inkwell.

I had no problem revealing myself with absolute truth; however, I felt dizzy and at pain whenever I spread what was inside me on paper and in my diary. I began to feel, as Adam expressed, that there was someone who could read me while writing, and there was someone who could trace me to put all my diary and words to the whole world. He would rewrite history according to the language of the age. He must read my thoughts and those of my predecessors and translate into a language understood by the reader despite his whereabouts. I understood it was not going to be an easy task; however, success is always with the sincere who believes in what he does; perhaps he could dedicate our stories to my soul that yearns to an age yet to come.

Nothing remained but to unfold my Adamite, that red man transferred by the Middle Eastern sun to the darkness of the region as if he were one of its citizens. He came as a traveller to explore Dilmunia and discover its waters, mountains, plateaus and skies, its relics and treasures buried under its sands. In no time its people and its peculiar characteristics impressed him. He used to say that the Dilmunian represented a Middle Eastern slot that represented the whole world in many respects. A man that preserves its history and heritage but looks forward to a brighter future. He lives on a small island but sees his role as pioneer of change in the region. What happens in Dilmunia, we find by the passage of time, finds its way to neighbouring states affecting and getting affected as well. All countries around him were attracting him: Persians, Unitarians, Ottomans, the British, and before them were the Portuguese, Ya'arebs and Qawasims. All these powers refused unilateral change. All wanted change in their own way, while Dilmunia wanted a dignified and emotional change that benefited the region first.

Adam came as if he were one of the conquerors. He settled there and drank its water and ate its food and communicated with its people and became known as "Adam of Dilmunia". He carried love, light, and goodness in his heart. I do not deny that light touched and attracted me unhesitatingly. The event of the sin was a beacon that carried light wherever he stepped.

Adam tried to enjoy the warmth of his second half; he found who shares his emotions and thoughts. That satanic sin was inharmonious in his life. I found him a sensational man that every woman desired to have, wherever she was. I agreed to accept engagement and marry him without clear answers. The man who regards a woman without answers is a good thing, better than a lover without questions. I was quite certain about the impossibility of consummation, the four conditions and the unfeasibility of our connection. Islam, despite the range of freedom, imposes restrictions on the marriage of a woman to one of the People of the Book, because it expects that the offspring would follow the faith of their father. This is a condition that none can leap over; many cannot digest. Is not love a fate that should have its legislation also?

I found the love in Adam's heart was stronger than all the satanic powers together in the hearts of all the people of Dilmunia. Perhaps it was a case of benign egotism. I preferred to extract the love energy from his heart, which was similar in form and most of the energy of my father, Abu Rashed. The energy of love that inundates man is capable of changing the world from its infernal state into a green oasis where humanity beautifies in angelic qualities. This energy embedded in the heart of every man, but the difficult task is how to reach it by digging inside the soul to the loving energy. Unless that massive energy inundates us, we remain captives of our desires and our sick satanic motives.

Man, you have to search for love in your heart and extract that energy, and then only you can rise higher than he who has harmed you. You will rise above using oppressive carnal power and the abusive language because you shall know that love is the master of evidence.

A Final Word

In many instances, the events of this novel intersect with facts and historical events; however, the whole content, the title and stories and events are all fictitious. Any resemblance between characters and historical personalities is mere coincidence. The novel itself is originally not liable to interpretation as it is not a historical or documentary reference.

Rasool Darwish
June 19, 2015